BEACHED WEDDING

A FRIENDS TO LOVERS SLOW BURN ROMANCE

DANI COLLINS

DANI COLLINS

JOIN DANI'S VIP LIST

Want the inside gossip and sneak peeks at what's next? You'll be notified when a new release arrives, when a price drops, and other VIP-only deals.

Join Dani's List Now

IT WAS MY JOB TO GET THE GROOM TO THE WEDDING.

I failed.

I'm still hungover from the bachelor party when I arrive in Oahu and ruin Ashley's life. She was expecting to marry my best mate, but on the way to the airport, he confessed he didn't want to marry her. They only knew each other three months, but Ashley is devastated.

Now we're stuck with her family and the groom's parents —who've always treated me like a son. I'd love to abandon ship, but Ashley needs a friend and that's what I am. It's the only thing I can be.

But as we spend the week together, and she realizes she was more in love with a wedding and moving to Sydney than she was with her groom, things change between us. Falling for my best friend's bride will sink more than a friendship. We're partners in a surf shop on the brink of expansion. Am I headed for a wipeout? Or the longest, most perfect ride of my life?

ASHLEY

$\mathcal{I}$ was stepping onto the curb at International
Arrivals of the Honolulu airport when my phone
rang. My smile of anticipation fell away.

Izzy. *I knew it.* My maid-of-honor wasn't coming.

Not a crisis. My sister was offended that I had asked Izzy
instead of her. Whitney was dying to take over, but what was
going *on* with Izzy?

I accepted her call and tried to put a smile in my voice.

"Hi." I braced the cool petals strung around my neck so I
wouldn't bruise them as I hurried down the sidewalk toward
doors where a handful of people with luggage loitered.

"Why am I hearing honking?" Izzy asked.

"I'm at the airport. Traffic is bonkers. I thought I would be
late." My fault. I asked my ride-share driver to stop for leis,
thinking it would be romantic. Now I was sweaty and
stressed. Pretty much my signature look.

"What are you doing at the airport?" Izzy was scandalized.
"Diva the hell out of this week. I would."

She would. For most of my life, I have been striving to

1

become more like Izzy. Izzy does what she wants and says 'no' when she doesn't want to do something. She makes zero apologies for either.

I'm getting better. It had only taken twenty-six years, but I was finally clawing forward with my own life, getting married in Hawaii to a great guy then moving to Australia with him. No more compromising and settling and doing as I'm told. No more apologizing for everything all the time.

"Sorry, hang on a sec," I heard myself say as I entered the airport. I could have bitten my tongue in half for the reflexive apology. I read the arrivals screen. "Okay, their flight landed." I drew a calming breath and moved into a corner to wait.

"I can't believe you left the beach. I can't *wait* to get there."

"You're still coming?"

"Of course. Why would you think not?"

Because she had waited until the last second to book and wasn't arriving until the day before the wedding. Because she was tapping a keyboard right now, and lately seemed to have ten things better to do than give me her full attention.

But anytime I asked if something was wrong, she deflected and blew me off.

"I'm just stressing," I excused. And gritted my teeth at myself for being less than honest. "My head went to worst-case when I saw you were calling instead of texting."

"I need my fingers to finish entering these numbers..." More tapping. "But I wanted to know if the resort has a shop where I can buy a bathing suit? That scream you woke up to this morning? That was me trying on my old one."

Unlikely. Izzy was gorgeous, but, "I did hear that." I relaxed into the warm wall at my back. The airport was open-air and as hot and humid as the rest of the island. "There's a shop, but it's expensive." The mismatched tops and bottoms started at eighty dollars, but Izzy had a great salary and wasn't footing the bill on her own wedding. "Now that I've seen what a cluster fu...nction—" I smiled and corrected myself as a mom with two kids came to stand near me. "—what a challenge traffic can be, I'll leave more time when I come back for you."

"*Don't.* Seriously, climb into bed with Shane and send Fox to pick me up." Izzy's tone lowered to a smoldering sexiness. "Tell him I can't wait to see him again."

I don't know why it bothered me, but for the last three months, Izzy had been making jokes about rekindling things with Fox and something about it put me off. She was the maid-of-honor. It was practically law that she slam the best man.

I knew Fox a lot better now, though. When Izzy and I had met him and Shane on our first night out after arriving in Sydney, we'd all been looking for a good time, not a long time. Everything about those early days had been pure fun. I didn't begrudge either of them getting their rocks off, especially if they had nothing better to do while they were here on vacation.

But something in Izzy's jokes sounded forced. Which made me think she didn't really want Fox. That made me want to question her motives and made me defensive on his behalf.

Which was not my place. If he was willing to be used by her or anyone else, what business of it was mine? None. They were grownups. They could figure it out.

Maybe I was tired of the chase and thought they should be, too. That's all this was. I went along with Izzy's suggestion because that's what best friends do.

"I'll see what kind of shape he's in. They might be jet-lagged or still recovering from the stag party."

"I thought that was last weekend. Didn't they go surfing?"

"They had a do-over. Quite a piss-up, sounds like. I got a text from Shane last night that he and Fox were taking a taxi to the airport because they were still drunk. That's why I decided to meet them here. They're renting a car and I wasn't sure they'd be sober enough to drive it. This way I'll be on the paperwork and can come back for you."

"Are you listening to yourself? That's way too much micro-managing for a bride."

"I know, but..." Normally I would trust Fox to sort it, but the stakes were really high. My mother was dying to find fault with my groom. I didn't expect everything to be perfect this week, but I would do whatever necessary so things ran smoothly.

"When I get there, I want to see you in a bikini, a wedding dress, then a bikini," Izzy stated. "That's it."

"Aw." I layered my voice with a sentimental pang. "You sound like Shane."

"That guy has gone three months without sex. Good luck wearing anything."

I chuckled, but it came out weak. I wasn't like Izzy in that way either, inclined to overshare about what went on in the bedroom. Shane and I were fine in the sack, but we didn't exactly tear each other's clothes off. I wasn't convinced anyone ever felt as porny and horny as books and movies made out.

Was I suffering FOMO over those who did? Sure. But I'd been raised to keep my expectations low. Focus on needs, not wants, so there was less room for disappointment.

And I was marrying a gorgeous surfy-dude who had great parents and a growing business. He was giving me an excuse to move to Australia. I had no reason to be greedy.

I glanced up as a swell of travelers began streaming past me. They were mostly Asian so it was probably a different flight. Shane and Fox were coming straight from Sydney.

"Seriously, I— Oh, hang on, Ash." Izzy muffled the phone while she spoke to someone.

I bit back a sigh, wondering if she even wanted to see me. We'd been best friends growing up, but she barely talked to me in the three months that I'd been back in Canada.

Granted she was four hours away from our home town, working at a demanding job in Winnipeg, living it up with all her city friends, but her parents still lived near me. She hadn't come back once to see them or me. Every time I had suggested coming to stay with her in the Peg, Izzy had had other plans. She often took days to respond to a text. I felt like I was an unwelcome reminder that we came from a dot on the map that was more of a zit in the armpit of the country.

I genuinely hadn't expected her to accept maid-of-honor duty. I asked because she was the one who had coaxed me to go to Australia with her last year, something I wouldn't have done on my own. Then she drew me into meeting Shane after chatting up Fox. Everything about that trip had started out fantastic.

Within the week, however, Izzy abruptly went back to Canada, ditching me for the bank job she currently held.

It was a really good job. I couldn't blame her. And her abandonment had turned out fine for me, obviously, but given how easily she had left me alone in a strange country, I had been expecting a regretful excuse the entire time I'd been planning this wedding.

Izzy came back on the line. "That was a hot-goss alert about a mat leave. They want me to apply to cover it. Guess I can't marry Fox and move to Oz after all. Do you think he'd move here?"

"The market for surf shops in Manitoba *is* wide open."

"Right? It's one of those things you don't know you need until it's here."

"Ask him when you see him. They've talked about expanding into California, since Fox is American, but with the price of real estate there— Oh. I just heard someone say 'G'day.' Might be their flight. I'll hang up."

"'kay. See you in forty-eight hours plus traffic."

"Can't wait. Travel safe."

I pushed off the wall and dropped my phone into my bag, bouncing on my toes in my excitement to see the man who was changing my life.

FOX

I detoured into the men's room and dry-heaved until my lungs threatened to squeeze out of me like toothpaste. As I did, my sunglasses dropped off the collar of my shirt and hit the water in the bowl. Brilliant. At least they floated as advertised so I had *that* going for me.

Plucking the glasses from the toilet, I leaned against the wall, wishing it was colder, but the airport was open to the elements. No A/C. I ought to be used to the heat and most days I could stand it, but not today. Not with this humidity.

Not with this hangover.

I was shaking and lived inside each of my next three breaths, waiting for the nausea to pass. When I was pretty sure I could move without retching, I swiped my wrist across my mouth and opened the door of the stall. I braced there and met the reflected gaze of the man washing his hands.

"Rough flight?"

"Yeah." The whole plane had listened to me alternately snore and lose my guts for ten hours. I should have stayed drunk. The minute I'd taken my seat on the plane alone, my conscience had begun to squirm. Now, I was crawling out from judgment-impaired drunk to a hard case of DTs and felt ill in a whole new way.

What kind of asshat talked a man into jilting his bride? I *like* Ashley. Shane could do a helluva lot worse. I should have kept my trap shut.

But no. I'd been 'a good mate' so here I was, drunk-sober and seedy, sick with the realization I had thrown a lever that would derail lives.

The other guy left. I washed and dried my sunglasses then hung my clammy face over the sink. I splashed cold water on my unshaven cheeks and into my mouth, rinsed and spat and stood straight. My head took a minute to catch up with the change in altitude. My stomach dipped and rolled until I found my equilibrium. Another cold sweat shivered over my ashy-brown skin.

I didn't meet my own eyes in the mirror, but I did glance at my phone to see a text from Ashley.

ASH

I'm here to surprise Shane. Where are you?
Don't leave the airport without me.

Fucking brilliant.

Curling fetal under an airport urinal started to look like perfectly rational behavior. With luck the EMTs might turn up with a shot of antipsychotic medication and lock me up for a decade or two.

Why had I even got on the plane?

Will you tell her? I can't. Those eyes.

I'd been too drunk to parse out that I should have refused. That was the pitiful truth. I'd been steeped in some kind of hero complex, convinced I was doing what was right by both of them.

Fucking idiot.

I shouldered my duffel with our company logo and left the men's room, distantly recalling my suit was in the garment bag with Shane's, the bag that had stayed in the taxi.

It's fine, mate. I'll make sure she's not mad. Who did I think I was, promising dumb shit like that? Ashley was going to knee me in the raisins and I deserved it.

I shuffled through the flow of customs and followed the crowd toward the exit.

My stomach pitched again and I accepted the suffering as my due, but when I reached to my collar for my sunglasses, I realized I'd left them beside the sink in the can. I would have to go back through security to retrieve them and doubted I could do that without a boarding pass. I had a vague memory of hooking my hat on the back of the door and I actually wanted to cry. The sunshine was going to pierce my skull like a diamond drill—

Ow. There it was.

"Fox! Aloha!"

Despite my legal status of 'walking dead,' my heart lifted at the sight of Ashley. I'd missed her. A half-smile tugged one corner of my mouth.

She always made me smile. It was her sincerity and the way she radiated warmth. She had bouncy brown hair and big brown eyes and I especially enjoyed the fact she always tried to dress to the nines but, by her own admission, only made it to seven and a half. Today that meant full make-up, a pretty sundress that bared her shoulders topped with a thick, ruffled lei of pink and white flowers. Her hair framed her face in windswept waves. On her feet, she wore dollar-store flip-flops on toes overdue for fresh polish.

She was real. Earthy and funny. Bright and nice. She did not deserve to be thrown over by anyone. What the *hell* had I done?

"Good to see you, Ash." I slouched for the hug she offered, but the cringe that briefly soured my face couldn't be helped, not when I was accosted by a fresh slant of sun and the thick blanket of humidity and the sickly-sweet aroma off the leis.

"Oh, wow," she said with a wince of her own, drawing back.

"Yeah, I need a shower. Bad." The whore's bath in the chemical toilet hadn't taken.

"Where's Shane? Not stuck in customs." She looked around me.

"He didn't text you?" Let there be a God.

"About?" She frowned with concern and looked past me again.

I rubbed where the sun radiated against my short, recently-barbered curls. I stepped into the shade. Then I grabbed the proverbial bandage and yanked, even though it was attached to something inside me and turned me inside out.

"He didn't come."

Ashley gave a half-gurgling chuckle as if she knew her leg was being pulled and she appreciated the effort, but it wouldn't work.

"Is he in the john? It sounds like you guys were *really* drunk. It's okay. You can sleep it off by the pool."

I clenched my molars against a fresh lurch in my gut.

"He didn't get on the plane, Ash. The wedding's off."

ASHLEY

"*Y*ou're the best man, Fox. You had *one job*," I said with another husk of a laugh, but this one caught like a fish bone in my throat. A huge block of ice was forming in my chest.

Because Fox wasn't smiling. He *flinched.*

He looked like a crust of bread that was starting to mold. His brown skin wore tones of gray as he leaned on the wall, shoulders hunched. His expression was ill with regret or remorse or some other emotion that was very *not good.*

My stomach clenched so hard, I couldn't draw a full breath. I searched his hazel eyes for the teasing light I'd seen there a thousand times. I liked Fox. A lot. I had from the moment Izzy had dragged him across the bar in Sydney and said, "This is Fox. He said we should come meet his friends."

Fox had a subtler personality than Shane's outgoing Aussie charisma, but he had a wicked sense of humor and his rock-solid demeanor was always reassuring. After Izzy had flown home, I spent the rest of my three-month holiday living with Shane in the house he owned with his best friend and business partner. Fox and I had often bonded over being fish out of water, him the Yank and me the Canuck. He razzed me *all the time.*

But he was never mean.

I looked toward the doors again. Doors that had stopped opening because everyone on his flight had come through and moved on.

"Is he *alive?*" I blurted.

"Yes." His head jerked slightly.

"He texted me that he was on his way."

"When?" He narrowed his eyes.

"When you were getting in the taxi." I scrolled to show him the handful of texts I'd received from Shane last night.

SHANE

Looking forward to sleeping on the plane. See you soon.

"What happened? Was he too sick to fly?" I looked toward the interior of the terminal, wondering when the next flight to Sydney would leave. Could I book Shane on a different one?

Fox lifted a helpless hand. His sigh was pained. "He told me he doesn't want to get married, Ash."

My concern for my fiance fell off its horse. My brain did a few rolling tumbles as I absorbed what Fox was saying, but I didn't want to hear it.

"At all?" My lips had gone numb.

Fox was wearing a pity face while we both stood here clutching our stomachs.

"Or like, right now?" I tried. "Because I know he didn't want to do it in Hawaii."

There were cheaper places to stay and surf, Shane had

argued, like Thailand. And the best surf on Oahu was played out by the end of March.

My family would have had to fly a lot further, though. Hawaii had been a stretch, not just financially, but because tropical vacations weren't 'us.' If I wanted an outdoor wedding, Mom had argued, I should hold it in the gazebo at the Riverside Community Park.

"I kept it as small as possible." I was still at a loss, dimly hearing myself trying to talk Fox into making Shane appear out of thin air. "If he wants to do it in Australia—"

Fox was shaking his head. "He doesn't want to marry at all."

I didn't want to let it into my head. It was too big. This wasn't just a humiliation in front of a church full of guests. This was a calling off of the most courageous thing I'd ever done. My few boxes of personal effects were on a ship in the middle of the ocean.

As that hit, I began to grow legit hysterical.

"He can't just *not show up*. And send *you* to tell me. His parents are having breakfast with my family right now. Do they know? *No.*" I stabbed my phone to call Shane, glaring at Fox. "What did he say? Oh my God. Is he seeing someone?" It had been three months since I'd left, but—

"No." Fox's tone was quiet, but firm.

"Is it cold feet?" I held up a finger to silence Fox as Shane's voice came on the line.

"G'day. This is Shane at Togs and Boards. I'm not here. Try Fox at..."

I waited for the beep and said, "Shane, what's going on? Call me." I ended the call and texted:

Call me.

I stared at the screen, waiting for the text to get marked 'Read' but it didn't even say 'Delivered.' Had he turned his phone off?

The flutters in my middle grew into a swarm of angry hornets.

"Can you call someone? Gunz or Shwickie? See if he's with them? Tell them he needs to call me." I realized I was trembling like someone going into shock. I had to blink to read the signage as I tried to determine the shortest route to the departure level. My passport was in the safe at the hotel. I would have to get it before I could do anything. Then I would have to explain to Mom—

He couldn't *do* this to me. He couldn't leave me here with nowhere to go.

I touched my chest, trying to calm my racing heart.

Fox texted someone, but the lack of a responding ding and the look on his face told me he didn't expect much to come of it.

"He's probably surfing," he said.

I bit my trembling lip and nodded, doing what I always did when I'd rather be screaming that my hair was fire. I kept my cool and concentrated on solutions.

"Let's go to the hotel. I'll check flights, pack, then go find him."

Fox hesitated. "I don't think that'll help, Ash."

"Well, he can't call off our wedding without even talking to me! You had a car booked, didn't you?"

"Yeah." He pushed off the wall. "Okay, sure. Let's get the car and go to the hotel. I have to tell his parents. They'll be worried if he doesn't check in."

I yanked the leis off my neck and dropped them in the first garbage can I saw.

ASHLEY

*T*hirty minutes later, I was stalking Shane on social media, trying to give Fox some privacy as he braced his hands on his knees and spat on the floor of the parking garage.

The guy behind the rental counter had asked if Fox was going to throw up in the car. I assured him he was fine, but had to wonder.

"That's alcohol poisoning," I said as he straightened and came toward me in a wobbling step. "That's not like you." Shane and all his friends enjoyed a good piss-up now and again, but Fox was usually the caretaker who stayed sober enough to ensure everyone got home safely. "What were you drinking?"

"Couldn't tell you." He swiped the back of his wrist across his mouth. "But I'm never drinking it again."

I studied his haggard profile sheened with perspiration above his shadow of stubble. Pity stirred in me, but I wanted to grab him by the shirt front and give him a shake, too.

"Where did you go?" What *happened* to make Shane back out on me?

"The usual crawl, but we started way too early and forgot to quit." He hooked his thumbs in the waistband of his jeans. "I don't know what got into me."

The self-disgust in his expression seemed to go deeper than regret over a bender. He looked on the verge of saying something.

I instinctively braced myself, but he flicked his gaze past me.

"G231? The Audi?"

I turned to see the red convertible. Very Shane.

"I wasn't paying attention to what it was." I had signed the paperwork while trying to compose appropriate texts to Shane and all his friends. I hadn't found the right words to ask if anyone had heard from him without revealing he'd dumped me.

I wasn't ready to accept that I'd been dumped. I kept thinking that if I could just talk to him, he would still have time to get here before the ceremony. I'd planned it so we would have a few days to acclimatize and pamper before the wedding on Wednesday. Afterward, we would enjoy another day of vacation with both families before I headed into the sunset to enjoy my exciting new life with my new husband.

"Want the top down?" Fox asked.

"Sure," I murmured and deleted what I'd started to text.

Fox took the key fob and walked to the rear of the car, popped the trunk and left his duffel bag inside it.

"Hey!" he called to an attendant. "I'll give you ten bucks for your hat. Twenty," he upped when the kid hesitated. Fox patted his own butt. His shoulders tensed. "Fuck me. Where'd I leave my wallet?"

"You gave it to me." I dug it out of my bag. The rental clerk hadn't been happy about my signing Fox's name to the paperwork, but with Fox rushing outside to gasp like a carp and a line of people waiting, standard procedure hadn't been the priority.

Fox found a twenty, exchanged it for the ball cap, and jammed the hat on his head. He shaped the brim as he dragged it low over his eyes, then he climbed into the driver's seat long enough to retract the roof. By the time I hit Send, he was walking around to the passenger side. He reclined his seat as I settled behind the wheel. I was pretty sure he was asleep before I'd finished adjusting the mirrors.

I didn't mind him passing out on me. I needed time to process. Before I pulled out of the spot, I checked once more for a message from Shane.

Nothing. Also very Shane. He didn't like emotional confrontations or talking about feelings. What man did? Fox was probably right. Shane was likely stacking surfboards and mates into his jeep, heading off-grid. That's what he'd done when a flash-flood had taken out the shop's storage room. He'd flown to the west coast and hadn't come back until the water had gone down and he was mentally ready to deal with the mess. The two times he and I had had a heated disagreement, he'd done the same thing, leaving me to wonder for days where we stood.

We hadn't had a fight this time, though. Everything had seemed fine until...this.

I glanced at Fox. With a sigh that was more of a whimper, I started looking for the exit.

FOX

"*I*'m okay. Just lost."

The sound of Ashley's voice dragged me back to consciousness.

I edged the brim of my hat up to see her accepting a tissue from a woman holding a toddler. The boy was staring at me without any self-consciousness, the way little nippers did before they were taught it was rude. As if I had something to teach him about human behavior, which I most definitely did not. Very poor example here, kid. Look away.

For some reason, Ashley had driven us into a family neighborhood. Shrubs bloomed in pinks and yellows, palm trees rustled overhead and a dog barked in the distance.

She blew her nose and tried to laugh off her tears. "I'm having a bit of a day."

The woman eyed me with suspicion.

"What's going on?" I brought my seat upright. I hadn't slept long, maybe an hour, but it was enough to make a difference. My head was splitting, but some of that was caffeine withdrawal. I hadn't dared accept anything on the plane, but now my stomach whispered that grease and salt would be greeted politely.

"I took the wrong direction out of Honolulu. Then I saw signs that said I was heading to the marine base so I got off the highway." Ashley's eyes were red and her chin crinkled. "Now I'm lost."

Hell yes, she was. My heart stumbled as I looked into her forsaken gaze. I tried to find words, but the ones I needed to say would have to wait a little longer.

"I would love a coffee." I appealed to the stranger. "Is there anywhere nearby?"

She directed us to a grocery store with a take-away counter a few blocks away.

"Thanks. We'll use the GPS to find our way from there," I said, fishing for my phone.

Ashley smiled weakly at the woman and continued up the road.

"I knew there was a way to get back to the resort on this side of the island. I thought all I had to do was keep the water on my right and I'd get there eventually. It was a dumb idea."

"It's okay. I like the scenic route." I was dreading telling Shane's parents that things had gone off-book. Getting lost on the way to doing that suited me really well.

Ashley parked and came into the store with me, veering down an aisle while I made for the deli counter where I ordered a breakfast panini. I didn't even know what time it was, but a few minutes later, I was washing down extra-strength Tylenol with a syrupy orange electrolyte replacement, waiting on my sandwich and a gallon of red-eye coffee, when Ashley appeared beside me.

She held a basket with a bottle of premixed marguerites.

I grimaced in rejection.

"I'm entitled," she said sullenly.

She was, but, "at least get real tequila. That premixed stuff is a recipe for flushing your sunglasses."

Her mouth twitched. "Voice of experience?"

"This morning. At the airport. The good ones that the sales rep gave me."

"The cute one? Too bad. That's really gross."

"Tell me about it."

She sighed and picked up the bottle to return it.

"Wait." I took my bagged sandwich from the clerk. "You want a bacon and egg sandwich?"

She stared with longing at mine. The corners of her mouth wobbled. "I won't fit into my wedding dress if I eat that."

Ah, shit. I closed my eyes.

"I haven't eaten anything but salad for *three months.* No alcohol, no bread. No cream in my coffee. It's disgusting without cream, by the way. Your mouth is a dead zone. And why did I bother? My boobs have disappeared and I still have an ass like a delivery truck. Now I'm not even going to wear the dress that maxed out my credit card?"

"Extra bacon, extra cheese," I said to the clerk so he wouldn't see Ashley blinking her damp lashes. "And a mocha frap with whip cream and caramel. If you have chocolate shavings—?"

"Fox, don't. What if—"

"Ashley." I grabbed her hand and gave it a squeeze. "If you tell me one more time that you're afraid to eat because it makes your ass look fat, I'm going to send you for shock therapy. Your ass delivers." I met her gaze and something like vertigo hit me, as if I'd rolled over a speedbump unprepared, rattling my brain.

Her eyes went wide and her hand flexed in mine, but she didn't pull away.

An impression of having overstepped hung in the air between us. This had only happened a couple of times before because I didn't *let* it happen, but I was suddenly thinking about the way she turned a regular day into Valentine's Day by putting on a pair of yoga pants. I nearly swallowed my tongue trying to find my voice.

"We're going to eat a sandwich, get our heads on straight, then talk," I said, releasing her hand and mentally pushing away those very wrong thoughts. She was my *friend*. Not...

No. Just no.

"No offense, Fox, but I don't want to talk to you." She hugged herself. "I want to talk to *Shane*. I keep thinking I could fix this if he would pick up, but I'm so mad, I would probably make things worse. I don't understand what *happened?*"

I drew a breath that burned. Words crowded into my mouth, some that wouldn't entirely make sense, but I didn't want to get into it here where men with short haircuts and stiff bearing would witness a White woman reaming a Black man a new one.

"C'mon." I headed toward the cash. On the way, I threw some potato chips and a few pieces of fruit into my basket, grabbed the first pair of sunglasses I saw that had a polarized sticker, and started on my tongue-scorching, crude-oil coffee while I paid.

Life-force seeped back into my bloodstream one cell at a time, bringing with it profound humility. I took the keys and ate as I drove. Five minutes up the coast, I saw a sign for a state park and pulled in.

Ashley lowered her frothy coffee and glared at the van

across the parking lot. It had a wedding bell logo on it. "Seriously?"

I polished the last bite of my sandwich and went to the trunk to dig through my duffle—which was when I realized I had grabbed Shane's bag from the taxi.

Fucking brilliant.

I found a pair of board shorts and jerked my head to steer Ashley to the mostly empty beach where I stripped to my boxer briefs.

"Fox!"

I had no pride left. No fucks to give. I walked straight into the water.

A reef protected the bay so the water was a glassy, shallow aquamarine. Almost too warm. When I was waist-deep, I threw myself forward in a shallow dive, swimming as far as I could without taking a breath, letting the worst of my travel grime and hangover rinse away.

When I felt marginally less disgraceful, I slogged back to the beach.

Ashley was waiting with the straw of her coffee tucked into one corner of her mouth.

"Sins all gone?" she asked.

"Where do you think the garbage island came from?" I jerked my chin toward the ocean, then slicked the water from the tight curls I kept trimmed to a quarter inch so my hair actually had a chance at drying between dips. "Turn."

"Why— Oh!" She squeaked as I dragged my wet briefs off my hips and wrung them out. "Get us arrested for public nudity, then," she said to the three palm trees up on the lawn. "This day couldn't possibly get worse."

"You'd think," I muttered, pulling on Shane's boardies. "Got any sunscreen?"

She pivoted and gave me an are-you-kidding-me eye roll before she dug through her bag. I often teased her about her shoulder bag because it was like one of those bottomless, cartoon-magic bags that had whatever was needed in the moment. Lip balm, wet wipes, an elastic band. One time, I locked myself out of the shop and she'd handed me a key, asking, "Does this one work?"

Ever since then, I would say something like, *I cracked my board, Ash. Got a spare in your bag?*

Have a look, she would say as she offered it. *I think it's under the parachute.*

As she handed me the sunscreen, she said, "I have a lady razor in here if you want to clean up that bikini line?"

"I said no peeking."

She snickered and it made me feel unreasonably good to make her smile.

I didn't smile back, though. Emotion hit me so hard, I had to take a step to keep my balance. I blamed the hangover and the rush of blood sugar after twelve hours of fasting, but my throat tightened with a weird emotion. My conscience was slamming up against my genuine affection for her and it was leaving a mark.

I smeared the cream all over my arms and chest, admitting, "I took Shane for lunch the day before we were supposed to fly out. I wanted to know if he'd talked to you about signing the pre-nup I had drawn up."

Her plastic cup landed on the sand and the top popped off. Coffee and the last of the whipped cream spattered the tops of my feet. She blinked at me, her big brown eyes wounded and brimming with stunned betrayal.

Guess not.

My heart grew heavier yet shriveled at the same time.

"It's not about not trusting you," I said.

"'course not."

"Please see it from my point of view. Shane and I are partners. Everything I have is in the business and the house. I'm entitled to protect my half."

She folded her arms and turned to stare out at the water. "What did Shane say?"

"That he hadn't sent it to you yet." I finished my legs and used my wet boxers to wipe the coffee off my feet before I smoothed sunscreen over the tops of them.

"So you, what? Got him drunk to make him sign?"

"No." I straightened, insulted, and decided to find a shirt rather than ask her to do my back. "We read through the draft, made a few notes, then dropped it at the lawyer's office. The receptionist promised to email the final copy to him so you two could e-sign it before the wedding. Then we went back to the pub."

We should have gone back to work. Gone surfing. Gone home to pack. Anywhere but the pub.

Getting that document finalized had felt momentous for both of us, though. The marriage was real. Everything would change. We'd both known it.

"Shane and I did a couple of shots. He texted the guys to join us. It turned into a crawl before we took the party back to the house and kept it going on the beach. Shane and I didn't talk about the prenup again until we were in the taxi." I dropped the sunscreen on my pile of clothes and rubbed the residue from my palms into my face and the back of my neck. I was avoiding her eyes. "You're my friend, Ashley. This isn't anything against you."

She was looking at me like I'd tricked her into betting all her money on a horse that had to be shot.

"Shane cares about you. He does. But in the taxi, he said he kept thinking that I was right to ask him sign something, but that you two shouldn't need a prenup. Not if you plan to stay married? I said, 'Do you?'"

She folded protective arms across her middle.

I had felt exactly this full of dread at the potent silence in the back of the car. My gut filled with a fresh bag of cement.

"What did he say?" she prompted shakily.

"Nothing," I said flatly. "I asked him if he was having second thoughts. He said he was."

A tiny noise, the kind of whimper small creatures made when they were trapped and suffering and only wanted to die, squeaked in her throat.

It rang like a piledriver in my ears. I swallowed, thinking I might have rushed the gun on eating. I made myself say the rest and hoped only words came out of my mouth.

"I asked him if he loved you. Like, the way his parents love each other. Get through anything love. He said his mum and dad had been after him to propose to you. You were going home and they thought you were good for him, that it was time he grew up. He thought so, too."

"He doesn't love me?" The break in her voice cracked something in my ears.

I took a breath, but it didn't seem to have any air in it, only thick, hot humidity. My lungs burned.

"Shane said that signing the prenup was like admitting he expected to divorce you. I asked him if he did expect that and he said he couldn't see being with you forever."

Her gasp went into my chest like a blade, but I didn't falter. I finished her off.

"I said if he was going into your marriage thinking it wouldn't last, then he shouldn't marry you at all."

"*You* said that." Her eyes were bleak.

"I did." And as sorry as I was for hurting her, I didn't *say* I was sorry. I still believed I had done right by both of them.

I'd had a front row seat on their relationship. They were a pair of puppies who frolicked and nipped and growled, always in play mode with each other. When things got real or difficult, they retreated from each other. Shane appealed to Ashley because she had had to grow up too young and Shane was very much a Peter Pan free-spirit. He was fun. That's why everyone loved him. Shane liked Ash because she enabled him to stay exactly as he was. She washed the dishes and picked up his socks, fetched groceries and reminded him to visit the dentist.

Her mouth began to tremble.

I held out a hand, an offer to hug. It was a plea not to be hated. "We got to the airport and he said he couldn't get on the plane."

"He was *drunk*."

"He was." We'd both been swaying and slurring our words, but a moment of acute sobriety had cut through the fog. Shane had hugged me and said 'Thanks, mate.'

"You could have made him come and tell me himself." Her voice rang with a deep well of hurt. Injury done to her by Shane and by me.

"He didn't want to face his parents." Or her. Evasion of difficult conversations was an art for Shane. That's why I'd had to pick my moment to press him on the prenup. Shane had side-stepped several times and had only faced it when we ran out of time.

Maybe I was as guilty as everyone else of enabling Shane to skirt responsibility, though. I knew his avoidance of something didn't mean he wasn't brooding privately. Looking back, I could see the way he'd tensed up every time I mentioned asking Ashley to sign. I would bet my share in T&B that Shane had known deep down, from the moment he'd put Ashley on the plane with a ring on her finger, that he hadn't really wanted to marry her.

Standing outside the airport in Sydney yesterday, we'd both known that if he came to Hawaii, he would buckle to Ashley and his parents and the pressure of the moment. He would marry her and they'd be stuck in a marriage that was doomed.

That wasn't fair to either of them.

My drunk logic had concluded that, as the best man, I was duty-bound to back him up, but this was *so* shitty. It sucked *so hard* to face her.

"Ashley, you know what I came from," I said gently. "I wasn't going to stand there and watch a train wreck happen."

"You don't know that's what would have happened. You didn't even give me a chance. You didn't give *us* a chance!"

Her sudden outburst lashed at me and maybe she was right, but, "Did you love *him*, Ash? Hell and high water kind of love?"

She jerked back. "Don't you question my motives. You just screwed my entire life. You could have had this talk with Shane three months ago, before I put my life in a box and sent it to Australia. Do I *love* him? I quit my job and sold my car to buy plane tickets for my family to be here for my wedding day. What do *you* think?"

"I think you're angry," I said in a level voice, trying to keep this from escalating, but I was sharply aware she hadn't said, *Yes. I love Shane.* "You want to blame someone and I'm fine being that person." I gathered our things, including the plastic cup still dripping whipped cream and iced coffee. It was caked with sand. "But would you rather be in a new country, living in his house and sleeping in his bed, maybe carrying his kid when you found out he hadn't really wanted to marry you?"

She paled. "No. But what am I supposed to do now? Go back to Canada? To *nothing?*"

It wasn't 'nothing.' She had family. I knew it was a complicated one. Wasn't everyone's? But they loved her.

I didn't say that, though. I walked to the trash bin and threw away the cup.

My conscience contorted into a knot, squeezing and hurting every inch of me as I turned back and said what had cut through my inebriation in the back of the cab.

"I love Shane like a brother, Ash. But he gave up and walked away before you even got married. What does that tell you about your chances?"

She blinked at me with weepy bewilderment.

"He wasn't going to stick. Not for the long haul." Not in the way she deserved.

"He never loved me? That's what you're saying? My whole relationship with him was a lie and I'm the idiot who didn't see it?"

"Don't." I felt scraped hollow inside, seeing how hurt she was, but they'd really only had three months together, then three months apart. Did she really believe that was enough to base a lifetime commitment on?

"Shane thinks prettier than reality. You know that." It was what made him such an excellent salesman and was a big reason why Togs and Boards was so successful. Everyone took the gulp of Kool-Aid Shane handed them and climbed aboard the train bound for pots of gold. Even me. "If he led you on, it wasn't malicious. He always believes things will work out and lots of times they do." Other times, I scrambled behind him to make sure whatever Shane had blindly promised didn't bank-rupt us.

"But *you* thought we'd wind up divorced. And that I would come after *your* company. So you blew up my marriage before we had a chance to fail."

I didn't see it that way, but, "Yeah, I guess I did."

"Well, fuck you, Fox."

She needed a punching bag. I accepted that. It still hurt like hell.

"I left my coffee in the car. I'll wait for you there." At least I'd had the sense to keep the key fob. I didn't fancy walking the length of the island in this heat.

ASHLEY

My hair was definitely on fire. I definitely wanted to scream and cry and rage. I thought about pulling a Fox, stripping naked and wading into the ocean, but never coming back.

Why would he do this to me? Why?

Because he was Fox. He was forever catching my arm if we crossed a street together, in case I forgot to look for traffic on my right because they drove on the other side of the road in Australia. Shane was a heavy-pour kind of host while Fox always brought me a water if I had more than two glasses of alcohol. More often than not, he also brought me a burger or some other substantial meal to soak up whatever I was drinking.

I would love to say I was special, but Fox had dedicated his life to keeping Shane out of trouble, too. Shane was impulsive and wildly optimistic and never would have paid the mortgage on time if his fiscally-responsible housemate hadn't looked after that pesky detail. Same with Togs and Boards. Shane was a geek for sports equipment and outdoor gadgets, but he would have made all the usual rookie mistakes of overextending during start-up if Fox hadn't set budgets and limited their inventory. *Fox* had had the idea to hire me to give their social media a shot in the arm in exchange for staying in their house for free.

I still wanted to kill him. What did Fox know about me and Shane?

More than I did, apparently, if Shane had confided to him that he didn't want to marry me without informing *me*.

I shouldn't be surprised that his parents had pressured him into proposing, either. His, 'What do you think? Should we get married?' hadn't exactly brimmed with loving sentiment.

I'd been stunned that he'd said that much. That he had *cared* that much. Shane could have anyone. Why me? I mean, there's nothing wrong with me that a little therapy wouldn't cure. I'm plump in the rear and lean in the self-esteem, but I'm nice. I'm cute. I can be funny.

But Shane is an intrepid, entrepreneurial, barrel-chasing surfer where I'm a prairie girl who can hardly swim. Not in rolling waves, anyway. Shane isn't afraid to break rules whereas I abide by the speed limit. I would wet myself before I'd use a handicapped stall and I'm chronically apologetic. Which I'm working on.

I'm working on all of it because if Shane's best friend had abandoned him a week into his three-month trip of a lifetime, Shane wouldn't have clung to the handful of people he had just met. He would have struck out on his own, making friends and having spur-of-the-moment adventures along the way.

I'm so *tired* of being predictable, practical, timid little Ashley. That's why I went to Australia in the first place. I was trying really hard to make bold choices and live my life with courage, the way people like Shane and Izzy and Fox did.

So I had answered Shane's tepid proposal with a fervent, "Yes!"

Did I *love* Shane? Maybe not the way I had always hoped to love someone, but the soul mate mythology has been extensively tested by my sister and proven largely self-delusional. Shane is a solid guy with a real job who respects and appreciates me. At least, that's what I'd believed at the time. He made me laugh and told me I looked pretty and made me feel needed and valued. What more could anyone want in a life partner?

What had he wanted that I don't possess? That's what really gnawed at me. I wasn't super confident, but I'm not fully insecure, either. Maybe I was never an A student, but I'm a solid B plus. Same as my cup size, incidentally. And I'm a team player. I worked very hard to look out for Shane's business, taking on its success as a personal mission.

I sniffed, realizing that fresh tears were filling my sinuses. I had been crying when I pulled off the highway while Fox slept, but that had been panic at being lost and general overwhelm. As soon as I talked to Shane, I kept telling myself, everything would get ironed out. All I needed to do was get to the hotel. Fox would help me get Shane on the phone and we'd persuade him to show up.

That wasn't going to happen, though. This was real. And Fox wasn't on my side. He didn't *want* me to marry his best friend. Because he thought I'd go after their business if and when Shane and I fell apart. That hurt. A lot. Not just Fox's lack of faith in our relationship, but his lack of faith in *me*. I had done a ton of things to support Togs and Boards. I redesigned their whole website. What about that?

I was so *mad*. At Fox and Shane and myself.

But so what? Being angry or sad or so humiliated I wanted to dig myself into a hole in the ground had never done a damn thing to change my circumstances. I had still had to get up and look at Mom over the breakfast table and face my teachers and fellow students and skeptical social workers. Life happened and you had to roll with it.

So I tried to think constructively. I had to tell my family that the wedding was off. Then what? Go back to Pine Grove and start over there?

That thought was enough to make my eyes water all over again.

I was hot and sweaty, sniveling and soggy. I didn't even have the balled-up tissue that woman had given me earlier.

I went into the public washroom where I blew my nose and washed off my smeared make-up. Ugh. With my red nose and shadowy racoon eyes, I looked like someone had died.

Only my girlish dreams.

When I came out of the toilet, I found the path blocked by an easel that obviously belonged to the wedding van. It had a chalkboard propped on it that read: *Happily Ever After is this way.*

I followed the arrow with my gaze and saw Fox leaning on the red convertible, sipping his coffee. He had pulled on a plain blue shirt and left it unbuttoned. The brown strip of skin down his chest was burnished by the late morning sun. His bellybutton was hidden by a small crease as he slouched. His abs were pure muscle bisected by a fine line of hair.

Why couldn't he be stupid and ugly and hateful? Instead, he was strong and steady and watched me approach as though he'd been keeping an eye out for me the whole time, prepared to come after me if I did something rash.

I trudged over and glared at him, aware I was punishing the wrong person, but he was here and Shane was not. Also, who asked him to be the voice of reason anyway? That was my job, thanks, and I had decided to take a vacation from that.

Vacation.

I tipped back my head and looked hopelessly at the expanse of clear, intense blue sky.

"What am I supposed to do? Blow what little money I have left in Hawaii for a week? Then go back to where I came from? Go to Australia—*where all my stuff is*—and have no home or job there, either?" No friends even. Everyone I knew in that country was part of Shane's circle.

Fox straightened off the car. His mouth hung crooked. "I'll help if you come to Oz."

"Gee, thanks, but I've had enough of your help." I threw myself into the passenger seat, set my elbow on the edge of the open window, then jerked away from the burn of hot metal. I glared at the women in plum-colored dresses arriving to lead their best friend down the aisle. They were smiling and excited. Dumb cows.

Fox climbed behind the wheel, waited a beat as though expecting me to look at him.

I refused to. After a minute, he sighed and pulled away.

FOX

*U*nder any other circumstance, this would have been a perfect day. The island landscape was spectacular, the traffic minimal, the music upbeat and the weather glorious. I was driving a convertible on an empty road with a woman by my side.

A woman who hated my guts.

I wanted to hold her hand. Comfort her. The more my hangover receded, the heavier my conscience weighed. What could I do, though? Not one damned thing.

It was hitting me that I was stuck here for a week unless I changed my flight. Much as I'd love to get the hell out of dodge, however, I was worried about Ash.

I was worried she wouldn't get over her mad. I was a good friend. *Shane had said so.* It was eating at me that I had stomped all over my friendship with her, but I didn't know how to make up for it. How could I? There was nothing.

Around and around my brain went, looking for a solution until, an hour later, we arrived at the resort.

I didn't know how the parking worked so I pulled up at

the valet stand. Ashley wasn't talking to me and slammed out of the car the minute I put the car in park. She stalked away without a word.

"Ash." I rose from my side, guts stretching thin as I felt an urge to follow her while my feet stayed rooted in guilt.

"I have to see Mom. The Holloways are in four-oh-two," she tossed over her shoulder.

"Are you staying in the resort, sir?" A bellman wearing a hotel shirt held out a hand for the car's fob.

"Yes, but I'm not checked in yet. I have to—" Oh, hell. Was it my job to inform the hotel that the wedding was off? I looked for Ashley, but she was gone. "I'm here for a wedding. The groom's parents are already here and expecting me. I need to speak to them before I do anything else." I didn't know how tight the security was, but I remembered I was in the States and needed to tip. I offered a twenty.

"I'll leave your luggage with the concierge and tap you into the elevator." The bellman pocketed the bill.

"Thanks. I'll be back as soon as I can."

We crossed a helluva nice open-air lobby with views of the surf that didn't quit. Maybe I *would* stick around. There was no problem too big that couldn't be outrun on a surfboard for a few hours.

The bellman tagged the reader in the elevator and pressed the floor number for me. I nodded my thanks, then let out a breath as the doors closed.

Shane's parents, Eddie and Sandy, had always been good to me. Coming from divorce, I was kind of fascinated by their lifelong devotion to each other, especially because they'd been through a lot over the years. I always wondered what their secret was and I *hated* that I was going to upset them when they were expecting a happy event.

I knocked, only realizing then that they might be at the pool.

Sandy opened the door with a wide smile that faltered as she saw it was me, not the son she was expecting.

"G'day, Fox. Shane isn't with you?" The permanent crinkle of maternal concern in her brow deepened. "He hasn't answered any of my texts." She backed up to let me into a room with a king bed, a desk and a chair.

The door was open to the balcony where Eddie was rising from his seat there.

"Shane's totally fine," I assured them. "But no, he's not here."

"I told her he'd want to see his girl." Eddie's body was stooped from a lifetime as a brickie. He kept hold of his beer and spoke through the open door. "Sandy wanted him to be able to find us when he arrived, but see? He's with Ashley. We can go down to the pool and Shane can catch up to us when he's ready. Beer?" he offered me.

"*No.* Thank you. But I will come in for a minute, if you don't mind." I waved for Sandy to precede me out to the small balcony. "Shane is fine," I repeated firmly, meeting Sandy's anxious blue gaze. "Not hurt or anything, but he isn't here. He decided not to come."

Sandy touched the gold pendant of a fingerprint that she always wore. "Do you mean he was delayed? Or...?"

"The wedding is off."

"Ah, shit." Eddie lowered back into his chair and took a pull off his beer.

"Oh, Ashley," Sandy said on a pained sigh. "Oh, dear."

"Yeah." I drew a deep breath and braced myself to confess the rest.

ASHLEY

$\mathcal{M}$y mom, sister, and niece were all staying in a villa rented by Whitney's new boyfriend, Oliver, who had brought his son, Ryan.

I wasn't sure what to make of them. Ryan was four, fairly well-behaved and actually pretty cute, but Oliver came off as a bit of a saint—which made me suspicious. Whitney had become more discerning as she closed in on thirty, but from the time she'd turned up pregnant in high school, she always seemed to have a man of some kind hanging around and they weren't always top shelf.

Whether that made my older sister a blind romantic or a codependent, I wasn't sure, but I had returned from three months in Australia to discover a stranger had a key to our apartment. I hadn't cared how nice Oliver *seemed*. Especially because he'd leaped on the wedding in Hawaii idea almost as fast as Whitney had, insisting on reserving a villa and paying for it. Granted he owned a plumbing company and seemed to be doing well, but he had an ex-wife and paid her support. Where did all his money come from?

According to Whitney, his divorced had been very civilized. No one yelled. Teachers never reported anyone to the authorities and the police had never come to his door.

Even so, who signed up for a week of living with his girlfriend's mother after only a few months of dating? Oliver's claim that it was 'a great chance for everyone to get to know each other better' sounded shifty. I wanted to know what he *really* wanted.

My mom, Joanna, had gone along with the villa proposal because it meant she would have a full kitchen. "We'll barely afford groceries at those prices," she had declared after reading reviews online. "In *American* dollars," she stressed. "We are *not* eating out."

So we had crammed ourselves into this villa yesterday evening after twenty hours of travel and a stop at the market for a week's worth of food.

Fliss, who was twelve going on forty, let me in. She had gone through a growth spurt while I'd been in Australia. She was almost as tall as me now, stick-thin with subtle curves. Whitney had said she could start wearing make-up, but Fliss wasn't in the hurry to grow up that Whit had been.

Fliss kept her ash-blond hair in a careless clip and preferred shapeless hoodies rather than tight jeans or dresses. She was academic and introverted and sarcastic. I adored her to pieces, but she was giving me the cold shoulder. Disappearing to Australia for an extended holiday was one thing. Moving there was a betrayal of our bond. She would probably take the news that the wedding was off better than anyone.

I could stand my niece being pleased by my misfortune. The smug 'You should have known better' from Mom was going to kill me. Quitting a good job and booking a three-month trip to a foreign country last year had been reckless and pointless. Marrying a man I barely knew? One who ran a surf shack—her words—and didn't have a trade or profession? One who lived in a money pit of a beach house and disappeared up the coast with his boys' club at a moment's notice? Nothing good could come of this.

And nothing will, Mom. You were right all along.

Fliss poked her head out the door after I came in, hesitating to close it.

"Isn't Shane with you?" Her eyes widened as she realized I'd been crying. "Are you okay?"

"Not really." I moved further into the two-bedroom bungalow and smiled weakly at Ryan on the sofa. He held a game controller. "Are you two here by yourself?" There was no one in the kitchen and both bedroom doors stood open.

Ryan pointed his elbow toward the door to the patio. "They're outside. Can we keep playing?" he asked Fliss.

"In a sec." Fliss might have been about to ask me what was wrong, but the screen door abruptly scraped open.

"Hi!" Whitney appeared in a bikini top and short-shorts. Her blond hair was freshly blown out, bangs cutting a wispy line across her graceful eyebrows. She wore full make-up and sandals with a low heel. "We were just saying you two ought to be here by now. Where's Shane?" She glanced around with a welcoming smile, then responded to a questioning voice on the patio, "Yes, they're here. Come out," she urged with a wave as she ducked back outside.

I bit back a groan of frustration and forced myself to walk out to where the red brick patio was surrounded by thick, well-watered lawn. The grass ended abruptly between the trunks of a pair of palms that framed the azure waves crashing onto a tiny, private beach. A warm breeze came off the water as a fine, cooling mist. It condensed on the table and chairs that sat beneath an open yellow sun umbrella.

Mom and Oliver rose. Everyone wore a welcoming smile and looked beyond me to the empty space where Shane was supposed to be.

As I searched for the words I needed, Whitney asked, "Did Shane go see his parents?"

"No." I hugged myself a little harder.

"Nap?" Oliver took off his cap to scratch his balding head, waiting for Joanna and Whitney to sit before he sank back into his own chair. "How long was his flight?"

I unclenched my jaw and admitted, "He didn't get on the plane. He's not here."

Whitney snorted in exactly the way I had when Fox had said it. Like it was a joke. Except it stung so deep when she did it, I couldn't help but glare at her.

"Seriously?" Whitney sobered. "Did he miss it?"

"He doesn't want to get married." Saying it aloud sent a fresh wave of humiliation through me, one that nearly closed my throat. *This is what I get for reaching too high.*

Mom snapped her spine straight, nearly coming out of her chair again. "I don't understand."

Me, neither. "He stayed in Sydney. The wedding's off." And saying it aloud made it *so real.*

"Are you being serious right now?" Whitney's eyes were round with disbelief.

"Well, you knew he didn't want to marry in Hawaii," Mom scolded. *Scolded.* "I told you—"

"Mom!" I bit out. "Can we save the post-mortem for after the body is cold? *God.*"

"What are you going to do?" Whitney asked, frowning with confusion. "About moving?"

"I don't know, do I?"

"Don't yell at me. It's not my fault."

"Can I do anything?" Oliver wore a concerned frown. "Talk to the hotel for you?"

Oh, God. I dropped my head into my hand. I hadn't even thought of that.

"Yes," Mom said decisively. "Get your money back. Whitney, call to change our flights—"

"No!" Whitney cried. "This is our vacation. We're here. We're staying. But are you moving back in here with us?" Whit wrinkled her nose. It had been fine for a night, but, "Maybe you and Fliss can share the pullout and Ryan can have Fliss's bed in Mom's room? It was fine for him to be in our room last night, but not all week."

"My stuff's in the hotel." I had walked it over before I left for the airport. I had registered and asked them to leave it in our suite, anticipating that Shane and I would be going straight up there when we got back.

I was going to have to quit thinking this day couldn't get worse, because it definitely could.

"I'll come with you," Fliss offered. She was suddenly right beside me, pushing in for a hug the way she had been doing all her life.

I automatically closed my arms around her wiry frame. For one second, I let myself cling to the youngest, slightest, most supportive person here.

"I'll do it myself," I said into hair I'd been combing since it had first grown in. It took everything in me to keep from breaking down. "I need to be by myself for a bit."

"Are you sure?" Fliss's mouth was pulling down with deep empathy.

I scraped the heel of my hand beneath each eye and nodded, then walked out, struggling to see the paved pathway into the hotel.

FOX

*S*andy was deeply upset on Ashley's behalf and wanted to see her. She and Eddie had eaten breakfast at the Barnes' villa this morning so they knew where they were going.

I probably owed Ashley's family an apology, but doubted Ashley wanted to see me. Also, despite passing out on the plane and napping in the car, I was gassing out. I went as far as the lobby with the Holloways then veered toward the concierge desk to retrieve my luggage, planning to check in and get a shower, then catch a nap in a real bed.

"Hi. The valet said he'd leave my luggage with you. It came out of a red Audi. Shane Holloway?" I remembered it had his name on it.

"Right. Barnes-Holloway. You were already checked in so we put it in your room. Do you need a key?" The concierge offered me a card in its little folder with the room number and the wifi password.

"Yeah, but—" Shit. I was too tired to say, *I was drunk. Mistakes were made.* I offered a half-hearted, "Thanks, mate."

I would fetch my useless luggage before Ashley got in there and read the tag and thought Shane had shown up after all. Then I would drag my sorry ass back down here to check into my own room.

I had booked a standard room for myself. One where I had expected to listen to parents yelling at their kids in the pool, maybe have someone next to me play their TV too loud and complain it was too hot to go to the beach.

Ashley had booked her and Shane on the Vista level. I stepped out of the elevator and walked through the Vista Club lounge on the way to the room. A young woman in a housekeeping uniform looked up from replacing a carafe of complimentary coffee and greeted me with a warm, "Aloha."

"G'day." The view through the floor to ceiling windows was nothing but ocean and sky. Whitecaps speckled the water and a few wispy clouds floated near the horizon. Directly below, frondy palms danced above a rocky point where the surf smashed itself into sparkling drops.

This level was way too nice for my tight fists, but Shane loved his creature-comforts. Oh, right. I turned back to the woman.

"There was a problem with my luggage. I'm going to need a toothbrush and a razor. Is there a disposable one the hotel offers or do I have to go to the gift shop?"

"I can help you." She disappeared into a housekeeping closet and came out with a selection of toiletries. "Anything else?"

Thank you, Vista level.

"This will do for now, thanks." I needed underwear, but I'd check the gift shop for that. At least Shane and I were roughly the same size. I could wear the rest of his clothes until I bought my own.

I carried on to the room, tapped the lock with my card, and entered.

I honestly hadn't believed there was more shit that could hit any more fans, but I was wrong.

The ocean view suite was big enough for a king bed, a full lounge, a small dining table and a wall of windows onto a lanai that ran the length of the oversized room. There was a full outdoor lounge and a small breakfast table out there.

Ashley sat up on the bed. Tears were running down her flushed, persecuted expression. Her surprised kick knocked over one of the towels sculpted into a swan that sat in the middle of the bed. There were two of them, encircled by rose petals that had been shaped like a heart that—yep—was now broken.

The door fell closed behind me with an overly loud *clunk*.

I took in the rest of the purgatory I had underwritten. A bottle of champagne sat in a sweaty bucket in a stand beside the sofa. On the end table stood a pair of champagne flutes. One glass wore a bow tie, the other had a small bouquet tied to its stem.

Over on the desk, a cellophane wrapped basket held water bottles, more wine, chocolates and protein snacks to fuel active honeymooners. A heart-shaped, cellophane balloon floated above it, imprinted with a scrolling, *I Do!*

The honeymoon package add-on had sounded like a great wedding gift two weeks ago, when I hadn't had a clue what else to get them.

"This room is on your card, isn't it?" Ashley said. "They told me it was prepaid when I checked in, but I didn't think about that at all. I just got my key, walked in, and fell apart."

"It's fine," I assured her, eyeing her warily. "I accidentally grabbed Shane's luggage. They brought it up here. I was afraid you'd see it and think he was here." I set the toiletries on the dresser beside the printed note that read, *We want your stay to be memorable!*

Job done.

"I'll grab it and go sort it." I glanced for the bag, but wound up looking at Ash. I got tangled up in the shattered misery of her doe-eyes. The ceiling pressed down on me. I wanted so badly to be fix this for her.

"Um." I cleared my throat. "Closet?" I paused on my way there to look through the door-less archway into the bathroom. It was cavernous with a double-sink vanity and a bathtub separate from the shower. There were shutters in the wall over the tub. They were open, framing Ashley on the bed.

"So you can watch your wife have a bath?" she guessed with a dubious wrinkle of her brow.

"I think it's so you can enjoy the view from the tub." I bit back my grin as I nodded at the windows beyond her, not wanting to laugh at where her mind had gone. Especially because I was titillated by the idea of watching a woman in a tub, soapy bubbles slithering down narrow shoulders to the tops of small breasts that—

Nope. Not the time or place, sport. Definitely not the woman.

I turned my back on the tub and glanced into a shower big enough for a family of five plus a shaggy dog. There was a bench along the back with a retractable clothes line above it. Three different showerheads offered the full carwash experience.

Lots of room for—

Where the hell was this coming from? I was definitely in recovery mode if I was thinking about sex, but no.

"Okay, this is weird." The shower was enclosed by an oversized barn door of frosted glass on rollers. It either closed off the shower or the adjacent toilet stall, but not both. "Nothing says honeymoon like watching your partner take a dump. Am I right?"

I leaned to glance at her through the opening over the tub.

"Finally, a silver lining to having my wedding called off." She drew her knees up to her chest and hugged them.

I came out of the bathroom. "Sandy went looking for you at your mom's villa. She feels terrible."

"It's not her fault."

"No." They hadn't blamed me, either. I wished they had. I wanted to be punished.

"They're so nice. I wanted to be part of their family from the first time I met them."

"Same," I said, meaning it. I loved my foster parents, but their marriage had fallen apart years ago, leaving it in two pieces on either side of the Pacific. Shane's family was broken, too, but there was a lot of glue in the form of love. In the way Sandy poured it over everyone, especially Shane's friends.

I moved to the night table and plucked a tissue out of the box, handed it to her.

Ashley eyed me as though considering my comment, then blew her nose. She discarded it off the bed where a handful were already balled up on the carpet. She took a fresh one and used it to dry her eyes and cheeks and down along her jaw into her throat.

"How did your mom take it?" I asked.

She flinched. Shrugged and muttered, "She told me so."

"What does that mean?"

"That she knew it wouldn't work out. You weren't the only one who didn't believe he loved me."

"Ash." I sat on the edge of the bed so my hip was near her bare feet. I had an urge to bracelet her ankle with my hand. It was mostly coming from a place of wanting to offer comfort, but rubbing a woman's leg, even if it was her shinbone, and even if you were friends, might come across as a pass. Especially when she was in such a bad place.

Her skin always looked incredible, though. Soft and smooth and tanned. My palm itched. I shifted so that I was sitting more with my back to her. I hung my hands between my knees and rubbed my palms together to erase the prickling sensation in them.

"I haven't even told the hotel yet. I just wanted to be alone. Then I came up here and got hit in the face with this...surprise pity party." She threw the handful of rose petals into the air. "I don't know what to do, Fox." She hugged her knees again and set her cheek atop them. "I have a flight booked to Australia in five days. Do I get on it? Go back to Canada? What?"

"It's a lot," I agreed. "Do you want me to talk to the hotel for you? They probably have a protocol for this." I wondered how often weddings were called off. I suspected most people went through with it once they got this far, even if they knew it was a terrible idea. My foster parents had, mostly because they'd been saddled with me.

"Are you going to change your flight and go back right away?" she asked.

"I don't know. I was going to get some sleep before I made any decisions." The far side of the bed called to me, drunken swans, crushed rose petals, and all.

"I guess I'll pack and go to the villa. Whitney wants to stay." Ashley sighed. "Mom's never had a proper vacation and she already paid for the groceries. She won't let them go to waste. She won't let me hear the end of what a bust this has been, though. What are Eddie and Sandy going to do?"

"I didn't ask, but they're traveling by cruise ship. I expect they'll stay as planned."

Her sigh was heavy and deeply sad.

"Listen. Stay here." I wound up with my hand on top of her foot as the words impulsively left my mouth. "I'll square it up with Shane when I get back. It's the least we can do."

"Don't feel *sorry* for me."

"I don't. Well, it's guilty conscience, for sure." I rubbed the top of her foot.

Her gaze flickered to where I was touching her and a tiny frown of consternation appeared between her brows. I brought my hand back to my own thigh.

"You need time to figure out your next steps. As your friend—and I swear to you I am your friend—I want to give you the space to work out what to do."

Our gazes hit and clung. I could see the conflict in her. She used to trust me. Now I saw doubt. It didn't matter that I deserved it. It still hurt. Maybe it hurt worse because I deserved it.

My hand twitched, wanting to reach out again. Wanting to restore her faith in me.

The ring of the phone on the night table startled us both.

Ashley gave it a grim look of dread. "Who do you think that is?"

I leaned forward and answered it, cutting off the second ring. "'Lo?"

"Aloha. This is Kalani in the spa." Her voice was gently inflected with a Hawaiian accent. "Everything is ready for your couple's massage. Are you on your way?"

Ashley overheard. Her eyes widened in horror.

I bit back a curse. Honeymoon package. *Such* a great idea.

"It was supposed to be a surprise," I said, speaking to both of them. "I don't think it's going to happen."

"You've already paid for it," Kalani pointed out.

Paying for something I didn't use went against everything I believed in.

"Just a sec." I muffled the phone against my stomach. "I booked this package as your wedding gift." I waved at the decorations and baskets. "It comes with a couple's massage."

It was the sort of pampering Shane would never think to arrange for a woman, but I had thought it would be a nice touch for Ashley. She was as much a penny-pincher as I was and rarely did anything to treat herself.

"Why do you hate me?" She shook her head with astonished disbelief.

I opened my mouth to grovel. I felt *awful*. More than anything, I wanted to get back to the friendship that meant so much to me.

So that's where I went, to the place where we were comfortable and trusting enough to mess with each other.

"It's your chin," I said gravely. "It's too pointy. You know I've never been able to get past it."

Her expression wavered between crumpling with sorrow and flashing into outrage. After a second, she curled her fingers against her mouth and looked away. A tiny snort came out of her.

"It's not the moustache?" she asked.

"No, the moustache suits you."

"You're a horrible person." Her eyes were gleaming with tears, but there was a smile in her voice.

"I am a terrible person," I agreed, heart lifting at that glimmer of humor. "Shane said to book the massage for when he arrived because airplane seats do in his back." I suspected it had also been an exit strategy from meeting Ashley's family, but that didn't change the fact I was out three hundred bucks if we didn't get our asses downstairs. "I have to pay for it either way. What do you say? You're stressed out. I feel like a sack of rocks. Let's get a massage."

I didn't wait for her to agree, just brought the phone to my ear.

"We'll be right there."

ASHELY

"*A*re you wearing underwear?" I asked Fox when we were in the elevator.

He gave me a startled look.

"I mean during the massage. They always tell me to take off as much as I'm comfortable removing and I never know when to stop."

"I think when you stop feeling comfortable?" He quirked a brow at me. "I don't actually have any, just the pair still damp from my swim. I'll wear Shane's shirts and boardies, but I won't wear his grundies."

"Oh." So he was naked under that robe? A vision started to form in my head before I hurriedly erased it, but my cheeks still tingled with a blush. I shrugged inside my robe. "I kept my thong on."

"Oh." He turned his nose to the front of the car. Cleared his throat. "I've only had a massage in Thailand and they don't care. Not that kind," he added quickly, cutting me a stern glance.

"Right." I rolled my eyes, smirking.

He frowned at my skepticism. "I'm fussy about who touches my junk. I sure as hell don't pay strangers to play with it."

You didn't know Izzy, I wanted to say, but bit my lips into a line, unsure why I cared one way or another. I found a quirky smile.

"Since I've seen what you're like if someone asks to borrow your pen, I'm inclined to believe you."

"I don't even like to share a bar of soap," he muttered. "Probably because I spent so much time with one in my mouth as a kid."

"Soap? Or junk?" I batted innocent lashes at him.

He pursed his mouth. "I'm going to let you have that because you're my friend and you need cheering up."

I grinned, marginally cheered. Bantering with Fox was always fun. I'd missed him.

More than Shane? I brushed that thought aside, but it didn't erase the troubling knowledge that if I didn't move to Australia, I wouldn't see Fox again.

That thought hit me like a sucker punch, landing so hard I had to take a deep breath to absorb it.

The elevator doors opened. Fox stuck out a hand to hold them open while I ducked my face and scooted out ahead of him, disturbed. All my emotions were at eleven right now, I reasoned. I wouldn't lose touch with him just because he forced my wedding to be called off. We could still be friends. Couldn't we?

Maybe I could still go to Australia and— No. I couldn't. My plan had hinged on having a home and a job. Fox might be willing to keep me on at T&B, but I couldn't work with Shane. I didn't want to. Not anymore.

This was so weird. How was I this upset at the idea of not seeing Fox, yet totally fine with the prospect of moving around the world and probably never seeing Izzy again?

Fox checked us in at Reception and handed me one of the forms on a clipboard to fill in my medical history. I tried to put things back to silly banter by holding out my pen.

"Can we switch?"

"Sure." He absently offered his pen and didn't get the joke until I failed to take his. "Oh. You're hilarious."

I had thought so, but now I wondered what it meant that he was willing to let me use his pen without question.

It meant nothing. He could get a fresh one from the desk if he wanted. I was being silly.

A woman named Inga came to get us a few minutes later. She led us outside to a hut big enough for two massage tables and a shelf full of towels. One wall was open to the surf. A gentle breeze wafted in with the lulling noise of the churning waves.

"This is my husband, Ikaika," Inga introduced.

The Hawaiian looked like a pro wrestler who broke sturdy men like Fox over his meaty thigh to make kindling for a luau. He shook Fox's hand and glanced over his paperwork while Inga did the same with mine. They asked about allergies and other concerns.

"I'll get handouts and your gift basket while you're having your lesson," Ikaika said.

"Wait. What lesson?" Fox and I spoke over each another.

"I'm going to show you some techniques so you can give each other a massage anytime you want." Inga smiled and nodded at Ikaika as he left.

"Oh. Um..." I cast an uncertain look at Fox.

He shrugged.

"Before you start, make sure you have everything the way you want it." Inga indicated the room. "You don't want oil on your hands before you set your phone to Do Not Disturb or realize the music is too loud. Have some towels handy," she advised as she set a couple of hand towels on the end of one massage table. "I can close the curtain if the light or the breeze will disturb you?"

"I don't mind if it's open." I glanced at Fox.

He nod-shrugged, looking as panic-lost as I felt.

"Good. Ashley why don't you sit on the edge of the table here." Inga patted the massage table. "And Fox if you leave your robe on, but drop it off your shoulders? Expose as much of your back— Perfect," she said as Fox turned his back and loosened the robe, catching the terrycloth on his bent elbows while making sure to keep the bottom half closed.

Inga adjusted the collar where it draped across his lower back and steered him with a hand on his upper arm. "Now stand in front of Ashley. Open your legs," she instructed me.

"I thought you were going to demonstrate," I said, thinking my voice sounded thin.

"It's a practical lesson." Inga cheerfully pressed Fox into place.

Fox seemed clumsy for the first time in his life. He gave me a look over his shoulder that could only be described as a cat going into a carrier that held the smell of the vet.

I hesitated, but Inga took hold of my knee and, *Whoop*. I wound up splaying my thighs to give Fox a space to back into. I swallowed as my knees sank into the folds of robe draping his flat hips. My vision filled with the wall of his contoured back.

"Ikaika's handout will summarize all the tips I give you

and includes a map to guide you through a fifteen-minute massage. That's usually a nice amount of time so you're both fully relaxed, but not so tired you can't do other things." Inga winked.

Hahaha. I bit back growing hysteria. "We're not actually, um, lovers." My throat dried up on the word.

"You're saving it for the wedding night? How sweet!" Inga moved to get the oil.

Fox swung a look over his shoulder again, astounded hilarity widening his eyes.

I slapped my hand over my mouth and made an agreeing, "Mmm-hmm," noise.

He dipped his head and his shoulders jerked with suppressed laughter.

Shane was going to get such a kick out of this, I thought with a private giggle, then sobered as reality rolled back in like a storm surge.

"This will be good for you," Inga was saying as she came back. She tipped a dime-sized spot of oil into my palm. "It will help you get used to touching each other. You want to rub your palms to warm it." She rubbed her dry hands together to demonstrate. "When you touch your partner, relax your hands. Tell him with your touch that he should relax. The more surface you touch, the more relaxing the massage."

I held my hands above Fox's shoulders, sensing his tension as he waited. Tentatively I set my oily hands against his skin. He was warm and smooth and his hard muscles flexed under my hesitant strokes. Goosebumps came up on his arm. I instinctively drifted my hand there to smooth them away.

His tricep twitched and the hollow of his spine deepened.

A weird swirling sensation, like laughter but different,

accosted the pit of my belly. My scalp prickled and I had to consciously draw my next breath. I was hyper-aware of the width of Fox's hips between my splayed knees. Of the little knicks and scars on his skin from being tumbled in the waves.

"I, um..." Fox cleared his throat. "I had a physiotherapist work on my leg when I pulled a hamstring. He did a deep tissue thing." He sounded gruff. His shoulders seemed to be hardening, not relaxing beneath my touch. "Shouldn't she be digging in with her thumbs?"

"You can bruise the muscle if you don't know what you're doing. That's not very romantic. Leave the serious treatment to the experts and let this be a sensual experience. Long, sweeping strokes," Inga coached, motioning for me to paint the oil across every inch of skin I could reach. "Any time you can't think of what to do, go back to these long, easy strokes. It can be very hypnotic for both of you."

It was. I was trying to dismiss this as an objective task like washing a wall, but Fox's skin was drum tight across firm muscles. I couldn't remember ever touching a man so thoroughly and deliberately. Not without being in a lip lock or other intimate scenario. It was like petting a big, powerful animal. Soothing, yet dangerous. Exciting.

"Do you like it?" Inga asked Fox. "Tell her. You'll want to remember to do that during sex, too. Communication is everything."

"Oh, my God." I and lifted my hands off his back. I wanted to bury my face in them, but they were covered in oil.

Fox hitched his robe into place, chuckling dryly.

"Don't be embarrassed. Why don't you take over, Fox?"

"I think we've got it." He yanked his belt tight before he faced me. His cheeks were going red and there was a persecuted light in his eyes. *Please get me out of this.*

I opened my mouth to let him off the hook, but Inga spoke again, cajoling, "You'll want him to know how to rub your feet if you plan to get pregnant."

I met Fox's thunderstruck expression and the absurdity couldn't be contained any longer. We burst out laughing.

ASHLEY

*W*e got through the foot rub and Ikaika came back. For the next hour, none of us spoke while Fox and I were molded into a gob of warm clay.

I was lost to a hypnagogic state when Inga wafted a lemon scented cloth above my face to gently bring me back to the real world.

"Your fiance is fast asleep," she said softly. "I'll let you wake him. If you'd like to put on your robes and enjoy our relaxation lounge, I'll bring you some water and your complimentary champagne."

I nodded, brain emptied of my ability to think or talk. I waited for the door to close then sat up and glanced at Fox. He was on his back and dead to the world, softly snoring. I sluggishly pushed my arms into my robe and belted it before I moved across to wake him.

"Fox?" I nudged his shoulder. "Can you wake up? We have to go to the lounge, but you can go back to sleep there."

He sat up, but I could tell he wasn't really conscious. I made sure to keep the sheet draped across his lap as I helped him put on his robe, then I had to risk a glance to see if he had managed to belt it properly. He had. Whew.

I picked up his slippers and we staggered to the covered patio where Inga was leaving champagne and cucumber water on a table next to one of the double hammocks. All the other hammocks and loungers were occupied.

As I crawled in, Fox followed right on top of me. His weight sagged me onto him and he swept me into an absent, one-armed hug that shifted me half atop him. His legs tangled with mine. We were squished together like shredded cheese in a taco. His whole body went lax on a long sigh and he was asleep again.

It was pleasantly warm, but there was a breeze. Inga draped a light blanket over us, handed me one of the glasses of champagne, then nudged the hammock into a lulling sway before she walked away.

I didn't ruin the moment by thinking about whether it was inappropriate to be cuddled up with Fox. It wasn't like I'd never been jammed up against him in a backseat or on a couch. It felt nice, actually, to be snuggled when I was so blue.

I carefully sipped, letting the sweet bubbles settle on my tongue while I listened to the distant pulse of waves and allowed myself to relax into the solid warmth of Fox's body.

Relaxing wasn't something I did very often. I actually couldn't remember a time since elementary school when I hadn't been stressing and trying to take control of some aspect of my life. I'd gone straight from the drama of my parents' divorce to Whitney being pregnant to helping watch Fliss while Whitney finished high school and got her hair-styling certificate.

Once I graduated high school myself, I got a job at a bar and moved in with a workmate so Mom could sell our old house and buy a condo. I put myself through community college part-time between serving drinks and watching Fliss after school. My certificate in communications landed me a decent job by Pine Grove standards. I had reliable income if not a lot of it. The company supplied medical devices and offered decent benefits and a year-end bonus. I bought a used car, rented my own apartment with a bedroom and a den, and started a retirement savings plan.

Small towns were notorious for limited dating pools so I hadn't had much luck there. Plus, between Mom's lectures and Whit's addiction to deadbeats, I was cautious about letting a man into my life. I instinctively held them at arm's length, not liking to talk about my childhood or let my guard down.

When Whitney's love life had taken yet another nosedive a year ago, she and Fliss had moved in with me 'temporarily.' My relationship status had suffered even more as a result, but that was as much my fault as theirs. I couldn't be bothered dating once I had someone to come home to.

It had been crowded, all three of us living together, but the location had worked for Fliss's school and with Whitney helping pay rent, I'd been able to save for the first time. I'd been trying to decide whether to apply to university to finish my degree or look for a condo to buy when Izzy had come home for a visit.

She had left right after high school for Calgary, where she got her degree and began working in an accounting firm. Her job prospects were endless and her bank account had already been very healthy when her grandmother had left her some money.

"Come to Australia with me!" Izzy had said while we caught up over coffee.

Mom had been appalled that I would consider blowing my savings on something so frivolous. The plane fare was outrageous and backpacking like a hippie for three months? Why couldn't I wait until I was approved for a work visa at least?

Why can't you wait. That was Mom's eternal refrain. Wait, wait, wait.

It had already begun to frost at night. The idea of being somewhere warm while winter settled in had tipped the scale for me. So had the idea of 'being like Izzy.'

I pulled the pin, bought the ticket, quit my job, and climbed on the plane.

When Izzy had abruptly decided to fly home a week into our adventure, I hadn't been able to stomach crawling home to Mom's superior sigh.

Way to dodge that bullet, I thought sourly as I drained my champagne.

Fox had saved me, which had been very unexpected since I'd been getting a vibe off him that Izzy and I had already overstayed our welcome. Our night at the pub had turned into an invitation to accompany a group of their friends on a camp and surf weekend. Izzy had shared Fox's tent while we were away and kept doing so when we returned to the men's beach house a few days later.

I had moved slower with Shane. He hadn't pressured me at all, which was part of his charm. He flirted in an easygoing way and didn't ask a lot of questions. Taking the step into intimacy had felt casual, but not in the derogatory sense. Sex with him had been nice, but it hadn't been loaded with deep meaning or great expectations.

If Izzy and I had moved on in those following days, I probably would have kept Shane in my heart as a fond memory of my travels, like a hike that had been worth the shortness of breath because I had slept well afterward.

Instead, Izzy had picked up an email from a former colleague in Calgary who had moved to Winnipeg. He thought she'd be perfect for the team he was assembling at the branch of a bank there.

"Are you coming back with me?" Izzy had asked as she had looked up flights.

Without answering, I'd gone to the beach to soul-search. By that I mean sulk. Fox had found me and I had poured out my dilemma, repulsed by the idea of going back to Pine Grove so I could update a website selling medical devices.

"'Our vision care diagnostic tools will change the way you see patient outcomes,'" I quoted. "That's the sort of pun I'm reduced to, in order to keep my sanity."

He hadn't laughed. Or pitied me. "Could you do that kind of thing for T&B? Our website is a heaping pile of feces. I know because I made it myself. The good ones are so dear, though."

It always made me smile to hear him use Aussie expressions in his mostly-American accent.

I had fully intended to find my own place as soon as possible, not continue sleeping with Shane. The house itself had been a worksite since the men were constantly renovating one thing or other in their spare time.

Somehow our arrangement had turned into a quid pro quo, though. I retooled the website and taught them how to stay on-brand with social media. I worked the retail counter and caught up a bunch of filing and other admin in exchange for rent and groceries. That trade-off rescued my pride and allowed me to keep from draining my savings, but the whole time I was staying with them, I'd been anxious to earn my keep. I cooked and swept sawdust and kept my showers under two minutes. I helped Shane organize his parents' thirty-fifth wedding anniversary. Actually, I organized it. He paid for it, but at least I hadn't been seen as a freeloader.

Apparently, I'd been seen as his extremely well-organized, hard-working, gem of a girlfriend who would finally pin Shane's feet to the ground because, days before I was due to fly home, Shane proposed.

If I was honest, I'd been in a state of anxiety about accepting ever since. I had called it wedding jitters and natural stress over emigrating, but there'd been a part of me that had gone into existential crisis. Was I trying to be someone I wasn't? Or was this a natural discomfort at stepping outside my comfort zone. Was I being courageous? Or ignoring my gut at my own peril?

In quiet turmoil, I had listened to Mom list reasons it was a bad idea, which only made me dig in my heels and pick up shifts at the bar again, to pay for an overseas move and a destination wedding.

A wedding that wouldn't even happen.

God, I still had to track down the wedding planner and cancel the ceremony.

Maybe Mom was right. Our family wasn't meant for reaching high. We just fell farther and harder when we tried.

That wasn't something I would dwell on now. I twisted to set my empty glass beside the full one.

My movement rocked the hammock and disturbed Fox. He sucked in a startled breath and caught me in tight arms, as though he thought we were falling. His eyes blinked open, confused and hazed with sleep.

"It's okay," I said, touching his chest and feeling the knock of his heart through the robe. "Go back to sleep."

"I'm really sorry, Ash." The regret and sincerity that husked his tone cut past my turmoil and eroded my lingering anger.

"I know." I let myself relax, head going onto his shoulder with forgiveness.

He rubbed my back once. His breath exhaled, and he was fast asleep again.

I stayed where I was, not wanting to disturb him, but had to close my eyes against the sting of tears.

No more of that, I promised myself and inhaled the fragrant scent of the nearby flowers and salty trade winds from across the ocean. I focused on the simple human connection of reclining next to another live body. Fox smelled like... I concentrated, trying to pick apart the pieces of his specific scent. Surf and the essential oils Ikaika had used, maybe left-over sunscreen and a hint of something very familiar...

FOX

"*A*untie Ashley."

For the second time today, I snapped awake at Ashley's voice, completely disoriented. It was like being chundered in the waves and unexpectedly bursting to the surface to catch a breath. I had no recollection of leaving the massage table, yet here I was in a hammock with Ash, limbs stacked and bodies pressed close as a pair of kittens in a towel lined shoe box.

"What?" Ashley stiffened mid-yawn, seeming surprised to find herself here, too.

I shifted to disguise the fact that parts of me stirred that really ought to stay lifeless.

"Everyone is looking for you." The pretty young girl standing over us sounded exactly like Ash when she was annoyed. She looked outright scandalized.

"Fliss," I said, recognizing her from the times I'd met her over FaceTime. "G'day. Fox," I reminded, thinking by her frown that she reckoned I was some rando who'd crawled into this hammock while her aunt was unconscious.

"I know who you are."

Huh. I'd been under the impression we were on friendly terms, but she skewered me with a cold glare.

"What are you guys doing?"

I was still half-asleep so my filter wasn't fully in place. "Getting judged by a tween— *Ow.*"

Ashley's elbow was surprisingly sharp, even through the layers of terrycloth robe. She worked herself like a turtle on its back, trying to exit the hammock. She only made it sway while the blanket tangled around our legs. I felt the soft friction of her calf rub against my shin. My dick completely misread that and stretched more insistently.

"Is that lube?" Fliss accused, pointing at a basket next to a pair of champagne glasses, one empty, the other flat.

"Is it?" I couldn't remember a damned thing. "Was I roofied? What happened while I was out?"

"It's *massage oil.*" Ashley piled the blanket onto me and got her legs hooked over the edge of the hammock. "How do you even know what lube is?"

"It's called the internet. It exists to destroy childhood." Fliss turned the basket. "There's chocolate. Can I have some?"

"Shhh!" came from across the patio.

Ashley scowled and asked in a whisper, "Who's looking for me?"

"Everyone," Fliss whispered. "Mom. Grandma. Shane's mom. Izzy called and asked Mom if she should still come."

"I texted her that Shane didn't show." Ashley informed me over her shoulder.

"Mom told Izzy she could help with the search party if nothing else," Fliss said. "I said I'd look for you and Grandma got worried, like you were kidnapped or drowned and I would be too, if I left the villa. Where's your phone? How come you haven't answered our texts?"

"I left it in my room. Is Izzy coming or not?"

"I think she is. I'll text Mom that I found you." She thumbed her phone.

I worked at keeping my expression unchanged, but the vague apprehension that had been stalking me for weeks settled in like a bad cold. On the three or four calls Ashley had had with Izzy after Izzy had gone back to Canada, Izzy had been very flirtatious and suggestive, always offering to 'meet me halfway' if I had plans to visit the States.

She had also threatened to return to Oz, but never had, which had been a relief. Izzy was cute and funny. We'd had a good time for the few nights I'd known her, but we hadn't had much in common. She liked fashion and clubbing and umbrella drinks beside a pool. I'm practical and active and would rather stand in as a dart board at a pub than subject myself to electronica.

When she had left so unapologetically to take her dream job, her departure had made for a clean end to a relationship that hadn't had a future. I wasn't that keen to start it up again.

"Grandma wants to know if you're coming for dinner. The Holloways are already invited." Fliss read from her phone. "It's at seven."

"What time is it now?"

"Four fifty-six."

Ashley's spine sagged. She peered over her shoulder at me. "What are you doing for dinner?"

I didn't have much appetite for what sounded like an ambush but, "Being your wingman?"

"Fair—?"

"Don't," I ordered, cutting her off. "You'll only embarrass yourself."

"He doesn't like it when I try to say 'fair dinkum,'" she confided to Fliss, putting a hard 'r' in it purely to sound like a cretin and irritate me.

Fliss tucked her chin. "Pretty sure that's a loonie into Grandma's swear jar. She started one for Ryan."

"Inflation much? It was a quarter when you were four. She's punishing your mother. Don't fall for that racket. Grandma cusses like a sailor when you're not around."

"Shhh!" someone hissed insistently.

Ashley tsked and tried to stand, seemed to struggle to find her balance, but—I realized after I had plastered my hand on her ass—she was only trying to get her slippers onto her feet.

I wound up with a generous impression of her butt that immediately found a space in my brain that had been sitting empty, waiting for that precise information about temperature and breadth and suppleness.

She found her feet and swung around, flushed.

"Don't forget your lube." Fliss picked up the basket.

"For God's sake, Fliss." Ashley drained the flat champagne in a couple of gulps.

I was so lethargic, I could have stayed in this hammock the rest of my life, but I threw off the blanket and climbed out.

As I did, Ashley glanced to the pocket of my robe, asking, "Do you have—"

I flashed her.

I wasn't trying to. I was *trying* to kick into a slipper. My robe parted and yeah. That happened.

Ashley's thunderstruck gaze slammed into mine. I read clear as day that she was hoping I hadn't noticed that *she'd* noticed. She went bright red as she saw I had.

And we both knew I was standing at half-mast. I had just woken up, for Christ's sake. I had felt that glance of hers like a warm breath.

I did the only thing I could do. I owned it. If I apologized every time I got an inappropriate stiffy, that's all I'd do in this lifetime.

I shrugged and tucked and belted the robe tight while glancing to be sure the minor hadn't also caught an eyeful of x-rated material.

"What's this?" Fliss brought her nose out of the basket, but apparently sensed something was amiss. She looked back and forth between us. "What's wrong?"

I braced myself for Ashley to make some pithy, disparaging comment, but she only blushed harder and mumbled, "Nothing."

My ears did that vinyl record scratch noise. A pulse of electricity jolted to the ends of my fingers and gave a bright stab into my groin at the same time.

What the hell? Disgusted or offended or amused I could handle. She wasn't supposed to act *shy*. Like she had been caught perving on me and felt guilty for it. Like she hadn't realized she could make me grow wood and was feeling all feminine and flustered now that she knew she could.

She kept her gaze lowered, eyelashes a line of fine, mink hairs that cast a feathered shadow against cheeks still wearing a soft blush. It was so damned pretty and suggestive of a woman considering her options, I suffered a second, sharper pulse. This one was made of high-grade, red-light district neon and pulled my homewrecker to full attention.

I was positively lightheaded. If Fliss hadn't been there, I might have asked Ash what the hell was going on.

Or maybe not.

No, I decided. Whatever my gonads were thinking didn't bear thinking about. Ash was friend, not food. This was an awkward moment that needed to be obliterated as quickly and completely as possible.

ASHLEY

"*A*re you moving back into the villa with us?" Fliss asked as we walked to the elevator. "Grandma said you would."

I bit back a hard, *Dear God no.* "I'm going to stay in the suite."

I wanted to look at Fox for confirmation. His offer to cover the cost was really generous, but even if he had changed his mind, I would max out my credit card and treat myself. He was right. I needed my own space right now.

Fox used his room card on the elevator and pushed his hands into the pockets of his robe as he joined us inside. Definitely naked under there. And no worries about the bikini line. He kept things tidy around the mast.

I wanted to fan the self-conscious heat from my cheeks. It was so dumb! I'd seen him in his underwear before, including a few hours ago when he'd jumped into the water at the beach. When we'd been sharing a house, I'd had to avert my eyes from his morning wood. I hadn't grown up with men in the house, but I knew erections were a normal, frequent, uncontrollable thing. Heck, he'd probably seen my nipples loads of times, when it was cold out or I'd been braless under a pajama T-shirt.

Okay, that didn't help. Now I was blushing with embarrassment, wondering if he had ever been this disconcerted by my nipples as I was by his boner.

No. I didn't think he'd ever noticed I was a woman. Not in a sexual way. Izzy was his type, all sensual and pretty and colorful with golden eyes and high cheekbones and buckets of bedroom confidence. Sure, he was nice enough to say, "You scrub up well," if I put on a dress and some lip gloss, but he never flirted or acted like anything more than a friend who happened to be a straight male.

He was probably feeling better from his hangover. That's *all*. Maybe reacting to generic breasts and butt, not specifically *my* chest and chassis.

And I wasn't reacting to him. Why would I? Everything was normal.

Why wasn't everything normal?

"Oliver wants to go on a hike to a waterfall tomorrow," Fliss said gloomily.

"Hmm? Oh. That sounds nice."

"No, it doesn't." She curled her lip. "I don't want to go and Mom was like, 'Leave Ryan with Fliss and we'll have some couple time.' I told you she only brought me to babysit."

"Ugh. Been there," I teased. "Little kids are the worst."

Fliss narrowed her eyes in a warning look. "You are required by law to devote yourself to your niece. Ryan is my mom's boyfriend's kid. I barely know him." She bit her cuticle. "At least Oliver said it was a family vacation and we should do something together. Then he asked me what I wanted to do."

"What did you say?"

"I dunno. What is there to do? Do you want to come with us? Walk through a botanical garden and see a waterfall or whatever?"

"Mmm..." I pushed my mouth to the side, not keen to watch Whit and Oliver rub noses when I was feeling so scorned.

"See?" Fliss charged.

"We could take Ryan to the beach," Fox suggested as the elevator arrived on our floor. "Get some boogie boards and mess around in the surf."

Fliss flashed him a surprised frown.

He shrugged as we stepped off the elevator. "Kept me entertained as a kid."

"Still does. Let's be honest," I said.

"Guilty as charged. Who wants coffee?" He detoured to the side of the lounge we were passing through.

"*Yes.*" I was still fuzzy from my nap.

"That's how I feel. Like I'm this close to being human again." Fox pinched his fingers in the air. "Coffee and a shower and I'll be there. I got it." He waved me off as I started to put down the gift basket from Inga. He dropped a cube of sugar into my cup with a healthy dollop of cream and handed it to me, then started to pour the next one. "Fliss? How do you take yours?"

"No, thanks." Fliss seemed to be taking note that Fox hadn't had to ask how I take my coffee. She sent a frown of confusion between us as I hung back, waiting for Fox to catch up before continuing down the hall.

When Fox used his room card as we came to the door, Fliss halted in the hall. "Are you guys *sleeping* together?"

"*No.* When would we even— He just got here." I rolled my eyes, pretty sure these robes were made of a non-breathable polyester because I was suddenly so hot I was sweating to death inside it. "It was a dumb mix up. They thought Fox was Shane and gave him a key."

"I still have to sort that out," Fox recalled.

"I still have to call off my wedding."

"Want me come with you?"

"Would you mind?"

"Happy to."

I smiled, relieved. "Thanks."

"It'll cost you a shower, though. I gotta wash off this oil."

"Go for it. Enjoy your resurrection." I heard it as I said it and bit my lips.

He took a circumspect sip of his coffee. "Always do."

"Don't use all the hot water." My voice sounded like I was being strangled. "I want to rinse, too." Which was practically a suggestion for him to invite me to join him.

He didn't say a word, but his tongue bulged his cheek as he disappeared into the bathroom.

I watched him go, then noticed Fliss was watching me with one brow quirked.

"Fox was kind enough to order the honeymoon package as a wedding gift," I said as a distraction and waved at the pageantry.

Fliss wrinkled her nose in pity at what a tone-deaf move that had turned into, but she quickly brightened with awe.

"This is a really nice room. Can I go out here?" She rolled open the door and let in the scent of a salty breeze, stepping to the rail and peering out to the horizon. "This is amazing!"

"I haven't even been out here yet." I joined her. It was pretty fabulous, offering a panoramic view of white beards on the tips of waves, gulls soaring below puffy clouds, sky blue to sea blue, west to east. The wafting palms and shush of the waves immediately soothed me.

I set my coffee on the glass-topped wicker table that sat between matching chairs then went back for one of the snack baskets.

"Are we going to ruin our dinner? *Noice.*" Fliss sank into the cushions on the loveseat. "Or, are you, like, buying my silence?" She glanced back into the room.

"Fox owns the beach house with Shane. You know I lived with both of them. It's no big whoop that he asked to use my shower."

"But were you *sleeping* together when you were there? Okay, I'm sorry!" she hurried to say when I withdrew the chocolate bar I was about to offer. "You have to admit it was kind of freaky for me to find you guys like that, though."

I shoved a square of ethical trade, dark chocolate into my mouth before offering one to Fliss. I chased mine with a sip of coffee so the mocha flavor melted on my tongue. We both groaned in enjoyment.

"So what happened?" Fliss asked, reading the label on a kombucha and sending me a glance. I nodded and she opened it. "Did Fox say why Shane called it off?"

"Fox talked him out of it."

"Are you *serious?*"

I shrugged, stinging all over again. "Shane had doubts and Fox said if he wasn't sure, he shouldn't do it."

"So why are you being nice to him?" Fliss thumbed toward the rail. "Over and out with that guy."

I bit back a smirk and a sigh. I was always pretty honest with Fliss, but I wasn't sure how to explain this when I was still sorting through it myself.

"I don't think he was entirely wrong," I was forced to

admit. No matter how hurtful it was, "Fox had a point. Should I marry someone and move around the world for him if it only takes one conversation with his buddy for him to walk away?"

Fliss flattened her mouth and wrinkled her nose in acknowledgement. "What are you going to do, then? Aren't your clothes and stuff on the way there? Are you still moving?"

"I don't know. I guess I'll spend the week trying to figure it out."

Fliss ate another piece of chocolate. "What did he even say, though? Shane, I mean. Because I thought you and Shane were like, in love and everything."

"So did I." But did I? Did I? I bit my lip. "There's a difference between thinking you're in love and being in love, I guess."

"Like Mom," Fliss said with a scowl.

I was honest with Fliss, but I was also prudent about what I said to her. Whatever reservations I had about Whitney's relationships were my own. I would always listen to Fliss vent about my sister, but I didn't pile on. Whit was Fliss's mom and, for all her sometimes flighty ways, Whit worked very hard to provide for Fliss and be the best parent she could be. She was way more relaxed with Fliss than our mom had been and I knew that was a direct result of the tight leash Mom had kept on us.

I opened the tin of mixed nuts. Offered them.

"Has she said she loves Oliver?" I asked. "I haven't spent much time with him, but he seems like he has his life together."

"Maybe. I don't know," Fliss mumbled. "I like it better

when she tells me she's seeing someone, but that she isn't ready for him to meet me. Or if I only have to say hi to some stranger at the shop. Oliver is *always* around. Am I supposed to be friends with him? What do I have in common with a guy who unplugs toilets and makes pancakes on Saturday morning?"

"I thought those creatures were a myth. Like a sasquatch."

"Right?" Fliss chewed a handful of nuts. "I was really looking forward to being able to come see you in Australia. Maybe live there with you and go to school. I want to *do* something with my life."

Oof. My heart panged so hard it left a crack. "I hear that," I said wistfully.

"Mom wouldn't have let me anyway." Fliss slouched lower on her spine and took a pull off her kombucha. "She would say I could only go if she could go. Grandma would never let that happen." She sighed heavily. "At least if you stay in Pine Grove, I could go live with you if Oliver starts hanging around too much."

"Oh, Fliss." I squeezed her arm. "She's your mom. What-ever happens, she loves you and wants you with her. I do, too," I added to soften the blow. "But I'm only worth half a vote, like Grandma. One quarter if we gang up with you against your mom. Been there and lost, haven't we?"

Fliss wasn't in a mood to be teased out of her sulk.

"I hate being a kid," she announced, kicking her legs out straight. "It's *so hard*. And it's going to be *years* before I can do what I want."

"Yeah, well, here's news." I sat back in my chair. "Being an adult blows too."

"Looks pretty good from where I'm sitting."

Looks could be deceiving, but in this moment, as the tropical breeze wafted over us and the crash of the waves was the soundtrack to our moment of zen, she wasn't wrong.

FOX

*W*hen I stepped onto the balcony, I interrupted an argument over whether olives were nectar of the gods or pickled dog turds.

"Long pants? Or can I wear shorts?" I held up the best options from Shane's bag.

"Shorts are fine," Ashley said. Her smile faded as she slid her gaze to the towel around my waist, then up to my bare chest and finally to my eyes. She swallowed.

I turned my back on whatever *that* was and changed in the bathroom, throwing on a short-sleeved button shirt, but only closing two buttons. I'd had a cold shower, but I was sweating. Humidity. That's why. Also stupidity, but mostly humidity.

"Shower's all yours," I went out to tell her.

"Thanks. Help yourself." She nodded at the array of snacks as she rose.

I'd been intending to visit the registration desk, but my stomach gave a sharp clench of hunger. Ashley sent a sly look to Fliss and said, "Have some olives."

"I'm with you," I said as Ashley went to shower. "Pickled

dog turds." I scooped a handful of nuts though, and threw them into my mouth as I sank into the chair Ashley had vacated. I ate the cracker she'd left next on top of her coffee. It was smeared with a sweet-hot pepper jelly.

Fliss had been laughing when I first came out. Now her brow was low again, her bottom lip sticking out. Her owly expression deepened when I drained Ashley's coffee.

"She won't finish it," I said. "She hates coffee that's gone cold."

"She also hates it when people talk about her behind her back."

"Like we're doing right now?"

"I'm not." She sipped from whatever she was drinking.

Ah, twelve. Such a superior age. The way Ashley had been raised with Fliss was similar to the way I'd had younger siblings who weren't really siblings. I had a closer relationship with Vicky's kids in Oz, but that was mostly geography. I saw my foster dad, Gary, and his kids every few years. We talked online often enough that we picked up where we'd left off when I did see them. I loved them all, even when they went through this testy adolescent stage.

Kids usually liked me. I was always up for taking them into a pool or playing cards or throwing a frisbee. Last I'd heard from Ashley, Fliss had been looking forward to meeting me, but she was staring at her phone now, not giving me the time of day.

Was she still mad about finding us asleep in the hammock or, "Did Ash tell you I told Shane not to come?"

"Yes." She lifted her head to deliver that with eyelids lowered in condemnation. "Tell her I've gone back to the villa." She started to rise.

"Whale spout," I said as I saw the plume in the distance.

"Really?" She stayed on the loveseat, but sat taller.

"There's one over there, too." I pointed.

We watched in silence for a minute. She pointed when she saw one off to the left, then settled back into the sofa and ate a dry cracker, eyes pinned to the water.

"I could have told Shane to come even though he was having doubts," I admitted. "I was really drunk, which isn't an excuse. I'm just saying, there wasn't much going on up here when Shane said he didn't think he should get on the plane. Mostly I was thinking this was what was best for both of them."

"So it's not because you're...moving in or whatever?" This girl and her side-eye. She called me all sorts of sketchy.

"No." I bit back a smirk of humor that faded as I thought about the way Ash's gaze had tracked all over my chest.

"Because she told me you wanted them to sign a prenup. From here it seems like you either did it for yourself or for Shane. I don't see how this is good for Auntie Ashley."

I bit the inside of my cheek. "I've seen what it looks like if people get married who aren't in love." I glanced at her, saw I had her attention. "I'm American."

"I know."

"Half the time I pick up the Aussie accent so not everyone realizes that. I was born near Seattle. My mom died when I was two. She wasn't with my dad and I've never been able to find him." Vicky had told me she thought he was White, but I didn't even know that much about him.

"I thought your mom lived in Australia."

"I call Vicky 'Mom,' but she was my mom's best friend. My mom didn't have any family so she asked Vicky to take me if anything happened to her, so I wouldn't go into foster care.

Vicky promised she would because who thinks it will really happen?"

"She didn't want you?"

"It's the difference between planning a tropical wedding and being married," I said dryly. "One's a very romantic idea, the other is a lifelong reality. Vicky was a really good mom to me. She did her best and Gary—they were only dating when she took custody of me. He did what he thought was the right thing and proposed. They were already fighting by the time the wedding happened and their marriage turned out to be a huge mistake. Not violent or anything, but it was a lot of pressure. Kids are hard and marriage is hard. If you don't really love each other and it's not even your kid?"

"Shane and Auntie Ashley don't have kids."

"No, but have you met Sandy? They would have started a family pretty quick if she had anything to do with it. Then what happens if the marriage doesn't work out? I was eight when Vicky and Gary divorced. Gary was having an affair with Stephanie. She's his wife now and Vicky married Mitchell a year later. Mitchell and Stephanie never really understood why I had to be part of their lives. They wanted to have their own kids and make a fresh family that didn't have a weird foster kid in the background."

"That's mean."

"People want things to be simple." But yes, it had felt cruel. I was pretty sure Mitchell had taken the job in Sydney as an attempt to distance me from his life with Vicky. Or, at the very least, he hadn't cared that that would happen.

"Why did you go live with Vicky?"

"I bounced back and forth every week between them in the first two years, before Vicky and Mitchell moved to Sydney. I was going to stay with Gary because, you know. American." I pointed at my chest. "But his life got complicated and he sent me to Vicky. It was supposed to be temporary, but Eddie and Sandy moved in next door and they didn't mind having an extra kid hanging around." I'd been a bit of a placeholder, but Shane and I got on so I'd been welcomed very warmly. "Anyway, the moral of the story is, being married to someone you don't love ends in divorce and it's not fun for anyone, especially the kids."

"You don't think Shane loves Auntie Ashley?"

"I think he loves having her around. She's chill and funny and thoughtful. He loves her like you love a good friend."

"Is that how *you* love her?"

Pow. That one crashed like the full weight of a wave, one that would have pinned me to the bottom of the ocean and kept me there. I hadn't seen it coming *at all*.

She took a long swig of whatever she was drinking, but kept her eyes on me as though she knew exactly what bomb she'd dropped.

Note to self, don't underestimate the preteen.

"Yeah, I guess I do." My lungs felt compressed, like I'd been winded and talking was an effort. "Because I hate myself for hurting her, but I still think I did the right thing."

Her brows went up, unimpressed by my willingness to die on that hill. She chucked her chin toward a fresh plume of mist in the distance.

I acknowledged the whale, then smeared a couple of crackers, gave her one and ate one myself.

"What do *you* think she should do? Come home?" Fliss slanted me a look that seemed to genuinely want my thoughts on the matter.

I pondered every conversation I'd ever had with Ashley.

Thought about all the times she had gone along with whatever Shane wanted.

"Can I ask you something?" I offered another cracker. "I get the impression that your mom and your grandma have strong opinions. That Ash is the peacemaker. Goes along to get along. Is that accurate?"

"I don't know." She shrugged. "Mom and Grandma argue a lot. Grandma doesn't approve of Mom's choices." She lifted superior brows. "Grandma is a nurse. She likes everything organized and tidy and we should all be prepared for an emergency and don't take dumb risks or make your life harder than it needs to be. They fight about how to be a good parent."

"Is your mom a lot older than Ashley? Because—"

She shook her head. "Just three years. She had me when she was seventeen."

"That's young." And made sense, because the few times I'd seen Whitney on the tablet, she hadn't looked much older than Ash.

"My dad was the same age. Grandma could tell he wasn't ready to be one."

"So they didn't get married or try living together?"

"No. I hardly see him. He lives in Ontario and sends me birthday money. He said he started an education fund for me, but Grandma told me I shouldn't count my chickens." Fliss chewed a nail and looked at the damage. "Grandma always thinks Mom's boyfriends are deadbeats and says Mom shouldn't date at all. She thinks Mom should have got a better education than hairdressing—which Mom really likes because it's flexible and I can go to the shop after school. But Grandma thinks *her* way of being a single mom is the right way. Then Mom says something like if she's so perfect, how come her daughter wound up pregnant at seventeen and is only a hairdresser, but *her* daughter is on the honor roll and never skips."

"You like school?"

"I don't know. Our town is so small, it's like your choices are to go to STEM club or smoke pot behind the gas station."

"Feels like a missed opportunity. Hold the club meetings there and solve fossil-fuel emissions."

She snorted. "Sounds like something one of those potheads would say. But yeah, Mom and Grandma argue a lot while Auntie Ashley takes me for ice cream and tells me they'll sort it out and everything will be okay. Why? Do you think I'm awful for wanting her to stay home so I don't have to listen to all of that?" She had Ashley's eyes, big and earnest. Certain there was a right way to be and she would strive to be it.

"No."

"Because I missed her a lot when she was away. I was really mad when she said she was getting married and moving. She seemed so happy, though. And at least we were coming here for the wedding, but now what? I know I shouldn't be glad this happened, but I want her to come home with us." She exhaled and sent me another look, this one shadowed with guilt.

"And you don't want to thank me for it."

"No. I don't." She scowled. "And I don't want you to tell her to move to Australia anyway. Are you going to?"

I blew out a breath, leaning back in my chair as I considered it.

"I don't know what to tell her. Shane's an all-systems-go kind of bloke. When he wants something, he goes." I ran one palm against the other and shot my hand forward. "Half the time it's a great idea and succeeds beyond everyone's wildest dreams."

"Like your company?"

"Yes and no. I wouldn't have taken that kind of risk alone and I had concerns about doing it with him, but Shane would have done it without me. And he likely would have bankrupted himself in a year or two. That's not me being full of myself. I know both of us very well. I'm one of the few people who is willing to throw myself in front of the speeding train that is Shane and say, Stop. Think. Let's do it this way. He knows I don't get in his way unless it's important. We make a good team. But Ashley isn't aggressive enough to get what she wants out of him. I know how hard she had to push to get this." I pointed at the roof over the lanai. "To her mind, it was a fair compromise, but Shane fought her every inch of the way."

"And didn't show up," Fliss noted darkly.

"Exactly. So I guess whatever Ash does should be her choice and we should support her in whatever she chooses to do."

"The summer dress, then," Ashley said from the opening to the bedroom. She turned away with a scrap of pink and yellow in her hand.

ASHLEY

I sent Fliss to the villa while I went in search of the wedding planner. Fox shadowed me across the busy lobby, but I refused to look at him.

"I'm not sure why I'm a dick for saying you should decide your own future."

"I never said you were a dick." I was thinking it, but I hadn't said it. I flipped my hair and took a place in line at the concierge desk, glancing to the registration desk that had an even longer queue of guests checking in.

"It was implied," he drawled.

"Well, how am I supposed to react when I overhear you talking about me? Saying I'm not good enough to marry Shane?"

"I said 'aggressive.'"

"Because that's what everyone wants in a spouse."

"I meant his personality is stronger than yours and you don't always hold your own against it."

"Oh, that's a way less painful kick in the stomach." He

wasn't entirely wrong, though. Shane wasn't here. I had lost that fight in the most profound way.

Maybe that was the problem with my entire life. I didn't know how to fight for what I wanted. I always decided I wasn't as important as everyone else and wound up giving in, thinking, 'Maybe next time.'

"Hey, c'mon." Fox touched my arm.

I pulled my arms into a fold across my chest, drawing in like a pill bug that couldn't stand the vulnerability of being seen.

"I only meant you compromise too quickly and Shane rarely does at all."

"*You* compromise with him. All the time. I've seen it."

His jaw hardened. "I pick my battles. When I believe I'm right, I'm a bigger hard-ass than he is and he knows it. He wasn't getting married without signing that piece of paper, Ash. Neither of us would have got in that taxi if we hadn't finalized it, let alone got on the airplane. I know that hurts to hear, but it's the truth."

"*Do* you? Do you know how much I'm hurting right now?" I stared straight ahead after lobbing that cheap shot at him.

The harried person behind the desk finished with an elderly couple and smiled a greeting for me to approach.

"Hi. I'm trying to find Waiola. I left a voicemail, but do you know where I can find her?"

"She's gone home for the day." The clerk glanced at the clock. "Is there something I can help you with?"

"I have to c-cancel—" My voice broke even though I'd sworn I wouldn't get emotional anymore. "I have to cancel my wedding," I blurted past the thorny weight in my chest.

"I'm sorry to hear that." The clerk offered an empathetic wrinkle of her brows.

Fox came to stand beside me. The clerk flicked him a confused, "Are you—?"

"A friend." He set his hand in the middle of my back.

All the feelings cascaded through me then. Anger, hurt, humiliation and annoyance at the sheer inconvenience of what I faced. Massive disappointment. I felt so *cheated*. The one time I had tried to go after what I wanted, *this* was how it had panned out. I *had* fought for this wedding, not just against Shane's objections, but against Mom's. I had had to rein in Whitney's over-the-top suggestions and make room for Oliver and his son while setting up contingencies for Izzy's wobbly commitment all while trying not to buckle to the guilt of abandoning Fliss. I had scrimped and double-checked everything with Sandy and worried myself sleepless about how to mesh all the personalities for an entire week, so everyone would come away feeling as though all this effort was worth it.

The one person I hadn't worried about was Fox. He was always on my side, or so I had believed. He had helped me organize everything on the other end of my endless texts, always picking up my calls, willing to press Shane for answers, coordinating dates and making bookings.

Fox had rolled out the carpet to the edge of the cliff that I was currently falling off.

I wanted to smack him, I really did.

I also wanted to lean into him and bury my face in his chest and bawl my eyes out.

I let him talk for me as he asked, "What's the procedure for something like this?"

"I'll send an email to Events so they can inform Catering and everyone else. Waiola will be in touch to discuss whether any of your prepayment will be refunded."

Pretty much what I had expected. Flame, meet savings. Wasn't that a nice warm glow right before the stink of smoke and ashes choked out the sun?

"Thanks," I managed to say and started to turn away.

Fox stayed at the counter.

"There's also been a mix-up with my room." He glanced reluctantly toward the line at the registration desk as he pulled his keycard from his wallet. "I was checked into her suite, but I have a reservation under Felix Wiley. Is that something you can help me with?"

My miserable sense of abandonment mushroomed.

"You want to cancel your reservation?" The woman began tapping keys. "Normally we'd charge you if it's less than twenty-four hours, but we're turning people away because of the conference."

"Oh, no, I was—"

"Wait." I closed my eyes. "It's your room, Fox. Stay in it. Cancel his reservation," I told the woman. "I can move to the villa."

"No. I want you to have the suite," Fox said.

"You don't want to pay for two rooms." I knew he didn't.

"I'd sleep on the beach to save twenty bucks, you know that," Fox said wryly. "You need some space. I want to give you that, especially because this is my fault."

"I know, but I won't get any if I have that big room." Fliss was probably already planning to move in. Once Whitney caught wind, she would try to shift *me* back into the villa and take that room for her and Oliver. I would probably let her.

The clerk was holding onto a patient smile, but the people behind us were losing theirs.

"The sofa is a pullout, isn't it?" I asked the concierge.

"It is, yes."

"Can I sleep on it?" I asked Fox. "We can share the suite."

"I... Sure? I mean, I'll take the pullout, but okay. Thanks. Go ahead and cancel my other room and leave us in the suite," he told the woman.

As he tucked his keycard back into his wallet, I let out a breath I hadn't realized I'd been holding.

FOX

I had an urge to take Ashley's hand as we approached the villa.

Why? This wasn't a date. I looked for pockets in the boardies and only then realized my hands were empty.

"We should have brought wine or something."

"Mom's been planning the menu down to the last slice of toast since we booked the trip. We bought beer and wine when we bought the groceries." Ashley rapped the door once and entered without waiting for an invite.

A variety of energy hit me as we stepped into the villa. The boy on the couch stared at me with open curiosity. Fliss held a handful of cutlery and offered a super casual, definitely not guilty of oversharing, closed-lipped smile.

The man taking chairs from the kitchen table might have some North American native in him, but could have been a very well-tanned White guy. He paused to give me an unabashed once-over while the two women in the kitchen sent a silent but loudly implied *Hmmph*.

"We're all up to speed then," Ashley said, showing all her teeth. "Thanks, Fliss."

Fliss scuttled outside.

"Fox, this is my mom, Joanna, and my sister, Whitney." Ashley waved, but it wasn't really necessary. We'd all met online.

"Nice to meet you in person," I said with the smile I reserved for the customers who looked like they wanted to spend a lot of money on something they didn't know how to use, and would demand a refund later. The kind I wanted to be nice to, but wanted to steer away from setting me up for later blame.

Both women had their hands full of dishes and didn't offer to shake.

"Nice to meet you, too." Whitney's tight smile shrank her top lip. She was a pretty blonde with a yoga-mom vibe. She had always seemed warm and funny and outgoing whenever I'd overheard her talking to Ashley, but she was definitely throwing cold today.

Joanna had struck me as far more reserved and still did. She was shorter and plumper than her daughters with hair the same shiny dark brown as Ashley's, but hers had streaks of silver and was cut in a no-nonsense, boyish style.

"Make yourself at home," Joanna said, but I wasn't convinced she meant it.

"And this is Oliver, Whitney's boyfriend," Ashley said with a wave at the man who set down a chair so he could shake my hand. "Ryan is Oliver's son." Ashley nodded toward the sofa.

Oliver offered a friendly smile. He looked to be in his late thirties, had a receding hairline and the hint of a paunch. He shot a glance at Whitney, definitely checking up on whether he was allowed to like me or should hold me at arm's length.

"Need help taking the table outside?" I offered.

"We were debating whether to bother." Oliver gave the fruit bowl on the table a perplexed look. "The Holloways aren't coming so—"

"No? I should go see them," Ashley said. "Is dinner ready now or—"

Her mother was taking a tray of chicken wings out of the oven. "Sandy had a headache."

"I'll text them," I said. "We can drop by after dinner if she's feeling better."

"Tell them you'll bring some of this food," Joanna said. "Save them ordering in or going out."

Ashley angled her body to give him a bland, *This is my mother*, blink.

"I'm sure they'll appreciate that," I said, because it was true. I read Sandy's immediate reply. "Sandy says she'd love to see you." His phone dinged again. "And don't worry about sending food. They're eating leftovers from lunch."

"So we're only seven," Joanna said. "We can dish up in here, then. Some of us can eat off our laps, rather than move the table."

Ashley pulled salads from the fridge and took them to the chairless kitchen table.

"You want a beer, Fox?" Oliver offered.

"I'm on the wagon. I'll pour myself a tap water, thanks."

"I don't usually have more than one myself when I've got Ry-guy." Oliver bent and picked up the boy who'd come to hug his leg. "What's up, little man? Hungry?"

Ryan nodded and curled his arm around Oliver's neck. He tilted his head into his father's jaw, but he was staring pretty hard at me. Was I the first Black man he'd ever seen?

"Hi, Ryan. My real name is Felix, but most people call me Fox."

"Fliss said you would take us to the beach and we can try a boogie board," he said.

Ah. "I did say that. Do you want to? Do you surf? Hang ten?" I gave him the finger-thumb hang-loose sign.

Ryan didn't know if he wanted to shake his head or giggle. He wound up grinning at his father while Oliver folded Ryan's three fingers into his fist and left his pinky and thumb sticking out.

"Then go like that," Oliver coached Ryan to swivel his hand.

"You're a natural. Can you swim?" I asked.

"He's had lessons. Only in a pool, but he can get himself from one end to the other. We brought a life jacket for him to wear."

Ryan got a disgruntled look on his face.

"I call life jackets PFDs. You know what that stands for? Pretty Fine Duds. I love seeing people wear them. I'm an open-water lifeguard and people who think about staying safe in the ocean are my favorite kind of people. We'll see how the waves look in the morning, try to get out before it gets too hot. Sound good?"

Ryan nodded and slid down his father like an otter off a rock.

"Fliss!" Ryan ran outside. "He said he would take us!"

"He probably won't sleep," Oliver said with a chuckle. "Fliss said you two were offering to babysit, but we can all go to the beach after the walk."

Oliver had the same inclusive nature that Shane had, like a herd dog who needed everyone to stick together.

"No worries. It didn't sound like Ash or Fliss were that

keen on the gardens. Go for your walk with Whitney and catch up to us when you get back." Yeah, it was a blatant effort on my part to win Whitney over, but so what? "Ash and I can handle it."

"You got kids?" Oliver asked.

"Three little brothers and two little sisters." I didn't get into how they weren't really related to me. "The youngest is fourteen, but no one grows out of playing in the waves, not even me."

Oliver chuckled, started to say something, then caught himself as though he suddenly remembered he was supposed to be getting my measure, not making friends.

I didn't mind. I was doing the same thing. It might not be my place to be protective of Ashley's family, but I was protective of her. I would make no apologies about wanting to keep her from being hurt by association.

Whitney offered an empty plate to Oliver. "Do you want to fill this for Ry or should I do it?"

"I'll do it, thanks." He dropped a light kiss on her lips and turned to dig a serving spoon into the potato salad.

Whitney offered me a plate and gave me a flickering once-over as she did.

"So?" she prompted.

I didn't know how I was supposed to respond to that.

Ashley distracted me by touching my back as she leaned to take a plate, causing a light shiver to chase down my spine.

"Help yourself," she invited. She sent a look of warning to Whitney as she began filling her own plate.

"What?" Whitney took the next plate and dished up behind them. "I'm allowed to have questions."

Joanna waved for Fliss to go ahead of her before filling her plate last.

"Ask me anything," I said mildly, even though I knew every single ear was trained on me along with not-very-surreptitious stares.

"Why didn't you talk to Shane sooner?" Whitney demanded. "You could have saved us a crap ton of money."

"Come on, Whit," Ashley cut in. "You wanted to come here more than I did."

Whitney made a shut-up face at her sister and looked expectantly at me.

"I—" I hesitated to speak a truth that would only hurt Ashley more. *I didn't think Shane would let it get this far.* It was a sobering thought and I disguised it by shaking some hot sauce into a puddle on my plate. "I think we all got caught up, not addressing the reality of it."

"By that you mean how it affects your business? I would think that would have come up the minute Shane and Ashley got engaged," Whitney said.

"It did." I could be one hundred percent truthful about that. "I called our lawyer, got his opinion, and told Shane the next day that I expected him to sign a prenup to protect my share in the business and the house, even if he wasn't worried about his share."

"What's your store even worth? Because—"

"Whit!" Ashley hissed. "You're being so rude."

"Well, I don't understand how a bathing suit boutique is worth breaking up a wedding for."

"It's more than that." Ashley's color went up with her dander.

I wanted to pat her arm and say, 'Easy, tiger,' but I was also kind of heartened that she was coming to my defense.

"We carry a lot of high-end equipment," I said. "Designer sunglasses, wetsuits, boards, camping gear. On paper, Togs and Boards is worth two million. That'll double in the first year if our distribution deal goes through on our T&B branded products. We're aiming for ten in five years by expanding with at least two more shops. That's conservative. I'm confident it'll be three shops and annual revenue closer to fifteen."

"Oh." Whitney blinked.

"They bought the house for two million," Ashley threw in. "It will probably sell for five when they've finished fixing it up."

"You flip houses?" Oliver perked up. "I've always wanted to try that."

"The trick is to do it fast so you're not carrying the mortgage longer than a few months. We typically find something we can live in and do the reno as time allows, but living in a work site gets old real fast. With this one, we've become victims of our own success. Running T&B hasn't left much time for a side hustle. We used to flip two or three a year. This one has been going on for eight months and it's only half done. We've had to hire out a lot of things we usually do ourselves. We won't lose money, but we won't come away with as much profit as I initially projected."

"Wow. I didn't realize. I guess all of that is worth protecting," Whitney said in a small aside to Ashely.

"Thanks," I drawled. "I thought my assets were worth protecting when all I had was four thousand bucks and my girlfriend at the time walked away with it, but okay." *Glad I have your approval*, I conveyed, not meaning to get pissy, but shit. It had been a hard lesson and one that I hadn't needed to learn twice.

Whitney dropped her lashes and her mouth tightened. She shoved the spoon back into the pasta salad.

"I didn't know that," Ashley said as she led me outside.

"Long time ago," I dismissed.

"I'm impressed that you went from zero to where you are today. How old were you when that happened?"

"Twenty." I tugged my earlobe, glancing up self-consciously as Oliver and Whitney settled at the table with Ryan, listening in. "I was taking my business degree and those savings were my rent and groceries. I had to give up my lease and pull out of school, go back to working for Eddie."

"You worked for Eddie?" Joanna asked, coming to take the fourth seat at the table.

"On and off through the years." I nodded. "I don't have a trade, but I can swing a hammer and dig a hole. Shane was still on the circuit—"

"Surf competitions," Ashley explained to her family.

"He'd bought a run-down bungalow with some prize money and wanted to flip it, but he wasn't home to do the work. Eddie had done the same thing when he and Sandy first married. He gave me some pointers and I cracked at it while Shane was gone. Shane gave me a cut when he sold it and we kept at it while I finished my degree. By then, we were getting good at it so we kept it up after I graduated. When Shane was ready to retire from professional surfing, he suggested we open the shop. By then I had a decent little nest egg and thought he was out of his tree, asking me to gamble it on Togs and Boards, but he talked me round."

"And now you're, like, rich?" Fliss asked from the seat beside me. "A millionaire?"

"Honestly? The bank owns most of T&B. We keep our salary modest and reinvest a lot of our profit into our growth plan. We had a really good quarter, thanks to Ash's help with the website and the vlog. Speaking of that—" I glanced at her then belatedly recalled she wasn't marrying Shane and coming to work for us. I bit back a curse. "Never mind."

"What?" she prompted, wide-eyed with curiosity.

I scratched under my chin. "I was hoping to corner you at some point while we're here to help with a promotion proposal. Remember that one we did for the wetsuits, tying it into board purchases? I want something like it for the tents and camping gear. There's a deadline for getting the proposal to the suppliers. That's why I wanted to jump on it this week."

"What else have I got to do?" she said dryly.

"I'll pay you. Obviously." It hit me that her not marrying Shane was a loss to the company, something I hadn't fully computed yet. Ashley knew the business and the particular culture behind our brand. I had already folded her skill set into our expansion plans. Togs and Boards wasn't a house of cards that would fall under the first gust, but her absence was definitely a missing piece that would have to be re-tooled.

"You don't have to pay me." She frowned as she shoved a bite of food into her mouth.

"Of course, I do. Maybe we could work out a long-distance consultancy." I was thinking aloud.

She scowled harder.

"So you're definitely not going to Australia?" Fliss pressed.

"You still want her to work for you?" Whitney chimed in with a scathing smile. "Just not have a stake in your company by marrying your partner?"

"Whit, stop it. I can fight my own battles," Ashley snapped.

"Can you?" Whitney scoffed. "Because what he did to you sucks. And you're completely ignoring that."

"To *me*," Ashley repeated. "Not you. So back off."

Everything in me wanted to take Ashley's hand then. Especially as her eyes pooled with tears of frustration and her mouth trembled.

"Hey," I said gently, confining my touch to one bent knuckle grazing her elbow. "I can fight my own battles. It's okay if your sister wants to give me a hard time. She cares about you. That's nice."

"Oh, if you're enjoying this, then by all means." Ashley swept a Help Yourself wave toward her sister.

Whitney set down her cutlery with a clank, as though ready to take up the challenge.

"Getting name, income, and points of vulnerability is standard procedure in this family, isn't it?" Oliver spoke lightly as he gave Ryan's fingers a wipe. "My ex-wife thought Ashley was hitting on her when she chatted her up at the grocery store."

"She did not!" Ashley giggled and covered her mouth.

"Oh my *gawd*. You grilled her at the grocery store?" Whitney was horrified. "*When?*"

"How did she know who I was?" Ashley wasn't denying it, I noted with amusement.

"Not at first. She was flattered, actually, then you said something about just getting home from Australia and she put it together. She thought I might want to know that my girlfriend's sister was doing recon." Oliver was tickled, not offended.

"Too far." Whitney glared at Ashley.

"Your Aunt Gilly opened your father's mail more than once," Joanna mentioned idly.

"That's illegal!" Fliss snapped her head around.

"Very illegal," Ashley agreed. "She worked at the post office."

"She could have been fired and I didn't even listen to her. I should have." Joanna shook her head with regret.

"Aunt Gilly was such a badass." Whitney said wistfully. "I've always wanted to be like her."

"Me, too." Ashley turned to me and said in an awe-filled whisper, "She rode a *motorcycle.*"

"Which is why Aunt Gilly is not with us today," Joanna said tartly.

Ashley, Fliss, and Whitney all bounced looks off each other as they heaved simultaneous sighs of resignation.

ASHLEY

*a*fter dessert, Fox tried to help bring the dishes in and wash up, but Mom said, "Ashley and I can do it. Whitney, why don't you and the men take the children to the beach?"

Be more obvious, Mom.

I was mortified, but Fox took his marching orders in stride, disappearing with Whitney who threw a smirk over her shoulder. She'd be grilling him again while I wasn't there to referee. Divide and conquer. Classic Barnes passive aggressive strategy.

I started rinsing dishes before stacking them in the dishwasher.

"Fliss said you're staying in the hotel? That Fox is paying for your room?" Mom repurposed a clamshell container that had originally held cookies, filling it with the leftover wings.

"It was paid for on the company card. He feels bad."

"He feels bad enough to pay for two rooms, one of them the honeymoon suite?"

I didn't usually lie to her. There was no point. She found out anyway.

I clunked more plates into the dishwasher. "We're going to share the suite. It's more economical."

Highlighting Fox's thriftiness was worth a shot, but Joanna didn't embrace it.

"Ashley Margaret."

Just that. That's all it took to send a spike of defensiveness straight through me. Whatever I was doing, it was wrong. I had to smarten up *right now*.

"Move back in here," Mom insisted.

I almost always buckled to that tone like a basic belt, fast and without fuss.

Tonight, perversely, I dug in my heels. "We shared a house for three months. I'm going to sleep on the pullout."

"You can sleep on the pullout *here*."

"We're not having sex. He's trying to be a supportive friend."

"If you believe that, I have a bridge in your size." Joanna slammed the refrigerator door.

"Not all men are trying to get a woman into bed, Mom."

"Yes, I can see that from the way a man paid for this villa so my daughter would sleep with him in the room next to mine. Explain to me where I went wrong." Mom's tone fell from exasperated to frustrated. "Was it the lack of a father figure that makes you girls think you need a man in your life? Because I have tried so hard to show you in every way I can think of that a woman can survive without one."

"Maybe we want to do more than simply survive, Mom."

My sullen remark was met with silence. When I glanced at Mom, she was not taking that well, facial muscles stoic, eyes bright with offense.

My heart sank.

"I didn't mean you didn't provide well for us, Mom. You gave us a great life." I sealed my lips, knowing when to put down my shovel and stop digging.

"I did the best I could with what I had and when I leaned on someone, it was my sister. *You* have women you can rely on, yet here you are, allowing a man to pay for your hotel room."

"Mom—"

"No. Mock me for trying to teach you to get along on your own rather than putting your future into someone else's hands. It *is* your life as you so dearly love to tell me, but *I* won't exact a price later."

Wouldn't she?

"Do we really need to rip into each other right now?" Even as I said it, I heard it as the placating, back down, pleaser voice I had sworn to expunge from my soul. "What are you even angry about? That I didn't listen to you in the first place? That you turned out to be right and I shouldn't have trusted Shane and now look at the mess I have to clean up? It's *my* mess! I'm not here begging you to solve it for me. That's why I'm not moving in here."

"No, you're letting him clean it up for you."

"He caused it!"

We worked in thick silence for a few minutes, the clatter of dishes the only sound.

"I'm angry that you've been hurt and I wasn't able to prevent it," Mom admitted quietly. "Every time that happens, I feel inadequate and hate myself."

I should have left him sooner, Mom had confided once, years ago, on a rare day when she'd had a couple of glasses of wine.

He was becoming so moody. Drinking too much. But I thought he would change.

"You can't protect me forever," I said, rinsing soapy bubbles from a pot.

"But I want to." Mom didn't take the dripping pot. She shouldered the tea towel and set her arms around me and hugged me. "I'm sorry that you're going through this. Shane's parents are really nice and if he's like them, I can see why you trusted him and thought marrying him could work. But I'm glad you're coming home." She gave me another squeeze and set a kiss on my cheek. "I like being able to keep an eye on you."

I found a weak smile while a lump rose in my throat. "I love you, too, Mom."

The lump stayed and an intense wave of sadness gripped me as I experienced a moment of blinding clarity. *I didn't want to go back to Pine Grove. Not to live.*

FOX

"*I*'m sorry," Ashley said beside me as we left the villa and started up the path to the hotel.

"For what?" The air was sweet and warm, the surf pounded in my ears and my belly was full of home cooking. In this moment, life was pretty damned good.

"For my family putting you on the spot. For making you endure an awkward dinner."

"It wasn't that awkward. And observing family dynamics is a bit of a spectator sport for me. I never felt like a member of my own so I'm always interested in how other families function."

She halted to study me. "I didn't know you felt like that."

Oops. I was still a little dull in the head, jet-lagged and mellow. I was being more raw and honest than usual. For the most part, I shelved my family in the 'modern blended' section and let people make of it what they would. I didn't bother wishing things had been different because history couldn't be rewritten.

"Did I sound like I was whingeing? I didn't mean to. Let's

go this way. I'm curious." I pointed down a path that veered left, trying to deflect her.

"I didn't think you were whingeing. I just think it's funny you would look to us for how a family functions. Spoiler alert, we specialize in dysfunction."

"Every family has its quirks. Even the families that look super solid from the outside have their fractures and stress points. Look at Eddie and Sandy. Losing their son and Sandy being so injured? It's kind of amazing they made it through all that."

"I know, right? And even though they all love each other, Shane always had this wall between himself and them." She mimed an invisible one before her. "Is that just growing up? Why do we all feel so disconnected from our parents?"

"Do you feel disconnected from your mom? See, that's what I find fascinating. To me it looks like you have a really deep connection with your mother and sister and niece."

"All we do is bicker and pick at each other."

"Yeah, but it's all done with love."

"You don't think Vicky and Gary love you?" she asked very softly, but appalled hurt amplified her voice. Each syllable reverberated through me the way an earthquake would tremble the ground beneath my feet, threatening to knock me off balance.

"They do." My chest felt tight, making it difficult to find a tone of voice that wasn't strained or clipped. "In their way. It's mostly obligation, though."

"Do you really believe that?"

"I don't know. But I find it telling that I didn't consider going to Vicky when I was broke at twenty. You're twenty-six and your mother is offering you her bed at the villa."

"That's Mom's controlling, matriarchal energy. She wants

her little worker bees inside the hive so she can wax up the hole and sting any man who approaches. Men are more independent by nature. You're taught to be macho and proud about money. I can see you refusing to ask Vicky and Mitchell for help because you like to be self-sufficient."

Or because I'd only received minimal support as a child, which had forced me to *become* pathologically self-reliant. I didn't spell that out, though, only conceded, "It's true that I don't like asking Mitchell for anything." I brought my own beer to his house every single time.

"I wouldn't, either. He seems like a dickhead."

"Sometimes," I agreed, but I had to admit, "He and Vicky are the real deal. And moving to Sydney was a solid career move for him. My life would be very different if he hadn't kept a roof over my head for ten years. These days we got along well enough." Mitchell had achieved his goal of early retirement so he wasn't wound tight as a snake looking to strike.

We continued walking. The path came out by the pool which was full of twenty-somethings holding neon-colored cocktails. The path continued around to the green space that formed part of the headland visible from our room. Marquis tents were set up and music was blaring.

"Really?" Ash complained.

"It's the corporate event, not a wedding." I pointed out the logo for a big pharma company.

She stayed on the walkway, arms folded as she watched the milling crowd in cocktail dresses and button shirts with loosened ties.

"That's the dynamic *I'm* always trying to crack," she said. "What kind of life are you living when the company you work for pays you to go to Hawaii and throws a party like this? Izzy gets schmoozed like this. She flies to head office and it makes her sound so important."

"She's not," I said dryly. "They want her to believe she is. That's the point of events like this. Shane and I get wined and dined all the time. They're a sales pitch dressed up like a Broadway show and they definitely expect you to get in bed with them after. This is probably about some pill they're supposed to push when they get home. My favorite is when these events are billed as a 'team building exercise' and all that happens is people get legless and do something so incredibly stupid, they have to quit their job and change careers."

"You're such a cynic." She was smiling with affection as she said it and started walking again.

"I'd love to say I'll change, but it's not likely."

"Nice. I see what you did there."

"Thank you. I didn't expect you to get it."

"Now you're reaching."

I was, but I was also having fun.

We came to an entrance door to the hotel and I started to open it, but she said, "Mom is overprotective because my father was kind of abusive."

I dropped my hand from the door latch and tried not to say, 'What' or 'Really' or any of those other disbelieving words, but I didn't want to accept that she'd been hurt. As a *child*. It instantly made me sick.

After a stunned moment, I found my voice, but it was deep in the bottom of my chest, arid and flimsy. It felt as though it unspooled vital organs when I tried to use it.

"You don't say much about him. I wondered what she meant at dinner tonight, when she said she should have listened to your aunt." I wanted to ask what had happened, but wasn't sure I could bear to hear it. I left the silence for her to fill with as many words as she wanted to offer.

"He hit me once." She stayed in the shadows of the overhang. Her voice was really quiet, almost impossible to hear over the music floating from the party and the crash of the surf. "But it was only once and kind of an accident."

"Once is too many." My sharp retort bounced back to me off the stone path beneath our feet and wooden rafters overhead. My brain was splintering. I wanted to grab her close, hold her safe, but my whole body vibrated with bloodlust. Where was this bastard? No wonder they checked up on each other's boyfriends, quizzing exes in the grocery store.

"Mom thought so, too." She was hugging herself, still talking to her toes. "He didn't mean to, not really. He was dropping us off at school. Whit and I were in the back seat, fighting over a scarf. It belonged to Aunt Gilly, but we both wanted to wear it and he kept telling us neither of us could have it, but we wouldn't let it go. He parked in front of the school and he reached back to grab it. Impatient, you know?" Her voice shook a little. "He didn't mean to hit me, but he knocked me in the face hard enough my head hit the window."

I recoiled in unconscious reaction, appalled. Sickened. "How old were you?"

"Eight. Everyone saw. The crossing guard and one of the teachers, some parents and students coming off the bus. I started crying, obviously. My lip was bleeding and I had a goose egg and a fat lip. He said he was sorry. He felt bad, I know he did, but it turned into this huge thing. They took me inside so the nurse could check me. She had to call social services. The police came. It turns out he was drunk. Over the limit."

"Holy fuck. Did your mom know?"

"No. She worked nights and came home from her shift at the hospital to cops and a social worker at the door. She'd been thinking about leaving him because he was drinking so much. Gambling, too. Things were really bad between them. He was a long-haul truck driver, but he'd hurt his back so he hadn't worked in a year. He was angry all the time. In pain, I guess. Frustrated."

"You don't have to make excuses for him."

She flinched at the harshness of my voice.

I cleared my throat, tried to keep my inner beast on a tighter leash.

"They were having huge money problems. This was the final straw for Mom. She divorced him, but had to pay off a bunch of the debt he'd racked up on their cards. She got full custody of us and he wasn't allowed to see us until he went through rehab and started paying support. He didn't. Not right away. He would bang on the door in the middle of the night, sometimes yelling, sometimes begging us to let him come back. I would be cowering in Mom's bed and Whitney would be trying to let Dad in the door, convinced everything would be okay if we just put everything back to the way it had been. Mom would call the police and he'd go into the drunk tank for the night. It was really ugly."

"That's awful." I could hardly take it in. "How long did that go on?"

"A few years?"

"Where is he now?"

"In the oil patch. He calls sometimes. The last few times he swore he was sober. I know he feels really bad, but... I don't know. I don't really think of him if I can help it. We hardly ever talk about it." She shoved her fists under her elbows, shoulders hunched. "The whole thing made me really cautious about stepping out of line. Mom plays into it, not that I blame her. Her life was in turmoil and she had two kids to support. Three, once Whitney had Fliss. She comes off as controlling and critical, but she's trying to keep us safe."

"I can see that," I murmured.

"Whit acted out for years. They still fight, which makes me..." She rolled her hand near her stomach. "I don't like conflict. Bad things happen when you rock the boat, you know? So I've spent my whole life terrified to take the smallest chances and I'm so tired of being that way. When Shane asked me to marry him, I didn't want to regret *not* marrying and moving overseas. He's a good guy. He drinks, but he's a cheerful drunk. He gets all sentimental. Never sticks around for a fight. He never once pressured me to do anything—"

She faltered and looked off into the dark as if realizing she was sharing more than either of us might be comfortable with.

"Cuddles and puddles," I said mildly. It was what all of Shane's mates called him when he was hammered and full of hugs, proclaiming he loved everyone.

"Can you imagine if we married? Between Shane's aversion to hard conversations and my fear of conflict, we would have suffered a thousand cuts before we realized we ought to divorce." She sounded very sad.

I wanted to touch her, but made myself keep my hands at my sides. "I'm going to say this in case you need to hear it, but I hope you know your father's behavior is on him. None of that is your fault."

"Oh, it was my fault," she said with a creak of agony in her voice. "He told me several times that it was."

I closed my eyes, but couldn't close my ears.

"I shouldn't have fought with Whitney over something so stupid," she said tiredly, as though she'd heard these words a thousand times. "I should have told everyone it was an accident. I should have said I wanted to see him and not let Mom kick him out, even though he was so angry I was petrified of him."

"Oh, Ash." My hands came up and I showed her my palms, helpless before such hurtful acts against someone who was really very sensitive and kind. And she'd been just a kid. So vulnerable. "Come here."

She stepped into my hug and squeezed her arms around my waist so hard she pushed the breath from my lungs. Her whole body was trembling.

"You're okay. I've got you," I murmured, rubbing her back and pressing my lips to her hair, trying to press the dark memories out of her while my heart pounded in angry hurt and my closed eyes stung.

"It was a long time ago. I'm being stupid, but I keep thinking that I did something to cause this mess I'm in now. That I wanted too much. Is that why it's all gone horribly wrong again? Should I go back into my tiny little box and be happy there?"

"It is absolutely not your fault." *It's mine.* I sheltered her as best I could, chest aching.

"Thank you for saying that." She took a shaky breath and drew back to swipe her fingertips below each of her eyes. "I swore I wouldn't cry anymore on this trip. Not unless I stepped on a jellyfish." She forced an over-bright smile.

"You didn't cry that time when you did." There was a silver drip on her jaw. I dried it with the edge of my thumb. "You were tough as hell." So tough and so fragile I didn't know what to do with her. And I couldn't seem to stop touching her. My fingers tucked a strand of hair behind her ear before I realized I was doing it.

I deliberately dropped my hands to my sides again.

"Seriously." She caught one of my hands and brought it to her mouth to kiss my knuckle. "I'm so mad at you I want to scream, but I'm really glad you're here. Thank you."

I came dangerously close to hugging her again. I wanted to hold her and hold her and hold her. Never let her go.

Don't. My heart pounded with confusion, wanting to comfort, but there were lizard-brain instincts that needed to be stomped down, too.

I shifted my grip so our fingers were linked before I reached for the door.

"You still okay to see Sandy? We can check in with them in the morning if you'd rather."

"I want to see her. It's going to be painful, but I'd rather cram it into this already shitty day and hope tomorrow is a better one."

ASHLEY

I ducked into the ladies' room off the lobby to wash my face.

I couldn't believe I had told Fox all of that. I was still shaking. My childhood wasn't something I talked about with anyone. Small town living had meant that everyone seemed to know our business. I'd been stared at in school and whispered conversations had followed me for years. When I'd started applying for jobs as a teenager, more than one prospective employer had repeated 'Barnes' in a way that still made my skin crawl.

That's what had been nice about a boyfriend on the other side of the world. He hadn't known any of that and it had been bloody refreshing.

All through dinner, I'd been sitting on pins, watching Fox easily field pointed questions from Mom and Whit. I kept trying to picture Shane being comfortable with that, but as amiable as he was, Shane didn't like anyone prying. Everything I knew about his family troubles had come through Fox or Sandy. Shane hadn't shared much of it with me himself.

It shocked me to realize that.

How would Shane have reacted if I'd told him about my father? I had a feeling my anxiety would have sat in me like an abscess the rest of my life before I confessed it to him. He definitely wouldn't have said the right things if I had. Shane didn't know how to handle conflict and volatile, complex emotions. At best, he would have clammed up and booked us onto the next catamaran off this island.

Fox was always a steadying presence, like a pier that let the harshest storm waves batter him while he stood there and put up with it.

I eyed him as we rode up the elevator, wondering about his remark about feeling set apart from his own family, but I didn't bring it up on our short walk to the Holloway's room.

Sandy opened the door to my soft knock. "Oh, Ashley. I am *so* sorry."

"It's not your fault." I returned Sandy's hug and we held it for a long minute.

"Come to the balcony. Eddie's out here."

Sandy ushered us through their room and onto the balcony which was lit by the pool below. I accepted Eddie's hug and shoulder pat and leaned on the rail, motioning for them to take the chairs they'd already been occupying.

"What are your plans now?" Sandy asked.

I bit back a groan, thinking I really needed a decent answer to that, true or not. I focused on the immediate future instead.

"Enjoy the week as best I can. I think we agreed to take Fliss and Ryan to the beach tomorrow." I glanced at Fox.

"Oh?" Sandy followed my gaze to Fox and I thought I detected a deeper inquisitiveness come into her demeanor.

"Teach them to boogie board," Fox said. "Join us, if you like. Come show them how it's done."

His gentle tease eased Sandy's worried frown into a wistful chuckle.

"If the doctors would quit telling me I'm too young for a hip replacement, I would. Shane always says I'll sink like a stone once they finally— Tsk. I'm sorry Ashley."

"Sandy, it's fine," I insisted. "I'm upset, but you can talk about Shane. We're all here for the week. Let's skip the blame and make a nice memory the way we intended to."

"That's very generous of you." Sandy played with the pendant she always wore while glancing at Fox again. There was another question in her expression. "You're staying the week, too?"

"I am." Fox's voice took on a firm note. Resolve or something else that was matter-of-fact and stubborn.

I heard what he didn't say—that we were sharing a room.

"Moral support," I said with a grateful smile, holding his gaze, not mentioning the shared room either, which gave my conscience a pinch, but it was totally innocent. Convenient. We would be working.

"It's been a long day," Fox said, straightening off the rail. "Do you mind if we catch up with you tomorrow?"

"No, of course. You have a good night." Sandy showed us out, curious gaze staying on us until she had closed the door.

"It really has," I said as we were entering our suite. "Been a long day," I clarified when Fox sent me a quizzical look.

"Hell to the yes it has. I haven't slept in a bed in..." He looked toward the clock on the nightstand, then gave me a blank stare. "It's been so long, I can't math."

"Is that you telling me to take the pullout? Chivalry *is*

dead," I teased as I moved to haphazardly unpack my suitcase into the drawers.

"Is that you playing the jilted bride card again?"

It was silly trashing, but I forgot to laugh as I noticed a card on the bed.

"Too soon?" He came up behind me.

"Hmm? No." I showed him the card on the bed that was no longer sprinkled with rose petals. "We had turn-down service and room-service breakfast tomorrow. What do you want?"

We filled out the card and left it on the latch outside the door.

"This package was a very thoughtful gift, Fox. Thank you," I said sincerely. "As consolation prizes go, I'm feeling less gut-punched."

"Good. Because I thought these things in my wallet were coupons for discounts, but they're actually things I paid for." He drew the keycard folder from his wallet and fingered through the slips of paper. "That was the massage." He threw it away. "This is the board I reserved for Shane, but we also get snorkelling gear for two. You get two free cocktails at the pool." He gave me the voucher.

I smirked. "Not drinking for a while?"

"Possibly never again. And a dinner cruise." He showed me the slip. "On Monday. We missed it. That blows."

"You really don't know what day it is. That's tomorrow."

"But I flew out on Sunday."

"It's still Sunday."

"Good God. Talk about a long fucking day."

I chuckled, then, "Can I ask one more favor before we call it a night?" I finished unpacking and showed him my turquoise baby doll. "I brought this because I didn't think I would actually need pajamas."

He stared at it, looked kind of fixated, and swallowed loudly.

A fist of heat clenched low in my belly. A slow blush crept through me, climbing higher and higher until my breasts were tight and my throat constricted.

"I, um, would prefer to sleep in a T-shirt if you have an extra?"

"Oh. Sure." He turned away to paw into the duffel. "I thought you wanted to trade. Blue is *not* my color."

I chuckled weakly and opened one of the dresser drawers for him, inviting him to unpack into it. He did, offering a blue T-shirt I recognized.

"That's Shane's."

"I grabbed his bag. Remember?"

I had forgotten, but shook my head. "I'll figure out something else." I looked for my yoga shorts.

"He's not going to care if you borrow his shirt."

"You really need to quit loaning out things that don't belong to you, seeing as you can't even share a bar of soap."

It was supposed to be a chirpy little joke, but he dropped his hand to his side, shirt dangling from his loose grip.

"Are you serious right now? We're going back to the hair clip?"

"Forget it," I muttered as his tone took me right back to that morning when I'd had to lock myself in Shane's bedroom to hide my tears.

"The package was open and there were still two more in it. It was right there on the shelf. It was exactly like the toothbrush I gave her from the drawer. Were they made of elephant ivory? I don't understand why it was a big deal."

My blood pressure rose despite my best efforts at keeping

this as meaningless as it ought to be. The house had been a fairly communal living space, probably because it wasn't something the men were planning to keep. It wasn't *home*. Friends slept on the sofa all the time and both Fox and Shane were pretty relaxed about loaning tools or equipment or vehicles.

"I couldn't get them in Australia," I muttered.

"But you had *four*. Jasmine used it for five seconds. Were you worried she had lice? What?"

And there it was, the mockery and complete disregard of my feelings that had gutted me that morning. I didn't understand why it felt like such a knife to the gut, but it did.

"You know what? I'll wear my *wedding dress* to bed." I whirled into the bathroom only to realize there was no door to slam. "What a stupid bathroom!"

I stood there, impotent and furious, able to hear him exhale with impatience.

"We're too tired for this, you know that, right?"

He'd been sleeping on and off all freaking day, but okay.

"Let's not say things that can't get unsaid. I should have asked first. Okay?" He was dealing his words out slow and precise. "I honestly didn't think you would mind, but I should have asked and I shouldn't have laughed when you got upset. I honestly thought you were playing it up."

I stood there out of sight, eyes clenched shut against my reflection so I wouldn't see my cringe of mortification. Yes, it had been an overreaction, but I was still so *mad*. Why?

"I don't understand why you're still angry," he continued in that ultra-civil voice from the main room. "But I accept that you are. I'm sorry. Wear the T-shirt or don't. I'm going to bed."

"You laughed at me," I blurted, and immediately wanted to

swallow the words, but more came out. "And so did your girlfriend."

A thump of silence, then, "*Ex*-girlfriend."

"She slept in your room!"

"I slept on the couch and why does it matter?" His voice was suddenly close enough to snap my eyes open.

We stared at each other in the glare of the bathroom vanity lights surrounding the mirror, neither of us able to hide our tension or hurt or frustration. I felt hideously exposed. My heart pounded as though I'd come face to face with a mountain lion.

"I didn't enjoy having someone I didn't know laughing at me. I thought you and I were friends, but you paired up against me to make me the butt of your stupid joke." That's what had hurt, that he'd taken that woman's side against me.

Fox stared at me for a long minute, expression inscrutable. His jaw worked as if he wanted to say something, but thought better of it.

"I was using you to get her to leave," he finally admitted through tight lips. "I could tell she was sizing up the house, thinking if Shane's girlfriend was living there then I'd welcome permanent company too. I didn't want to start up with her again. That's why I slept on the couch when she was more than willing to share the bed. Your snap-show made it easy to tell her she should probably look elsewhere for long term accommodation."

"Why did you even bring her home from the pub if you didn't want her around?"

"I don't know. She had just got back into Sydney. She needed a place to flop for the night. I thought I wanted sex, then I didn't. The T-shirt's on the bed. Go to sleep." Seconds later, the pullout creaked as he yanked its frame from the sofa.

FOX

I exchanged the voucher for the board at a shack run by a sleepy local kid.

"Shane not with you?" the kid asked.

"Nah, mate, sorry."

He looked pretty crestfallen. He'd probably volunteered to open early for the chance to meet an idol.

I wondered if and when word would get out that Shane had canceled his wedding. We'd played it up online. Anyone who followed surfing closely knew the former champion was getting married in Hawaii. I should probably ask Ashley to help me draft a statement, but I wasn't sure how that would go over.

It was one more piece of mental plastic floating in my head as I clasped the board beneath my arm and headed down to the water.

I'd slept well enough, but the minute my phone had pinged with the depth-sounder that was my alarm, my brain had swelled with every word I had exchanged with Ashley last night.

That shit about her Dad, for instance. I sincerely hoped I never met him. No wonder she was always going the extra mile and trying to keep the peace. That was a lot to carry, especially when she'd been a kid.

She didn't usually pick fights either. That regurgitation of our argument over Jasmine had caught me off guard.

I still regretted bringing Jasmine home that night. She had been planning to meet a friend who was finishing a shift at a different pub. The beach house had been closer and she'd casually suggested coming home with me. I thought, *What the hell.* We'd managed to stay friends through a couple of on and off spells. She traveled a lot, so she preferred to keep things casual. She was only planning to stay in Sydney until she'd built up her savings for another overseas trip. I hadn't been with anyone since Izzy and could have used the exercise.

I'd changed my mind by the time we were pulling into the drive, though. Jasmine had been surprised when I'd given her the bedroom and I'd wondered what the hell I was doing myself.

The next morning, she'd been gently prying. I'd been trying to hurry her along, unable to explain even to myself why I was reluctant to start up with her again. She was funny, knew everyone in our circle, had her own goals and wasn't looking for any man to complete her. We were both doing our own thing which kept us from gelling into anything serious, but we were comfortable with that and each other.

So comfortable, she'd been taking the piss with me, siding with Ashley if Ashley would only recall events correctly, but she seemed to have taken Jasmine's remarks as ridicule.

Until that day, I had never seen Ashley get angry and, God help me, hadn't taken her seriously because of that. And the fact it was over a damned hair clip. I'd been pretty fucking patronizing, not that I'd recognized it at the time. I hadn't realized how genuinely furious she was until she'd refused to speak to me for days after.

She'd been right, too. They didn't carry them in Oz. I'd searched four different shops without success. I might as well have been browsing the tampon aisle, I'd been so out of my depth as I picked over scrunchies and pins and all the other doo-dads in the hairbrush section. I'd had to ask a mother with two little girls to advise me and still came home with the wrong kind. Ash had been gracious enough to accept it as a peace offering, but it had been another few days until she had fully thawed.

I crossed the cool sand and waded into the water with purpose, grunting when a swell rolled against my thighs and soaked my balls, sending a familiar jolt through me. I dropped onto the board and began to paddle.

I had never understood why Ashley had been so damned mad over a stupid two-dollar hairclip. I hadn't dared bring it up again and ask for clarification, either. I wasn't a masochist. Then, last night, for a minute there, she had sounded almost jealous.

My heart thunked in my chest, but I told myself it was my imagination. What kind of Freudian-ass self-delusion was it that I had manifested a thought like that?

It sure as hell hadn't been my finest hour when I'd let Ashley's temper nudge Jasmine out the door. I'd been embarrassed, sending Jasmine mixed signals by bringing her home then leaving her to sleep alone. On her way out, she had sent a speculative glance toward Shane's closed bedroom door, the one Ashley had slammed.

I'd been relieved she was gone and tried to forget the

whole thing, but Ashley's wounded silence had nearly killed me.

A chop of water hit me in the face, reminding me to pay attention. As the next glassy swell approached, I dove through it and, like magic, my head cleared of all but what was immediately before me—ocean and sky glowing a predawn silver with streaks of purple and pink on the horizon. The world was no longer pressing down on me. I was inside it. Part of it.

My muscles tingled and warmed as I stretched into longer, more determined paddles. I arched my back, dug deep to pull myself up the face of the next swell and rode over the crest, sliding down its backside. I paddled again, licking salt spray from my lips.

Soon I was exchanging nods and "G'day," with a handful of locals sitting on their boards. The sun cracked a sparkle across the water as my turn came up. I eyed the set coming in, dropped onto my stomach and began to paddle.

The wave pushed and lifted me. Still on my stomach, I clung to its peak as I angled left, leaning my weight on my inside rail while watching to make sure my line stayed clear. With nothing in my head but balance and timing and keeping that delicate pressure on one side, I popped up, bringing my feet under me. I lifted my hands, heels doing the work to carve into the wave as I picked up speed and swooped down.

Here was the ride. The wind rushed across my face and cut through my boardies and rashie. My body absorbed the energy of the ocean through my feet against the board. Every shade of green and blue and white-gold hit my retinas. The wave started to curl over me and I crouched into a tight stance to stay inside the barrel. As I trailed my fingers in the wall beside me, it was like punching into the space between time and reality. I was everything and nothing. Magnificent and vulnerable. I was jacked with adrenaline and basking in euphoria. I was completely in control, but purely a passenger on this board and this planet.

The wave began to collapse. I fishtailed out of it and my speed slowed. My board wobbled and I let myself fall.

As my ears filled with the growl of the sea, my vision turned to bubbles and foam. My lungs starved for air as the weight of the wave fell over me, chundering me into its belly.

ASHLEY

I woke and knew I was alone even though I couldn't see over the back of the sofa to the pullout. Not that Fox had been snoring or anything. I had woken in the night and tried not to toss and turn too much, very aware of him sleeping in the room with me.

Now there was a distinct emptiness that made the room seem huge and hollow.

Dawn patrol, I guess. Most serious surfers preferred it, but Shane's morning exit had always been announced by a loud whiz, the banging of cupboards, and the rattle of a board off the rack. The fact Fox had slipped away so quietly that I'd slept through it gave me a niggling sense he hadn't wanted to talk to me.

I never should have brought up that stupid hair clip. It had been a joke that had gone off the rails and why had I even gone there? Why?

And why hadn't he told me before that he had been trying to get Jasmine out of the house? I had subliminally sensed he was pitting us against one another. That had been part of my anger that day. It was a dick move. Fox was usually more forthright. If he didn't want to do something, he said so up front.

I skimmed open the drapes to a glorious morning and stepped onto the lanai. A handful of surfers were sitting on their boards outside the small bay next to the resort, but I couldn't tell if Fox was among them. I squinted at a man with a cap of black hair and wide shoulders in a neon green swim shirt, but his bearing wasn't Fox's and his skin looked too light.

The door mechanism hummed and I stepped into the room as Fox entered. He wore T&B boardshorts with a sunset pattern and one of their short-sleeved rashies in silver with a panel of blue down the sides. It was so tight, I could see his nipples along with every contour of his torso, right down to his washboard abs and the indent of his navel.

I jerked my gaze up to find him coming back from taking inventory of my ribbed tank and skin-tight yoga shorts. He could probably see my nipples, too. It wasn't cold outside, but it was breezy. I crossed my arms.

"I was looking for you, wondering if you would be back in time for breakfast." I tried to find a smile of greeting, but our altercation last night had left static in the line.

"I had to." He showed me the 'Relaxing Within' tag he had left on the latch outside the door as he left to surf. "Otherwise, they might not have delivered it." He moved the card to the inside.

Such thoughtfulness didn't seem like the mark of a man holding a grudge over last night's argument.

"You sleep okay?" he asked.

"I did," I lied. "How was the water?"

"Good."

Ugh. Might as well ask about the weather.

"I'm going to change and hang these in the shower." He plucked at his rashie then dug into a drawer on his way to the bathroom.

I watched him go, wanting things to be okay between us and not sure how to make it happen. After a second, I heard the water running and the tap of a razor against the side of the sink. While he was out of sight, I put a sports bra on under my shirt.

Breakfast arrived and I brought it to the table on the lanai, glancing up from my phone when he joined me. His jaw was clean. He wore fresh board shorts with a sleeveless T-shirt. A waft of sunscreen and a hint of minty freshness arrived with him.

"You hear from Shane?" he asked, nodding at my phone.

"No. I was seeing what sorts of jobs are available to someone with my vast experience in writing advertorials for medical devices." I set aside my phone and lifted the lids off the plates.

"Where? Sydney?"

"Anywhere." I tried to shrug off my predicament. "When one door closes there's another fish in the sea, right? Those sausages look good."

He moved one to my plate and stole a chunk of hash-browned potato from mine. "What do you mean 'anywhere?'"

"Australia, but also Canada. Vancouver, Calgary, Toronto... I've been given a choice so I feel like I should exercise it. How did you settle on staying in Oz? Have you ever considered going back to Seattle?"

He paused in pouring coffee for both of us, brows low over his perplexed gaze. He finished what he was doing then set down the carafe.

"Let's see. Rain?" He weighed one hand in the air, then held out the other. "Sunshine."

"Mmm. Forty below in Pine Grove or forty above in Australia." I copied the motion. "These are tough choices, aren't they? Seriously, though. Was that all it was? Weather?"

"It wasn't a conscious choice." He tucked into his plate. "I was only going to do a year of school in Oz while Gary and Stephanie got through their son being a premie and got into their new house. But once I was on the Aussie school cycle, I didn't want to fall back half a year by enrolling in Seattle. I visited Gary over school breaks and we talked about me coming back to finish high school, but the year I turned fifteen, Eddie offered me and Shane work with his clean-up crew. If I had realized he wanted a couple of strong backs on a wheelbarrow and we'd be picking up broken bricks in the heat, I might have made a different decision." His grin went sideways, wry. "But it was a legit job. Everyone agreed it was a good thing to be able to live and work in two different countries so I got all my documents in order. I was prepared to go to the States for work once I got my degree, but by then Shane and I were flipping houses and talking Togs and Boards. Here we are."

"Does the US even feel like home anymore?"

"It feels like my hometown. I see Gary and the kids every year or two. It's a place that feels nostalgic and familiar, but also changes enough between visits that I know it's not my life anymore. Why? What are you thinking?" He was watching me closely, as though he was invested in whatever I decided. Maybe he was. It could be awkward for him and Shane if I went to live in Australia anyway.

"I'm thinking I need to make some phone calls to the shipping company, find out how my stuff will be handled if I'm not there to physically receive it, ask if I can redirect it. I can't see starting my life from scratch in Sydney, where I won't have anyone. That's a little further out of my comfort zone than I'm comfortable with."

"You have me."

"No, I don't." I said it gently, but it was true. "You'd be my first call if I was arrested, I promise. But I can't work for you and Shane. I can't hang out with your crowd. I'm out of the club." My voice quavered. I swallowed and squinched up my nose to hide the way my chin wanted to crinkle. "I'm sad about that, but *c'est la vie.*"

"We can all still be friends, Ash."

"I refuse to be one of those cast-off sheilas who hover around you and Shane looking for a way back in."

His face blanked to a warning stiffness. "I happen to think it's a mark of decency that I'm on speaking terms with every woman I've ever slept with, including the one who took all my money." He jabbed his fork into another cube of my potatoes. "Not that I'd cross the street to say hello if I could avoid her, but I wouldn't push her into traffic. Shane's the same. You two will be fine after this blows over. Come to Sydney if you want to. I can still hire you."

"I'll just forget the part where Shane stood me up for our wedding, then?" I got up and found my wallet in my bag. My engagement ring was in a zipped pocket. I set the ring on the table next to his plate. "I took that off so I wouldn't lose it while swimming. Maybe that was bad mojo and the reason this happened. You might as well take it back to him."

He barely looked at it. "You're really not coming to Oz?"

"Not to live, no. And I won't make a point of seeing him if I don't have to. Neither of us will enjoy it."

"What are you going to do then?" He sent an angry frown

toward my phone. "Go to some *other* strange city where you don't know anyone? No." He didn't give me the chance to answer. "If you're not going home, come work for me. At least until you figure out what your next move is."

"I'm pretty sure I heard you say yesterday that whatever I did should be my decision."

"If it's something you've thought through, then yes, I'll cheerlead you all the way. But running away? That's a knee-jerk reaction."

"It's called a fresh start." I sat and added cream and sugar to my coffee, giving it a vigorous stir with my spoon. "Because here's what I'm thinking. I can go to Sydney, where I'm not wanted, or I can go home to lick my wounds. *Or* I can see this as an opportunity to do whatever *I* want."

"And that's what you want? To be alone somewhere unfamiliar? No one wants that unless they're hiding from the law."

"Well, I *wanted* to be married, didn't I? That's not a dig," I added in a mutter, bracing my elbows on either side of my plate, holding my heavy head. "Getting married was a dumb idea. I see that now."

After a stunned silence, he asked, "Do you really believe that?"

"I don't know. Yes. If I was only doing it for the sake of doing it, then yes. Will you please put that away so I won't stress about it?" I nodded at the ring.

He carried it into the room and I heard the Velcro on his wallet tear.

When he came back out again, I picked up my fork, but only pushed my scrambled eggs around without eating any. "I keep thinking about something Mom said last night."

"When she pulled you by the ear into the kitchen?" He sat back down. "I wondered if I should ask about that."

"She wasn't really mad."

"Just disappointed?"

"Pretty much. She said that she's tried all her life to show us that a woman doesn't need a man to survive so she doesn't understand why I hitched my wagon to one. Maybe she could see that Shane and I weren't lovestruck enough to justify a complete change of life. Maybe that's why she wasn't supportive of what I was doing."

Mom knew how to be supportive. She'd encouraged me when I'd started college and had offered to help financially if I wanted to finish my degree.

"I don't want to knock her because she made a lot of sacrifices for us," I continued. "But she's independent to a fault. I don't think she's dated once since the divorce. If she has, it's been on the down-low. And she quietly puts on us this guilt trip that we've held her back from pursuing her own life. She didn't want either of us to move out, though. Even though it allowed her to sell the house and buy a condo with a mortgage that was more affordable. She's finally making progress financially, putting away money for retirement, after years of struggle."

"That's good."

"I know. But I think she's afraid to get involved with someone in case they try to take that from her. Anytime we suggest she set up a dating profile, she says, 'I have you girls.' I don't want to be the reason she doesn't have companionship. And I don't want to be her only source of companionship. Just because *she* doesn't want a man or sex doesn't mean I shouldn't. Or does it? Am I rationalizing being selfish?"

"Wow. I'm going to need more coffee to tackle that." He poured a fresh cup and blew across it. Drank a little and set down his cup. "Promoting abstinence is one of those things that looks great on paper and proves largely ineffective in real life. Sex remains popular."

I found myself wondering exactly how much sex Fox liked. The normal amount? More? Aside from Jasmine, he'd never brought anyone else home and had mostly come home every night. On the few occasions when he hadn't, I hadn't quizzed him and he'd usually offered an excuse like having had too much to drink so he had slept on a friend's couch.

"Unless your mother is suggesting you engage in casual sex, your only option is to allow someone into your life on a more permanent basis," he said.

"Exactly! It's not like I don't know how to live alone. I can pay my bills and unplug a sink when it backs up. But after a few years of that, it was kind of nice when Whit and Fliss moved in. I liked having someone to come home to. I know how to tell a guy I'm not interested without needing a ring as a repelling device, but maybe Mom had a point that I was marrying because it's what I thought I was supposed to want. I'm twenty-six. This is when you're supposed to get your act together, right? Getting married and moving to the other side of the world made me feel like I was taking charge of my future instead of just existing."

"Twenty-six," he scoffed with a shake of his head. "Such a baby. Definitely too young to marry."

"You're thirty-two. *Such* an old man." I rolled my eyes at him. "What if marriage is something I want, though? Is that a bad aspiration? Do *you* want a wife? Or is Mom right and tying yourself to a man is an outdated institution that subjugates women?"

"This discussion feels way above my pay grade."

"Coward." I stabbed the sausage he'd given me, not bothering to cut it. I held it on my fork and bit the tip off, chewed and swallowed. "But if I don't want to marry and have kids—if my Mom says I'm not *allowed* to want that—what do I want? That is the crisis I'm in."

"Ah, you're in pre-life crisis. Been there."

"That's exactly what this is." I nodded. "I don't know what I want, but I'm pretty sure I'd like children at some point. The clock is ticking, though. Anything I want to accomplish should be done now before I have them." I set down the sausage and sat back. "And doesn't that sound like I'm eager to live a spontaneous life? *Pfff.*" I sipped my coffee, disgusted with myself. "But I saw how having Fliss put a kink in Whit's life. Sure, she could have become a lawyer if that's what she really wanted, but she was starting from further back and would have had to fight harder than someone without kids. I should take advantage of the advantage I have, right?"

"Did you and Shane talk about having kids?"

"Did *you?*" I tried to keep a straight face, but mirth bubbled up against my best efforts. There was a running joke amongst their friend group that Shane and Fox were an old married couple since they'd been living together for a decade.

"No." Fox gave her a pithy look. "He's always been concerned about losing his figure."

"He's not even here to defend himself!" But I giggled more, before admitting, "Shane was very much on the fence. I get why he was wary, but I thought I could talk him round." Was that the way it should be, though? One partner badgering the other into becoming a parent? It ought to be something both wanted from the outset.

"You have to be on the same page about kids or you're doomed," Fox said as though voicing my thoughts. "We're all sold a story on how fulfilling family life is, but I know for a fact that Gary didn't have his eyes open when he proposed to

Vicky. He thought he was rescuing her and manning up. He didn't have any idea what he was really in for."

"Which was?" I wanted to hear more about his family.

"A lot more than making the mortgage payment and driving me to soccer practice on Saturday. They both worked, but Gary never made my lunch, never dropped me at school, never stayed home when I was sick. He's a good guy. He was trying to be a dad the only way he knew, but he didn't have to be my dad at all. I look back and I can see he was expecting praise for his great sacrifice and never once saw that Vicky had dinner on the table every night and got the laundry folded while making sure I brushed my teeth. I was mad when they divorced. My life was unstable for years, but I can see why she decided taking care of one person would be a helluva lot easier than taking care of two."

"Yet she remarried and had more kids with Mitchell."

"Mitchell never did more as a parent than Gary did, either. But he's rich enough that Vicky didn't have to work outside the home. The imbalance between their contributions wasn't as glaring. Personality-wise, they're a way better fit."

"And Gary's wife? Stephanie is a doctor, isn't she?"

"Dermatologist. After Michael, she hired a nanny so she could go back to work six weeks after giving birth to the other two. I'm not judging her. She's just very type-A. It's hard to be around someone wound that tight. I can't help thinking there's a difference between having it all and having too much."

"You're such a feminist."

"And I have burned my bra to prove it."

I was grinning as we settled back onto our even keel, but a strange poignancy tightened my throat, one I wasn't ready to examine. I dropped a dollop of yogurt on my fruit cup and stirred it into mango, blueberries, and strawberries.

"I go back and forth on marriage." Fox sounded introspective. "It's something that will probably happen one day, but I'm not in a hurry. I've been focusing on making money, building the business. I refuse to bring a woman into my life just to have someone to pick up after me." He glanced at me as though he knew he was maligning his best mate along with my willingness to put up with an untidy boyfriend.

Shane had needed a lot of managing. I had known that and thought the trade-off would be worth it. But what would I have gained? An exit out of Pine Grove and a decent job, but would that have been fair to Shane? Didn't *he* deserve someone who felt more for him?

I was no longer hungry for the psychedelic fruit on my spoon.

"I always reckoned I'd get married when I found someone I *had* to marry. Not pregnant," Fox hurried to add when my brows went up. "Someone I needed in my life every single day."

"That's sweet." Romantic almost.

He looked sheepish. Maybe even blushing a little. We were both smiling in amusement, but also with something deeper. Our gazes seemed to be locked and my scalp prickled. The tingle continued all the way down my arms, tightening my breasts.

"What, um. What about kids?" I rubbed my arms, trying to erase the sensation. "Do you want a family?"

"Sometimes," he said gravely. "I see someone like Oliver with Ryan and I think, yeah, I want that, but with the state of the planet, it seems irresponsible to bring anyone else on board. There are plenty of kids out there like me, who need a family, but there's a part of me that wants, I don't know. Someone who looks like me."

His voice echoed with isolation. I'd never seen him look so somber. His soul was right here, hovering restlessly beneath the surface of his otherwise undisturbed demeanor, like a massive creature that almost poked through, then sank deep again before I was able to fully see it.

"Vain, right?" He dismissed his yearning with a twist of his lips.

"No. It's human. I love when people think Fliss is my sister. Or my daughter." I snickered.

"That happens? You would have been her age when you had her."

"I was fourteen, but yeah. I love the scandalized glares." My phone pinged and I glanced at the screen. "Speak of the devil. Fliss says Ryan is asking what time we're going to the beach."

"Didn't see that coming, did we? Soon as we finish eating works for me."

"I have to talk to Waiola first."

He nodded and stole another potato, then another.

I was glad he would come with me to call off the wedding. I was really glad to be back to the solid foundation of our friendship, but a different clock had begun ticking in my head, one that counted down my remaining four days with him.

My options were as wide and endless as the ocean beyond the balcony rail, but I didn't want unlimited options. I didn't want to pursue wild goals in far flung fields.

I wanted to stay right here. In this moment. With him.

FOX

"*W*here did Auntie Ashley go?" Fliss was breathless as she staggered out of the surf clutching her surf board.

"Ryan needed the bathroom. You're doing really good," I told her.

"Hardly." She grabbed at my arm as a wave hit the backs of her knees and she almost toppled into the water.

I steadied her with a grin. "Don't turn your back on the waves. Maybe ease up on the drinking, too."

She forgot her hostility toward me and giggled, found her footing, and turned to watch another guest pop up to a crouch and slither along the face of a modest swell, tumbling into the wash a few seconds later.

"How long did it take you to get good?"

"Keeping in mind that 'good' is subjective, not long. But I was taught by a pro. Sandy took us every day, before and after school. We barely had time for homework. Definitely no time for getting into trouble."

Fliss's face blanked. "Sandy surfs?"

"When she was younger. You didn't know that? She's famous in Oz. She's in their sports hall of fame and everything."

Her brow crinkled, suspecting I was having a go. Given Sandy was sixty, had a bad limp, and her mobility issues had caused her to gain a lot of weight, it was easy to miss how athletic she still was.

"Struth," I said. "These days she only gets out maybe once a week as part of her work with an adaptive surf club for people with disabilities. That's what gave Ash the idea for our Do It Your Way segments."

"Oh, like when Shane interviews someone who uses a wheelchair or has low vision, but they learn to surf. I like those. They make me think that I don't have to do everything exactly like everyone else. Just think outside the box and you can do anything."

"Exactly. Thank you. It was such an obvious fit for us, but Shane and I didn't see it. I only knew our sales had plateaued and it was eating at me because our reputation was solid. Ash did an online survey to find out more about our customer base and we learned that T&B was seen as only for elite athletes. Part of that was the Holloway legacy. Also, Shane was only interviewing top level surfers."

"I like those, too. Like, the girl on the wave that was so huge?" Her eyes went big. "I thought she was going to die."

"We'll keep doing those," I said with a chuckle. "But once we started mixing it up with competitive and adaptive and weekend warriors who bring dogs or kids, our customer base exploded."

"Did you compete?"

"Nah. I always tagged along for Shane's training, but Sandy pretty much birthed her sons in the ocean and taught them to swim before they could walk. I couldn't catch up to that."

"Shane has a brother?" Fliss shaded her eyes as she looked up at me, puzzled by this new information.

Oops. Not my story to tell, but, "Marcus died in the car accident that wrecked Sandy's hip."

"Oh. Did Shane get hurt?"

"Sandy was on her way to fetch him from a friend's house. Eddie was at work. It was someone trying to outrun the police on a rainy afternoon."

"That's awful."

"Yeah. It happened about a year before I went to Sydney. They moved in next door to Vicky and Mitchell a few weeks after I arrived. I had started school, but hadn't made any friends. I was pretty much hating my entire life. Vicky saw a boy my age and dragged me over to help carry boxes into their house."

"How old were you?"

"Ten. I got in the way more than anything, but Sandy was still on crutches and appreciated the help." From then on, she invited me along on whatever they were doing. Surfing, camping trips, a night at the movies.

I suspected their family had needed a leg that propped up the dinner table after one had been broken out. I didn't match, but at least I kept the whole thing from collapsing. I didn't mind because at least I had a place where I felt wanted. Back then, as far as Mitchell had been concerned, I was a fifth wheel.

Ryan hurled himself into the water at my feet, splashing us as he landed on his hands and knees in a retreating wave. He popped his wet head up. He wore a grin and his eyelashes sparkled.

"You're a nut," I said.

"We just saw Eddie and Sandy." Ashley came up with Ryan's PFD dangling off one arm. "They said they're buying if we want a burger."

Ashley wore a straw hat, sunnies, and a white bathing suit cover-up that was more eyelet than yarn. It somehow made her hot pink bikini, with its demi-cups and metal rings that revealed her side-boob, even sexier. The skirt barely covered her juicy ass before fluttering against her honey-gold thighs.

With a heroic effort, I forced my gaze back to Ryan.

"I'm hungry," Ryan stood to declare. He promptly got knocked over by a wave.

I crouched to catch his arm before he was dragged into deeper water. Ryan was taking his beating like a champ, laughing as he blinked and coughed up a mouthful of seawater.

"I could eat." Fliss nodded with enthusiasm.

"We should get out of the sun for a while," I said.

"Can we come back after lunch?" Ryan asked as we gathered our things.

"We should check in at the villa, see if your Dad and Whitney are back," Ashley said.

"I'll return the boards and meet you at the restaurant," I said as Fliss rinsed them in the surf and stacked them.

"Thanks." Ashley made such a pretty picture with her sun-kissed cheeks and relaxed smile as she looked up at me, I had an impulse to kiss her.

What the fuck, Wiley.

I made myself walk away, disturbed by these thoughts that would not stay behind the firewall, but our conversation from this morning kept coming back into my mind. I hadn't fully articulated my thoughts on marriage and family to myself until I'd said them aloud to her. It felt strange, as though my robe had slipped open again. I wasn't ashamed, but I felt like I'd revealed too much.

And what was with her being so adamant against coming to Sydney? If she wanted to stretch her wings beyond Pine Grove, why *not* Sydney?

Why did I even care? She was a grown woman. She could make her own choices.

I just didn't like the idea of being out of the picture, completely oblivious when life's inevitable garbage truck rolled over in front of her.

I hiked back to the open-air restaurant and saw Ashley greeting Whitney and Oliver. She hugged her sister, but her profile was really stiff. Her smile seemed forced. Fliss stood beside them, her expression that of a beauty pageant's second runner up. She wore a weak smile on an otherwise devastated face.

"G'day," I said as I joined them. The stench of the proverbial garbage truck was thick on the air. "How was the botanical garden?"

"Life changing." Whitney stretched her arm toward me, ensuring her hand was in a slant of sunshine.

The diamond ring on her finger flashed with shards of broken light.

ASHLEY

"**O**liver proposed," I informed Fox, trying to bury my 'can you believe that' screech deep in my chest, but *seriously?*

"Congratulations." Fox reached past me to shake Oliver's hand.

A waiter approached with menus and asked if we needed a bigger table.

"Join us," Eddie insisted to Whit and Oliver.

"We only came to share the news," Whitney protested. "Mom was organizing lunch at the villa."

"Let me buy," Oliver insisted. He was glowing like a bride. "Text Joanna to join us."

"Mom never looks at her phone. Fliss, run and ask Grandma to join us," Whit ordered.

Fliss was hungry and tired, but she disappeared so fast, people probably thought she had robbed the place.

Oliver offered me a smile of remorse.

"I didn't mean to be insensitive by proposing when you're..." He couldn't even finish the sentence. "I've been planning this since we booked the trip, thinking I would do it after the wedding. Then I honestly meant to put it off until we were home again. But when we got to the waterfall..." He looked at Whitney, gaze all helpless and hapless and smitten.

Oh, God. How could I hate him when he looked at my sister like that?

"It was so perfect." Whitney locked eyes with him, expression equally sappy and soft. "The sun was coming through the trees in little beams, making a rainbow in the spray. No one else was around. The birds were singing and the air smelled amazing. I'll never forget it. I said I loved him and he said he loved me and we kissed. Then..." She blinked fast and gave a little sniff of gathering tears. "He asked me."

My heart panged at how romantic it sounded.

"I couldn't help it!" Oliver laughed at himself, blushing. "I had been meaning to put the ring in the safe but it was in my wallet. The words popped out. I nearly dropped it."

"He went down on one *knee.*" Whitney pressed both her hands to her chest. "I couldn't even speak." She was laughing and flushed. She was freaking ecstatic and she deserved it. She really did.

But oh, my heart throbbed with envy. With a recognition that I didn't have that and *hadn't* had it. That's what really stung. I hadn't believed it was possible. Not for *us.*

But maybe it just wasn't for *me?*

"That sounds really beautiful, Whit. I'm happy for you. Truly," I said through the gall I was trying to choke back. I *was* happy for her. And I refused to see it as insult to injury, but that didn't stop my gut from roiling with icky emotions like jealousy and offense.

Fox slid into the chair beside me and gave my knee a commiserating squeeze.

I wanted to fall into him and let him wrap his strong arms around me and squish me into his chest and pat my head and say, *There there.*

But I had to smile and report on Ryan's excellent manners and terrific form while we'd all played in the waves.

We ordered drinks and Fliss returned with Mom as we were deciding on communal plates for starters.

Fliss had her head ducked, but her eyes were red. Fox must have noticed, too. He stood and said very casually, "Have my chair, Fliss. I need more room for my legs."

It was exactly the same amount of room on the far side of the table, but Fliss mumbled "Thanks," and sank into the chair beside me, which put her on the end, so I screened her from her mother and the rest of the table. Her hair fell to hide her expression as she studied the menu. She sniffed, but I was the only one who heard it.

"Are you having the wedding now?" Ryan asked Whitney with innocent confusion.

My brain went through the proverbial windshield. Beside me, Fliss sucked her tongue into her lungs and made a choking noise.

"I've already arranged for my refund," I blurted.

"Not on this trip," Whitney said with an affectionate smile at her soon-to-be stepson. "We'll decide about wedding dates and everything else once we get home." Her smile faded as she realized Fliss was using Ashley as a human shield and refusing to look at her.

Oh, kiddo. I deflected attention by pointing to a cat wandering between the tables. "I heard there were a lot of feral cats here. That must be one of them."

"Looks well fed," Fox remarked.

Sandy inadvertently steered the conversation back into

rocky waters, joking with Joanna, "At least your mother-of-the-bride dress won't go to waste."

"I'm moving in with you," Fliss said through gritted teeth to me.

Across the table, Fox sent a concerned look to her, then searched my gaze. I gave him a half-hearted smile.

We got through the meal and, as we rose to leave, Whitney invited everyone to the villa for dinner. "Oliver and I were planning to barbecue anyway."

"We missed you last night. Please come," Mom coaxed the Holloways.

"That's very kind," Sandy glanced at Eddie who nodded. "We'd love to."

"We have plans," I said a little too loudly. "Sunset dinner cruise," I added when everyone looked at me with surprise. "It was already booked and paid for. We can't cancel or change it." I had no idea if that was true, but looked to Fox to back me up.

"It's part of that prepaid package I bought for her and Shane."

"The romance package," Whitney recalled with a hard smile. "No, you don't want to waste that."

"We could drop by the villa afterward," Fox said. "The sun sets around seven. I doubt they'll keep us out much later than that."

"We'll text." I sent that promise to Fliss, but her how-could-you-abandon-me glower didn't budge. "I have to make some calls about my stuff now that Sydney's awake, but you can come hang out in our room if you want," I offered in an attempt to mollify her.

"I'm dying to see all these balloons and baskets I've heard about," Whitney said brightly. "I'll walk up with you."

Fliss made an injured noise and said, "I'll go read my book."

"I want to see the balloons." Ryan looked appealingly at Whitney.

"I'll bring you one, sweetie." Whitney smoothed his hair. "I want to talk to Auntie Ashley. You go with your dad and I'll bring it to the villa. Sound good?"

Ryan nodded and Whitney exchanged a light kiss with her intended before we all broke up and went different directions.

A thick silence fell between Whitney, Fox, and me once the Holloways got off on their floor.

"Have you checked out the fitness room?" Whitney asked Fox, pointing to the plaque beside one of the elevator buttons. "I've been meaning to see if there's a yoga class we could do with Fliss."

"I was thinking that, too, but I haven't looked up their schedule yet," I said.

"Would you mind fetching one for us?" Whitney asked Fox as the doors opened on the Vista level. She used her sweetest voice and added a pretty-please bat of her lashes.

"Really?" I said flatly. "If you want to talk to me alone, just say so."

"I assumed Fox was smart enough to figure that out."

"I've been meaning to check out the gym." He handed me the overstuffed beach bag he had carried up from the restaurant, but made sure to meet my gaze and give me a chance to signal that I wanted him to stay with me.

I might not want to talk to my sister right now, but I wasn't afraid to.

"Thank you," Whit said of his understanding.

He stayed in the elevator and I led Whitney through the coffee lounge.

"Anything you have to say you can say in front of him," I muttered over my shoulder.

"Yes, I can tell you're very close. What is *up* with that?"

"He's my friend." I ignored the burn of what felt like a guilty conscience. I didn't have anything to be ashamed of. Except maybe some ill-advised ogling *after* he'd told me I'd been thrown over. A bit of weepy leaning on him last night. A teensy shred of anticipation for a quiet dinner with him tonight away from the madding crowd of my family and Whitney's impending happily-ever-after.

Whitney didn't need to know about this weird, new, misguided attraction I was suffering, though. She had a litany of crimes and misdemeanors she wanted firmly placed on Fox's record.

"He broke up your wedding. He's staying in your room—"

"Technically, I'm staying in his room. And he took the pullout 'cause he's a gentleman."

"He's seducing you with massages and dinner cruises."

"I'm not even going to dignify that." I shuffled through my bag in search of the keycard as we stood outside my door. "You don't get to judge me. I'm going through a lot and you are *not* helping."

"What was I supposed to say? Sorry Oliver, but I can't accept your extremely romantic and heartfelt marriage proposal because my sister's feelings are more important than ours? It's not my fault your wedding fell through. And I'm sorry it did, I really am. But I'm *happy*. For the first time in my life, I'm genuinely in love. I want you to be happy for me."

"I am." I didn't sound it. Not really.

I found the card, but didn't use it. I faced my sister and spoke from the heart.

"Oliver seems like a really good guy. Ryan wouldn't be

such a happy, confident, well-adjusted kid if his dad was a deadbeat. I'm glad you've found someone who makes your life better. I am genuinely happy for you."

"Thank you," Whit said, and we shared a hug.

"But your timing sucks," I added as I tapped the card against the mechanism and pushed into the suite.

"Holy Christmas," Whitney gasped as we entered.

The spectacle was worse since the resort had delivered what Fox had called a 'Sorry for your loss' bouquet—which was a rearrangement of the wedding flowers I had already paid for. The note said the Events team regretted they wouldn't be able to provide the celebration I'd been anticipating. If there was anything they could do to improve my stay, they encouraged me to reach out and very much hoped they could serve me in future.

"This view is killer." Whitney opened the door onto the lanai and stepped out.

I moved to stand beside her and set my bare hands on the rail. "That's a really pretty ring," I said of the sparkler on her finger.

"Oh, Sissy." She threw her arm around me and used the endearment that was only ever in play when we were making up after a mad. "You'll get through this. We always do. At least we haven't given up your apartment yet. You can have it to yourself once Fliss and I move in with Oliver—"

She cut herself off as I pulled away and looked to the horizon. She read my stubborn jaw like a neon sign. Her breath sucked in with the energy of a thousand older-sisters.

"You are not going to Oz to be with *him?*" She waved at the interior of the suite. "*No.*"

"Would you please stop acting like I'm madly in love with Fox?"

"*You* stop acting like it and maybe I will."

"Oh my God. Even if I was, which I'm *not*—" For some reason my voice stumbled over that. "—you have had some very sketchy relationships with some very sketchy dudes. I've always accepted your choices."

"Sure you have," she said on a chortle of outrage. "You've been treating Oliver like he's radioactive waste since you met him."

I couldn't deny that, but I only looked to my nails. "What about Fliss? She isn't happy about this."

"Forgive me for not ruining the moment by telling Oliver I need to run it past the tribunal of women who think they all get a vote on how I live my life."

The irony of making that statement seconds after her bossy command about how I should live *my* life went completely over her blonde ponytail.

"Fliss and I will work things out," she insisted. "We always do. *You* are the one in the witness box. What are you going to do now that you're not marrying Shane?"

"I don't know," I ground out. "And I'm sick of everyone asking me that as if I had a Plan B in case my groom didn't show up. Maybe you should take a lesson from this. Make a contingency plan for if Oliver backs out," I said with a facetious smile.

Whitney's brows flexed in hurt, but after a second her mouth went sideways with rueful empathy. She drummed her gel-polished nails on the rail and cocked her head.

"Rebound sex has always been Step One for me after a break up. Maybe you should give Tall, Dark, and Convenient a go since you're not going to see him ag— Oh. Hi. That was fast." She smiled into the suite.

I closed my eyes, refusing to turn around. I considered

throwing myself over the rail and ending it all right now. What further humiliation could I possibly have left to live for?

"They don't let you work out unless you have closed-toe shoes," Fox said. "Here's your schedule."

"You're a peach." Whitney took the page Fox handed her.

I turned, but kept my gaze lowered, unable to look at Fox.

"I didn't mean to interrupt. I just came to drop that and tell you I'm heading to the shops to buy some shoes."

"We're done. I need to go talk to Fliss," Whitney said. "And Mom. Surprise surprise, she has opinions, too." She aimed a flat smile at me and looped me into another hug. "I'm sorry our timing was so awful. Please don't be mad. It's ruining my vacation."

"I'm sorry you think I treat Oliver like he's radioactive waste. I only meant to treat him like he has a cold sore. One of those really bad ones like you had that time—"

"Oh, shut up." Whit pushed away from me. "Enjoy your cruise. I'll see you both later."

As Whitney stepped from the lanai into the suite, Fox drew a bottle of champagne from the fridge. He cast me a questioning glance.

"Good idea." I nodded agreement that he should give it to Whitney. "You and Oliver enjoy that. Congratulations."

"Really?" Whitney took it and studied the label. It was askew after being in the melted ice bucket all night, but it put a huge smile on her face. "Thank you."

"All part of the prepaid romance package," I said sweetly.

Whitney gave Fox a rueful head tilt. "Thank you, Fox," she said as though her mother had poked her in the back to remind her to use her manners. "For this and for giving us our moment of girl time."

"No worries."

Whitney left and I had a hard time meeting Fox's gaze. When I finally tried, he wasn't looking at me. He was searching his wallet for something.

"Do you need anything while I'm out?" he asked.

"I'm sorry," I said to get his attention. "I don't know what to say about what you overheard except that Whitney's MO is not mine."

He didn't pretend he didn't know what I was talking about. He found the valet ticket and closed his wallet.

"I'd like to say you don't have to say anything, but I think we need to say something."

"To who?" I asked with alarm.

"Each other."

My heart dropped about ten feet and stayed there, crushed under the elephant that had muscled its way into the room.

Oh, who was I kidding? That pachyderm had been here this whole time, pressing on both of us, using its trunk to goose places it shouldn't.

I knew I was violently red because my face hurt as though I had the worst sunburn of my life. My whole being dripped guilt and mortification.

"Fox, if I—" I didn't even know what to say.

"Stop." He held up his empty hand, then ran it over his face —which had darkened with embarrassment. He squeezed the back of his neck. "I know you're not the type to pick up the nearest warm body in search of comfort. Or use me to punish Shane. I know you're not like that, but you are in a bad place. I want to be here for you, but we're pretending we're mature enough to share a room without overtones and the tones are *everywhere*." He waved at a lemon-yellow bra I'd left on the foot of the bed.

"You're attractive, Ash. It's not like I've never noticed.

Sometimes I wonder if you realize how hot you are, which is a tiny bit frustrating because I've always wanted to tell you that and couldn't. Now I'm saying it and..." He pressed his lips flat and lifted helpless hands. "It makes this worse."

My stomach was tight, as though braced for a blow, but all those words had been the opposite of a punch. A caress. Swirls of taboo excitement worked through my abdomen.

I shook my head, fearful. I wanted to put the brakes on something that was rolling away uncontrolled. I stood there both humiliated at being unable to stifle my attraction toward him while I hungrily ate up his reluctant compliments. Should I tell him I thought he was hot, too? I had noticed, too. He had those wide shoulders and high cheekbones and those golden-hazel eyes that made me feel gilded in light. His abs were obscenely sexy. So was his ass.

He licked his lips and his gaze came up from where my bathing suit peeked through the eyelets of my dress. He swallowed.

I couldn't breathe.

"I don't mean to see you as anything but a friend and I refuse to lose you as one," he said, voice strained but firm. "I won't crawl into bed with my best mate's ex, either. So we need to agree that whatever this is..." He waved between us. "...can't happen."

"I'm so embarrassed." I hung my head in my hands, wanting to curl into a ball. "I've put you in a terrible position. I'll move to the villa."

"No," he insisted gruffly. "I want you to stay here." He was staring out the doors to the furthest point on the horizon, all the way to Asia. "I want to spend as much time as possible with you because I'm worried I won't see you after this. Not soon, anyway."

"Oh, Fox." My shoulders fell and so did the corners of my mouth.

"Yeah," he said heavily. "You don't realize how much someone means to you until they're in a different time zone. I've missed you," he admitted sheepishly, then chuckled. "So do the neighbors. They keep asking if you can feed their cat when they want to go away for the weekend. And the kids at the shop." He was grinning, but it was kind of melancholy. "People come in and ask for you. That rep who likes you so much. The one who also thinks you're hot."

Also.

"He only flirted with me because I was the owner's girlfriend."

"And there it is." Fox shook his head in exasperation. "I swear that wanker sat in his car for ten minutes, checking his teeth and retying his tie, before he came last month. I thought he was going to cry when I told him you'd gone back to Canada."

"Pull the other one." I offered my ankle.

"But you still think he wanted *Shane's* attention. You're not hard to look at, Ash. You have a great laugh and you're kind and patient and smart. Any man would have a crush on you." He cleared his throat. "Which isn't what this is. It's just..." He ran his hand over his face.

What?

I couldn't bring myself to ask, afraid of the answer. Afraid I would have to start labeling my own thoughts and feelings and petty disdain for women who had thrown themselves at him when he'd only been trying to help them buy a wetsuit.

I wanted the floor to open up. I wanted to pack and leave and not have to face him. I wanted to stay right here and not miss a second of the time I had with him, even when it was agonizingly awkward.

"I missed you, too," I admitted, relieved to have that much off my chest, even though it caused a wide river of what-ifs to open between us. Impossible possibilities we could never explore.

I cleared my throat and tried to steer us back into neutral waters. "I'm extra glad you're here because who else can I talk to about the fact that my *fucking sister*..." I leaned forward in belated outrage. "Got fucking *engaged*. The day after my own wedding was cancelled?"

"Okay." He put up a hand and bit his lips together. "It's not funny, but..."

"Oh, it's hysterical. *I'm* hysterical."

We held a look of bewildered hilarity at the perverseness of the situation. All of my pent-up anger and hurt and humiliation... All of it seemed to poof into a jagged chuckle of what-can-you-do? We both laughed it out, but my eyes watered.

"There's no use being mad, is there?" I said after I had grabbed a tissue and blew my nose into it. "I'm not getting married and she is. So what?"

"I think that's a healthy attitude." He nodded.

"Thank you. I mean that. You are a good friend. Someday we will have a beer and laugh for real over this entire nightmare."

"I might still be on iced tea, but that's sounds like a plan."

"Stomach still sour?"

"Touching that champagne bottle nearly turned me green."

I chuckled. Nodded. Fell silent. Wistful.

"I have to ask you something else," Fox said with a wince of reluctance.

"What?" I braced myself.

"How do you feel about helping me draft a statement that the wedding is off? Shane won't do it. I've already had a couple texts from friends, asking me why we haven't posted any photos yet. We talked up the wedding online. Fans will be expecting something."

"Oh gawd." He was right, but, "I don't know what to say. Artistic differences?"

"That's better than saying he stood you up." He winced.

"I'm won't smear your brand, Fox."

"I don't expect you to lie."

"This is just one of those things that didn't work out. Let me think about it while I make my calls about my stuff."

"Thanks. I'll run out and grab what I need, but I'll come right back to help with the statement."

"We can work on that marketing proposal too, if you want."

"You really don't mind?" He searched my gaze. "You don't have to be this nice, you know."

"Of course, I do. Otherwise, I have to revoke my Canadian citizenship."

His mouth twitched. "Back soon."

I nodded. Business as usual. Nothing to see here folks.

Except a giant elephant that had been acknowledged and was still here.

FOX

*I*t's not a date. I kept telling myself that as I shaved and flossed and buttoned on a shirt I'd bought with briefs, shoes, and sunscreen that didn't smell like a tropical fruit salad. Not that I minded smelling like Ash, but my attempt to set things firmly back into the friend-zone had wound up making me that much more aware of every word I spoke or every look she sent my way.

I zipped the fly of my new shorts and smoothed my eyebrows and ignored the tingle of anticipation in my balls. I gave myself a hard look in the mirror over the dresser.

Not a fucking date, mate.

Ashley was in the shower and this damned open-concept suite allowed me to hear the interrupted spray of water, indicating her movements, painting pictures I didn't need in my head. The fragrance of shampoo and soap carried on the air, signaling all the wrong things to little Fox.

I stepped onto the lanai with my phone and tried not to think of the way Ash had felt on the sofa cushions beside me this afternoon, as we'd passed my laptop back and forth. Our elbows had brushed and she'd smelled like ocean and sunscreen and the familiar scent of *her* as we crafted the marketing proposal for Togs and Boards.

She was so damned good at this stuff. Shane was the dreamer and could talk up Togs & Boards unceasingly, but he was a face-to-face, hand-shake closer. I was a bean-counter. I could manage the hell out of numbers and inventory and logistics.

Ash bridged the gap between our skill-sets really well. It killed me that she wasn't going to join our team after all. I texted Shane. I often threw random notes at him as a sort of agenda so we could scroll through the next time we were in a room, talking business.

> We need to talk about staffing. I'll have to hire someone else if Ash isn't joining us.

SHANE:

Are you back?

I ALMOST DROPPED MY PHONE. My arteries felt scorched by adrenaline as I quickly thumbed out a reply.

> Still in H. Staying the week.

SHANE:

...

SHANE:

How did she take it?

> Upset. But coping.

Was it a lie? I didn't think so. I admired her resilience.

SHANE:

She still there?

Everyone is.

Easier than changing flights.

SHANE:

Tell her I'm sorry.

I did.

I watched the indecisive dots play across my screen again.

"I'm ready," Ash said, stepping onto the lanai in low-heeled sandals.

I guiltily clicked off the screen as lifted my head.

Her dress was a white, body-hugging mini with a halter front. The skirt was cut like an upside-down tulip and was covered in tropical flowers. She went on tiptoes so her legs were slender and a mile long while she gave a little spin to show me how the dress closed across her lower back, but left the upper half bare except for a criss-cross of spaghetti straps.

No bra.

Her hair bounced loose around her shoulders as she faced me again. She'd kept her make-up light, only darkening her lashes and glossing her lips.

I made myself look at that pretty smile and not allow a longer stare at the front of her dress.

I'd seen her braless beneath clothes before. I'd managed not to turn it into an erotic fantasy before. What the hell was wrong with me that all I could think about was finding the dark shadow of her nipples and biting through that pristine fabric?

Her smile faltered. "Do I pass?"

"Almost. Turn around again," I requested, mouth dry. "You left the price tag on."

"Oh, there's a shock." She laughed. "I always need revision. I'll get my scissors."

I checked my phone, but Shane had gone dark again.

Blowing out a careful breath, I followed her into the suite. She brought me a pair of nail scissors that were too small for my big fingers. I managed to snip the tag then ran my fingertip beneath the edge of the dress where it was pressed to her spine. The backs of my knuckles absorbed the warmth of her lower back as I felt for the sharp T of plastic that was lodged in the seam somewhere.

She smelled like all those delicious things I'd been trying to ignore. Her shoulders twitched and her entire back looked...kissable. My mouth watered and my scalp prickled.

"That's it," I said, fishing the tiny piece of plastic from the fabric and setting everything in her palm.

"Thanks." She ducked her head, but I caught the flush on her cheeks as she went back to the bathroom.

Not a date, mate.

But when she came back and said, "Now?"

"Perfect," I declared. And I meant it.

ASHLEY

*S*ince Fox wasn't drinking and it was such a nice evening, he drove us to the marina in the convertible rather than us catching the shuttle.

The ticket claimed, 'There will be no snorkeling from the sunset cruise,' but it was the same catamaran that was used for day trips to the reef. It was about seventy feet long with two sets of stairs over each of the pontoons down to the diving platform in the stern. A polished, vintage wooden surfboard was mounted in the space between the stairwells, painted with the slogan, 'Sorry, I had a board meeting.'

The catamaran was nice, though. Sleek and white with a dolphin theme throughout. There was a settee and dining area beneath slanted windows inside, but everyone sprinkled themselves outside. Some chose the small foredeck while others chose the U-shaped bench seat on the aft deck.

About thirty guests were aboard with us ranging in age from an elderly couple to a family with school-aged kids. The captain introduced himself and his first mate, Tala, a burly man who served us a round of drinks as the cat made its way out of the harbor.

Once the rigging went up, the temperature cooled off to a pleasant breeze.

"I don't know what I was picturing, but it wasn't this," Fox said about an hour in.

We'd just finished our appetizer of premade sushi rolls and were enjoying the view of the rocky shore from the starboard rail—a sailing term I only knew from one of those memory devices that stuck purely because it made little sense. 'Port' and 'left' both had four letters. 'Starboard' had an 'r' in it like 'right.' 'Port' also had an 'r,' obviously, but it still worked. I was standing on the righthand side of the cat, therefore I was on the starboard side.

"I thought there'd be a bubble machine at least," I said. "Maybe a dance floor so we could waltz to the top twenty ukulele hits."

"Or learn hula. When am I going to cross that off my bucket list?" Fox asked.

"I think this is as much of the stereotypical Hawaiian experience as you're likely to get." I offered him the triangle of pineapple garnish from my drink.

"Thanks." He took it, started to eat it in one bite, then said, "Fuck!" He spat it into the water and yelled, "Man overboard!" at the top of his lungs.

"What?" I followed his pointed arm.

Against the shore, I thought I glimpsed a flash of red, but the sun and the swells hid it again before I could be sure.

While people gasped and crowded up to us, Fox grabbed my arm hard and pointed it alongside his own. "Do you see the red? That's a shirt. You see it?"

I nodded jerkily. "I do. Yes."

A swell receded and I saw a man clinging to a jagged rock. He had the broken half of surfboard in his hand. As a wave crashed into him, the surfboard popped up and disappeared, leaving the man clinging to the rock with both hands.

"Keep pointing. Do not look away," Fox ordered, still gripping my arm so hard he might leave bruises. "The cat won't be able to get close enough. Keep pointing." In my periphery, I was aware of him ripping open his shirt.

"What are you doing?" I cried, arm already aching, but I kept watch on that poor swimmer struggling to keep his head above water, fighting against getting dashed to pieces. "You can't go in there!"

"I'll take a board."

He slipped away and other guests took his place at the rail. I heard someone shout, "Use the life ring!"

"We're all accounted for," the first-mate said breathlessly.

"There." I kept pointing with both fingers before I dropped my tired arm. "A surfer. In trouble." *Where was Fox?* I could hear him swearing near the stern.

Someone fired a bright orange life ring into the water. It trailed a string of rope, but it wasn't nearly far enough. What the hell was *that* supposed to do?

Amid a few gasps, there was a bigger splash, then another. Fox came into my field of view, on his stomach on a board, paddling toward the life ring. He scooped it up as he went by it and kept right on going toward the surfer.

"Is there enough rope?" I cried.

"Someone's feeding it out," a woman said behind me, voice trembling. "Will he be okay?"

"He's an open water life guard," I said, but that didn't make him a superhero. He wasn't invincible. The water was choppy, the waves coming in big sets. There could be rip currents and rocks he couldn't see. What the hell was he thinking? "Don't they have a jet ski or a life boat or something?"

"The first mate is launching an inflatable."

The sails abruptly went slack, ruffling and snapping above us.

The flash of the orange life ring was disappearing and reappearing between the swells, allowing me to track Fox while I kept my gaze fixed on the red shirt.

Fox neared the surfer. He probably shouted, but whatever he said was carried away on the wind. He sat up on the board and threw the ring at the surfer.

The surfer's relief was palpable even from this distance. He started to reach for the ring, but a fresh wave slapped him into the rocks again. He was gone, then seconds later, his arm was through the ring. He let go of the rock and weakly kicked toward Fox.

Fox had hold of the rope and dragged the man toward him while the waves pitched both of them toward the rocks. When the men clutched each other's forearms, Fox wobbled, nearly unseated from the board, but he managed to drag the man onto it.

A huge cheer went up.

Don't cheer. This isn't over!

I reminded myself to breathe and finally let my arm drop to clutch the rail.

Fox got the ring over the man's head and under one arm, then positioned the man on the surfboard in front of him. With the man's legs under his armpits, Fox hung off the back of the surfboard and began battling through the waves, coming back toward us.

This was the real fight. Twice they had to duck through a crushing chandelier of a cresting wave. I expected both of them to get washed away at any second. My heart hammered in my throat each time they disappeared. When they came up for air, I sucked in a breath myself then held it again as another wave cascaded over them.

Suddenly the rope went taut. I realized the guests had caught up all the slack and were pulling them toward the boat while Fox continued to paddle.

I moved my curled knuckles from my pounding heart to my mouth as the men drew near enough I could hear Fox reassuring, "You're all right, mate," while the surfer clung weakly and coughed up sea water.

Tala told everyone to get back and asked one guest to help bring the victim aboard. The surfer was so weak, he folded onto the deck. A beach towel was handed over and Tala dried him vigorously, pausing to let him cough, then resuming.

Fox needed help handing up the surfboard. It was the decorative board and it was heavy enough that two men had to grab it. They grunted as they hefted it up to the deck. Finally, Fox came up from the platform, chest heaving with exertion. Everyone cheered and gave him a round of applause.

Another towel was offered and he said, "Ta," as he wound it around his blue boxer briefs. He waved off the accolades with a self-conscious cringe.

"That was probably the stupidest thing I've ever done. Don't try that at home, kids." He aimed that at the youngsters.

"It was *so* stupid!" I cried and launched myself at him.

FOX

I was still amped with adrenaline, heart pounding and lungs aching so hard, I thought my chest would burst. Ashley nearly knocked me off my wet, slippery feet and back into the water.

I closed my arms around her and staggered to catch my balance, something soaring in me at the feel of her crashing against me.

Her cheek pressed hotly to my cold chest. All of her was warm and there was so much naked back beneath these sexy criss-crossed strings that tangled up my fingers. I'd been trying not to think licentious thoughts about her, but now her slight shoulders were under my palms and her hair was soft and sticking to my wet skin. Her lips were damned near touching my nipple and her arms squeezed tight around me.

My nose nuzzled itself into the silky waves of her hair and my hands shifted on her back, trying to find a safe space. I wound up on that strip of fabric above the curve of her ass— which felt really intimate and not friend-zone at all, but nice. Really very nice.

"You scared me!" she accused, pulling back to glare up at me with those huge, dark eyes of hers. Her lashes were spiked with dampness, her mouth pink and trembling.

"I'm fine." My voice had to be dredged from deep in my chest. I lifted one hand off her to stroke a damp strand of hair off her cheek and before I knew what I was doing, my fingers followed that flyaway mass to cup the base of her skull. My mouth was against hers.

It was pure instinct of the moment. We both froze before it became a real kiss. Her eyes were open, but I didn't see rejection there. Only awareness that this was the line we had promised each other we wouldn't cross. If I had drawn away in that second, it would have been nothing more than a stolen peck.

But her hand shifted against my waist. Her lips moved under mine. She might have pressed up onto her toes, but my arm tightened in the same instant, catching the pliant weight of her as the boat rocked beneath our feet. I enjoyed the sensation of gathering her in and up into a taut line against me. I liked it a lot.

And however it happened, one way or another, we were kissing proper.

And *fuck* did it feel good.

Her eyelids fluttered closed. I let my own drift shut, letting this become a dream. Letting myself sink into the fullness of the kiss.

Her lips were soft and receptive, parting and shifting in response to the hungry pull of mine. Her lips clung and opened wider with invitation for me to take more. I did, stealing a deep potent taste with a stroke of my tongue. I wanted to *consume* her.

All the nerves and muscles in me that had fought the beast

of the ocean switched into that other biological urge. Fast. No gentle stir of desire here. Lust jabbed like a knife into my groin, tightening my belly and filling my mind with an imperative to press her beneath me. To cover her and spread her thighs with my own and—

Someone laughed.

I made myself drag my head up. My heart was still on the verge of exploding, but now it was for a different reason.

Ash blinked as though waking up. Her mouth was shiny, her dress wet enough I could see the dark circles of her areolas topped by the sharp points of her hard nipples.

The only thing that saved me from showing more wood than that antique surfboard was the fact I was pressed up against her and wearing a towel over my clammy underwear.

"I'm in my jocks," I reminded her. "Any idea where my clothes went?"

Embarrassment flashed into her eyes. She ducked away. "Here."

I was dimly aware of the people around us making teasing remarks and laughing over our kiss. Ashley was trying to find a good-sport smile as she handed over my clothes.

"Good thing I didn't go commando," I told the goggling faces, trying not to think about how profound—and completely inappropriate—that kiss had been.

I clutched the towel and crouched next to the first mate who was still assessing the man I'd rescued.

"I can treat him while you..." I circled my finger to indicate the dinner cruise that had been interrupted.

"That'd be great, thanks." Tala rose and asked for volunteers to help bring the life boat back on board.

"Let's get you into a cabin. You can rest and warm up," I

said, helping the weak surfer to his feet. "And that's the entertainment portion of tonight's cruise, ladies and gentlemen. Be sure to give us five stars when you review online."

I didn't look at Ashley as I helped the man below deck.

ASHLEY

$\mathcal{F}$ox stayed below until the cat was motoring into the marina, giving me lots of time to overthink our kiss while trying to pretend I was enjoying the company of strangers.

The rest of the meal had been served with an apology for cutting short the cruise. The captain was taking the surfer back to shore so he could get medical attention, in case he had injuries beyond the nasty cut on his leg that Fox cleaned and closed with butterfly bandages.

"We'll talk to the tour company about compensation. We really appreciate your understanding," Tala said, offering an extra round of drinks.

I had polished two of the hard lemonades I'd been offered which did nothing to erase the taste of salt and Fox from my lips. Or ease my nerves when Fox finally came above deck.

Was he mad at me? Was our kiss my fault? I could have pulled away at the last second. We had pretty much sworn a blood oath that nothing like that would happen between us and it had barely happened anyway! It was a fluke. Curiosity. He had pulled back before I'd had nearly enough.

I was freaking out over the way he'd pulled away and *moved* away. His mouth had felt really good, soft and supple and strong and knee-weakeningly hungry. I could have kissed him forever.

I had wanted to, much to my shame. It was a terrible realization to have about a friend. Why had I let it happen? I didn't want to mess up what we had, either.

Maybe we could pretend it hadn't happened at all?

"How is he?" I asked, apprehensively searching his eyes for clues to his thoughts.

Fox had his guard up. Way up. His shoulders were like a yoke made of iron. He barely met my gaze before he tracked it restlessly across the water.

"Still spitting seawater, but he'll be right. He bought a house thinking he could surf straight out his front door. Didn't ask any locals about rip currents or other hazards."

"Kook." I didn't know everything about surf culture, but I knew what the idiots who failed to recognize their own limits were called, especially when they wrecked everyone else's fun.

The purse of disgust on Fox's mouth agreed.

"I said I'd take him to the clinic and drive him home." Fox's gaze struck mine for a split-second before he looked away again. "Do you mind taking the shuttle back? Will you be okay going to the villa alone?"

"Of course." I didn't want to believe he was volunteering in order to avoid me, but that's what it felt like, leaving my heart feeling stretched thin.

"He offered me a private heli-tour tomorrow as a thank you."

"Oh. That's nice. He's either really grateful or he's sizing you up for a kidney."

"At least he's being a gentleman and buying me breakfast first."

I smiled, but it trembled. I couldn't think of anything witty to add. I couldn't stop thinking about our kiss. *Oh, shoot*, I recalled with a thud in my heart. I had to tell him about the photo and the video.

I opened my mouth, but Fox said, "He, uh, saw us..." His flinty gaze touched my cheek and ear. "You're invited. On the heli-tour."

My insides did a lift and swoop as if we'd crested a particularly rough wave, even though we were moving very slowly in the sheltered waters of the marina.

Whatever he read in my eyes made his expression turn cautious.

Keep it casual, I reminded myself with mild panic. *Friends.*

"Do I want a free aerial view of the island? Who wouldn't?" Hard to get into too much trouble wearing seatbelts and shouting over the drumming noise of a helicopter. "Unless you'd rather go alone. Is he the pilot? Because..."

"No." The corners of his mouth deepened. "He owns the chopper, though. Sounds like he has one of everything."

"How is he so rich?" I glanced over my shoulder, but the surfer was still below. "Is he famous? Why didn't anyone recognize him?"

"He sold an app," Fox said dryly.

"How is that still a thing? Was it an app for making apps? Because I feel like everything else has been invented by now. And is that what buys you a mansion with a private beach? You and I have to put on our thinking caps so *we* can buy a house on a beach."

It was our usual, garden-variety banter, but it landed like a fart in an elevator when he said, "I have one."

"Right. Forgot." I was forgetting a lot of things, most especially that I'd been engaged his best friend, the man who owned that house with him. That's why I wasn't supposed to suck Fox's face.

My stomach cramped and I stared blindly at the boats we were passing as we closed in on the slip.

"Ash—"

"There's a picture," I blurted while keeping my voice low.

"Of?" he asked with dread.

"Us. And a video."

"Fair dinkum?" He pivoted to face me, saying in a quiet hiss, "It lasted five seconds."

Definitely wasn't happy about our kiss. I held up a hand and he swung back to the rail. His jaw muscle pulsed and his biceps flexed.

"There's no video of that. Margorie, the older lady, took a snap of us—" I glanced over my shoulder. "*Hugging.*"

It wasn't a hug. It looked like the cover of a romance novel, him shirtless and dappled with beads of water, me clutching at him, hair windswept, my expression all limpid and smoldering as I looked up at him.

"I don't know if she'll post it." Margorie had promised to send it to me, though. "The mom with her hair in a bun? She filmed the rescue. That's definitely getting uploaded. She was already trying to do it, but we were out of range. I thought about saying T&B might pay her for it, but if she knew she might get more traction by tagging Shane..." It had been a tough call. "I got her details."

"How does it look?" Fox asked uneasily.

"Honestly? Really dramatic and exciting. Everyone is

sounding all worried, then they cheer when you get him. I wouldn't be surprised if it gets picked up by some networks. You should capitalize on it." I wrinkled my nose, already knowing he would hate that idea. Shane was the face of the company. Fox liked his role behind the scenes.

He grimaced. "I'll get so much blowback on the safety side."

"You will. That's why it has viral potential. Everyone will have an opinion. You might even wind up with your very own troll."

"Lucky me."

"The price of success, my friend." I faltered in lifting a hand to pat his arm. That word felt as though it was made of sharp edges as it lingered on my tongue. I dropped my hand back to my side, but pressed on with my attempt to pretend that's all we were. "Instead of Shane Says, you could call it Fox Freaks."

"You've had time to think about it and that's the best you could come up with?"

"Feats? Frolics? Doesn't have the same ring of urgency. Or insanity."

His choke of humor was laden with self-disgust.

"I need my ass kicked for being so reckless." He ran a hand over his hair, started to say something else, then pinned his mouth shut. His nostrils flared and his brows lowered with dismay.

We'd both done something reckless.

As the catamaran engine finally cut off, my stomach churned with worry that we'd made a huge mistake. The kind that couldn't be undone.

ASHLEY

S ince the cruise had been cut short, I arrived at the villa early enough that the Holloways were still there. By then, the video had been uploaded and I'd been texted the link by the passenger who had filmed it. I was able to show everyone why Fox was absent. The rescue had everyone gasping.

Eddie said "Bloody idiot" with exasperation. Sandy had opinions on surfers who got themselves into trouble out of sheer ignorance. Then she gave me some pointers on how T&B could share the video and frame it to help people understand they were putting others in danger when they were thoughtless about their own safety.

"Can I watch it again?" Fliss asked.

"Sure." I handed her my phone, then asked Whitney, "How was the champagne? Good enough that I can ask a favor?"

Whitney lifted amused brows. "Such as?"

"Harry, the guy Fox saved... He offered Fox a heli-tour tomorrow." I wasn't sure if Fox really wanted me to go, but... God help me, I wanted to spend as much time with him as I could. "I'm supposed to pick up Izzy from the airport tomorrow."

"We can do that," Oliver said brightly. "We're happy to."

"No, you and Ry go kayaking like you planned," Whitney said to her intended. "I'll go. Fliss can come with me. I want some mommy-daughter bonding time."

Fliss lifted her head from staring at my phone and curled her lip at Whit. "Then take Grandma."

"Grandma has been invited to join the Holloways on a tour of the resort," Mom said.

"In a golf cart," Sandy explained. "I can't do long walks with my hip."

"That sounds fun." I was pleased to hear that Mom was doing something besides planning meals and deadheading the resort's already well-tended flower baskets.

"Yeah," Whitney said. "Way to wheel out of your comfort zone, Mom."

I slanted her an admonishing smirk. Behind her, Fliss was still on the sofa, still looking at my phone as it pinged with an incoming text.

Fliss's eyes bulged and she snapped an accusatory glare at me.

"What?" I instinctively moved toward her. "Something from Shane?"

"No," Fliss said with disdain. She slapped the phone into my hand. "I thought vacations were supposed to be fun. This one sucks. I'm going for a walk."

Oh, frig. The photo from Margorie of me and Fox hugging had come through.

I clicked off the phone and glanced with dread around the room, trying to think how I would defend myself, but everyone was watching Fliss kick into her flip-flops, completely misinterpreting her tantrum.

"It's one hour to the airport," Whitney said with tested patience. "You said you didn't want to go kayaking."

"It's too late to go out walking around," Mom said. "It's dark. Practically your bedtime."

"The four-year-old is still up!" Fliss pointed at Ryan where he was playing Go Fish at the table with Eddie and Oliver.

"I'll go with her," I said, snatching up my bag.

Fliss's teeth lined up against her tight bottom lip, as though she wanted to tell me to eff-off, but after a quick glance at Ryan, she stormed out without saying it.

I jammed my feet into my sandals and hurried after her.

Fliss stayed where the path was paved and lit. Bugs fluttered against the lights overhead and a couple of teenagers were goofing around on the tennis courts. A tiger-striped cat saw us coming and shot into the shelter of a nearby shrub.

"I know what it looks like. That's not what it was," I said as I came alongside her.

Fliss threw me a look of pity. "I'm so sick of being treated like a little kid who doesn't understand what's going on or have any choice about anything."

"I know you're upset about your mom and Oliver. I'm sorry I went out tonight instead of hanging out with you. Do you want to talk about it?"

"And say what? She's going to marry him whether I want her to or not."

"Are you mad that she's getting married or that she didn't talk to you about it first?"

"I don't know!"

"Well, at least let her tell you how she thinks it will be. Then you can tell her what you're worried about."

"Sure, I'll go on a super fun car ride tomorrow to the airport so Mom can tell me how great Oliver is. Can't you get Izzy with the helicopter? This is all really fucking stupid." She plopped onto a bench.

I ignored the curse. Truth is, I never stopped her from swearing and barely filtered my own language around her. Hadn't for years. I sat down beside her.

"I heard Mom tell Oliver that she told you to go to bed with Fox and get it over with. Have you?"

"What? No. And I won't." That felt like a lie as I said it. Because I wanted to. Not as revenge or rebound, but because I wanted to. Oh gawd.

I tried not to let that realization show on my face as Fliss chewed her nail and stared at me so hard, I felt the heat of it against my skin.

"I was really scared for him tonight," I admitted, experiencing a fresh shiver in my chest. "It made me realize how much I care about him."

"So what are you going to do?" She sounded both belligerent and anxious.

"Nothing," I said, and feared it was another lie.

Fliss wanted reassurance that Auntie Ashley would be there for her through this latest upheaval in her life. I wanted to be there for her. Love wasn't selfish, I reminded myself. My needs didn't matter. They never had.

"I— Being with Fox is impossible." I was reminding myself as much her. "He's not just the best friend of my ex-fiance. They're business partners. They own a house together."

"It'd be like having an affair with a married man. Like you caused their divorce." Fliss said it gravely. It wasn't a joke. Then her face crumpled a little. "I don't even get why mom wants to get married. Sure, have a boyfriend. Have sex. I don't care. But why make us all live together and everything?"

"You're sounding a little like Grandma."

"Harsh. Why did *you* want to get married, though? Just so you could move away? Did you even love Shane? Because now you're into Fox. It's very Twilight."

"Why are you so mean?"

"I'm twelve." Fliss bent and rubbed her fingers and thumb, trying to coax one of the feral cats closer. It grew skittish and retreated into the dark. She straightened and gave me a disgruntled look. "Don't tell me I'll understand when I'm older. Explain it to me now."

"I wasn't going to say that." I usually did try to explain things to her in an age-appropriate way, but this one was hard. I barely had a grasp on it myself. "First of all, grownups aren't that smart, sorry to tell you. We're basically a bunch of twelve-year-olds who can drink and drive. Not at the same time," I hurried to add.

She rolled her eyes.

"We want kids to believe we've got shit figured out because life would be really freaking scary for you if you knew we were as confused as you are, but we are." I slouched deeper on the bench, tilting my head back to look at the stars. "I've been thinking a lot about marriage and how important it is to me and why."

This afternoon, when I'd been trying to write the press release about why the wedding had been cancelled, I'd realized how much I'd been thinking about a wedding and not the marriage itself.

"Want to know a secret? I hadn't even read the vows we were supposed to take. When Fox first told me that Shane didn't expect us to stay married, I was really upset. Because

I'm stubborn, right? I can make anything work. That's what I thought when he said Shane felt that way. Like, 'I'll show him.' But is that a good reason to be in a marriage?"

Fliss was bent again, offering her empty hand to a skittish kitten, but I was pretty sure she was listening so I kept talking.

"Shane and I would have come here and said those vows if Fox hadn't stopped us. They're supposed to be promises and we probably wouldn't have meant them. Realizing that made me think a lot about whether I'll ever be able to say anything like that to anyone and mean it."

"Grandma has told us a million times that we don't need to get married." Fliss sat up and looked at me.

"I know. But I still had this sense that I should. And I always expected I would. I'm not sure why."

"Peer pressure?"

"You'd think we grow out of it, but we don't. The messages are everywhere, right? Don't you feel as though you're expected to marry and have kids?"

"Everyone at school is like, 'Josh is so cute. I want to have his babies.'" She made a gagging noise, tongue curling out to her chin. "I'm like, do you know how babies come out of you? Because, no thank you."

"And we *know* we're supposed to be skinny and eat vegan even though no one says it to our face."

"And have clear skin and wear the right clothes."

"And men are supposed to be sex machines and women are supposed to naturally love children, even though kids can be very challenging and petulant."

"And children are supposed to be respectful of their elders, even when they can tell when an adult is talking down to them."

We made faces at each other and jostled elbows.

"So you don't want to get married anymore?" Fliss asked.

"I don't know." I looked back at the stars. I kept thinking about what Fox had said about wanting to see someone every day. About missing me. "I can't say I never will, but..." But the man who inspired the closest thing I had to that feeling in me felt firmly out of my reach. "I think—please don't tell Grandma I said this. I think I wanted to show *her* that I could get married and make it work."

"Because she got a divorce from Grandpa? And thought you should never marry?"

Fliss didn't know all the gory details of that time, only that my dad was an alcoholic who hadn't wanted to seek help and that was the main reason Grandma wasn't married to him anymore.

"I guess," I said. "Like I wanted to prove to her that I was smart enough to make a better choice than she had, maybe. I wasn't really making a choice, though," I realized. "I was still doing what I thought was acceptable. What I thought Grandma could accept as a valid reason for me to leave Pine Grove and all of you. I understand why she wants us to live this small, careful, safe little life and stay close to her. It makes *her* feel safe. But it's stifling."

"Tell me about it," Fliss muttered, then cut me a glance. "Do you think that's what Mom is doing? Showing Grandma she can do it better?"

"No. I think she really loves Oliver."

Fliss grimaced.

"Look. Being twelve sucks." I picked up her hand and squeezed it between my own. "It also sucks when you feel like your Mom controls your whole life. Believe me, I *know*. But your mom loves you, same as Grandma loves me. She wants to give you a good life, but she also wants to *have* a good life.

Your mom wants to feel loved and have someone who will be in her life when you decide to get the fuck out of Pine Grove yourself."

"In *six* years." She pulled her hand away from mine.

"At least you're not waiting until you're *twenty*-six. And it's not like I'll never come back to see you. We'll still text and call—"

"It's not the same!"

"I know, but Fliss, nothing stays the same." I started to add more, hesitated, then decided to give her the courtesy of being raw and real. "Are you going to stay twelve and need me exactly this same amount? You already don't."

She snapped a look at me and I could tell she wasn't sure if she wanted to deny that or assure me that she didn't need me *at all*. Twelve. Such a ridiculously difficult age for the person in it, let alone the people around them.

"I wasn't much older than you when your mom had you," I reminded her. "Grandma was working and your Dad..." I shrugged because I barely knew the guy and his absence had made things less complicated in the long run so I didn't run him down to his daughter. "Your mom's friends were doing what teenagers do. They weren't around to help her. I was the one she leaned on and I don't resent it. I love you, Fliss. I love you *so much*, but you're finally old enough that I *can* leave. I can think about what I want to do, rather than what Grandma thinks I should do, or what your mom needs me to do. You've already started making a life of your own. You'd rather hang out at Sofia's than hang out with me. Which is *fine*."

She had her arms folded and wasn't looking at me, but I could see a gloss on her eyes.

"This is the age where you're going to want more and more independence. Growing up is like learning to walk. You want cushions to fall back on, but once you figure it out, you keep going with it. You never go back to *not* walking. Not if you can help it. Shane was my cushion. He's gone and I stumbled and it hurts, but I have to pick myself up and keep trying. I can't go backwards."

"You thought you would feel more independent by getting *married?* Grownups really are stupid."

"We really are. But you realize I'm not leaving you at the pound, right? She's your mom. And wherever I end up, you can come visit."

"Promise?"

"Pinky promise." I offered mine.

After a discontented sigh, she hooked hers into it and gave it a jiggle.

FOX

*A*shley was beside me, soft hands whispering across my bare chest, lips touching my throat. Her hair fell to tickle my shoulder and the short blue nightgown she wore was slippery beneath my palms, heating under my touch as I grasped her waist and drew her onto me. I ran my hands down her back, slow, savoring the feel of her, sleek and smooth and lovely.

She parted her legs over my hips, settling intense heat against my cock while her mouth found mine in the dark. The soft mounds of her breasts were squashed against my chest. I wanted her nipples in my mouth, but I didn't want to stop kissing her or lose that volcanic heat crushing my rocket.

This was the kiss of life that was the prelude to the little death. I was hard and throbbing, aching to be inside her, but wanting to play it out. Savor. My greedy hands flowed down to the lace that cut across the tops of her thighs. I drew circles with my palms on her bare cheeks so the silk rode up. I let my fingers follow the strap of her thong into the crease of her ass, reaching to probe beneath into slippery heat.

I groaned with gratification, wanting inside her so bad—
"Fox?"

I snapped my eyes open. I was so close to losing my load, I had to clench my fist around my throbbing cock. My heart was pounding, the room dark, my breath broken.

"Are you having a nightmare?"

She was still in the bed on the other side of the room, thank God. Not standing over me, witnessing me nearly succumb to a wet dream.

"Yeah," I lied belatedly, voice rasped with acute sexual frustration. "What time is it?"

Her body shifted across the sheets. It was the most erotic sound I'd ever heard in my life. "Five eighteen. Are you going to surf?"

If I could climb out of bed without breaking my dick off, "Yeah."

"Do you want to talk about your dream? Was it about the rescue?"

"No." I hoped like hell she couldn't see I was tenting the front of my briefs as I made my walk to the bathroom. I couldn't even take a piss, I was so hard. My balls were still tight, my skin damp and so sensitive, I felt every molecule in the air as I moved through it. My heart was thudding unevenly, pushing blood around that didn't know where to go.

The waves would cool my jets, but I'd have to sport this trophy all the way through the lobby and down to the beach. Fucking brilliant.

What was even happening to me? I'd always thought Ash was hot and sure, I'd ogled a few times, keeping it subtle and always reminding myself she was off limits. *She still was.*

I splashed cold water on my face and the back of my neck,

rinsed my mouth, thought about a story I'd once heard about a torn scrotum. That scared enough starch out of Fox junior, I could step into my borrowed boardies and shirt. I held a towel in front of me as I searched out my keycard, dimly aware that Ashley was sitting up in that big, wide, sweet-smelling bed, peering through the dark, watching me leave.

It was So. Fucking. Hard.

ASHLEY

*A*s the helicopter banked, I resisted the force that pressed me into Fox, not wanting him to think I was literally pushing up on him. Each time I did end up squashed against him, he subtly pulled away with what felt like avoidance. On the next tilt, he was in my space, though, so I really didn't know how to interpret it.

He'd been withdrawn when he returned from surfing, but when I asked if he would prefer to do this heli-tour alone, he'd given me the impatient look he threw at me when I stared longingly at a cookie and said, "No thanks."

"It's going to be fantastic. You have to come."

That had been before we were smooshed shoulder to shoulder, hip to hip, thigh to thigh next to the pilot in the front of the chopper. The windshield was a see-through bubble that extended below our feet. We'd opted for the 'doors off' experience and were strapped in securely, but I felt as though we would tumble straight into the scenery with each tilt.

On the next angle, Fox seemed to fall away next to me. I

grabbed his wrist as if I was some James Bond stunt double, capable of hauling his dangling ass back into this aircraft should he actually fall out.

"It's like a motorcycle, you nut." His humor-laced voice cut the music playing in the headset. "Lean with it, not against it. Unless you feel sick?"

"No, I'm just scared. This is the best and worst roller coaster ride of my life."

"We're totally safe. Here." He slid his arm under mine so we were linked, forearms aligned as he wove our fingers together. He hugged my elbow securely into the warmth of his side. "Better?"

Not really. The chopper dipped at that moment, making my stomach swoop. I squeaked in surprise and clung to his arm, but we were both laughing and so was the pilot.

Down we went until we were skimming above turquoise water that smashed itself into shattered rainbows against black, pillowed rocks of hardened lava. It was breathtaking.

Fox flashed me a grin and I stared at his teeth for several awe-filled heartbeats, both of us exhilarated by racing across this wonderland.

I couldn't see his eyes behind his sunglasses, but my lips began to tingle. His smile faded. He rolled his lips together before he turned his attention out the door again.

The loss was so palpable, my throat hurt, but the chopper climbed then, pressing me into my seat. Soon we were flying over crumpled peaks of tropical jungle. I had thought the east coast of the island a startlingly rural contrast to the concrete metropolis of Honolulu and the sprawl near the military base. The ridges below us were nothing but steep valleys of undisturbed greenery, the isolation giving the impression no human had ever set foot there.

A few minutes later, our pilot landed us ever so gently on a rocky outcropping. Before us, the acid-washed denim ocean stretched endlessly, its edges decorated with white frills of waves hitting the seams of yellow sand on the shoreline. The bowl of the sky was pressed over it, the foothills below us rugged and lush with tangled jungle.

The music stopped and we removed our headsets. As the rotors slowed, I took a few calming breaths, appreciating how the world had grown silent and still. A cool breeze cut through the cockpit, skating across my bare arms and legs.

"This is unbelievable," I murmured.

"It really is," Fox agreed.

"I have a picnic for you," the pilot said.

"I don't know where I'll put it," I said, setting a hand across my stomach.

Harry, the surfer Fox had rescued, had fed us a robust breakfast of eggs benny, quinoa porridge, and tropical fruit with Greek yoghurt before he'd sent us on our way.

"It's just champagne, cheese, and fruit. Swim first," the pilot suggested. "Come back when you're hungry."

"Swim?" I looked from the cliff that dropped away before us to the craggy peak behind us.

The pilot unbuckled, but stayed in his seat as he pointed out a barely discernible path into the jungle.

"The trail is officially closed. The final leg to the top is called Cardiac Arrest. Three guesses why that is." He lifted a disparaging brow. "People still hike it, though. It takes about five hours from the bottom. If the heat or their heart doesn't do them in, a nasty fall can. This is where the rescue chopper lands." He glanced at his watch. "You should have the pool to yourself for a while, though. Go down, not up. You'll see the waterfall and the pool in about ten minutes."

I followed Fox out of his side of the helicopter. He took my hand and I gripped it tightly, knees still spongey from the flight.

"I didn't know we'd be hiking." I'd worn a sundress and sandals, but even though the path was a steep incline down, there were plenty of rocks and branches to hold onto.

A few minutes later, as I began to wonder if we'd made a wrong turn, the musical trickle of a waterfall drew us. I didn't see it until we were pretty much standing in the narrow stream that fed it, though.

The water dropped a few feet into a handful of smaller pools and finally into a big one that sat like a garden of Eden amid the thick jungle that surrounded it. We picked our way down and Fox reached back to help me as we reached the edge of the pool.

The water was placid and deep blue. A single beam of sunshine cut through the opening in the canopy to glitter against its surface.

"I feel like Adam and Eve," I said in a near whisper. Innocent of sin.

Except they weren't. *I* wasn't.

I glanced guiltily at him. He wasn't looking at me, but his brow pulled with remorse, as though some thought or other was torturing him.

"I didn't know we'd be swimming or I would have worn my bathing suit." I slipped out of my sandals and waded across the slippery rocks to my shins, holding my skirt above the surface of the water.

He didn't follow, only stood looking across to the waterfall, expression tense and inscrutable.

"Are you mad at me?" I asked.

"No." Quick and sure, but sharp.

"You sound mad." I waded a little further, holding the skirt a little higher while lifting my gaze to the walls of greenery around us. Birds twittered and odd little flowers bloomed next to broad, variegated leaves.

"I'm not mad at *you*," Fox said grudgingly.

"Who then? Yourself? Because we kissed? Just pretend it didn't happen. That's what I'm doing." I was also pretending it was working, apparently.

The sounds of nature filled the silence, idyllic, but the remoteness seemed amplified by the distance between us. I wasn't even facing him, but I could feel him behind me on the shore, close enough to reach out and touch me.

He wouldn't, though. We were too far apart in other ways.

"The irony is..." His voice dried up.

I glanced over my shoulder and he was still looking off to the side, gaze faraway. He seemed reluctant to go on. His mouth twisted and his sardonic tone seemed aimed at himself.

"I want to talk it out, but there's no one to talk to. That's why I stayed so late at Harry's last night. Sometimes it's easier to talk to a stranger, but he doesn't get it. He doesn't have a business partner who's been there for him all his life. He comes from money so he doesn't get how hard I worked to get what I have. Which is chicken scratch compared to the way he lives."

"Don't disparage what you've achieved."

"I'm not. I'm just saying it was a failed effort to use him as a sounding board."

"And you can't talk to Shane because he's not here. And it's me." The words seemed to stick like a spear in my breastbone. "I'm the problem."

"I wouldn't talk to him anyway. We don't do girl talk.

That's why it took until the last minute and more alcohol than any man should consume for our frank discussion in the cab." His hand skimmed his hair, then he made an impatient noise of ironic-laughter. "You're right. You're the problem and you're also the person I want to talk to about it. When I call you my friend, that's what I mean. I trust you enough to tell you anything. More than I'd ever tell Shane. Turns out *you're* my best friend. I bet you didn't know that, did you, Ash?" The words gusted out of him on a laugh that held the force of a small hurricane.

I didn't even know how to respond to that. It was lovely, but it also made me feel more wretched about this ridiculous situation.

My hands crushed the cotton fabric of my dress as I realized I was suffering a similar frustration. I didn't want to talk to my sister or Izzy about these conflicted feelings I was having, or the attraction that grew by the minute, fuzzing all my well-developed sense of caution. I wanted *Fox* to help me make sense of this and he was the source of it.

"Which makes Shane my brother, I suppose," he mused. "Because I've never had thoughts about him like the ones coming into my head about you."

A wobbly smile tried to land on my mouth. I pressed curled fingers against it, closing my eyes against a hot sting. My hem landed in the water and I felt the skirt weigh heavier on my hip. I came out a few steps so I could wring it out.

"When we get back, I'll get my own room."

"No," I pleaded softly, straightening. Experiencing such a profound loneliness, I didn't know how to process it. "What you said yesterday about seeing as much as possible of each other... I want that, too."

"Ash." His palm came out, beseeching. "That wasn't a

nightmare this morning. I was dreaming about you." He was glowing with a hard blush. He dropped his hand to his side. "It was pretty graphic."

My whole body prickled with a shivery tingle and my ears rang. How graphic?

"It was all I could do not to crawl into bed with you. I can't..."

Don't say it, don't say it—

"I wanted you to," I blurted.

He physically jolted. Paled, maybe, but he was standing in a shadow so it was hard to tell.

"After you left, I imagined you coming back," I confessed in a scraped-thin voice. "Joining me."

His hands hung at his sides, but his fists curled tight. His voice was strained. "Are you saying—"

I fought to swallow and barely nodded, but it was enough to make him seem to expand inside his own skin, hardening to granite. He stepped into the water so he was right in front of me. The fierce light in his eyes made the embers of passion still in my belly flare hot.

I'd never felt so exposed in my life, but I met his searing gaze and let him read my guilty secret in my blush. The best orgasm of my life had come by my own hand with thoughts of him delivering it. Flutters of uncertainty struck my middle as I let that hover unspoken but acknowledged between them.

"Why would you tell me that?" His voice was almost scary, it was so gritty. It abraded and caressed at the same time.

"I thought—" I could hardly breathe, let alone talk. "I thought we were being honest."

"Not that fucking honest!" His voice bounced off the rock wall above them. "Jesus, Ash."

Then he clasped either side of my head and his mouth

slammed down on mine so hard and thorough and powerful, I was nearly driven to the ground by the force of it.

My feet slid and I grasped at his forearms. He shot his arm around me, pulling me up against the solid strength of his body.

It should have felt abrupt or rough or objectifying, but it was what we had both been craving. His full lips became my everything, claiming mercilessly while giving up his entire soul to me at the same time. I tasted his wildness, his greed, but also his helplessness. His agony.

That's what was in me. Yearning and selfishness and shadows of self-reproach that I pushed to the edges so I could glory in the golden light. The taste of him. The feel of his warm sides and strong back beneath my splayed hands.

We melded into one another, bodies pressing, arms closing tight. Clinging. Transmitting to each other the fear we would be torn apart.

For a few minutes, it was only this, locked in a stolen kiss that neither of us should want, but neither wanted to end. It was sweet and lurid. Blatant and explicit and so rare, I wanted to hang onto it forever. He was hard and thick against my stomach. The ache that had kept me awake most of the night returned. I knew he felt exactly as I did, *knew it*, and it made the shared kiss all the more profound.

"Tell me to stop." His breath wafted against my lips as he nipped at my jaw and took my earlobe in his teeth.

"I can't."

He sucked in a harsh breath as though I'd stabbed him. His head went back and he groaned his torment at the sky.

I was shaking and ran my trembling hands over his tensile strength, savoring every sensation, every texture and scent while a distant clock ticked in my head. I had never felt this way, as though the sky pressed down and the earth pressed up and the only escape was into his arms.

"I can't...not want to touch you," I breathed and claimed more. The cords at the base of his neck, the balls of his shoulders, the flex of his biceps and the meaty firmness of his twitching pecs all filled my greedy touch. He was so hard and wide and strong. Hot and fierce and tender as he smoothed his hand down my hair and pressed a kiss to my crown as he drew me in tighter and closer, sheltered and held prisoner.

Stopped.

"Ash..."

"I know, I know." I trembled as he pressed me into this tiny space—this single moment.

But I wasn't ready for it to be over. I offered my mouth.

With a vanquished groan, he covered my lips with fresh reverence. His fingers against my throat absorbed the vibration of my tortured moan while I drank and drank the sensation of him slaking his thirst for me.

We can't, we can't, that infernal voice warned in the back of my head. But when he drew me out of the water and backed himself against a mossy boulder and set his feet wide then drew me to sprawl half over him, I joyfully went. My breasts mashed flat against his chest and my hands found his hairy thighs beneath the edge of his shorts, stroking and making him hiss with pleasure.

His mouth was trailing down my neck now, light fingers sliding the strap of my dress off my shoulder and taking the strap of my bra with it. He claimed all of that real estate with soft wet bites of his mouth and an erotic dart of his tongue into the hollow beneath my ear and along the line of my collarbone.

I held my breath, skin shivering pleasantly while wires of

tension drew electric and taut into my erogenous zones. My nipples tightened with anticipation. I hadn't known something so small could cause so much havoc, making every inch of my skin feel too tight and ultra-sensitive. I melted more heavily against him, stomach taking the impression of his erection. When he tickled his fingertips against my spine, I arched and he groaned with pleasure.

I liked that noise. I wanted to make him do it again and ran my hands under his T-shirt. He picked up his arms and I followed the motion, blindly throwing his T-shirt to the ground, gaze pinned to his mouth. *Come back, come back.*

He slouched a little further down the rock and cradled my jaw in his big hand as he slanted his head and kissed me deeply. Like it was all we would ever have, but all we would ever need.

I tried to lift my arms to go around his neck and my bra strap cut across my arm. I whisked it down and pulled my arm free of it, then swept the other one away before I twined both arms behind his neck, loving the feel of my naked chest against his.

He kissed me once, brief and hard, then clamped one arm around me while he pushed off the rock with the other. He turned us. My feet caught and stumbled on the uneven rocks, but he held me securely and now my back was against the moss on the rock. He kept one arm behind me to cushion me against it while the other eased the front of my dress all the way to my waist.

I sucked in a breath at the sensation of cool air and the avid heat in his gaze, worshipful yet so visceral he didn't even have to touch me to make wet heat rush heavily between my thighs. When he caressed with light fingers, gently shaping around the side of one breast, I trembled. He danced the backs of his fingers beneath the other and I bit my lip, knees going soft.

"Fox," I murmured shyly.

"You're so pretty, Ash." His voice, so coarse and moved, raised goosebumps all over my body. "Beautiful."

I usually felt very average, but not today. As he caressed me so reverently, my eyes dampened with emotion. I *felt* beautiful. Like a freaking goddess who was more a spirit of nature than a being, one who had come up against another force of nature in the type of storm that left scars across the landscape. The kind of heat and energy that cracked and bolted like lightning, capable of melding two things into one. Indelible.

I shivered again, realizing this would never be the sort of encounter I might have with another man. For me, sex was pleasant and sensual, but a bit routine, like washing my hair. I could go through the steps and feel refreshed afterward, but nothing in my life was different afterward.

This would change everything. It was carnal and intimate and *meaningful*.

This was the point where I should tell him to stop, but I didn't. Couldn't. I looked down at the breasts that captivated him. At my own nipples, beige with pink tips, sharpened to tight points by arousal and the cool mist coating the air.

I watched him lick his lips and dip his head.

I curled my toes and closed my eyes and still wasn't prepared for the heat. For the pull that sent a sharp jab of acute arousal straight into my pussy and dragged a groan from deep in my chest. A pulse point seemed to throb and grow in strength between my legs, calling to him.

My hands went to his shoulders, his hair. This wasn't new, I acknowledged distantly, but it felt new. It felt like nothing I'd ever experienced. *This* wasn't a sharing of self but loss. Surrender. Not to him. To *need*. To this thing that gripped both of us equally.

All I knew was Fox. His smell and the shape of his shoulder and the feel of him shifting between my thighs.

I ought to feel excruciatingly wrong, doing this with him, but a bizarre tenderness filled me. Something that wanted to savor and memorize the textures from his thick, crinkly hair to the fabric of his shorts against my inner thigh. I wanted to breathe him in. Lick him. Bite.

He moved to my other breast and I made a garbled sound, arching myself flagrantly. My knee came up and I felt him press more firmly into the space I'd created, keeping me in place with this weight.

He lifted his head and cupped my face, kissed me with such tenderness I could have cried. The stiff line of his erection met the pulsing folds of my mound and I sighed.

He rocked and the sensation coaxed another noise of abandonment from me, driving my arousal to higher and higher degrees.

"I won't get pregnant," I confided when his lips trailed across my cheek.

He stilled his mouth against my skin. He dropped his head against my shoulder while his whole body seemed to slump in defeat.

"I had a physical before I came away—" I realized I was starting to sound desperate.

All the beauty from this moment bled away. I *was* desperate. Because I could tell that I'd ruined it. I wanted to cry, I was so angry with myself. With him, for being more noble than I could ever hope to be.

He was shaking. He lifted his head as though it weighed

more than he could manage. The regret in his eyes arrowed straight into my heart, cracking it into jagged pieces.

"We can't. You know we can't." He licked his lips and rubbed his thumb against my cheek in a caress that was probably meant to soothe, but it felt as though it would break the skin and leave an open wound. "This was too much. Incredible," he breathed with a restless track of his gaze over my face and hair. "But too much. It shouldn't have happened. Can't."

He drew away in a hunch like an old man, catching my hand as it fell off his shoulder. He tried to kiss my knuckles, but I yanked my hand away, stupefied by the plunge from arousal to incredible pain.

He flinched and his gaze held mine. Begged forgiveness.

"Let's go for a swim. Cool off."

I wanted to tell him to fuck off, that swimming was the last thing I wanted to do.

But since the waterfall was the only place to hide my tears, I skimmed off all but my underwear and waded into the pool.

FOX

Harry, you son of a bitch, I was still thinking when we landed on the man's lawn.

My new friend hadn't understood the problem, but had believed he knew the solution. He'd sent us to swim alone, trying to engineer exactly the close encounter we'd had.

I had treaded water as far from Ashley as I could get, seriously considering hiking down the entire mountain and hitchhiking to the resort, just to avoid further temptation.

To avoid the bitterness in her profile.

I couldn't believe she had admitted to entertaining fantasies starring *me*. It was one thing for my subconscious to sideswipe me with an erotic dream, quite another to process her *conjuring* sexual encounters between us. Her candor had pretty much mule-kicked me off whatever high horse I'd been on. I'd had to kiss her. Had to.

And *of course* reality was infinitely better than my dreams.

I don't know how I stopped. I really don't. The fact she'd been ready to go all the way had nearly undone me. I was all about consent and always checked in before things went too far, but things had been going far and fast and had felt *right*. In a way I'd never experienced.

My chest was still tight with regret at turning her down. Hell, my balls were punishing me with a dull ache that extended into my stomach and down the insides of my thighs.

Now I only had the memory of kissing her and sucking her nipples and it was a pearl in an oyster, digging at me, yet I couldn't resist turning it over and over, allowing it to take up more and more space inside me, glittering and precious and liable to kill me if it was ever pried out of me.

Harry's butler met us. Harry had expected us to be gone at least another hour and had run out for a follow-up appointment with his doctor. We could enjoy his pool if we wanted to wait for him to return.

I glanced at Ashley. She had been pretending fascination with anything that wasn't me for the last hour. She had taken a seat in the back of the helicopter for the flight back, too, apparently no longer caring if I plummeted to my death.

"We're expected back at the hotel." Or rather, Ashley expected me to take her back to the hotel and I'd disappointed her enough for one day. "Thank Harry and let him know I'll give him a call to thank him myself. It was great."

"You didn't touch the picnic," the pilot reminded me. "Take it with you."

Like we needed another bottle of champagne, but the butler carried it to the car for us and set it in the back seat. As I rolled away a minute later, toward the gate at the end of the driveway, I touched Ashley's wrist.

"Hey," I said.

"Can we not?" She moved her hand into her lap and kept her head turned away.

Been here, done this. My sigh burned into the bottom of my lungs.

I racked my brain as we crawled through congestion toward the resort, pulling over to put the roof up when rain started to spit. Ten minutes later, the squall became so intense, pouring in such voluminous buckets, I pulled over again to wait it out.

"What are you doing?"

"It'll pass in a minute."

She *tsked* and put on the A/C to combat the humidity and the fog gathering on the insides of the windows.

"Ash—"

"I don't want to talk about it."

"Because you don't have a solution, either. Do you?" Sexual frustration added a layer of aggression to my voice that came across like blame. I didn't mean for that to happen, but this wasn't easy for me, either. "Say we have sex. Then you go to wherever the hell you think you're going and I'll feel like I took advantage of you. So will you, by the way."

"You don't know me."

"Like hell I don't." She had been genuinely hurt when Izzy had promised to travel with her then dumped her. That had been a *trip*. Not physical intimacy. "And what do I tell Shane? Nothing? Let it sit on my conscience like a tumor? What if you and I try to give this a serious go? Now we *have* to tell Shane. *I talked him out of marrying you.* Shane pretends he doesn't have feelings, but he does. He would be rightfully pissed and probably would demand I buy him out—which I can't. He's not in a position to buy me out, either. So now we dissolve what we've built? Take a loss on the house? Even if he walked out and left T&B for me to run, I need his celebrity endorsement. That's our brand. The business wouldn't survive without him so every way I look at this, I'm screwed."

"So long as your priorities are straight," she muttered.

"That is fucking unfair. Tell me there's a way you and I can see what this is—" I pointed between us. "—that won't cost me everything, including people I genuinely care about. Tell me. I'll do it."

"Don't yell at me," she snapped, eyes gleaming with unshed tears.

I recalled her experience with her father's anger and clenched my hands on the steering wheel, trying to rein in my anger so I didn't scare her.

"You think I don't know how shitty this is?" she asked. "I know I can't go to Sydney with you. I'll never be part of your life if I do. Shane's mates are never going to accept me if I've moved on to his bestie like some kind of two-timing slut."

"*Don't.*" I would never let anyone call her something like that, especially her.

"I'm not keen to be the girl who broke up T&B, either. You think Eddie and Sandy are going to keep being nice to me if I'm with you? No. You did the right thing, Fox. Is that what you need to hear? Thank you for saving us both. Okay?" Angry tears stood on her cheeks and she swept them away.

"The thing that bites most is that it's more of the same. No matter what I want..." Her voice cracked and her hands clenched into fists. "I'm always forced to lower my expectations. Get married in Hawaii? Heck, no. I can't even get *laid* in Hawaii. Career? I can go back to my job in Pine Grove that pays the bills, but I can't have a career I enjoy. I *wanted* that job at T&B! Do you realize that? I felt like I did good work there."

"You did."

"Nice to know, but who cares? Because someone else gets to have that job. Not me."

"I keep telling you, we can find a way to...keep you on. Somehow."

"This is not about finding the compromise! It's the fact that settling is all I ever do because that's all I'm allowed to do. So fine. I'll settle for being friends except, wait, we can't be friends anymore because I ruined everything by letting you touch my boobs. I'll go home and go back to not even wishing."

"Ash—"

She cut into my attempt to reason with her. "The rain is letting up. I want to get back. Unless that's too much to ask?"

My hands were still clenched around the steering wheel. I wanted to shake it loose from the car and throw it across the road with a primal scream, but I gritted my teeth and pulled into traffic. This was *such* a cluster-fuck.

At the resort, I left the car with the valet and carried the basket into the hotel.

"You gave your room key to Fliss," I reminded Ash when she started digging into her bag on the way to the elevator. I fumbled my wallet from my pocket.

"I'm looking for my phone. I haven't checked my messages."

"I heard from Shane," I finally remembered to tell her.

"When?" She snapped her head up, bag still agape. "What did he say?"

"Yesterday. I meant to tell you, but we went on the cruise and..." I shrugged. Had it slipped my mind? Or had I shoved it out of the way?

"And?"

"He's sorry."

She stared at me until the doors opened for us. Then she choked out a husk of a laugh.

"Great. That fixes everything. Thanks." I used my card on the reader and she stabbed the button. As soon as the door s opened and she shot off down the hall to the room.

I gathered my patience and followed, catching up to her at the locked door where I touched the card to the reader. I schooled my expression as we entered, expecting Fliss to be here, but there was a whole gaggle of female voices.

"Oh, *hello*." Izzy came in from the balcony.

ASHLEY

*I*zzy was so many things that I would never be. Her skin was flawless and bright with a natural golden hue, like a topaz. She was tall and slender and never bemoaned her modest chest. She had the confidence to go without make-up and wear her hair in a faux-hawk, letting it flop boyishly over her feminine features.

Most of all, Izzy knew what it was like to have sex with Fox.

That was all I could think as I hugged her. I didn't want to think of it. It certainly didn't make me feel good. It made me feel small and insecure. Envious. *Jealous.*

"Oliver and Ryan are still kayaking," Whitney said, coming in from the lanai behind her. "We decided to steal some of your wine and enjoy the view. Mom is still out with the Holloways."

Behind Whitney, Fliss scratched her elbow and looked sullen, but remorseful, as if she'd done something wrong by letting her mom and Izzy into our suite.

"No problem. Thanks for making the trek to the airport.

How was traffic?" I pretended I didn't notice the way Izzy smoothly moved to hug Fox.

"I don't know if I'm supposed to be nice or angry with you for busting up the wedding." Izzy's voice held a scold. "Either way, it's good to see you."

"You, too," he said politely. He still held the basket from Harry in one arm and pulled away to set it on the dining table.

"We left too early," Fliss said, watching Fox.

"But that was okay," Whitney insisted with a tense glance at her daughter. "It gave us time for a froyo and a chat."

Fliss derided that with a curl of her lip, but continued to stare at the basket. "You got another one? What's in it?"

"Stuff that won't travel." Fox opened it. "Help yourself."

Izzy and Whitney moved with Fliss, all drawn like magnets.

"Oh, my God!" Izzy snatched up the champagne and hung her mouth open as she displayed it to Whitney.

"Wow." Whitney crowded around the basket, scooping out jars and crackers and packets of truffles. "This is really high-end stuff."

"I'll leave you to your tickle fights and go for a work out," Fox said, tense beneath his sardonic expression. He crossed to the dresser for a fresh pair of board shorts, sending a more somber look toward me as he passed. "I'll talk to the front desk, too."

About getting his own room. I bit the inside of my bottom lip, nodded once, stomach tight against a crease of nausea as he left.

"There're glasses and everything." Whitney was saying, drawing the flutes from the basket and sidling a glance at me. "What exactly was Fox planning? And what stopped him from execution?"

"Nothing," I said with annoyance, trying not to blush or look guilty. Or devastated. "It's from Harry, the guy he saved."

"How was the heli-tour?" Fliss asked.

"Really cool." I tried to find the enthusiasm I'd felt on the first half of the flight. "He took us over the water to where lava was spitting into the ocean, making clouds of steam. Then we stopped on the top of a mountain and hiked to a grotto. Swam a bit, but we weren't hungry so we came straight back."

Three pairs of eyes stared at me, seeming to expect a higher level of gushing.

I shifted uncomfortably, feeling transparent. Could they tell Fox and I had had an encounter that had left me in agony?

"Well, it sounds like taking you on that tour was the least he could do after wrecking your wedding," Izzy pronounced. "I say we celebrate all the single ladies."

"Hey," Whitney said with a frown of consternation.

"Unless you *want* to be with someone. Then you get to celebrate that," Izzy corrected easily. "What do you say?" she asked me as she showcased the champagne like a game show hostess.

"What the hell." I nodded for Izzy to peel the foil off the cork. According to Fox, if I wanted to drown my sorrows, I should do it with the good stuff.

FOX

I worked myself to quivering exhaustion on every machine, then ran on the treadmill until I was empty. After grabbing a shower and a protein shake, I booked my own room. They had *one*. I went back to the suite to pack up my stuff.

I was hoping the women had made their way to the villa. I couldn't face Ashley's baleful glare again.

I'll go back to not even wishing.

I wasn't trying to disillusion her. I was trying to hang on to what I had—which included her. And I wouldn't be flat broke if Shane and I dissolved the business, but it would still hurt. I enjoyed a certain level of security because I had fought for it. I wanted to keep it.

As a child, I'd had a constant sense of being adrift with very few anchor points, all of them borrowed and tenuous. Creating this feeling of having roots and community had been years of blood, sweat, and tears. The next house I bought was going to be *mine*.

As for the business, I never wanted to go back to working

for The Man. I liked *being* The Man. I loved owning T&B, loved having the control to set goals and achieve milestones.

Granted, some of that had felt a little colorless after Ashley had gone back to Canada. In the short time she'd been there, she'd become a fixture in my days. When she'd gone home, I'd known it was temporary, but it had been a taste of what life would be like without her and I hadn't liked it.

A bleak space was opening in front of me, one that I was fighting looking into. That's why I had stuck around this week, to put off having to face losing her from my life.

I pinched the bridge of my nose where the protein shake was driving a cold spike of ice cream headache into my sinuses.

If Ash and I couldn't find our way back to being friends, if I couldn't at least know she was on the other end of a text or a call, I didn't know what I would do. I had to figure out how to smooth things over with her.

Without sleeping with her.

But oh, I wanted to sleep with her. Talons of want were lodged in my guts, reminding me why I had to pack and leave her room. Put more space where I didn't want it. It was for the best, even if it killed me.

I stepped out of the elevator and immediately came across Fliss in the lounge, curled into a corner of the sofa, reading a book.

"I thought it was lady time on the lanai?"

"They're all getting drunk." She didn't lift her eyes from her page.

"Perhaps I won't rush in there, then." I dropped onto the other end of the sofa, still nursing my protein drink, relieved.

But was I? Maybe Ash was telling her sister and Izzy that we'd made out. I didn't care what the other women thought of me. Not really. But I cared if Ashley was hurt and angry enough to talk down about me.

I glanced at Fliss to see if she was giving me the stink-eye.

She was watching me over the top of her book. The cover had gold embossed lettering and a scene of a misty pond with a band of robed sorcerers. A huge eye was superimposed above them.

"I won't bug you if you want to read."

She dipped her nose into her book, but almost immediately dropped it into her lap.

"How did you feel when your foster mom got married? Did she *ask* if you wanted to move to Australia? Or did she just take you there against your will?"

"Does Oliver want you and your mom to move?" That was news. "Where?"

"No. Mom said we'll stay in Pine Grove and I don't even have to change schools, but I still have to live with a guy I don't know. And now I'll have a stepbrother who's like, four. What if Mom gets pregnant? Then I'll be like Auntie Ashley and have to look after a baby that isn't even mine. And I know I'll love it and everything. I don't even mind Ryan. He's cute, but kids are a lot of work. Everyone thinks babysitting is just watching TV and making sure the stove is off. It's not. Babies cry and you have to figure out why. And stinky diapers *stink*."

"Babies are messy," I agreed. "Families are."

"I *know* family is messy. Have you seen mine? This is one long week of diarrhea." She rose to make herself a coffee. "But I think that's what Mom is trying to do, make us look like a 'normal' family. It's, like, the only thing she's ever wanted in her life because Grandpa was a deadbeat and my dad flaked out on her. But I don't care if I don't have a dad. I *like* living with Auntie Ashley. I don't care if people think it's weird."

"People give you a hard time about that?" My big brother protective instincts leapt to their feet and growled.

"Not really. Just this one girl asked me if I had two moms and laughed. I don't even like her and so what if I did? I mean, read the room. We've moved on." She rolled her eyes.

Damn, I liked this girl.

"What do you like most about living with Ash? What do you think will change if you live with Oliver?"

"Everything." She tasted her coffee and stirred another sugar into it. "With Auntie Ashley, she stands up for me against Mom. Mom never lets me forget that I'm her kid and half the time she acts like Grandma and says I should listen and do what I'm told because she said so. But Auntie Ashley treats me like I'm allowed to have a say and makes us talk things out. Now Oliver will have his own opinion and who do you think Mom will side with? He doesn't even know me or what I want."

"It takes time to get used to each other, that's for sure."

She came back and curled a leg beneath her as she sat.

I'd seen Ash sit like that a thousand times. Fliss was so like her, it was laughable. Endearing. It made me picture a little girl with Ash's big brown eyes chirping back at me over some adults-know-better edict, melting my heart while she tested my patience. The idea was so sweet, my throat ached.

I shook my head to clear the vision. "For what it's worth, Oliver seems like a good guy. Like he wants to be a good parent."

"I should still get a choice over whether I want him to be *my* parent."

"You know that almost no one gets that choice, right?"

"I guess," she mumbled against the rim of her cup.

"I always wanted a 'real' parent," I said, using my fingers to quote around the word.

"You didn't feel like you had one?" She was wearing Ashley's exact look of compassion, chin tucked and eyes wide.

"Not really." I didn't tell her it would have felt different if Vicky and Gary had been fighting to keep me, rather than fighting over who had to take me.

"But you must have been stoked to see kangaroos and koala bears in real life, when you went to Australia?"

"I was," I admitted, nodding as I recalled the excitement that had hit when I was getting on the plane. "No one warned me about the freaking spiders, though." Or snakes or jellyfish or crocs.

A smile of morbid curiosity spread across her face. "Auntie Ashley said some of them are really big. She showed me a photo of one she saw at a campsite that was as big as her hand." She splayed her fingers wide.

"That was only a teenager. I've seen bigger." I set my hands in the air as though framing a dinner plate.

"For real?" She hung her tongue out. "Barf. I'm never going there."

It was a throwaway remark, but knocked me onto my proverbial ass. It was one more reminder that her aunt wouldn't be there as a reason for Fliss to come visit.

She sipped her coffee. "Do you like your stepfather?"

"Mitchell is okay." I tried not to rehash the past since there was no changing it and I'd mostly made peace with it. "We never fought or anything. I did all my chores and got good grades. Spent a lot of time at Shane's so I wasn't in the way too much. He still calls me his wife's foster son, though. Even though his kids look like they could be my biological siblings.

It's always made me feel like he wants people to know I'm not his, you know?"

"He sounds like a dick. What was your stepmom like?"

"Stephanie calls me her stepson and treats me more like a member of their family, but she's hard to be around. Really high strung. She's a doctor and they have three kids plus they breed standard poodles. She keeps a lot of balls in the air and runs everything like a military operation." I chopped my hand against my palm. "Are you coming for Christmas? What time do you arrive? How long are you staying? Can you watch the kids on Tuesday so we can go to a holiday party? That was a conversation I had with her last week."

"It's *March.*"

"That's Stephanie." I sipped my shake and found it empty so I rattled it, hoping for a final taste. "As a kid, it was really hard to relax around her because I felt like I was one more thing she had to manage. I kind of preferred Mitchell's indifferent attitude. He didn't make me feel super welcome, but he didn't act like I was a huge burden, either. I was just a fact of life he couldn't avoid, like paying taxes or sweeping the garage. And I had Shane next door so I was glad to stay in Oz."

"And Eddie and Sandy were nice to you?"

"Very nice," I assured her, privately smiling at the anxious look she was giving me. *So* much like Ashley. "They invited me to come along all the time. Eddie calls all of Shane's mates 'son' and means it. Like they've adopted all of us. It means a lot."

It was why I couldn't bear to further damage my relationship with them by taking up with the woman they had thought would be their daughter-in-law.

"Are you saying I should make friends with Josh who lives next door to Oliver?" She made a face of revulsion.

"What's wrong with him? Is he one of the potheads who hangs around behind the gas station?"

"Jock," she said pithily. "Doesn't even know I'm alive. Not that I care." She tried to sound dismissive, but I read confused speculation in her disgruntled expression.

You poor, poor kid. I wouldn't go back to middle-school insecurities for all the money in the world. But where was I right now? If not co-starring in a high school love triangle? God knew I didn't have the lead.

"Tell him you learned to surf over spring break. That'll get his attention."

"Are you referring to my failed attempts to drown myself?"

"You'll get better."

"When?" she scoffed.

"What are you doing right now?"

"Really? You want to go surfing? With me? Right now?"

"Why not?" I could use the distraction as much as she could. I wasn't in a hurry to face Ashley again, especially if she was talking to her sister and Izzy about me.

"I already have my suit." She plucked the string that was tied around her neck beneath the collar of her striped T-shirt.

"Text your mom so she knows where you are and let's go."

ASHLEY

*D*rinking while depressed only made you more depressed. That was the great epiphany I was experiencing. I was being careful not to fall past the tipping point, where I would start to confess stupid things to Izzy and Whit, but I had consumed enough that I felt both drunk and hungover which only compounded my misery.

Izzy and Whitney insisted the best way to combat my blues was dancing at the bar.

I tried talking them into getting something to eat at one of the restaurants, but they had picked their way through the baskets of snacks all afternoon. None of us was genuinely hungry. Even so, I didn't relish being around a bunch of corporate toads getting hammered as they waited for the ska-reggae-punk band to start. The DJ was warming them up with eighties classics and the whole bar was singing with Journey's, "Don't stop...be-leee-ving..."

Whitney called Fliss and yelled over the music, "Tell Grandma the DJ is playing her housecleaning soundtrack. Tell her to come dance to it for a change."

Izzy laughed gustily, but I only managed a weak smile.

Whitney begged Fliss to babysit Ryan so the grownups could come to the bar. Mom wasn't interested and promised to stay with Fliss and Ryan. Eddie and Sandy appreciated her invitation when she called their room, but declined.

Oliver turned up ten minutes later. He had a bruise on his cheek where Ryan had accidentally clipped him with a paddle while they had kayaked. He went straight to the dancefloor with Whitney.

"Come *on*," Izzy insisted, clapping her hands over her head as she tried to drag me after them, singing, "Girls just wanna have fu-un..."

"I'll watch the drinks," I insisted. "Go." I hated that I was being such a wet blanket. This was their vacation and they wanted to enjoy it. It wasn't their fault I'd been rejected twice in one week.

My stomach felt like it was rotting. My head was pounding and my heart was aching. My self-esteem wasn't even on the floor. It had been swept from the unfinished basement into the garbage bin and taken by the diesel truck to be shoveled into an incinerator.

But I wouldn't cry. I refused to cry.

This too shall pass, I assured myself, and tried to think of where I would go if not Sydney or Pine Grove.

The high-top table joggled slightly. A middle-aged man with the glow of double-shot screwdrivers leaned on it. *Oh, God.*

"Can I join you for a drink?" The music had switched to Livin' on a Prayer.

"I've had two men treat me like shit back to back. You're risking your life by even speaking to me."

He drew back. "How about I buy you a drink and leave you alone?"

"My hero. Make it a soda with lime."

He nodded and walked to the bar, leaving me thinking maybe I should have given him a chance.

Someone else sat down. I went from affronted to excited as I recognized Fox, then back to affronted as he eyed the array of drinks on the table.

"They're not all mine." I sipped the blue-vomit special that I'd barely touched. It was so sweet it was making me gag.

"Soda with lime," he said as a server came by with the water the other guy had ordered for me.

"How did you know where we were?" I asked.

"I called the villa. I moved my things to my own room." He slid a keycard toward me. When I widened my eyes, he said, "That's the spare for yours."

My wobbling heart tumbled to its hands and knees, getting skinned afresh.

"Thanks." I plucked it from him and stuffed it into the pocket on my miniskirt. "Why didn't you save a few bucks and share Izzy's room?"

"Don't do that."

I reached to sip my water. "You don't get to tell me what to do."

"Yeah, I do. I'm your friend and I care about you. I get to tell you when you're hurting both of us."

"Right. *Friends.*" The word scraped a layer off the back of my throat. My eyes lost focus. Or filled with tears. Why did this have to be so horrible?

Human League cried, *Don't You Want Me, Baby...*

"Oh, my gawd." I choked on a laugh of sheer torture.

His water arrived.

"Thanks." Fox offered his credit card, drawing a circle over the table to indicate he would pick up the tab for whatever was currently owed.

"You always say you're so cheap, but then you do things like that," I said as the server walked away. "Why?"

"It's a round of drinks," he dismissed.

"But you're paying for my suite, too. Did you get your own?"

"They only had a standard queen."

"But would you have if they did?"

"Are you trying to pick a fight? No, I wouldn't, but this isn't complicated, Ash. I don't spend money on myself because I'd rather save it for things I really want. I'm frugal, not cheap. I shout drinks when I'm out with a group and buy dinner when I'm on a date. When I need something, I get the least expensive one that will do the trick. When I *want* something, I wait until I can afford the very best so it will last forever."

I held his intense stare as I sifted through a statement that was actually very complicated. Was he saying that I wasn't something he wanted or needed? That he would wait? That he couldn't afford me? Maybe, like Shane, he didn't think we would last forever so why start?

The music switched over to a rhythmic strum of a guitar. Rick Springfield's chesty voice began to croon, "Jessie is a friend…"

"Oh, *come on*," I cried to the gods.

I looked for my purse, forgetting that I hadn't brought one. Just my room card and a credit card.

Fox touched my wrist. "Did you say anything to anyone?"

"No!" I scowled. "What is there to say?" I made herself drain the soda water, stomach sloshing with rejection, but I needed to hydrate or I'd feel even worse tomorrow.

Fox's hand stayed on my arm, thumb playing against my skin. It was nothing. A tiny feather of a caress, but it felt so good. So achingly good that I stood there paralyzed the way cats go limp at a grip on their ruff, submissive and starting to purr.

And Rick Springfield wished that he had *Jessie's Girl*...

Fox's touch abruptly dropped away and suddenly we were surrounded.

Whitney and Izzy reached for their drinks. Oliver asked Fox if he wanted a beer then disappeared to the bar to get one for himself.

"Where are you going?" Whitney scolded as I stood.

"Bed."

Duran Duran began singing Hungry Like the Wolf. Izzy grabbed Fox's hand. "Come on." She was already tick-tocking her hips.

I didn't stick around to see if he went to grind it out with her. I ignored Whitney's, "No, stay," and went to my empty room where I downed two extra-strength ibuprofens and shoved myself under the sheet, begging sleep to come before any tears arrived.

ASHLEY

A papery noise woke me. I wasn't sure if I'd heard it or if it was a remnant of a dream, but I was awake now, blinking at the clock.

Six a.m. on the wedding day that wasn't.

My head was dull and so was my stomach, but my hangover was mostly emotional. I made a cup of coffee and took it to the lanai.

The surf wasn't doing much and there were only a couple of stragglers out there. I saw a man who looked like Fox coming in. He stood up in the wash and tucked his board under his arm, pausing to glance up.

It was Fox. Looking for me.

I lifted a hand, chest tight.

He lifted his.

Why couldn't I hate him? It would be so much easier if I could hate his guts.

He started walking toward the resort and I watched until he disappeared. When I finished my coffee, I walked in to make another. Something on the floor by the door caught my eye. An envelope. The sound of it being pushed under the door must have been the noise that woke me.

I set aside the empty cup and picked up the envelope addressed to 'the soon-to-be Mr. and Mrs. Holloway.'

"Oh no," I groaned, sitting down to open it, already knowing what it was.

Yep. Two sealed envelopes fell out. One was a pastel green with my handwritten, 'Shane' on its front, care of Waiola and this resort. The other was a business envelope with the T&B logo on it. My name was written in block letters above the address.

Open it? Burn it?

With shaking fingers, I opened the one I'd written.

Dear Shane,

I'm packing up the last of my things to ship tomor-row. I still can't believe I'm doing this, but I'm really excited to start my new life with you.

I didn't imagine that first night that we would come this far. I only wanted to have a small adventure when I left for Australia. Meeting you was the luckiest thing that has ever happened to me. I'm never lucky!

Thank you for being you. You're always a gentleman and you make me laugh all the time, which is what I love most about you. That and your friends. Someone famous said "A man is known by the company he keeps." (I looked it up, lots of people claim to have said it, but it remains true.) You surround yourself with the best people which tells me how lucky I am to be marrying you. I feel like I've finally found the place I'm supposed to be. See you at the altar...

I pressed the page to my chest, wincing at how revealing this was. Ugh.

Was that really all I'd seen in him? His friends? Because if I was honest, there was only one friend who had consistently included me and made me feel welcome. One friend I had wished to see every single day. One who made me laugh and feel smart and important and, lately, confused and sexy and filled with yearning and despair.

I dropped the letter to the cushion beside me and rose to make a fresh cup of coffee, then hunted out what remained of the box of truffles, needing fortification before I read Shane's letter to me.

I was kind of shocked he'd gone through with it. When Waiola had suggested it, I had thought it sounded like a lovely keepsake from our special day, but Shane wasn't romantic. I had had to bug Fox to talk him into it and send it on time. I would bet anything that Fox's DNA was on the back of the stamp.

Which said a lot about why I was reading these alone on my non-wedding day.

I let another truffle melt in my mouth as I sat and carefully tore the seal. The letter was on a standard A4 page, but folded weird to fit into the envelope. A yellow sticky note on the outside held Fox's handwriting.

I didn't read what he wrote, but I hope he knows how lucky he is. I love you both and hope you crazy kids knock this out of the park. Can't wait to see you again. Love, Fox

I unfolded Shane's letter. It was typewritten.

Ash,

I'm not sure what to say. Fox said to tell you how awesome you are and that I can't wait to see you again. You are. I'm sure Hawaii will be great. If I'm beside you when you read this, you can tell me how wrong I was about not wanting to do our wedding there, haha.

I don't know how to write mushy

stuff, but we make a good team. I know
that you make me better and my folks
adore you. I'm sure the wedding will be
great and we'll be really happy.
See you soon,
Shane

I swallowed the lump of chocolate, but it went down like a rock. I reminded myself to breathe as I absorbed the contrast in the two notes. Fox had used the word 'love' twice while Shane hadn't used it at all.

Which was true to character for both of them. Shane wasn't good a mushy stuff unless he was loaded. Then he wanted to hug everyone and tell you what a great mate you were and how much he appreciated you.

Fox wasn't mushy, either, but he wasn't afraid to say something like 'I love you both' if he meant it.

My biggest takeaway was that Fox had been rooting for us to succeed, but he'd also seen that we wouldn't. Maybe he had protected himself with the prenup stuff and talking Shane out of coming, but he had actually protected all three of us from a painful, messy, inevitable breakup.

Because Shane didn't love me. I didn't love him. Not the way people should love each other if they were marrying and planning to spend their lives together. Not the way I ought to if I was leaving my family and home for him.

The hotel phone was on the table beside me. I jabbed for the operator and asked for Felix Wiley's room.

"G'day," he said after the second ring.

"Can I come talk to you?" I realized my voice was quavering and that I didn't even know what I wanted to talk to him about, only that I needed to see him.

"Sure. I was going to text, ask if you want to meet for breakfast. Are you okay? Shit. What's happened now?"

"Nothing. I don't know. Can I come to your room?" I was already kicking into my flip-flops.

"Sure. Two-forty-two." His voice rang with confusion.

I dropped the phone on the sofa and stayed in the robe, barely remembering to shove my keycard into the pocket before I hurried down the hall to the elevator.

FOX

I dropped the cordless phone back onto its charger. I had just hung my wet togs and pulled on a dry pair of boardies. I'd been trying to work out how to smooth things over with Ash, thinking if she was up and willing to wave at me, she might be willing to join me for breakfast.

Yesterday had been every type of hell, seeing her happy when we were flying, touching her... In so many ways we were ideal for one another. Separate but the same.

But so wrong in other ways. Our fight in the car had grated on me for hours.

I had used Fliss a little, taking her surfing. She was fun and keeping an eye on her as she fell again and again had distracted me, but she also fed that part of me that would take any scrap of Ashley. Her laugh was so like her aunt's, it was like a voicemail I obsessively listened to, trying to store it for future. And Fliss had revealed odd tidbits and minutia of their lives in Pine Grove. Learning there was a shop near Joanna's place where she and Ash loaded up on penny candy before going to the movies made no real difference to my life, but I ate it up all the same.

I'd felt Ash's absence all the more for only hearing about her, not seeing her. It had physically hurt me to pack my things into Shane's duffel and drag my ass down to my own room. It was small by comparison. Claustrophobic. But what did it matter how I felt? I kept hurting her and I deserved to suffer for it.

I'd been worried about her, too, even though I knew she was with her sister and Izzy. She was still upset if they were drinking all afternoon. I had needed to check up on her so I'd called over to the villa.

The last thing I'd wanted to do was go to a noisy bar and try to talk to her. I'd wanted to dance with Izzy even less.

Ashley had looked as miserable as I'd ever seen her when I saw some a-hole with a burned neck above the collar of his corporate polo shirt hitting on her.

A green haze had crossed my vision at that moment that wasn't healthy. I didn't have any right to that type of reaction, but it was there all the same.

Fortunately, she got rid of the guy before I'd acted like an ass to a hapless stranger.

I kept thinking about how she kept saying she couldn't come to Sydney, that she didn't want to go back and didn't know how to move forward. She'd been at similar loose ends when Izzy had left her in Australia. She'd been wringing her hands, staring at the ocean and looking very anxious when I caught up to her that morning. She wasn't ready to fly home, but didn't know how to strike out on her own.

"Any recommendations on where I should go?" she'd asked meekly, eyebrows pulled into a frown of uncertainty.

I'd known her less than a week, but I'd already picked her

brains about how to improve our website. Offering her a 'consulting' job to make those changes had been spur of the moment, but had made sense. And she'd been great at it.

For as long as I could remember, I'd been knuckling down, staying focused on building stability for myself. Building my savings and building the company.

The fact was, there was a part of me that was insanely jealous that she had nothing but options before her. The urge to drop everything and bum around the world with her while she figured things out was obscenely tempting.

I couldn't, though. I had responsibilities. A business to run. A life I'd worked my guts out to create.

The sudden rap on my door made me jump.

"That was fast," I said as I let her in.

She waved a piece of paper in front of me.

"You were right. He never loved me. I didn't love him. This entire thing was a stupid idea and I never should have let it get this far. You did me a solid and I can't be mad, but I am anyway. I don't know what to *do*." She was on the verge of tears and it tore me up.

"What is that?" I held out my hand.

She stood there with the paper dangling in a limp pinch at her side, mouth down at the corners, so desolate I held out my hands to her.

"Ash. Babe..." I don't know where the endearment came from, but she was sad and I couldn't stand it. "Show me. What's going on?"

"It's Shane's love letter. And *yours*."

"My— What?" My heart nearly lurched out of my throat. My whole face instantly hurt with a hard blush.

I caught the flash of a yellow sticky note and recalled adding it to Shane's Letter from the Groom. I tried to

233

remember what I'd said, but all I could really remember was that the first barbs of real doubt had sunk into me when Shane didn't even want to write a freaking letter to the woman he was planning to marry. And I remember being worried he would hurt Ashley if he refused something so small. What did it mean for their future if he couldn't do that one little thing?

"What did I say?" I asked.

"That you love us both." She shook the page again.

Fuck. I was suddenly freefalling from yesterday's helicopter straight into the crater of a volcano. I couldn't breathe.

"I do." I had to clear my throat. "As a friend. I didn't break you up for *me*." Had I? I squeezed the back of my neck. "Is that what you think?"

"No. I don't know." She was searching my eyes.

I opened my mouth, but my voice was lost at sea. Wave after wave was swallowing and chundering me, throwing me around so all I could do was flail and gasp for breath.

"I wanted this for both of you." That wasn't a lie. "If Shane was the one for you, if you were both in love..." My throat was so dry, my voice turned to a rasp. "Then I wanted this day to be everything you wanted it to be."

"Then you don't love me. Like that." Her shoulder hitched and her mouth trembled.

I tried to shake my head because I *couldn't* love her as anything more than a friend. I couldn't.

"I can't," I said. But I was starting to think I did.

ASHELY

I can't. Not, *I don't.*

I felt dizzy and sucked in a breath because I'd forgotten to do that in the last few seconds.

I waited for him to say something that would further clarify how he felt, but all I saw was anguished conflict behind his eyes. He yanked his gaze from mine, but his expression was tortured. It held all the hunger and surrender and defensive wariness that was making my stomach clench.

The silence was spooling out, leaving nothing but the rush of my blood pounding in my ears.

Because we stood on a precipice. One where saying the wrong words, saying *those* words, would change everything.

In that second, I achieved a type of clarity. Fox was my friend. He'd become my very best friend. He was my confidante. Maybe even a soul mate.

He was everything I wanted in a partner and I wanted to tell him that. I wanted to say the words I was longing to hear. They crowded in my throat with my heart, battling for space, but I swallowed all of it into a dull ache in the middle of my chest. It sat there like a dry wish bone, sharply pronged and piercing, strained apart and on the point of splintering.

Because I couldn't ask him to destroy his own life by loving me. Love didn't break things. Love protected and caught you when you were weak, the way Fox kept doing for me. Love sacrificed for the ones who held your heart.

Which meant that once again, I would have to lower my expectations, but this time it didn't feel like settling. It hurt. It hurt so deeply I could hardly breathe, but I held that hurt inside me so I wouldn't hurt him and something about doing *that* felt inordinately good.

"Thank you," I said, looking to the flash of yellow. Reading again, 'Love, Fox.' "This would have been perfect, if Shane had been the man I loved."

It was the closest I would come to telling him who I really did love. Because it was him. I was realizing that in real time, never expecting it to fill me with such an intense ache of longing and joy.

"Ash." He closed his eyes and a spasm of pain flexed across his face.

"It's okay." I moved to hug him, one hand still clutching the note. I didn't let the embrace turn into anything more than a hug, though. We were friends. That's *all*.

I closed my eyes and accepted that. I let the side of my face rest on his bare chest and listened to his heart and told myself to be grateful for this much.

His arms closed around me, equally careful. Equally caring. I felt his chin rest on my hair. He released a shaky sigh that made my hair shift in a tickle against my scalp. It was the most beautifully imperfect moment of my life.

Words of longing and love crowded my tongue again. I wanted to turn my lips against the muscles of his chest. I wanted to rub my face against him, lift my chin and invite his kiss. Against my best intentions, my heartrate changed.

Tension invaded his muscles.

I started to pull away.

His arms, so gentle one second ago, hardened with resistance, holding me in place.

"Don't go," he said with an edge of desperation in his voice.

"Fox..." Now the paper fell to the floor so I could splay both hands on the warmth of back. He was so tense, I instinctively moved my hands, trying to soothe.

His chest expanded with a deep, shaken breath.

We held a long stare. Said nothing because anything we said right now could not be unsaid later.

Without really making a conscious decision about it, I leaned into him a tiny, tiny bit. An invitation.

He started to lower his head. Hesitated. Then he exhaled against my mouth right before he smothered my lips with his own.

Everything we weren't saying came spilling out in our actions. Deep yearning sealed us in a long, wet, hungry kiss. Frustration made it bruising and trust made the strength in his arms safe instead of scary. I clung to him. I told him with the dig of my fingertips into his flesh that I wanted everything he was. I wanted everything he was willing to give me.

Yesterday's lust returned in a flood. An unending wave that swelled and submerged, turning our kiss messy and blatant. His tongue swept into my mouth with a faint flavor of mint. I sucked on his bottom lip until he groaned and dragged me harder into the shape of his wood, then I scraped him with my teeth as I released him. He slanted his head and ravaged my mouth without mercy. There was no other word for it. He kissed the hell out of me until my knees weakened and I hung off his neck.

He caught me. Of course he did. His strong arm held me firm, never letting me fall. When I lifted my head, we were both panting. I gripped his shoulders, trying to find my balance. I watched his nostrils flare and his tongue slip across his bottom lip.

If he pushed me away again, I would cry. I really would.

He looked down. Allowed a small space between us that brought a sting to my eyes. I tried to gather myself to bear this rejection. Again.

He dragged at the belt on my robe, loosening it, then pushing it open.

A tiny shudder went through me. Relief. Joy.

I'd slept in a thong because I'd been too lazy to do anything but strip and fall into bed last night.

His breath left him in a jagged laugh. His hot hand went to my stomach, burning my skin as he drew a flat circle.

"I'm not stopping, Ash." His voice was something I'd never heard, gritty enough to make my scalp prickle. "Not unless you tell me to."

He dipped his head and tongued my nipple. One arm locked across my back and the other hand slid to my ass.

I felt every single callus on his palm as he massaged my cheeks. Every whirl in the pattern of his fingerprints as he caressed the backs of my thighs while opening his mouth over my nipple in wet suction.

So many sensations accosted me, I squirmed, but his arms tightened, holding me in place. The onslaught sent pulses of pleasure directly into my pussy, making me ache while juices

gathered and dampened my thong. I moved my hands help-
lessly over his shoulders and the back of his neck, alarmed at
how intense this was, but all I could really think was, *Don't
stop. More. I need more.*

I was so *hot.* I shook the robe off my shoulders and tried to
drag my arms out of the sleeves.

Fox straightened, throwing me a look between triumph
and defeat as he helped me free myself, then he backed me
toward the bed.

We kissed again. He kissed me as he followed me down.
Kissed me and kissed me as we settled on the mattress and I
opened my legs so his weight was between my thighs. I curled
my legs around him and roamed my hands over his satiny
back.

Time slowed. There was nothing but long, lazy kisses that
strayed over cheeks and jaw and neck. His breath whorled
against my ear. I inhaled the scent of ocean in the crook of his
neck and sucked on his earlobe, smiling when he went taut.

He didn't stop his lovely slow caresses. His hand on my
thigh lazily climbed to my waist and ribcage and up to cup my
breast, driving me mad with anticipation before he finally got
there. Then I gasped as he played his thumb in light circles
around my nipple.

My hands shaped his shoulders and the hollow of his
spine, then found the waistband of his shorts and slipped
inside to enjoy the way his glutes flexed under my feathery
touch. *Mine,* I thought. *All mine.*

Now there was only this—the thing we really wanted to
communicate. The words that had to remain unspoken, but
were there on his lips as his mouth returned to mine. He
kissed me tenderly. Lovingly.

He took my hand in his and set kisses in my palm and

against the underside of my wrist and nuzzled the sensitive skin inside my elbow.

It was profound and mildly awful because it was too deliberate. I wanted to be swept away so we could pretend later that this wasn't a conscious decision, but it was. I wanted this. With him. Only him.

I wanted to tell him I had never felt like this with any other man—so natural and delicious and *glad*. But I didn't want comparisons. I didn't want anything inside this moment but us.

I rolled against him in a press of joy and a cling of need, throwing myself more deeply into this experience to dampen intrusive thoughts.

He fell onto his back and pulled me over him. The playful move left me straddling his hips, startled, but then laughing in exhilaration.

"Damn." He lazily played his fingers against my waist and hips and up, watching his hands as he slid them across my skin and cupped my breasts, plumping them before he swept his touch around to my shoulder blades. He urged me to come down, so my chest was above his chin. He turned his head to capture one nipple, drawing hard enough to make me squeak at the intensity of the sensation that pierced between my thighs.

"Hurt?" His hot breath wafted against the damp, beaded nipple. His tongue circled, fueling that rush of heat into my thong.

"No," I sobbed. "It's good. I like it."

He took the other one, made me groan and clench my pussy muscles on another burst of wetness. I lifted my hips off him, self-conscious.

"What's wrong?"

"Nothing." I straightened my arms, blushing. "I'm really turned on."

"I know. I like it." He looked down my front. His hands climbed my thighs so his thumbs were in the sensitive crease at the tops of my legs. His lashes hooded his eyes as he grazed the pad of his thumb against the gusset of my thong.

He made a noise that was low and pleased and used a tiny bit more pressure, just enough to have me biting my lip and dancing my hips to follow the movement.

He slid his thumb beneath, skimmed fine hairs in a frustratingly light, yet more deliberate, caress.

"Fox," I breathed.

"Like?" He slid the fabric aside and watched as he delicately parted my slippery folds.

"Yes." When he grazed my clit, my eyelids fluttered closed. A fresh pulse of heat released. I bit my lip, so swollen and sensitive, he barely had to touch my clit and I was quivering in anticipation.

I was more aroused than I'd ever been in my life. Aching so intensely that, before I realized what I was doing, I had set my hand over his and was showing him, pressing his touch deeper into my cleft, rocking in time to his circling. Biting my lip. So close—

I abruptly moved his hand away. "I'm sorry."

"Don't even," he growled, bringing his thumb to his mouth to taste. "I want more of that."

In an agile twist, I was on my back on the mattress, arms splaying out to catch myself before I'd realized that I had already landed safely. He pulled my thong down my legs, sliding away as he did.

When he brushed my legs open and settled between, so casual and confident, I forgot how to breathe. A wet kiss touched my inner thigh, making me twitch. He steadied me with a warm hand at the top of my thigh, stroking to coax me to open my legs wider. His hot breath clouded on my mound.

He groaned and licked on either side of my outer lips before flicking once with his tongue.

I jolted at the lash of pleasure, tensing as I braced for it to happen again.

He made a noise of amused pity. "I'll be gentle," he promised.

"Oh, please don't be," I groaned, letting my legs fall fully open.

Another chuckle wafted across my flesh, bringing every cell alive to the nearness of his mouth. He parted me with his fingers and settled in to grow very acquainted with the most intimate part of me.

This was Fox, I was thinking through my haze of lust, but nothing about this felt strange or wrong. Not when he was doing such glorious things. He pressed a finger into me. *Two.*

I moaned.

He paused. "Okay?" His touch retreated.

"So good," I managed to stutter.

His fingers slid back, arriving deep, stretching me in the most delicious way.

He was driving me insane. I lifted my hips into his mouth, moaning unreservedly and suddenly peaking. Quaking. Coming hard while he kept fucking me with his mouth and hand.

He didn't let up until I was weak and trembling, thighs splayed, body twitching all over. Even then, he played a little more, until fresh swirls of desire began singing in my blood.

He rose over me and took tastes of my nipples on the way

back to my mouth, causing fresh havoc in nerve endings that should have been spent.

"I liked that," he said against my mouth.

"Me, too," I breathed. "A lot."

We shared a smile. A kiss.

"Condoms are in the bathroom." His gaze checked in. Are we really doing this?

"Hurry back." I caressed his ear, his shoulder, the line of his collarbone and down the center of his chest as he pulled away.

I liked the way his cock pressed so insistently against the front of his shorts, and the way he dragged them down and kicked out of them on the way the bathroom, letting me watch the flex of his firmly muscled ass.

When he came back, his erection was in his fist.

I'd seen him in shorts and togs and underwear more than fully clothed, but the full effect of him naked and aroused was somewhere between soft-porn firefighter calendar and old-world artistry.

Fox was physically perfect. His wide shoulders and muscled chest narrowed to stacked abs and flat hips. Tidy patches of hair arrowed down to that dark erection jutting so fiercely from between his thick, tense thighs.

My heart took a little skip of erotic excitement. I watched him open the condom and roll it on, thinking again that this wasn't something we could pretend 'just happened.' We were two adults making a choice. Maybe a bad one.

It didn't feel bad as he came back down on the bed, knees sliding between mine and pushing my legs apart.

I slid my hands between us so I could fondle the shape of him, squeezing to test how thick and hard he was, then caressing balls drawn tight with arousal. He closed his eyes as

I stroked him, head sinking to hang heavily against my shoulder.

We kissed again, lengthy dirty kisses with a lot of tongue and moaning. I bent my knee and lifted my hips, silently urging him to give me what I wanted.

"Okay?" he murmured, sliding his touch to feel how wet I was.

So much more than okay. I nodded and guided his tip to ride against my clit for a few rocks of my hips, enjoying the friction before letting him catch at my entrance.

He made a growling noise and his body shook as he pressed that wide dome into me, filling me with a smooth, thick invasion of his flesh.

I drew my weak knees to his sides. He settled his weight fully against me, all of him snug and deep, filling me up. He was iron hard inside me and I gripped him with my inner muscles, eyes closed, reveling in the feel of him lodged within me.

I cupped the back of his neck and drew him close enough to nibble at the edge of his jaw, his lips.

He withdrew and returned. The move was slow and deliberate and delivered such a delicious rake of pleasure, I gasped and arched.

A wicked noise of amusement filled my ears. His satisfaction turned to torment as he did it again. This was too good. It was more pleasure than either of us deserved. And more than I could endure for long. It would be over far too soon and this was all I would ever have.

Maybe he realized that, too, because he held the pace to those careful, heavy strokes, drawing this out, holding us on a plain of abject joy while we groaned in ecstatic torture.

It was no use. The inevitable crept over us, locking us with tension, demanding more. I dug my nails into him and he deepened his strokes. I lifted my hips to meet his thrusts and he quickened them, losing what remained of his control.

Climax hit like a sledgehammer, engulfing me in waves of joy, tearing cries of elation from my throat while he drove deep and shuddered in equal surrender.

FOX

*S*he hadn't said she loved me.

I hadn't said it either, but that didn't mean I wasn't feeling it. What a blind idiot I was! Ash was sweet and fun and I *had* wanted her wedding day to be perfect. I had wanted Shane to see what a treasure he'd found in her and for them to both have a good life together.

I hadn't torpedoed their wedding for this. To end up with her lying against me like this, after I'd left to discard the condom and came back to gather her close, so her legs entwined with mine.

I didn't know what to say, but her breaths fell into a measured cadence, telling me she was drifting to sleep. I didn't have to say anything. I could brood to my heart's content.

*Dis*content.

Fuck. Until the last couple of days, this was something I had deliberately and determinedly not imagined happening between us ever. Ashley had been my roommate and work-mate and someone I liked seeing every day, but that was it.

Any sexual attraction I'd experienced had been firmly ignored because that's what you did when women were employees or in relationships or showed zero interest in your dick.

If she'd been attracted to me during her time in Oz, she hadn't revealed it. Even after the kiss on the dinner cruise, I had thought we could go back to being friends.

It wasn't until things had gone off the rails on the heli-tour that I'd started to think we had both been harboring more sexual attraction than we'd wanted to admit. Our fight in the car had made it impossible to pretend it didn't exist, but this?

So you don't love me. Like that.

I didn't know how I felt beyond wishing this wasn't so fucking impossible. How did she feel, I wondered? Because in the car she'd said something about showing up for a wedding and not even getting laid.

I couldn't believe she would be so cold-blooded as to fuck the best man as revenge against her absent groom. Not when her hug had felt so damned final. Like she was saying goodbye to me. Or to this.

She had tried to leave before we crossed this line, but I hadn't been able to let her go. *I* was the one who had kept her here. And kissed her. And let it turn into this.

Sure, she had kissed me back and locked her legs around me as though she would never let me go.

But she hadn't said she loved me and I didn't know if she was sparing me from having to make hard decisions or if she was taking her sister's advice and cleansing her palate with some rebound sex.

Ah hell. I hated myself for even thinking that. For doubting her. But this...whatever it was...had come on so fast. And it was too intense. It was like dropping into the most perfectly formed wave, the kind that almost never happened, but when you found that kind of nirvana... Well, it became all you could think about. A fixation. You chased it until you found it again.

Which scared the hell out of me because I *couldn't*. *We* couldn't.

Not right now. Not without deep costs.

Give me time, I silently begged her. I played my fingers in the tails of her hair. I needed time to figure out what to do. Maybe in a year—

The ring of the room phone jarred me out of my ruminations and startled her awake. She sucked in a breath.

"You're okay," I murmured, cuddling her closer.

She made a noise that might have been dismay or remorse at realizing where she was, but she only withdrew her arm from where it was draped over my waist and curled it between us where the other was tucked like the wing of a bird.

The phone rang again. I stayed where I was, holding her nude warmth against my own.

"Aren't you going to get it?" she asked.

"No."

"Who is it?"

"I don't know."

It rang again, annoying. My phone had been buzzing as well, but it was over on the chair where I'd left it last night, face down on the cushion and muffled, so it was easier to ignore. I'd quit looking at it when people had begun texting to ask why Shane wasn't responding to the statement I'd posted, asking if Shane was okay and whether there was anything they could do.

"Whitney wouldn't know to look for me here, but she might be trying to find me." Ash rolled onto her back. "We

248

have a pedicure this morning." Her enthusiasm level was that of the average colonoscopy patient. "Izzy made us wait to get them until today so she could come. Mom cancelled hers, but Whit insisted the rest of us keep our appointment. What time is it?"

She lifted onto her elbow to see the clock. Sighed. Her gaze came back to mine, troubled and searching.

"I have to shower and..." Her mouth pouted ruefully. She let her hand rest on my stomach. "Are you mad?"

Those eyes. Defensive and vulnerable and capable of toppling countries if she only understood the power she wielded with that liquid gaze of hers.

"No." I was still telling myself this was another erotic dream that could be tucked away as a private aberration. I swept the fall of her hair behind her ear. "You?"

She caught my hand and spoke into my palm. "No."

But shadows entered her eyes right before she hid them with her lowered lashes. She rolled away and sat up on the far side of the mattress and stayed there. Her narrow back slowly lengthened as she straightened her shoulders, gathering herself.

I stacked my hands behind my head so I wouldn't reach for her. I watched as she rose and sought out her underwear, then stepped into it. She absently traced her thumbs around her hips to smooth out the twists. It was a tiny thing to notice and enjoy, but I did.

She shrugged on the robe and bent on the way to the door to pick up the letter from Shane. She folded it carefully, tucking it into the pocket of her robe, looking again at the yellow sticky note I'd left on the front of it. She glanced back as she opened the door, more beautiful than anything I ever seen, flushed with sex and slumber, mouth pink and eyes wide with— Christ almighty. If that wasn't love shining in those big brown eyes then the emotion didn't exist.

My chest filled with thorns and roses. Yearning and gratification.

She walked out, leaving a hook in my chest that pulled me to sit up. I almost called her back, but the door clipped shut and I dropped my head into my hands in defeat.

Because I had nothing to say. I had no plan, no offers or promises I could make. Every part of my life that I wanted to share with her would be dismantled by the very act of asking her to share it.

What else could I do, though? Pretend this hadn't happened? This hadn't been a quick fuck or rebound sex. It had been intimate and meaningful. What we'd just done would have been life altering even without all the repercussions threatening in the background.

My phone on the chair pinged with yet another incoming text.

I swore and walked over planning to shut it off. Maybe crush it under my heel or drop it over the balcony. Anything to make it shut the hell up.

I glanced at the screen, though.

"Oh, fuck."

ASHLEY

"*H*old the elevator!"

I shot my hand into the crack and almost got it pinched for my effort, but I hit the stopper and the doors clunked open again.

Someone at the back of the crowded car sighed impatiently.

The elevators were busy, full of conference-goers and families needing breakfast and sporty types who liked a morning run. I'd had to wait a few minutes for one to even arrive and someone from the dinner cruise had come along to chat while I did. I'd had to find polite words when my brain was still in bed with Fox.

We'd had sex. Really good sex. The kind of sex that made it impossible to imagine sleeping with anyone else ever again. I couldn't sleep with *him* again, though. Even I, with my aspirations that were doomed to crash, had enough grasp of reality to know when something really was too grandiose to wish for.

So I'd walked away and here Fox was, racing after me,

making my heart soar to unimaginable heights. He'd pulled on boardies but nothing else, not even flipflops.

That wasn't the face of a man chasing down a woman in an airport or holding a boombox above his head to woo her, though. That was grim disaster shouldering in to stand before me while the doors closed behind him.

"What?" I asked with growing dread.

"Shane's here."

"What?" My reaction was dramatic enough that all the heads in the elevator turned to stare at me. "Here?" I pointed at the floor. "In the hotel?" Was I screeching? I think I was screeching.

"On his way. He landed an hour ago and was renting a car."

"What does he want?"

The elevator stopped and Fox shifted into my space to allow a handful of people to get off around him, then he stepped back, giving me room again. "He wanted me to fetch him. I was surfing and missed his text."

Then I had called Fox on the hotel phone. He let me into his room and we'd—

I covered my mouth.

The elevator stopped again. More people got off while we stood there in dumb silence.

When we arrived on my floor we stepped out, but didn't move.

"He's definitely on his way here."

"Yes," Fox confirmed tersely.

"He didn't come all this way to see you or his parents. You'll all be home in a few days. He wants to see me." *Why?* I didn't want to see him. Not now.

Not after this morning.

Oh God. I looked at Fox and guilt, so much guilt, pulsed

between us. It was like the force that pushed magnets away from one another. He looked to the end of the hall and the hardness in his profile hit me like a slap.

A familiar, grotesque, frightened feeling was awakening inside me, the one that said I was to blame for this. I was the screw up. Everything was wrong and it was all my fault.

"We should talk," Fox said grudgingly through his teeth.

"About what? Tell him whatever you want. I don't want to see him." With growing agitation, I paced down the hall to the suite. My hand shook as I touched the room card to the door lock.

I pushed into the room and Shane turned from the open bag on the foot of the bed. He was dripping wet and completely naked.

"There you are."

ASHLEY

"*M*ate." Fox put up a hand like he was shielding his vision from the flash of an arc weld.

I ducked my head, even though Shane's clean shave was something I'd seen before. He was easy to admire in his birthday suit, tanned and ripped and beautifully proportioned, but not now. Not ever again.

"Quit being coy. You both know I drip dry." He found some boardies and stepped into them. "All right. White wobbly bits tucked away. Pair o' wussies."

"What are you doing here?" I was still in shock that he'd come to Hawaii. When I'd said I didn't intend to talk to him, I meant it.

"Surprise." He pitched the word weakly while he pushed his arms wide in a slow-motion, big finish pose. "I texted that I was coming," he said to Fox.

"I just saw it a minute ago." Fox held up the phone he clutched in one hand. He indicated this room with other. "How did you get in here?"

"I told the desk I had a reservation and they gave me a key.

I wanted to see you," he said to me, mouth pulling into an uncomfortable smile. "I texted you that I was coming up. When you weren't here, I reckoned I'd shower then find you. Were you two at the pool?"

"No, um—" My gaze fell with self-reproach and snagged on the letter I'd written to him. It sat open on the sofa cushion where I'd left it. I shot forward to fold it and shove it into the pocket of my robe with the other one.

"What was that?" Shane asked with a sharp frown.

"Nothing." I eyed him, wondering if he had read it before he'd showered.

My stomach was churning like a washing machine full of loose change and gum. *I don't want to do this.* It struck me that Fox had done me a huge favor, ending my engagement by proxy. In a perfect world, I wouldn't have had to face Shane ever again, or at least not until I'd had some time to get over all of this.

Of course, this wasn't a perfect world. It was a world that was determined to play my pain for laughs because here Shane was, three days late and a pair of shorts short.

Shane shot a hairy eyeball look toward Fox, one that made my heart clutch. I couldn't face his finding out what we'd just done. I hadn't processed it and wasn't ready to defend it. I wasn't sure I could.

"It was my letter to you," I blurted. "For our wedding day."

Throwing that out there was a gamble. I didn't want to start a game of disparagement or finger pointing. A dim part of me hoped it would propel him to leave. One of the things I liked most about Shane was that we had never really fought. The minute we'd started to disagree, when the butterflies of anxiety would start in my middle, he always vanished.

That hadn't been particularly cool. Mostly it had left me

feeling responsible for the discord, same as always. Then Fox would give me some insight into Shane's guilt over being the reason his mother and brother were on the road the day Marcus died. Or how he never dealt with any of his emotions because he'd have to start with the loss of his brother and who in their right mind wanted to rake over that kind of pain if they could avoid it?

Shane didn't leave, though. His shoulders dropped a notch and he held both his palms out to me in a plea.

"Ash, I'm sorry. It was a shitty thing to do, not getting on the plane. I was drunk. Really crook for two days. I didn't even look at my phone. When I sobered up and told the guys what I'd done, they couldn't believe what a bloody idiot I was. Fucking Gunz said it was past time one of us married a girl," Shane said in an aside to Fox.

Fox managed a weak snort, but his shoulders were bunched defensively. His arms were crossed and his face was stiff as carved mahogany.

"Apology accepted," I said tentatively. Please God let that be the only reason he was here.

"Just like that?" Shane's smile flickered.

Fox didn't move, but I felt his gaze transfer from Shane to me and penetrate like a laser.

"Of course. You didn't have to come all this way. You could have called." My heart was beginning to fatigue, it had been sustaining this raised pace for way too long. The butterflies inside me were turning to bees and beginning to swarm, making all of me feel as though I was vibrating. Was it possible to die of adrenaline poisoning? Because I think I was about to.

Shane's head went back. "Giz a minute, Fox." He jerked his

head toward the door, inviting him to leave without looking at him.

Fox didn't move.

After a charged second, Shane snapped him a hard look.

I kept my focus on Shane, but my voice shook. "You were right to call it off."

"You don't want to get married?" Shane's arms crossed. He sounded more confounded than anything, which wasn't a surprise. He was used to getting what he wanted, sometimes by working for it, more often by being good-natured and good looking.

"I already cancelled and got some of the money back. We can't get married. And..." I was hugging myself so hard I could barely breathe. "I don't want to."

"Okay, but..." He jerked a shoulder. "Shouldn't we talk about it?"

"Why?"

"Because..." He gave his wet hair a ruffle, then swiped his palm on the seat of his boardies.

This confrontation wasn't loud or violent or hurtful, but it was doing a number on me. Standing up for myself always left me wondering if I had a right to do such a thing. I tried to ignore the anxiety and waved a trembling hand at Fox.

"One friend told you not to marry me and that was enough for you to call off our wedding. Now another one said you should marry me and here you are. Fox, do you want to weigh in with a fresh 'Don't bother?' I'm pretty sure that's all he needs."

Fox's shoulders were like mountains, his feet planted like a tap root.

"Do you want to marry him?" Fox asked me.

"*No.*" And he ought to know that. I glared at him, unable to believe he'd even have to ask, but I could see his faith in me was paper thin. Barely there at all.

I turned away so I wouldn't reveal how deeply that cut.

"Ash, come on," Shane muttered. "It was cold feet."

I shook my head. "No. It was you listening to your gut. And I've had time to hear mine. We don't love each other, Shane. Not the way we should."

"That's not true." He took a few steps to come alongside me and sent an irritated glance toward Fox. "Come on, mate. Step outside or something. I can't talk properly with you here."

Still Fox didn't move, not that I could see him because I had my back to him and my eyes were growing wet. Drawing a full breath was an effort. I *hated* hard conversations like this. It took me right back to my childhood when one heated argument with my sister had ruined our family. I crushed the sleeves of my robe in my fists.

"Fox kept us from making a huge mistake. I care for you, but we don't have what it takes to make a life together."

"How can you say that? We're great together."

"We weren't *together*, Shane. Not really. We lived alongside each other. Adjacent. Not participating in each other's lives."

"We slept in the same bed. We drove to work and spent the day with each other."

"I worked with *Fox*. Half the time you sent me to visit your parents by myself. You never showed any interest in meeting my family." I had made excuses for that. Things had happened fast and I had thought there would be lots of time for that after we were married.

"I talked to them over the tablet," Shane grumbled. "They live on the other side of the planet, Ash. How was I supposed to get to know them?"

"You know what I mean. You never asked about them. You and I don't share our thoughts and feelings. Not the important ones. Do you know anything about my father? Have you ever told me *anything* about Marcus?"

"No." His voice hardened. "But I don't talk to anyone about him. It's not *you*." He gave his jaw a rub. "I don't understand why anyone thinks there's value in wading through painful shit. There isn't. All right?"

"See? That!" I pointed at him. "That's it exactly. Remember when I told you my dad is an alcoholic? That was your reaction. You didn't want to hear it!"

"Because I thought you were telling me I shouldn't drink."

"Maybe you shouldn't," I cried. "Maybe I think you drink too much and that's why we shouldn't get married."

"I don't drink that much. Not every day," he defended. "I don't do it when I *shouldn't*."

"Except when you're supposed to get on a plane for your *wedding*. Then suddenly you're too drunk to fly!" I was shaking so hard I was afraid I would start to cry.

"Ash, it's okay." Fox came as far as the end of the sofa, one hand out in an offer of reassurance.

It struck me that as many times as I'd ripped into him over the last few days, I hadn't felt *this* upset doing it. I didn't know if that meant I felt safe with him, but it sure told me I didn't feel safe confronting Shane. I was probably only doing it *because* Fox was here as a buffer. A safety net.

I sniffed back my tears, trying to hang onto my composure.

"For Christ's sake, Fox. It's your fault I didn't get on that plane. *Tell her that.*"

"I did. And you said you didn't want to marry her so why are you here?" Fox asked tersely. "Do you want a wife? A woman in the house? Do you want *Ashley*? Because she's got her own baggage. If you don't want to deal with yours, don't sign on to carry someone else's."

Shane gave him an affronted stare. "Screw you very much, then. Your assistance is not required. *Christ.*"

"This doesn't have to be ugly," I blurted, growing agitated that Fox and Shane were swiping at each other. "Waiting until the last second to back out was a dick move, but you were right to do it, Shane. We don't have what it takes. We would have wound up divorced."

"You don't know that!"

"I *do*. Look at us right now." I pointed between us. "This is you and me unable to reconcile after a break up. This was going to happen so it's better we do it before we're locked into marriage and all the rest."

"You're not even trying to reconcile." His arms were at his sides, but his gaze moved between me and Fox, growing suspicious. "Why not?"

"Because we're not right for each other." My stomach cramped and I turned to stare blindly out the windows, refusing to betray Fox by looking at him, but my heart was twisting beyond what I thought it could bear.

"And you've got someone else who is?" Shane asked scathingly.

The smack of his voice, so ripe with fury at being betrayed, hit me like a bus. I spun around, but he was glaring at Fox, saying, "You fucking asshole."

FOX

*S*hane snatched up his bag and headed to the door.

"Mate—" I tried to get in his way and got a rough brush-off.

"Not *your* mate. Not anymore. You're dead to me. Both of yous." Shane flung open the door and walked through it.

I leapt to catch it, snapping a look at Ash. She was so pale even her lips were white.

I had to go after Shane, though. Had to try to salvage something, even though I didn't know what I would say. I caught up to him at the elevator.

"Keep walking or I will knock your teeth down your throat," Shane bit out without looking at me.

A couple coming from the opposite end of the hall faltered. The guy turned his date around and they went the other way.

"Look, I have a room. Let's talk this out." I touched my pocket, realized I'd left my room key in my room downstairs. My phone was on the table in Ashley's suite.

"Nothing to talk about," Shane said.

The doors opened and I stepped inside the car with him.

"You have a death wish? You reek of sex, you prick."

"I know what you're thinking," I said grimly. "This wasn't going on when she was in Oz."

"Fuck you, it wasn't. Why else would you tell me not to marry her?"

"Because you didn't love her." I had never spoken so harshly to anyone. "And nothing happened until this morning when she got the letter from you that was so lukewarm, she couldn't kid herself any longer. So I'll tell you what else didn't happen. You and Ashley."

"Really? Why's that? With you in the house, getting in the way all the time?"

Don't engage. Don't engage.

"Four times," I blurted, showing that many fingers. "Four times I said I'd find my own place and you talked me into staying to finish the house. I'd say you're like the mafia, but you're more like a toddler with a security blanket."

Shane dropped his bag and shoved me into a corner.

I lurched off the wall before the pain of contact had penetrated and shoved Shane to the other side. Things would have got very rough if the elevator hadn't stopped and opened.

"Shane?" Sandy gasped. "Good Lord! What are you doing here?" She dropped the bulging plastic bag she was holding and came into the elevator to hug him. "The wedding's back on?" She was beaming.

"*No.*" Shane gave her an abrupt one-armed hug between snatching up his bag and stepping out of the elevator.

She set out a hand to hold the door, blinking in confusion.

"Is your room on this floor?" Shane demanded. "Or—"

"I was heading to the laundry." She grew flustered as she stepped out and picked up her bag. She glanced between us.

"Don't look at that prick. He busted up me and Ash so he could move on her."

"That's not true. Sandy—"

She didn't look surprised, though. More like this was news that confirmed something she already believed. She sent me a disheartened look that might as well have been a kick in the stomach.

Angry frustration gripped me. I was hurt that she immediately believed the worst, but guilty because Shane's accusation wasn't completely wrong.

The doors started to close and I said, "We'll talk later, when you've cooled down." Knocking each other around wasn't going to solve anything.

"Go fuck yourself." Shane started down the hall.

"We're this way, love," I heard Sandy say.

If she looked back at me, I didn't see it. The doors sealed and I leaned against the wall as the floor dropped. I was sick with myself for letting things fall apart so badly. I tried to push the button for Ashley's floor, but the elevator finished its descent to the lobby.

Now I couldn't get back to the vista level without a card keyed for it. I didn't even have my own room key.

Brilliant. Just fucking brilliant.

I crossed to the lobby telephone, but Ash didn't pick up. I left a message that I'd be in the take away shop in the lobby, then sat there eating a breakfast bagel I charged to my room.

What had even just happened? How had things turned inside out so quickly?

Walking into the suite to see Shane there, naked, had been a punch in the gut. Not one of guilt, though. A green-hazed possessiveness had knocked me off balance. Shane and I could take the piss and get competitive with one another, but we were always on the same side. Suddenly, he'd been a rival. A threat.

Shane had sensed it right away. He'd made jokes, had given us the benefit of the doubt by asking if we'd been to the pool, but suspicion had hung in the air like a whiff of smoke. Shane and Ash didn't know each other down to the last eyelid twitch, but Shane and I did. We had both had our fur up from the second we'd laid eyes on one another.

Refusing to leave when he asked me to had betrayed things further. I had been hanging on her every word, listening for the revelation I dreaded—but maybe wanted?

The acknowledgement of *us* hadn't come from her lips, though. That had stung, but maybe she'd been scared to say it.

The way she'd grown so upset as she shot down Shane's attempt to make up had tied my guts into knots. The only other time I'd seen her get worked up like that had been the hairclip incident, when she'd thought I was picking on her. How had I thought that was harmless and cute? The consequences of pushing back scared her. I saw that now and I'd been compelled to stick around and let her know she was safe. She wasn't alone. I would *always* have her back.

My feelings must have been painted ten-feet tall across my face, 'cause Shane had seen 'em and read the situation without any effort.

Twenty minutes later, I remembered that she was supposed to get a pedicure. I ate the fruit cup with yoghurt I'd ordered for her and debated trying to find her at the spa, but I wasn't up for post-analysis in front of her sister and Izzy, though. Shane's and Sandy's contempt were quite enough for the moment, thanks.

The front desk refused to give me access to Ash's room, even though I assured them I only wanted to retrieve the phone I'd left there. I managed to talk them into a spare card for my own room, at least.

The blankets on the bed were still tousled. I made a half-hearted effort to straighten them, but it didn't help sort out the disarray in my head. An hour ago, I'd been trying to think how I could possibly go back to Oz and keep this from Shane and carry on as normal.

So much for that. My whole life was unraveling and I wasn't even sure of Ashley's motives. Why had she fallen into this bed with me?

What did I want her to reason to be? I'd been the one who was adamant we maintain our friendship, but we'd given into lust and I hadn't had time to come to terms with that. I didn't know what I wanted to happen.

Did I want her to share my life? Because, after the cluster-fuck I'd just created, she was justified in asking, 'What life?'

Fuck. What the hell was I going to do?

ASHLEY

I heard the phone while I was in the shower and didn't bother listening to the message, presuming it was a reminder from Whitney to bring the sunglasses she'd left here yesterday. I texted that I was running late and would meet them in the spa. Then I pulled a sundress over my damp body and combed out my wet hair. No time for make-up, even though my eyes were still red from the reactive tears I'd shed while in the shower.

Fox's stricken look as Shane had walked out on us was sitting against my heart like a razor blade, digging in with each beat. *My fault, my fault, my fault.*

I cringed, grabbed my purse and kicked into my flipflops, then hurried down to the far end of the hall, to the elevator that went directly to the spa. It was only when I stood alone in the lingering scent of essential oils that I allowed myself to wonder how Fox was making out with Shane.

A glance at my phone only told me Whitney was in the spa, waiting for me.

The doors opened and I saw her sitting next to Fliss in the

waiting area. Fliss lifted her gaze from her phone long enough to send me a why-am-I-here look.

"Thank you," Whitney breathed as she shoved her sunglasses onto her face, covering make-up that looked stark against her green-tinged complexion.

Izzy came in from the stairway entrance. She wore sunglasses with rhinestones on their arms. Her denim shorts had an overall bib and she wore a neon blue crop-top beneath.

"Were we *actually* dancing on the ceiling last night?" Izzy asked. "'Cause I woke up on the floor and I feel like I fell twelve feet. Getting pedicures was a way better idea when I thought we'd be partying tonight instead of last night."

I smiled, but it didn't stick.

"Why do you look hungover?" Izzy asked me with disgust. "You left early."

I hadn't decided how much to say, but figured I had to at least warn them.

"Shane's here."

Izzy dropped her sunglasses down her nose to blink her thick lashes at me. Whit made a strangled noise and Fliss asked, "Does that mean the wedding is on again?"

"*No.*"

"I was just asking." Fliss went back to reading her phone.

I hadn't meant to sound so bitchy, but I'd spent a lot of yesterday deconstructing my engagement with Whit and Izzy. Today's conversation with Shane might not have been easy, but I'd had time to process that we really had been doomed. That had helped me articulate it to him, unpleasant as that had been.

"Is everyone here? Please come in," a technician invited, leading the four of us to two pairs of massage chairs facing each other. "Shall I bring a round of mimosas? I'll need I.D.," she told Fliss.

"I'm twelve. I don't want anything." Fliss didn't want to be here. None of us did, but we should have cancelled two days ago if we didn't want to be charged for it. When I had tried to do that, Whitney had insisted we should spoil ourselves. So here we were, day undeniably spoiled.

"Have you talked to him?" Izzy asked as we all kicked off our flip-flops and sat down to sink our feet into our respective footbaths.

"He was in my room. I had no choice."

"Really?" Whitney paused in fingering through the magazines on the table between us. "Did he walk in on you and Fox sharing a room and come to a completely logical conclusion?"

Fliss lifted her gaze from the chair controller she was using to try out all the rolls and bumps of the mechanical massage.

The young women arranging instruments at our feet exchanged not-so-subtle looks of 'this is going to be good.'

"No." I scowled at Whitney. "Other way around, if you must know." I smiled a thank you for the mimosa as it arrived and wet my dry throat. "We walked in on him coming out of the shower. Completely starkers." It was an irrelevant detail that was a useful distraction.

"Ooh, I'd like to see that," Izzy mused. "What did he want? Don't say a wedding."

"He did," I admitted flatly. "I said 'no thank you.'"

"How did he take that?" Izzy asked, growing more concerned.

"Not well." I glanced at my phone, disturbed that there was nothing from Fox.

"Why not? *Did* he jump to conclusions about you and Fox?" Whitney asked, taking on her Law and Order voice. "Better yet, do you continue to deny these accusations are unjustified?"

"Whit," I said tiredly.

"I noticed he left right after you did last night."

"You said you weren't going to sleep with him," Fliss said. "Did you?"

"Hold on," Izzy demanded, putting up a hand. "Are you and Fox a thing? Why didn't you *tell* me? Is that why he told Shane not to marry you?"

"No! *Gawd.*" I caught another wide-eyed 'holy shit' look zing between the techs. "We're just friends. Were. Are. It's complicated." I clenched my eyes shut, wishing I could disappear. Wishing I could chew off the foot I'd shoved in my mouth because I was well and truly trapped.

"We're going to need a bottle of tequila, lime wedges, and salt," Izzy said sweetly to her tech. "Four glasses, and you'll have to overlook Fliss's lack of i.d. This is crash-course, Sister's Traveling Pants, high-grade gossip. We cannot leave her in the field."

"I'm glad you're enjoying this." I thought about storming out, but with my feet all soapy, I'd probably do a Bambi on ice and provide even more entertainment. Maybe even earn a trip to the hospital to get a bone set.

"So, what are you going to do?" Fliss asked. "Marry Fox instead? And go to Australia like you planned?"

"No," Whitney answered for me. "What rebounds in Hawaii stays here."

"It's not a rebound! I don't know what it is, but it's not that." What could it be, though? I'd cost him his best friend, his home, his career. No wonder he wasn't texting me.

How *much* did he hate me? That was the painful question I was trying not to answer.

"It's a rebound," Whitney insisted. "You got dumped and you've leapt on the next available man. There's no shame in it. I've done it—" She clammed up and smiled at her daughter.

"You won't let me eat sugar cereal, but you'll talk about casual sex in front of me? Good to know you'll be totally fine when I start doing it."

Whitney sent Fliss a stern look.

"One of the best things women can do for one another is avoid slut-shaming," Izzy said to Fliss before taking a sip from her narrow glass. "And Fox is actually a pretty good cure for a broken heart."

"Is that why *you* slept with him? To get over someone else?" I asked, wondering if *he* knew that.

"He hasn't exactly called. I don't think he cares," Izzy said dryly.

"Good grief. At this rate, I'm going to have to sleep with him just to keep up," Whitney said under her breath.

"We can be sister wives," Izzy said brightly. "Polyamory is all the rage these days."

I shot her a look, wondering if that was a dig about my unintended throuple with Fox and Shane.

"My friend Gillian has twin cousins who don't have the same dad." Fliss clicked off her phone. "They're a boy and a girl so you can't really tell, but their mom is polyamorous and got pregnant from both guys at the same time."

Izzy turned her head to scoff, "That isn't possible."

Fliss shrugged . "It happens with cats all the time."

Whitney set aside her magazine. "Is the tequila here yet?"

FOX

I wasn't really absorbing the information I was reading about the WWII pillbox—the small concrete bunker that I had wandered toward because I had nothing else to do—but the graveled voice beside me made me jump.

"You're dead, mate." Eddie peered out through the narrow window.

"No doubt." My intestines clenched in a combination of guilt and the sort of dread I hadn't experienced since I'd been young, when whatever passed for a home and stability had been yanked like a rug every few years, before I learned how to roll with it.

I had never learned to like it, though. In fact, I'd managed to forget how painful it was, but it was all coming back in vivid colors and it sucked *hard*.

"I didn't realize you were out here," I said.

"Sandy was doing laundry. I felt like a stroll." Eddie came out and stood looking at the rugged mounds of cooled lava pocked with tidepools that formed the shoreline.

I gave a meaningless nod and drew a breath. I'd have to say it.

"Do you have your phone on you? Did you know Shane is here?"

"Fair dinkum?" Eddie shoved his hand into his pocket and withdrew his phone, gave the screen a few swipes.

"Sandy saw him," I added. "I think he went to your room with her."

Had Shane really expected to slide back into place next to Ash? I was still trying to make sense of this morning's events, including why Shane had decided to show up after all.

Did he love her? Had I done the unthinkable and actually destroyed a marriage before letting them give it a shot?

"That's excellent." Eddie was grinning at his phone. "The wedding's back on?" His excited tone fell away as he looked at me. "Or not."

"Not." I gave the back of my neck a rub where sweat was trickling. "He asked her, but she said no."

"Hmph. Well, she was pretty hurt. Still, that's a shame." Eddie seemed about to say more, but only looked at his phone as he clicked it off and thoughtfully returned it to his pocket.

I had to come clean. Had to.

"Let's get out of the heat," I said and led Eddie to the path shaded by the trees.

"You've seen him?" Eddie asked as we got there. "I thought you'd be helping him drown his sorrows if he's not celebrating."

I swallowed a sick taste of bile in the back of my throat. "We had words."

"About?"

I gritted my teeth against a stronger thrust of nausea. This was *so hard*.

"I didn't mean for it to happen, Ed." I looked at the water, unable to look at this man who was a father-figure. "I hope you'll believe me when I say nothing happened before this morning, which doesn't make it right. I know that. But it wasn't as wrong as Shane thinks. Which doesn't matter because we can't go back from it." I released a frustrated sigh.

"You and Ashley." There was no doubt in his tone, only a strong, *I reckoned*.

Were we that obvious? Because *I* hadn't seen it.

I couldn't look him in the eye. I couldn't bear to see his disappointment or disgust. Not after Sandy had already cut me in half. I waited for him to say, *I taught you better.*

"I can't say I'm surprised."

"Ed, I *swear*—"

"Yeah, yeah, you were sharing her room for moral support. Oh, you didn't think we knew about that? We're not idiots."

I pinched the bridge of my nose. "It really was supposed to be moral support. We're *friends*."

"You could have been reading bible verses to each other for all I care, but it was clear to me you had feelings for her when you showed up here. Otherwise, you wouldn't have got on the plane. You would have texted her. Or me and Sandy, and told us to break it to her. No, you've always been..." Eddie looked to the water. Made another dismissive, impatient noise. "You've always been protective of our Shane. If that meant being sweet to his girl, well, that's all I thought it was between you and her. Until you got here. Then it was plain as day to me that it wasn't just Shane's heart you were tending, looking out for her the way you did."

My heart was in the sand and getting kicked along the path. I set a hand on my stomach where my clenched guts felt as though they were spilling out. I felt like a child. Obvious. Foolish, because I might have fooled myself, but no one else.

"It wasn't clear to me," I said in a rasp. "Or her. But Shane thinks... It doesn't matter what we did or when. He has every right to be angry. I just hope you and Sandy will believe me when I say I meant no disrespect to either of you. You've always been so kind to me. I wish I wasn't causing you more hurt."

They were some of the hardest words I'd ever had to say. I clamped my lips flat so they wouldn't quiver like a child's. Thankfully a line of tourists on horseback came toward us, forcing Eddie and me to separate to either side of the path. I used it as an excuse to send Eddie a final nod and started in the opposite direction from the resort.

"Hold up, there," Eddie demanded as the horses trotted into the trees.

One had dropped apples, leaving a pungent aroma that had both of us grimacing.

Eddie jerked his head, urging me to walk with him toward the hotel. He didn't speak until we could breathe freely again.

"Sandy and I have been suffering a lot of guilt since you told us Shane wasn't coming."

"Why? None of this is your fault." I waved that off.

"No, you listen." Eddie had a voice that had not only kept his sons and their high-energy mates in line, but had kept many a tradesman or worksite on task. "We got onto Shane pretty hard about Ashley. We should have kept our noses out, but she's a lovely girl. Sandy started dreaming about grandkids and you know I'll give her the moon if she wants it. We would both like to see Shane settled. That's a natural thing for a parent. And I'm embarrassed to say we thought it was time he found a woman to look after him instead of leaning on you."

"We're partners. I lean on him, too. We bring different things to the table."

"You're a good team, I agree. Shane knows how to work if he has to. Wouldn't have won a damned thing if he was truly lazy, but we spoiled him. I know that. You lose a child and your perspective changes. Why fight with him to take out the garbage? He'd suffered enough heartache in his life. It's not the best way to parent, but it was how we felt."

"I know. And you thought Ashley would make him happy. So did I."

"No. See that's where we messed up. We were thinking about how happy it would make *us* if he married her. Shane *is* happy. Was. And I suspect he proposed to her because he wanted to make us happy. He's a good boy at heart."

"He is." I winced one eye closed as I looked at the water through the filter of the trees. "You're not making me feel any less of a prick, Ed." My chest felt as though it was caving in on itself.

"We're all pricks sometimes. Shane was, three days ago. We'll still talk to him and we'll still talk to you." His heavy hand came down on my shoulder in a fatherly clap.

I rocked under the impact, both eyes closed now, afraid the sting in them would become too hot to contain. It was already spreading to my throat.

"Thank you," I said tightly. Earnestly. "I don't know that Sandy will feel the same, but it's kind of you."

"Kind? This isn't charity, you little shit. Do you remember the day Vicki dragged you over to help us move boxes? I'd never seen a more miserable face than yours—except on our boy. Twenty minutes later, you and Shane were laughing about something or other. I didn't care what sort of idiocy it was. We hadn't heard Shane laugh since the day of the crash. And before you say something stupid about that being the only reason we kept you around, or suggest you were some sort of substitute for Marcus, you aren't. You couldn't be. You're you. And you grew on us, ya big dumbass. We worry about you every bit as much as Shane. We want a good life for you, same as we want for Shane."

"Even if mine comes at the expense of Shane's happiness?" I asked skeptically.

"Well, that's the shits, isn't it? But no one says life is a pretty little rose garden. Where we come from, be thankful if all you've got is aphids. That's all this is, a nuisance detail you and Shane will have to work through."

"Never realized you were such an optimist, Eddie," I scoffed, still choked up.

"That's not optimism. It's perspective. You're not *dead*, Fox. Once Shane realizes that, he'll be grateful for the luxury of telling you what a maggot he thinks you are."

I had to laugh at that. It was ragged and pained, but a laugh all the same.

"Terrific. I can't wait."

ASHLEY

"**A**re you coming to the turtle beach with us?" Fliss asked as we finished up at the spa. Her moonglow purple toes had finally put a smile on her face. Whitney had gone with valentine red. Izzy wore neon green and I wore bubblegum pink. A safe choice because the rest of my life had drifted into such choppy waters.

"Sorry, hon. I forgot all about that." I thumbed through my string of unread texts, all well-wishes from friends in Pine Grove. Ugh. Fox and I had posted the statement to the T&B website, but I would have to post the link on my social media and stem all this salt they were rubbing into my wounds.

Still nothing from Fox, though. Was he making progress with Shane? Or so furious with me, he didn't want to talk to me? The longer this silence went on, the thicker the blanket of guilt weighed on me.

"You guys go ahead," I urged Fliss and Whitney. "Tell Mom I'll figure out something for dinner." Mom had already been stressing about how to rearrange her meal plan since the wedding dinner had been called off.

"Izzy?" Whitney invited. "Want to come see the turtles?"

"Pass, thanks. I have a hot date with a lounge chair next to the pool." Izzy nudged my elbow with her own. "Let me buy you lunch first. I haven't had breakfast."

"Me, neither. I'm starving," I confessed.

Whitney and Fliss headed back toward the villa and I followed Izzy to the restaurant.

"Looks pretty busy." Izzy made a face at the family in a booth chaotically trying to feed two little kids and a baby. "Let's see if the other one is open."

"It's expensive and I think they only do dinner."

"The beach one?" she suggested.

"It had a notice yesterday that they would be closed for a private event today." The pharmacists were still here. "Oh, wait. I have a coupon for the golf clubhouse." I had printed it before I left home and dug it out of my purse. "Want to try it?"

"Sure."

By the time we had walked the short distance in the midday heat, we both gratefully ordered the pineapple margarita that was on special. Even with the lingering champagne in my bloodstream, however, I couldn't relax as I sat across from Izzy. In the spa, we had thankfully moved on from discussing Fox and Shane and sex lives, but now all I could wonder was, "Are you judging me?"

"For ordering fries instead of salad?"

"*Pfft*. Diet firmly set alight and launched over the ocean in one of those paper balloons. After I starved myself to fit into that stupid dress, too." I propped my head on my hand and wondered what I could get for it.

Wedding dress, never worn. It probably had its own category on Marketplace.

"The whole time I was doing it, I was thinking, 'Izzy would

never punish herself like this. She'd order a dress that fit in the first place.' But you have such a great body, you could wear a Snuggie down the aisle and look great."

"So could you. Why do you put yourself down all the time?"

"I don't know. Mom and her 'be realistic' lectures? She made sure I didn't kid myself into thinking I was a super-model. Therefore, I must be hideously flawed and have to work every second to look like a human."

"She's not that bad. Is she?"

"No." I wrinkled my nose at my twisted self-esteem. "Mostly that's me suffering the messages society sends me, but where's the fun in taking responsibility for my own hang ups? Aren't our parents supposed to be the reason we all need therapy?"

"No kidding. The other day, I told my boss we should market a savings account for counselling. Parents won't need to go to confession, they can deposit their guilt as monthly contributions into their child's future cognitive therapy fund. They'd never have to feel bad about the fixations and phobias they bequeath us. Win-win."

"Did you get a promotion? Because that is seriously brilliant."

"I know." Izzy coolly sipped her drink and licked the salt from her lips.

"Yet another way I wish I could be like you. Bold. Innovative." It was supposed to be a cheeky compliment, but Izzy gave me an impatient frown.

"What's wrong with being like you?" she asked. "Why isn't that good enough?"

"Because I don't know how to do it," I moaned. "You accept people how they are, especially yourself. You don't make apologies for who you are, either. You say, 'Screw it' and go after whatever you want without letting it rot your stomach with anxiety. I went to Australia so I wouldn't be so freaking boring and came home engaged. How predictable is *that*?"

"You think you're boring and predictable?"

"Don't you?"

"No." Izzy seemed genuinely perplexed.

I faltered, then decided to wade all the way in.

"I guess I thought you must because you don't really want to hang out with me lately. Which is fine," I insisted, holding up a hand. "You live in the city and even I don't want to be in Pine Grove anymore. I don't blame you for not coming back or calling. You have a busy career and a life. But that's what I mean. You *do* things. Mom is all like, 'Keep your head down and save for a rainy day. Don't reach too high or you might fall down.' It's my fault that I listen. I know that. I thought I was changing by boldly marrying this Australian surfer, then I realized I wasn't. Not really. I was settling for what I thought was as good an offer as I was liable to get."

"Oof," Izzy admonished.

"I know. It sounds awful when I hear myself say it, especially because he's a really great guy. For someone else." I took a shaky breath. "Now I don't know what I'm doing because it turns out that being impulsive and going after what you want without giving a rat's ass for the consequences has consequences."

"Imagine," Izzy tucked her wedge of pineapple into her smile, nodding with sympathy. "I get what you're saying, though. It's hard to admit what we want and go after it, especially when it's something people don't expect us to want. Or *want* us to want."

"Exactly." I sighed, relieved to be understood.

Izzy rolled her lips inward, then pushed aside her drink and stacked her forearms before her on the table. She leaned in.

"Ash, I'm bi."

"Bi...? Bisexual?"

"Bicoastal," she said dryly. "Yes, bisexual."

I stared at her, genuinely dumbfounded. After a second, I managed to close my mouth, but my brain was a four-by-six, freshly hung, shiny blank whiteboard.

"I had no idea," I managed to say. "I mean, obviously that's cool. We're friends and I love you no matter what, but I'm feeling really stupid for not even suspecting. You're so open about how much you're into guys. It didn't occur to me that you might like girls, too."

"That's called hiding in plain sight. *Please* don't tell anyone, especially your family." For the first time since we were little, Izzy revealed a hint of insecurity.

"Of course not. Not if you don't want me to, but they wouldn't judge. I mean, Mom would give you the safe sex talk —again." I bit my smile, recalling how receptive we'd been the first time she'd lectured us, simply because we'd both got our period that summer.

Izzy snorted with old humor, too.

"But she ran a program at the women's resource center for years," I reminded her. "She's got a modern view on gender and attraction."

"I know. But my parents don't know. Neither does anyone at work. I don't want to be worrying it'll somehow get to all of those places before I figure out how to tell them myself."

"I'm one of the first people you told? Thank you for trusting me." I was genuinely touched. "And I'm sorry your parents are..." I pushed my mouth to the side. Izzy's father wrote papers for conservative think tank and her mother was very active in their church. "Stuck in their ways?"

"Mom literally tried to set me up on a blind date with an oil lobbyist the last time we talked. I march for climate change. *She knows that.* But she's really proud of me for getting that job at the bank." Izzy lifted her fists in a mini-cheer. "Because it means I can go back to work part time as a teller after I have kids."

"Oh, brutal." I had to chuckle. "And there was my mom pretty much taking us for spaying after Whit came home pregnant. Did you ever tell your mom that mine is the one who got you on the pill?"

"Do you want your mother's car lit on fire? Of course not."

We chuckled.

"This is why I love you," I said. "Even when everything feels broken, you make me laugh."

Our food arrived and we tucked in.

"So..." I asked around a French fry. "Do you have someone special?"

"Besides you?" Izzy asked, flashing me a cheeky grin. "I'm kidding. Don't get all full of yourself like you've won a trifecta or something."

I had to spit my food into my napkin so I wouldn't choke on it, I was laughing so hard. I took a deep drink of my slushy margarita, trying to get hold of myself.

"Oh, my God." I dabbed under my damp eyes with a fresh napkin. "Yeah, that's what I was thinking. That I'm irresistible. *Please* don't tell me that's why you invited me to Australia last year."

"No, that was..." Izzy grimaced before confessing, "I was getting over someone. My first *girl*friend. I presumed we would move in together and... It didn't work out. Obviously."

She forced a smile, but her eyes were sheened with old hurt. "So what you saw as me being bold and not giving a shit was standard, post-breakup madness. I wanted to run away from who I was. Fox was... I told myself I was going back to only dating guys. And he's a great guy. For someone else." She was mocking me with my own words, but being gentle about it.

Because she knew how hard it was hitting me.

The server came to ask if we wanted another round of drinks. We both nodded enthusiastically.

"When I got this job offer," Izzy said after the woman was gone, "I saw it as another way to go back to being who I'm expected to be. And all of this is literally why I brought up the therapy fund idea with my boss. I wanted to know if our benefits covered counselling. I realized I wasn't processing who I am as well as I could. Which is also why I was wishy-washy about making my travel arrangements and didn't fly in until yesterday. It took a while to get in with the doctor I wanted. I had my first appointment on Monday." Izzy apprehensively waited for my reaction.

"How did it go?"

"Pretty good."

"Good. But what I'm hearing is that your stomach *does* rot with anxiety." I pointed a fry at her. "And you've been keeping that from me. Unbelievable." I shook my head with dismay.

Izzy bit back a smile while her eyes dampened. "That's what I love about *you*," she said sincerely. "You're still my friend even though I wasn't completely honest with you about why I wanted to go to Oz and left you there to fend for yourself. I've been feeling guilty, wanting to explain it all. That's why I've been weird about hanging out. I knew we had to have this conversation, but I'm still not sure *how* to talk about it. Or how much I want to say. It's confusing."

"It's okay. Truly. I'm really glad you felt like you could tell me. And it's a good reminder to me that not everything is about me. Everyone has their own thing going on. It's as if everyone has their own lives and problems," I said with mock wonder.

"Right?" Izzy picked up her cutlery. "As if we're each the star of our own story and the rest of the world is our supporting cast."

"Oh, I never feel like a star. I'm more like a key grip. If I drop a light, it's all over. Cut! Start again. Everybody is giving me dirty looks."

"Hate to break it to you, but you're not important enough to ruin everything."

"Oh, Joanna. So nice to see you." I tilted my head in a scold at her.

We shared a grin, but mine faded as quickly as it formed.

"I feel like I screwed up Fox's life pretty badly without even trying."

"How? By sleeping with him?"

That and, "By wishing for a chance to see what we could have?"

"You think that *wishing* for a chance to see what you *might* have could ruin his life? You are full of yourself."

"And sleeping with him," I admitted with a grimace of guilt.

"Was it consensual? Did you force him?"

"You and I are not going to trade notes."

"I'm just saying, if it was something you both did, he shouldn't blame *you*. Is he trying to?"

"I don't know what he's thinking." I nudged my phone with its lack of messages. "He went after Shane who was *so* mad." My chest filled up with rusty nails all poking this way and that inside my lungs. "It's not just the house and the business. Shane's mom and dad are like family to Fox. If they turn their back on him, I wouldn't blame him for hating me."

"For God's sake, why is it all on you?"

"Because I knew we didn't have a chance at a future. Not the way things are with Shane." My voice dwindled with the rays of hope I'd been clinging to. "I knew we should have stayed friends, but I.... I wanted to be with him, even if it was only once. I listened to my heart, not my head." My libido, really. "Now my heart is going to wind up broken."

"Oh, sister," Izzy breathed. "Do I hear that."

Our drinks arrived and we tapped the salted rims.

FOX

*a*sh still wasn't answering in her room. She was long gone from the spa, wasn't at the pool or on the beach. I didn't know Izzy's last name so I couldn't see if Ash was with her in her room. She wasn't in any of the hotel restaurants and there was no one at the villa when I knocked.

That bothered me. My brain leapt to imagining she and her family had checked out and gone to Honolulu, to wait for their flight back to Pine Grove. Maybe she regretted sleeping with me that much. Maybe she was tired of this farce of a week that I'd caused her. Maybe she was rethinking her options, now that Shane had turned up and still wanted to marry her.

Even though neither had claimed to love the other.

I kept coming back to that because we hadn't said those words, either. We hadn't made any promises. We'd given in to a moment's temptation and... What?

I tried to believe Eddie was right, that Shane would come around, but I bumped into Sandy in the lobby, waiting for the elevator. She looked frazzled.

"Oh, Fox. I finally got the laundry on, but I needed more quarters." She showed me the rolled coins, expression shifting from a reflexive smile of warmth to something less certain.

"Shane in a mood to talk yet?" I asked.

"No, but listen." She touched my arm. "Ed and I have talked. You'll get your fair share. We have enough equity in the house we can mortgage it so Shane can buy you out. Eddie and I will come out of retirement and help him manage things. Ed ran his own business all those years. He knows what it takes. This looks like a disaster, but it's just a bump in the road."

It was surgery without anesthetic. Were they insane, risking their retirement savings on a business that was still only a few years old? It was in a growth stage, reliant on website visits and online sales, not on quoting a job and showing up to do the work. It was headed by a man they never said 'no' to.

"We'll talk more when we're back in Oz." Sandy gave my arm a final squeeze and offered a weak smile. "Things will work out one way or another. They always do."

"Sure." I let her take the elevator that arrived and said I was going for a swim, but I was reeling from the message the Holloways were pulling together and I wasn't one of them. Not anymore.

I went to the beach and threw myself into the surf so I could blame the salt for the sting in my eyes.

ASHLEY

J gave Izzy my cocktail vouchers for the pool bar and left her browsing bathing suits in the gift shop.

"I want to catch up with Fox," I said, "But come for dinner tonight at the villa."

"Love to. Can I bring anything besides my winning personality?"

"A bottomless enthusiasm for Go Fish. Ryan's always looking for a fresh mark."

"What are the stakes? Jelly beans? Should I stock up?"

"Defin— Oh!" I noticed Fox had messaged me through one of my social media accounts.

My phone is in your suite. Heading to my room now. Call me there when you get this.

"Well, that explains— I gotta go!" I hurried out of the shop and found a lobby phone only to see Fox come from where the business center was located.

When I was a kid, I used to pump so hard on the swings the ropes would go slack. That's exactly how I felt as I glimpsed him. Like I was suspended in mid-air at the very zenith of joy.

He wore a salmon-colored T-shirt with three buttons at the collar. It wasn't even tight, but hugged his wide shoulders and the sleeve cuffs accentuated his muscled biceps. His low-slung cargo shorts did the same for his legs and butt, hanging off his frame so beautifully, he was like a catwalk model. He ambled toward the elevators with an absent confidence that made heat swirl in my middle.

"Fox!" I called, voice wobbling like I had a case of Victorian vapors. I clapped the lobby phone back into its cradle and hurried after him.

"Hey," he said in greeting, brows pulling together with consternation. He didn't return my tentative smile.

A thick, invisible wall had come up between us. It was like a block of gelatin that condensed into a more solid, stickier, airless mass the closer I got to him.

He might look mouthwatering on the outside, but his eyes held the same wariness and weariness I'd seen when I'd picked him up from the airport a few days ago. He was show-ered and freshly shaved, but his cheeks were hollow.

Something in me sank so hard and fast, my knees grew soft and my head light.

"I didn't realize your phone was upstairs. I went for lunch with Izzy at the golf club. I'm really sorry." Really, really sorry. Sick with it, now that I could see there didn't seem to be anything but a few shreds of cordiality left between us.

He waved me to enter the elevator ahead of him. I used my card to take us up to my floor.

"Shane?" I asked apprehensively.

He shook his head.

"Fox—"

He shook that off, too. "It is what it is."

And that meant it was bad. My heart scraped the floor, dragging ten feet behind me as I led him to the suite.

"Do you want to talk about it?" I asked as we entered.

"Nothing to say. Shane wants me dead and his parents are talking about remortgaging their house to buy me out."

"Oh, my God." I left my bag on the floor and dropped onto the sofa, head landing in my hands. "I'm *so sorry.*"

"Are you?" he asked cryptically from where he was standing next to the table, pocketing his phone and key card.

"*Yes.*" I picked up my heat, appalled he would doubt it. "I never meant for any of this to happen. If you're thinking I went downstairs this morning planning revenge, no. I absolutely did not. I wanted..." I dropped my head back into my hands, heels of my palms pressing the sting into the backs of my eyes.

"What?" he prompted in a grating voice.

"It doesn't matter what I want. Everything I want turns to shit. I grabbed one tiny piece of what I wanted and unleashed a fury on you that you'll never forgive. I am so, so sorry."

"Ashley." His voice was suddenly right above me. He almost never said my whole name. I was always 'Ash,' the way my family called me. It made him sound grave. It made me feel like I was in deep, deep shit.

It took all my courage to look up at him because I didn't want to see his anger and blame and disappointment and hurt. I had hurt him and would never forgive *myself.*

"Why did you come to my room, then? What did you want? What *do* you want?" He searched my expression for something I was too terrified to reveal.

I thought about how I'd walked out of his room thinking that was all I would have with him. All I could have. Because I had learned to keep my expectations low and not reach. But I knew what I wanted.

"I want to love you. A little," I added quickly, because that already felt too big. Too much stretch. My eyes filled and my chin crinkled.

"And you're sorry you *did*?"

"*No*. I'm glad we did that, but I'm really sorry I wound up causing— Oh."

His strong hands took hold of my upper arms and drew me to me feet. "Jesus, Ash. You scared the hell out of me."

He wrapped his arms around me and nearly squeezed the air from my body. I had been about to fall apart and now he was squishing me back together.

"This has been a hell of a day, not knowing how you felt." His voice was a deep tremor in his chest. "Thinking— Yes. Love me. God. Please. Do you? Or do you only *want* to?" He drew back to look at me.

"I think I do, yeah," I admitted miserably, unable to keep my mouth steady. "And I know it might seem like I'm only turning to you because I'm scared to be on my own. I'm not. I'm scared to not have you in my life. That's been eating me up all week way more than Shane backing out of the wedding."

"Oh, babe." He pulled me back in and tucked my head beneath his chin, heart hammering against my cheek. "I felt awful. You weren't texting me back. I thought you must hate me."

"For what?" I hugged my arms tighter around him. "All I could think this morning was that I couldn't say what I wanted because it would put you in a terrible position. I didn't want you to feel obligated, like I expect you to choose me."

"I have chosen you. How do you not see that?" He pressed me away again. "I chose you when I didn't let you leave my room this morning. I didn't know what to say after, though. I was hoping for more than five minutes to figure it out." One side of his mouth pulled in a half-hearted rueful grin.

"What are you going to do? Because I'll get out of the way. I'll go back to Pine Grove and..." Wait for him? That would be excruciating.

"Is that what you want?" Tension settled into his jaw and his grip slid to my shoulders.

I shrugged under the weight of his hands, but my quivering lips said "No."

I might love him, but I wouldn't halt my life for him. Maybe I wasn't going to Australia as Mrs. Shane Holloway, but I wasn't going back to being timid Ashley Barnes, afraid to dream big and make mistakes.

Some mistakes were worth making. Even if he and I couldn't be together or fell apart tomorrow, I was already glad we had this one week between us. It was ours and no one could take it away from me. Not ever.

"Babe. Tell me what you want," he urged, giving my shoulders a squeeze.

I wanted him to keep calling me 'babe.' My mouth flickered with wistful humor.

"It's hard for me," I said softly. "To imagine I'm allowed to go after a bigger bite of the world." I didn't have a surf champion for a mom who had taught me that it was completely normal to follow the sun and my dreams.

Fox didn't either, but he had learned to be ambitious. Izzy was like that, too, even though her parents were like my mom —careful and content with a quiet, secure, conventional life. Maybe the biggest thing Izzy had revealed to me today was that underneath all that bravery, everyone was scared in their own way. No one liked to fail or be rejected or lose.

But you didn't get what you wanted unless you went for it, whatever 'it' was.

"Spit it out," Fox urged. "There are no wrong answers. You want marriage?"

"What?" My eyes almost fell out of my head. "*No.*"

"What then?" He withdrew slightly.

"I mean..." I set a placating hand on his chest. "Maybe. One day. I'm still sorting through my feelings on marriage. I was going into it for all the wrong reasons and it's not something I see as a goal anymore." I felt a little foolish that I ever did. "I was using marriage as something to give me independence. Because I saw it as the only way I could pry myself away from Mom and Pine Grove. No, I just think it would be nice if you and I could be together and see what we have."

"That would be nice." His gaze softened and he set a tender kiss on my mouth.

For a few seconds, as we held onto each other, all the shaking in me stopped. I hadn't destroyed what we had. Fox and I were okay. In this moment, everything was okay.

And maybe this was as much security as anyone had— moments of believing everything would be fine, even if it wouldn't. Even if you didn't know the way out of the mess you were in.

"You'll come to Australia?" he asked quietly. "We don't have to stay there, but you have to get your things and I have to move out." He sighed and stroked my hair. "We'll have to find a place to stay. Get jobs that might suck. But let's aim for spectacular and get there eventually."

"I envy your confidence."

"You doubt me? Us?" He frowned down at me.

"No?" My heart was pounding with equal parts excitement and overwhelm. "I don't want to look too far into the future." Monsters abided there. That was life. "Do you think we have it, though?" I asked cautiously. "Get-through-anything love?" Because this thing between us was very new and fragile and I didn't want to delude myself again.

Fox sobered. Then snorted with self-deprecation. "I was a prick to ask Shane that, wasn't I? But you don't know until you're tested and this has been a fucking week, Ash." He wasn't talking about the shortness of timeframe. He was referring to all the shit we'd been through since he landed.

"I definitely feel tested," I said on a strangled laugh, splaying my hand on my side. "What I do know is, Shane and I wouldn't have gotten as far as a wedding if you hadn't been on the other side, picking up his slack. He and I definitely didn't have it. But I'm right here with you now." I stroked my hand across the contours of his waist and lower back. "Even though I've wanted to kill you more than once since you landed."

He slid his around me again, but his expression was somber. "I do think we have it," he said. I'm gutted about Shane and his parents and I'm not giving up hope there, but if I lose my share in the business and the house... I can weather that. I don't want to lose *you*."

A fine tremble went through me, one that shifted tiny polarities in me to align with points inside him. It was recognition and connection and yes, a strange little bond that I suspected would only strengthen throughout our life together.

"That's how I feel," I said huskily. "I don't care where I work or if we can only afford a crappy little flat as long as I'm coming home to you."

"Babe." His hazel eyes were shiny as he touched his mouth to mine.

My heart turned over.

"I mean it," I murmured.

"I know you do. And I mean it when I tell you to expect more. It won't be a *crappy* flat. Be greedy. We're going to have it all."

And if we didn't, we would still have each other.

All the angst and worries churning inside me fell away. Beams of joy and gratitude and love glimmered through me, suffusing me with a radiance I could hardly contain.

We kissed again and it was better than all the ones that had come before. It was no longer stolen. This kiss was pure. Certain. It was given back and forth without reserve. Without guilt or hovering what-ifs.

It was the first of many deeply set stones that were the foundation of our future. The next was his lips pressing to the point of my shoulder. I closed my eyes and absorbed that beautiful imprint before I grazed my mouth against his Adam's apple. He swallowed.

We pressed our cheeks and breathed in each other's scent.

He said, "Every time I touch you, I wonder how I didn't realize sooner..."

"I know. I keep thinking this is how it's supposed to feel." I smoothed my hand across the muscles of his chest. The feel of him caused sensations to swirl and swell within me. "When I touch you, I feel it inside me."

His hands slowly shaped my lower back, igniting fires as he climbed his hands to my ribs then down to the top of my ass. He smoothed his palms over my hips and slowly brought them up to my shoulder blades, cradling me close again, but this embrace was no longer comforting and safe. I was beginning to glow. To *burn*.

"I didn't know I could love anyone like this," he confided with an emotive edge on his voice. The pulse in his throat was heavy against my palm.

"Me, either."

It awed and overwhelmed me, but I wasn't frightened. Not anymore. Even when he kissed me so deeply, I lost track of where we were and forgot to breathe. Even when my arousal became more than desire. More than want. Hunger. Need.

I swept my tongue into his mouth and pushed my hips into the thick pressure of his erection.

This wasn't me. I was never the sexual aggressor, but I needed him to know how much he meant to me. How deep this craving went for us to be physically *together*.

He groaned and brushed the straps of my sundress down my shoulders.

I pulled back. "It has to come over my head. My ass is too—"

His brows went up in a small warning.

"—spectacular for it to slide down over my hips."

His teeth flashed. "Hell yes, it is."

He shed his shirt and shorts, then helped me with the dress, lifting it off my upraised arms. I reached to unhook my bra and he caught a finger in my underwear, but only used that snag to draw me closer as I threw my bra away.

He was naked and hard and so incredibly sexy I nearly melted as my skin brushed his hot, tense frame.

I realized I was shaking when I watched my fingers tremble as I lightly traced across to the ball of his shoulder, down his biceps to his forearm.

"I want to rub myself all over you," I whispered and licked

at his dark brown nipple, beaded and tight beneath the pressure of my tongue.

He drew a shaken breath. His arms tightened around me. "Yes, please."

I released a breathy laugh against his chest, but I wanted to sob under the massive feelings swamping me.

"I'm serious," he whispered against my ear, making my scalp tighten. "I want you all over me." His fingertips were tracing the line where my thong disappeared between my cheeks. The tickling caress caused a hot rush of wetness into the cotton.

"I want you in me." I clasped my hand around the girth of him, squeezing firmly enough he pulsed in my hand and hissed a breath through his teeth.

He nipped at my mouth and backed me toward the bed, then we stood beside it, kissing deeply, tongues playing and both of us groaning at the gorgeous, lusty sexiness of it. His hands cupped my breasts and his thumbs circled my nipples. I stroked him and he pushed into my hand and I was pretty sure I was going to die from the ache in my pussy.

I released him to push the thong down and he threw himself onto the bed, then invited me with the beckon of his hands.

I straddled his hips and he said, "Babe. Up here." His strong hands took hold of my hips and he slid down the bed, encouraging me to move up.

"Another time." I'd never sat on a man's face in my life. For the first time, I was more intrigued than appalled, but, "Right now I really need to feel you in me."

I stood on my knees over him and used my fingers to part and spread my juices over and around, preparing to take him in.

"Keep doing that," he said in a low, graveled voice, hands moving restlessly on my thighs while he watched.

I slowed and showed him what I liked, rubbing up over my clit and sliding down to penetrate, growing hotter and hornier under his intense stare. I was getting really close. I bit my lip, slowing my touch. Slowing and slowing.

When I made a helpless noise and lifted my touch away, he dragged his incandescent gaze up to mine.

"Keep going. I want to watch."

I already felt unbearably vulnerable, but there was something in his soft command, something in this small bridge of trust we were building, that made me want to give him everything. I closed my eyes and touched myself again. I stroked my clit until I was wet and tense and arriving at the peak. Rolling over it.

A small cry tore from my throat as the climax hit. I buried two fingers deep inside me, waiting until the hardest pulses had faded before I let them slide free.

I dropped my hand away, panting, and blinked my eyes open.

I wasn't sure what I expected to see on his face, but beneath the lust, there was joy. Triumph. Love. It was the sweetest kick in the heart.

I melted onto him.

He kissed me and stroked me as if he'd been the one to deliver that orgasm. As if we'd been linked when it happened. As though we'd shared it.

"That was really sexy," he told me as he rolled me beneath him. He kissed along my hairline and into my neck and I feathered my fingertips down his spine and crooked one knee up, inviting him in.

"Condom?" he asked.

"I have an IUD." And I'd had a full physical before getting it. And yes, maybe that was yet another sign I hadn't been committed to the life I had thought I was starting with Shane. Much as I loved Fliss, she was the result of one forgotten pill. When I got pregnant, it would be because I was ready to be a mother.

"Really? I haven't been with anyone since the last time I was checked, but I always wear condoms. I don't know how long I'll last without one."

"I'll risk it." I smiled against his chin.

He levered himself onto one elbow, looking down between us as he guided the leaking tip of his cock to my slick, aching center. And finally, *finally*, he was pressing into me.

"Oh, that feels so good," I groaned, clamping my legs around him, encouraging the steely intrusion as he withdrew slightly before sinking deeper. I gripped him hard with my inner muscles, wanting to keep him forever.

"Keep telling me that," he said, trailing his lips across the line of my jaw. "Communication is key during sex. Or so I was told."

After a stunned second, I remembered he was quoting Inga and burst out laughing. He had to cage me with his big body and settle his weight heavily on my hips to keep us joined. We went back to kissing, but kept chuckling, calming, then falling into a fresh fit of giggles.

"Why did you *say* that?" I asked, running my hands over him, still snickering.

"So I wouldn't fucking explode. You feel really fucking great, Ash. I want to fuck you so hard."

An earthy groan left me. I cradled his strong-boned face in my hands and met the dance of lusty amusement in his eyes. "Do it."

Now he made a noise that was distinctly uncivilized and kissed me again, deep and filthy with lots of tongue. When he started to move, I felt it like taut violin strings that rang notes of pleasure with each measured withdrawal and return. I couldn't believe how incredible it felt. How powerful.

"Oh, fuck," I moaned throatily.

"Yeah," he gasped.

"Don't stop. It feels *so* good. Oh, *fuck.*"

He kept moving, deep and hard, like he was making me his.

It was incredible. I wanted him to hurry up and finish me yet keep me right here forever, subjecting me to this insanely gratifying, lascivious act.

His tempo picked up. Our flesh was slapping and I made noises that I hoped he realized were approval, even though I sounded pretty tortured. A wild flush of heat washed over me. The prickling tingles of climax neared. My pussy felt so swollen and overstimulated, I thought I'd burst.

"Harder." I could hardly speak. "Please. Oh God, Fox—"

He rose onto his knees and dragged my hips into his lap and slammed into me. The new angle and the sharp impact were enough to cause a deep contraction within me. Release hit, one that had me opening my mouth in a broken cry, unable to bear how good it was.

"I'm coming," he bit out, swearing and pounding into me. "Ash!" His ragged noises joined mine as he pulsed hotly inside me.

FOX

J had a nagging sense I should be thinking about our future. Something constructive. But I was too blissed out.

"Bloody oath, we're good together," I said through lips that still felt numb.

"You are," Ash murmured sleepily. "I've nev— Never mind."

I shifted so her head fell off my shoulder. I curled my arm under the pillow, dragging the other into place for her. Now we were nose to nose, bodies still close, legs still woven together.

She was blushing, her eyelids still swollen and heavy, her mouth soft. As she met my gaze, she bit her lip and looked embarrassed.

Concern edged into my zen. "What were you going to say?"

"It doesn't matter." She pulled the sheet from across her hip up to beneath her armpit.

"Tell me." I hooked my finger in the wisp of hair that

caught in the corner of her mouth and swept it away. "Was that okay? We finished pretty strong." My balls were still singing like a tuning fork. "If I was too rough, you have to tell me. Stop me."

"What? No. That's was awesome. I just said it was."

"No, you said I was good. Ash—"

She cut me off with a groan of frustration, then babbled out, "I was going to say I've never come at the same time like that. I thought simultaneous orgasms were a myth. And I didn't think I could, you know, get off without...helping myself."

"Oh. Wow. You are *really* blushing," I teased, rubbing my knuckle against her hot cheek. It was redder than an apple.

"Because I don't think we should compare." She grabbed my hand and pulled it under her chin, closing her eyes to hide whatever was in them. "I sure don't want you telling me how I stack up in your history file."

"You came this morning without—"

"I know. That's what I'm saying. I thought it was a fluke, but you're some kind of sex god with a magic penis. Congratulations. Your trophy will be mailed at a later date."

Christ, I loved her. Laughing, I caught my arm around her and dragged her close so we were belly to belly, spent dick against the still damp curls decorating her slit. The best feeling ever.

"I will never get tired of hearing that I make you come. Say it often, say it loud." I nipped her earlobe. "Say it when I'm inside you."

"Don't get arrogant." She pinched my stomach. "You've set a standard now. You'll have to live up to it."

"Challenge accepted. Wait. What exactly is the standard?" I pulled my head back to look at her. "Twice a day? I haven't been that randy since I first learned what masturbation was and really applied myself to getting good at it."

"You made your own bed," she said, tucking her arm beneath her head as she rolled onto her back.

"I did, didn't I?" I grew distracted by her pretty breast and the way it was drawn to sit up high and proud by her upraised arm. I caressed the underside where she had a light sprinkling of freckles, enjoying the freedom to explore and admire. I gave her nipple a kiss that turned into a taste, just because I could.

"I keep thinking this shouldn't be so comfortable, lying here naked with you like this. I refused to think of you this way for so long."

"Yeah, I had the door firmly locked on fantasies where you're concerned, too." I splayed a possessive hand over the swell of her breast so her damp, beaded nipple poked through my fingers. "I'm pretty excited we get to do this as much as we want from now on."

"Me, too." She smiled, but her smile immediately faded.

I moved my hand to her stomach. "What?"

"Nothing." She covered my hand. "I just remembered we can't stay in this bed forever. Then things got really big in my head really fast."

"Reality. *That* son of a bitch. I was hoping we could ignore it a little longer." The coiled snakes that had been in the pit of my gut over Shane awoke and slithered restlessly. I had brooded all day and hadn't come up with any miracle solutions.

Except this. Touching her. Reassuring myself I wasn't alone in this. That *this* was real.

I moved my thumb in a small caress, drawing a circle around her navel.

"My family has pretty much convinced themselves I'm going home with them," she said. "This won't be received well." Her fingers played over mine, tickling into the spaces between. "Whitney thinks you're a rebound. You're not."

"You told her about us?" I stilled my hand.

"I told her Shane was here and she figured out that *he* figured out..." Her stomach lifted and fell beneath my hand as she sighed. "Fliss is still coming to terms with getting a step-dad. Mom is going to have questions. Opinions." She dragged in another daunted breath and blew it out. "I just don't feel like having a huge fight with them. So maybe we stay here?"

"That's Plan B. But let's talk about how we'll break it to them."

"Actually, staying here is Plan Z. I'm the dumdum who offered to make dinner at the villa tonight. Mom didn't have anything planned because we were supposed to be eating the catered wedding dinner tonight. I would suggest taking them out, but we're a lot of mouths and we have to start thinking about our finances. Plus, given the possible *volume* of tonight's discussion, the privacy of the villa is the better venue."

"You really think it'll get heated?" This *would* be tricky. I couldn't stand by for anyone abusing Ash, not even people who loved her as much as I did.

"I think we have one chance to win them over. This is not a drill, soldier." She was joking, but genuine apprehension lurked behind her brave smile.

"I'll cook ribs on the barbecue," I stated. "With garlic pota-toes and a salad. I will not let you down."

I meant it, too.

ASHLEY

$\mathcal{W}$e returned from the grocery store as my family was unloading from Oliver's van and followed them from the parking lot to the villa.

"You're joining us for dinner, Fox?" Mom asked in more of an askance question than invitation, tone loaded with reserved judgment.

"Thanks, Whit." I sent my sister a flat smile since she had clearly been gossiping about us. "Fox is cooking, Mom. Izzy's coming, too. I'll text her, tell her we're back and she should come over whenever she's ready."

"Fun," Whit said, sending an amused glance at Fox.

I pointed a warning finger at her while Fox emptied the groceries onto the counter and said to Oliver, "Ash said I could bum a beer for the barbecue sauce."

"Waste of cheap beer, if you ask me," Oliver chided, but handed a can to him before he began pouring wine. "Ashley?"

"Later, maybe. Thanks." I needed a clear head.

Oliver handed a glass to Mom who promptly set it aside. He poured another for Whitney.

"Mom, I've got this," I said as Mom tried to unpack the cardboard box they'd used as a picnic basket on their outing today. "This kitchen is too small for all of us in here. Sit." I nodded at the stools on the far side of the breakfast bar. "Enjoy your wine. I need to talk to you about something."

Mom hesitated, then moved onto the stool across from where Fox was setting out a cutting board. I moved her wine so she could reach it and called Whitney back from heading outside to the patio with her own glass.

I glanced to where Fliss was setting up a video game with Ryan on the sofa. "I want you all to know that I've made a decision."

While Fox and I had meandered grocery aisles, he had coached me not to sugar-coat it. *If you don't sound sure, people think there's room to change your mind.* It was probably the best advice I'd ever received and the hardest to apply, but I was doing it.

"I'm going to Australia with Fox." Bam. No argument. There it was.

A resounded silence, then Fliss asked, "For how long?"

"For... I don't know." So much for sounding sure.

Fox paused in digging through a drawer and came to stand beside me. His warm hand settled in my lower back.

"Australia is where we're going to start." He sounded very sure. "Wherever we wind up, it will be together."

Another silence. Then Whitney said, "So you're not going with him as a roommate."

"We're a couple. Yes." I slid my arm around Fox's back, tucking myself against his solid, but relaxed frame. How was he this confident? Didn't he realize we were starting a fight we would have to finish? Why didn't he hate this as much as I did?

"So you're going with *this guy* instead of the other one," Whitney waved a dismissing hand at Fox. "She's using you to get back at Shane. You know that, right?"

"Whitney." I curled my fist into the fabric of Fox's T-shirt.

His hand slid to dig reassuringly into my waist. "Ash isn't like that. You know that as well as I do."

"Oh? You think you know her as well as I do? I beg to differ, cowboy." Whit was really working herself up, pointing aggressively at Fox, then at me. "You're taking advantage of her and no. *You* are coming home with us."

"Oof. I think you missed the 'young lady' tag on that. No, Whit. If I want to go to Australia, I will go to Australia. I was going anyway. Why are you upset?"

"I'm not upset!" Whitney yelled.

"Clearly." I could feel myself wanting to climb aboard the reaction train, but I was also genuinely puzzled by how mad she was. This was Mom's purview. Or the tween with an axe to grind, not the newly engaged woman who finally had her act together.

"Are you going to marry *him* now?" Whit asked with another wild wave at Fox.

"Maybe. Someday. Right now, Fox has a lot to sort out with Shane and the house. They might end their partnership." I looked up at Fox. He wore an impassive expression, but he wasn't completely unaffected by that hard fact. Now tension had crept into him. Defensive, maybe?

We were going to be okay, though. I was sure of it, even if my family wasn't.

"Right," Whitney said disparagingly. "So you're shacking up with a guy who stole you from his best friend, one who is losing his business *and* his house. You'll have *nothing*."

"I'll have *him*. God."

"Ash and I will be fine," Fox said in a deep voice brimming with quiet affront. His fingers were biting into my waist. "Better than fine. I look forward to proving it to you."

"And who's picking up the pieces when that doesn't happen?" Whitney charged.

"Why are you being like this?" I cried. "I was happy for you and Oliver. Why can't you be happy for me?"

"Because you are breaking up the family. *Again*. And this time it *is* your fault. This is bullshit. This is fucking *bullshit*."

I jerked, taking those words straight to the heart. Like a fucking *blade*.

My gasp had Fox closing his arms around me protectively while Whitney shot into the bedroom and slammed the door.

Into the profound silence, Fliss said, "It's okay. My mom is just upset. I think she got too much sun today."

We all looked over to see her hugging Ryan, glaring at all of us while Ryan's lip quivered.

"She'll put money in the swear jar later." Fliss rubbed the boy's back.

"I'll go see about collecting it." Oliver set down his beer. "It's okay, son." He gave Ryan a reassuring pat on his way into the bedroom.

Fliss gave Ryan another hug, then stood and held out her hand. "I bet you we can talk Grandma into letting us have ice cream before dinner."

"Take my wallet from my purse," Mom said.

Fliss did, and kept Ryan's hand as they walked out.

"Hey," Fox said, loosening his arms then giving me another gentle squeeze.

I blinked wet lashes, trying to shake off my shock. My profound hurt.

"This is not your fault, Ash." Fox pressed a kiss to my

temple, so tender it caused a fresh fracture across the break that Whitney had put in my sternum. "You're living your life. How people react is not something you can control."

I nodded and hugged myself into him, pushing my wet eyes against his T-shirt, but I didn't really believe him. Not after Whitney had said *that*.

"Pass me your sister's wine?" Mom set aside the glass she had just drained.

Fox released me and reached for Whitney's, handing it over while I swallowed and ran fingers under my eyes, trying to sniff back tears I refused to shed.

Mom looked thoughtfully at Fox. "He's right. You can't control how others people react or behave. I've tried. The swear jar barely works." Her gaze hit mine, dry and grave. "You did not break up our family, Ashley. I had to make choices based on your father's behavior. *His* behavior. That was on him and we recovered."

This wasn't something we talked about often, but Mom had said something like this to me in the past. I appreciated hearing it again, but I was still hurt and angry with Whit.

This time it is your fault. She didn't blame me for the past, but she was sure as hell blaming me now.

I looked at the bedroom door, torn between walking in there to tell her to fuck herself or walking out altogether.

"What are you making us, Fox?" Mom asked.

"Besides a hasty getaway?" I muttered.

He snorted. "I'm still here." He set out a bowl and found a knife.

We'll get through this, he seemed to be saying. *We can get through anything.*

Tears came back into my eyes.

"Barbecued ribs," he told Mom. "I'm cheating with the

sauce. I usually make it from scratch. When I'm being fancy, I use dark beer. This'll do, though." He had a bottle of prepared barbecue sauce, but was setting out fresh garlic and chopped parsley. "How were the turtles?"

"Bigger than I expected," Mom said. "They didn't move much, but one made its way into the water. We found a table in the shade where we could see them as we ate. Oh," she recalled. "Ryan found me a treasure while we were beach combing."

She dug into the pocket of her shirt and withdrew a square gold charm. It was engraved with the words 'Great-grandma.'

"He wanted me to have it because I'm a grandma and he thinks I'm great." She was both amused and affronted at the idea she was being called a great-grandmother.

"It's biologically possible," I reminded her. "Do you think Whit will have a baby with Oliver? Oooh, maybe she and Fliss can do that together."

"Bite your tongue," Mom ordered into her wine glass.

"Ruthless," Fox said with a chuckle and a shake of his head.

"You're originally from Seattle, aren't you, Fox?" Mom asked. "Do you ever think of moving back there?"

Oh, Mom. Be more obvious.

He glanced up from chopping the ribs into sections and dropping them into the bowl of sauce. "Seattle is a great place to visit, but no, I don't think I'd ever move back there. I've considered California a few times. Shane and I have discussed how and where to expand the business. We've talked about here, too. Those are long term goals, though. We've been concentrating on growing within Australia."

"And now...?" Mom probed. "Are you liable to lose your stake in the business?"

"Mom."

"It's okay," Fox assured me. "There are provisions in our partnership agreement on how to buy one another out if we decide we can't work together. It will be expensive and messy, but I'll come away with something. Enough for Ash and I to start fresh. What did you say the other day?" He glanced at me. "Something about viewing disaster as an opportunity to make choices that might not otherwise be available?"

"I doubt I was that eloquent, but sure, I'll take credit." I started washing vegetables for the salad.

"You can't work in the U.S.," Mom said to me, brows pulled with introspection. "You're better off in Australia where you have a visa now, so you can both work. Australia has universal health care, too. Sandy was telling me about their system. Honestly, I think our government could learn a few things," she added with a sigh.

"Mom's a nurse," I reminded Fox.

"Will you have to marry to put Ash on your plan?" she asked Fox.

"Mom. Put away your shotgun. You don't even want me to get married. Ever," I reminded.

"I never said 'never.' I'm just asking how it works."

Fox glanced up from starting to peel potatoes, mouth twitching with amusement.

"Truth is, there might be some hiccups with Ash's visa if she won't be working for T&B since the company sponsored her. If that happens, we'll reassess, but after she started running our social media, I had a few people ask me who we were using. We were cagey because she was trading work for rent, but there are definitely opportunities for her to do more of that."

"Medi Wear would hire you remotely, wouldn't they?"

Mom said, perking up. "They offered that when you put in your notice."

"Mom. Your rotors are showing." It was something Fliss said when Whit was being a helicopter mom.

"I just want to know you'll be all right," she said pithily. "And I'll say this once so it's out there. You can always come home if you run into trouble getting on your feet. With Fox, unless he's the source of the trouble."

"*Mom.*" But I was laughing now.

Fox caught my wrist in a signal to let him speak.

"I promise I won't be, but thank you, Joanna," he said sincerely. "I don't think it will take us long to find our groove. You raised a bright woman capable of making good decisions and I make pretty good ones myself. Eventually." He winked at me. "I'll be doing everything I can to make sure we're secure, but it means the world to me that you'd open your home to us if we were in a bind."

"I just wish it wasn't so far away."

"I was already planning to visit my family in Seattle this Christmas. The dates aren't firm, but we'll add a leg to come see you."

"Oh, that's too soon. Too expensive if you'll be starting new jobs."

"Shane and I fly a lot. I have a ton of points," Fox said.

"Even so, Seattle to Winnipeg is farther than people realize. Perhaps we could meet you in Seattle."

"Or California," I suggested. "Fliss would love that. So would Ryan." Whit could stay the fuck home. I wasn't going to forgive her soon.

Oliver came out of the bedroom as the potatoes were starting to boil. He looked for his son on the empty couch.

"They went for ice cream," I said.

He gave a philosophical shrug. "Need any help with dinner?"

"I was about to start the barbecue," Fox said, taking the bowl of sauce-coated ribs outside.

"Let me grab my beer. I'll join you." Oliver looked for the can I'd put back in the fridge.

I dried my hands on a tea towel and eyed the bedroom door, trying to figure out what I'd say.

"Maybe give her a minute?" Oliver winced as he saw where I was looking. "She's still upset. Embarrassed. Worried about how Fliss is taking this." He waved at himself. "She took it out on the wrong person."

I nodded and Oliver walked outside, then I looked at Mom.

"Should I go talk to her?" I asked.

"I will." Mom stood, but there was a knock on the main door.

"Izzy," I said, starting to dry my hands again.

"I'll let her in. I like him, by the way." Mom nodded toward the windows where we could see the backward baseball cap on Fox's head. "Which isn't to say I won't cut off his nuts and make it look like an accident if he hurts you again."

"I'll let him know," I said dryly, then impulsively gave her a hug. "Thanks."

"For?"

"Understanding. Not being mad. Loving me anyway."

"Always." She hugged me back, then went to open the door for Izzy.

FOX

*a*sh made a soft noise of protest when I pulled away from her at five.

"Shh. Go back to sleep," I whispered. "I'll be back soon."

"But you'll be cold and wet and you feel really good right now." She snuggled her butt deeper into the spoon of my body.

"You feel really good, too." Good enough my dick throbbed in protest. *Are you sure we have to go?* "I want to, though." I softened my departure with a kiss against her sweet-smelling neck.

"Will Shane be there?" She rolled onto her back to watch me rise and dress in the shorts and rashie I'd left out last night, after checking out of my room downstairs and moving back in here with her.

"I don't know." Shane would be up and paddling out, no question, but there were a thousand places to surf. He didn't have to do it here.

"I won't worry too much if you don't come back right away. Go for coffee or breakfast if he's up for it."

"Thanks." I gave her foot a squeeze through the covers as I left.

Shane wasn't at the equipment hut. It was a beautiful morning, the air still, the sky clear and glowing silver, the waves coming in on clean, measured sets.

I waded in, mind replaying dinner last night. Whitney had stayed in the bedroom, which had bothered Ash, but the rest of her family had warmed up to me. I'd been relieved by that, but I'd heard her mother's concerns loud and clear and it was more fuel to my fire in terms of working things out with Shane. I didn't want to lose the business.

I ducked under a wave and caught my breath with a shudder. The pressure to resolve things with my partner kept my shoulders tense. I tried to stretch it out in a long paddle, cresting the next wave, pushing through the crush toward the calm beyond the break line.

When I got there, a half dozen surfers were sitting on their boards.

"This fucking guy," Shane said with a disparaging glance.

The others chuckled, thinking it was a joke, but their humor died as they realized Shane was serious.

"Just here to surf, mate," I lied, sitting up on my board to study the sets coming in.

Silence reined and someone slid away, paddling in and dropping into the wave a moment later.

I was watching that surfer so I didn't realize Shane had skimmed close enough to kick at my board until I was tilting into the water. I went under with a *sploosh*.

"Grow up," I said as I surfaced and slid back onto my board.

"You grow up. I saw the video. You're a bloody idiot. You know that?"

"Didn't know you cared." And, because we'd screwed around like this a thousand times over the years, I brought up my own foot, curled my toes on the rail of Shane's board and gave it a hard, downward shove.

Shane was a seasoned bull rider, though. He kept his seat and only sneered. "I don't. Not for shitheads who insist on shoving in where they don't belong."

"That's where we're at?" Because that crossed a line. Shane *knew* how much of an outsider I'd always felt. Now he was saying all those years I'd been made to feel like part of his family had been me hanging on like a dag? He knew what a tender nerve that was for me.

"If you're punching that low, we really do have nothing left to say." I turned and began paddling to catch the next wave.

"Fox."

It wasn't my turn, but I flipped him the bird because there was only so much crow I would eat. Fucking prick, talking to me like that. All that history and what? Shane had only been tolerating me? Fuck. Him.

Seconds later, as I popped up, Shane dropped into my wave right in front of me.

I wanted to nail him, I really did. I waited until the last second to spin my board, delivering just enough of a clip with my board against his that we both wiped out and churned in the wash.

My board hit my shoulder and I came up spewing, blowing water out of my nose. My sinuses were stinging and my temper was at eleven.

I looked for Shane, saw him surface and shake his hair out of his eyes. That was as much notice as I gave him. I wanted to kill him, but I wouldn't let him die. He was breathing so that was enough. We were done.

I grabbed my board and pulled it under me, paddling in.

"This is your fault!" Shane yelled as he skimmed in on the wave behind me.

"Sure is, mate. Buying a ring, dodging the prenup, sulking in the taxi, not even willing to get on the fucking plane and tell her yourself? That was all me. I did that."

We waded toward the shore.

"*You* picked up her friend at the pub." Shane accused. "That's on *you*."

"She picked me up. *You* invited them to come camping with us."

"*You* hired her. You encouraged me to go along with all this wedding bullshit."

"Because I thought you loved her! I don't read your fucking mind." I reached down to peel the leash cuff from my ankle. "What's really giving you the shits? That you lost your girl? Or your *boy*?" I wanted to punch him for what he'd said out there, I really did.

"You think I don't know I'll be bankrupt in a year without you?" He sloshed out and yanked off his own leash, then jammed his board on end in the sand. "That is all I'm good at!" He pointed at the water. "I know that. The house, the business. Every fucking thing I want, you help me make happen. *I know that.* I wanted to believe I was finally getting something right outside the water. That *I* was doing it. I thought I had to at least try." His shoulders fell. "Marriage felt like such a heavy weight, though."

"Marriage is a weight. People are heavy. What do you want me to say? That I'll step aside and help you get it right with her? No. She's a human being and made up her own mind. And..." Fuck it. "I love her." I was both empowered and defeated by the scope of my feelings for her. "I didn't mean to.

I swear to you nothing happened until I got here. I didn't even realize how I felt until yesterday morning, right before we caught up to you."

"Fair dinkum?" Shane scoffed. "*I* knew you two had more than I did with her. Why do you think I felt so sick about marrying her? But you kept pushing all that wedding bullshit on me. I thought you knew better than I did. Now I don't even have my best mate anymore. So fuck you for that. This is all. Your. Fault." He pointed to punctuate each of those final words.

I threw back my head. "Well, fuck you for sleeping with her when you knew I cared about her more than you did. What else? Get it all out, possum."

"Fuck you for setting me up to take a beating from everyone we know by backing out of this wedding. That's why I came here, because you weren't there—" He pointed to the horizon. "—to tell me that I didn't have to give it one more go. Now I have to go back and tell everyone she's with you? Fuck you for embarrassing me like that."

"Fuck you for saying that thing about me not belonging anywhere. That was low. Unforgivably low. And fuck you for dropping in on me like that!" I pointed to the waves. "You want to give me a concussion?"

"I wanted to get your attention." Shane looked to his upright board and shifted his feet, voice losing some heat. "I didn't mean it the way you took it. Only that you're always sticking your nose in. You know you do it." He was back to accusing. "You're always trying to fix every little thing. Which reminds me, fuck *you* for risking your life, playing superhero for some stranger. I've lost a brother, mate. I am not losing another one. Not to stupid shit like that. Jesus Christ, Fox. Use some fucking sense."

318

"You look exactly like Ed. Say it," I prodded, leaning into the way we joked about what a hardass Eddie had been when we'd been young and stupid. "Tell me to quit pissing around and get my head on straight."

"*Fuck you.*" There wasn't any heat in that one, though.

Most of my ire was falling away. We shared a look of mutual disgust.

"This is a family resort," I reminded him. "Maybe we should clean it up."

"Not yet. Fuck you for busting up a good thing. What am I supposed to do without the business? Get back on the circuit? My body can't take that."

"We can still work together."

Shane snorted, eyeing me with skepticism. "Is she coming back with you?"

"Yes."

"To work at T&B?"

"That's up to you."

Shane's cheek ticked. "We kind of need her. I've been getting calls."

"I posted a statement."

"Yeah. And people want to know more. They always want more." Shane hung his hands on his hips. "I don't think we can live together. Not the three of us."

"Oh, mate, I am so tired of living with you. We are definitely paying someone to finish that house. Ash and I are getting our own place."

"You want to hire someone? Who?"

"I don't know. Let's talk it out over breakfast." I tilted my head toward the resort and whatever restaurant might be open.

"All right. But..." Shane nodded at the water. "We probably won't get back here soon. No sense wasting decent surf."

I wrapped the cuff around my ankle again and carried my board into the water. As I did, I let my gaze travel up the exterior of the hotel.

Ash stood at the rail of our lanai, a hotel robe belted around her. She saluted me with the cup in her hand.

I touched two fingers to my lips then dropped onto my board and paddled out.

ASHLEY

"*S*hane's asking his parents to join us for breakfast," Fox said when he returned and found me on the lanai.

"'Us' as in..."

"You, me, him...."

"You two are okay?"

"Okay," he confirmed, but I heard it as 'just okay.' Not great, but okay was better than blood feud so I'd take it.

He stripped naked right here on the lanai.

"Decorum," I reminded, waving at the handful of tourists out for an early morning stroll to the point below us.

"They can't see anything. I tried really hard to see up your robe from down on the beach. I was not satisfied."

"No? Want to try again?" I flicked the robe to expose my knee.

"No," he said firmly. "I mean, yes. Always. But I said we'd be right down because Sandy and Eddie have to check out and catch their cruise back to Oz." He bent to grip one arm rest of my chair. His other hand, cool and damp from the surf, ran beneath the fall of the robe up my thigh while he planted a kiss on my gasping mouth.

"Your hand is cold."

"You're nice and warm." He tried to explore my belly, but ran into the constriction of the robe's belt. We kissed again, lingering over it. Just when the tips of his fingers grazed into the notch of my thighs, sending a sharp tingle shooting between my legs, he pulled away. He was notably hard, gaze tempted as he studied me.

"If I promise to be quick?" I coaxed.

"Get in there." He jerked his head.

Ten minutes later, I was brushing my teeth, bumping into Fox as he shaved, both of us wearing silly, stupefied grins.

The euphoria of climax dissipated when I threw on my sundress and sandals, though.

He pulled on the shirt and shorts he'd worn yesterday.

"I'm nervous," I admitted as I picked up my bag and he pocketed his wallet.

"You can wait the rest of your life for a better day to face your problems, but they won't change until you do. Vicky says that all the time." He held the door for me.

"Is that why you always push in and sort things?"

"Do I really do that? Shane accused me of it this morning."

"You kind of do, yeah." As the door closed behind us, I slid under the arm he raised in invitation. We walked down the hall with arms around each other. "It isn't necessarily a bad thing. If you hadn't offered me a job, I wouldn't be here right now."

We arrived at the elevators and shared a look that held all the emotions. Amusement at our own expense. Remorse at how rough this week had been. Something deep that made my heart leap because this felt so inevitable and right.

"I don't expect you to save me, you know. I can figure things out on my own," I said.

"I don't want to save you. I want to keep you." He seemed to hear how possessive that sounded and smirked, rueful. "In my life, I mean. I think I knew that pretty much from the first hour we met. It didn't compute that I wanted to build my life around you until this week."

"I don't really understand why," I confessed. "I know why I want to be with you. You're amazing. Thoughtful and confident and funny and generous. I don't know what you see in me, though, to put yourself through all of this."

"Ash. You're tougher than you look, braver than you think. And, damn it, we put *each other* through the wringer this week. But we came out stronger. No?"

"Yeah." It seemed impossible and I was still a tiny bit boggled at having such an unwritten future, but I felt like I could handle whatever might come along. Maybe I *was* tougher than I knew.

FOX

*W*hat I didn't say was that it meant the world to me that Ash was taking a chance on me when my life was on such shaky ground. I knew I would always find a way to survive. I would always have an ancillary place with my foster families. Hopefully, I would repair things enough with the Holloways that I'd remain a part of their lives, too.

But I wasn't asking Ashley to be *part* of all those things. I wanted to create a life *with* her. It was a different sort of ambition. Bigger. I was both excited for what might come and terrified of letting her down.

As we left the elevator, she tucked her cool hand into mine.

We *were* stronger together. It wasn't a belief, it just was. I stood taller and faced the lingering animosity with Shane without flinching.

Shane was at a table set for five and watched us approach, gaze going from me to her and down to our joined hands.

"Your parents here?" I asked, noting Sandy's bag hanging off the arm of one chair.

"At the buffet," Shane nodded.

I drew out a chair for Ash.

"Any chance this is funny yet?" she asked wryly as she sank into it.

Shane paused in bringing his cup of coffee to his mouth. "Not until I stop living it and start telling it. Then it'll be hilarious."

She scratched her upper lip. I sat and squeezed her knee beneath the table. The fact was, I loved both of these wombats in different but equally ridiculous amounts. I really wanted them to be okay with each other.

The server brought coffee. Ash took her time adding milk and sugar. I watched Shane watch her. He was waiting for her to look at him.

"I should have told you myself," he said quietly when she finally lifted her gaze.

Her eyes widened. She cleared her throat. "I should have caught a clue from how hard I had to push that maybe you weren't that keen." She gave a what-can-you-do shrug.

"I liked having you at T&B. The videos took off. The staff bullshit disappeared."

"For you," she said on a choking laugh. "Because I was making the schedule and covered for them when they didn't show up. The bullshit disappeared because *I* ate it, rather than it going to you."

"That's what I mean."

She looked at me, nonplussed.

"I found it very freeing as well," I said, deadpan.

She shook her head in disgust, but we were all biting back smirks of amusement.

"Oh, thank you for this," Sandy said as she and Eddie

arrived with full plates. "I would have been worrying myself sick the whole way home if you lot were still not speaking."

"Shane said you've decided to keep the business as is," Eddie said, looking between me and Shane. "You reckon you can put this behind you and keep going on as before?"

"Did you keep your same flight back to Oz?" I asked Shane. He nodded.

"That gives us another day here to talk things out, but yeah. I think so."

"Ooh, are we going to have, like, team-building exercises?" Ashley asked with an innocent bat of her lashes, harking back to what I'd said about people who got legless and had to change careers.

"Been there, done that," I said with a warning look that made her snicker into her coffee. "One thought I had was for Ash and I to make the push into the Gold Coast now instead of next year. We could work remotely from there."

"I'll go," Shane said as though the decision was already made.

Breathing space, one way or another, was my goal, but Shane was probably the better candidate for going up north anyway. He had a better grasp on the surf community and how that intersected with retail. He had a good eye for real estate, too, especially where it would best be situated for our bread-and-butter clientele.

We fetched our own breakfast and talk turned to other things. When it was over, hugs and handshakes were given out all around.

"Your mother called over this morning to say goodbye," Sandy said to Ash. "I'm looking forward to her visiting you. We'll all get together, yes?"

"Of course."

"And you," Sandy said as she hugged me. She held on tight for an extra few seconds. "This isn't what we expected out of this trip, but that's life, isn't it? I'm pleased you've got someone who makes you smile as much as Ashley does."

"Me, too." My heart was firmly lodged in my throat. "I'll still keep an eye on him. Don't worry," I promised quietly.

"As if I could ever stop worrying about the bunch of yous." She was teary as she rubbed her lipstick off my cheek. "See you at home."

ASHLEY

*a*n hour later, I joined my family on the beach where
they were just settling in. Ryan asked for Fox the
minute I appeared.

"He'll be down in a while. He's talking with his friend
about their business."

"Oh?" Mom looked up from the book she was reading
under a shade umbrella.

"We had breakfast with the Holloways. Sandy's looking
forward to you visiting us."

"She's so lovely, isn't she?"

"She is. Now, before I do anything else, I'm going to get a
photo at the end of that point," I said, nodding at the rocky
outcropping that helped form this sheltered cove next to the
hotel. "I've been wanting to do it since we got here. Anyone
want to join?"

"I'm wiped," Fliss announced, rolling her soggy body over
on the flattened lounger next to Mom and reaching for a dish
of grapes. "I got up on the board *three times* on the other side,
but it took, like, a hundred tries."

"You were surfing this morning?"

"Uh huh. Oliver tried, too."

"I feel like an old pair of jeans, I spent so much time in the washing machine," he said.

"Ha. Good on you for making the effort," I said, wishing I'd caught some video of Fliss, but glad that she and Oliver had found something to bond over. "Iz?"

"I'm sort of living the dream," she said from her own lounger. She was gleaming with a fresh coat of sunscreen, face mostly hidden by sunglasses, body shaded by her own umbrella. "Do you mind if I make like a lizard?"

"No. It's your vacation, too. Enjoy it."

Oliver took Ryan back into the water, but Whitney stood and whisked her sarong around her waist, tying it off. "I'll come."

Great. I ignored the way Mom and Fliss and even Izzy watched us walk away.

We didn't talk as we wended our way between canoodling couples and energetic families and sedate retirees all staked out on the sand. When we reached the first lumps of pocked black rocks, Whitney finally spoke.

"I didn't think you were serious about him."

I tilted down my sunglasses to look over them. "Lack of apology not accepted."

"I'm not going to apologize. My feelings are valid and real," Whit muttered, picking her way onto the uneven rocks ahead of me.

"I am not breaking up this family! It was never my fault that Mom kicked Dad out and it isn't now. Ask Mom. We're not even broken." *So go to hell, Whit.*

"*I* feel like we're broken. Like we lost something a long time ago that I've wanted to get back to. I thought this was our chance to finally be...whole."

"You're getting married! You're moving in with Oliver. Taking Fliss. Even if I went back, you won't be there."

"You were only supposed to go away on vacation," she scolded. "Which was *fine*. When you said you were getting married and moving there, I pretended I was fine with it, but I'm *not*. I never was."

We came to a spot where the waves were crashing hard enough on the rocks that the spray overshot the ledge and hit our legs.

"Now you're not even getting married and you're *still* moving away. I'm so *mad* at you for leaving."

"Gosh, I wouldn't have guessed that from all the shit I've been taking from *all of you*. But we were always going to grow up and do our own thing, Whit. In fact, your own daughter is going to grow up in *six years* and go off and do her own thing. Brace yourself."

"Does Fox know you're this mean? Because I'm going to tell him."

I continued picking over the rough rocks toward the tip of the spit. When we got there, I started snapping photos of the ocean—as if I didn't already have a thousand photos of the endless quilt of blue-green beneath a ceiling of paler blue.

"Do you really love him?" Whit asked as she stood beside me.

"Do you really love Oliver?"

"So much," she said with a ring of despondency.

I lowered my phone. "Why is that such a bad thing?"

"Because Fliss is barely speaking to me."

"She's twelve. And Oliver seems really sweet. So is Ryan." I flipped the screen so we could take a selfie with the ocean behind us.

"Isn't he the cutest? I didn't expect to fall for him so hard, either."

For the space of a few snaps, we abandoned our differences, posing with wide smiles and duck lips and our favorite, somber and cheek-to-cheek, so we looked as much alike as possible.

"I'm just worried Oliver's ex— Well, you've met her." She sent me an exasperated look. "I mean, she seems nice, but it's still going to be weird to be her kid's stepmom and have Oliver acting like a dad to Fliss. I want so much for us to fit together and turn into a family, but what if we don't? What am I going to do if I don't have you to run to when I realize I've made another mistake? Mom just says 'I told you so.'"

I lifted my chin to where Oliver's red ballcap stood out next to Ryan's green sun shirt. Fliss was beside them, damp blonde hair drying in the breeze. "Isn't that your future husband purchasing your daughter's affection with ice cream? Pretty sure it's going to be okay."

"He's so worried they won't find common ground. All the way to the turtle beach, he encouraged her to tell him about the different versions of Sims. Mom and I were ready to throw ourselves from the van, but he was so patient and *interested.*"

"Definitely a keeper," I said as we began making our way back.

"Right?" Whitney smiled all soupy, then sobered. "But it's going to be hard on her. *Fliss* needs you, Ash. Who else can she complain to about me? Mom just agrees with her. At least you take my side sometimes. And help us get over our mad. She's *only* twelve. That's a lot of teen drama I'll have to face alone. Blood will be shed. Lives lost."

"And she can smell fear so I suggest you pull it together." I slid my arm around her and Whit dropped her own arm across my shoulder. We were sticky with sunscreen and we were picking our way across uneven boulders, forcing us more off balance than ever, but we clung to each other anyway. "She's not the nightmare you were, coming in after curfew smelling of coconut rum and cigarettes."

"Because you raised her right." Whitney squeezed me closer. "I love you *so much.* You know that, right?"

"How could I doubt it. We don't roll out a guilt trip like this for just anyone."

"Isn't that the truth?" Whit wrinkled her nose and grinned. "I used the good china and everything. A veritable *banquet* of guilt and you turned around and made me feel guilty for guilting you. That's a lot of love between us."

"It really is."

"It won't be the same if you're not there," Whit said, releasing me as we arrived back at the sand.

I wondered if I should tell her that Fliss had said the same thing to me.

"You'll tell me if things go sideways and you want me to come and get you, right?" Whit said with a frown of concern. "I'm giving you a hard time, but I won't if something happens and you need me. I promise."

"I know." I faced her. "And you know I'll come home if you really need me."

"I guess I do know that." She gave a little sigh of resignation. "At least tell me he's giving you screaming orgasms."

I'd already spotted Fox walking up the beach toward us. I knew Whitney was pitching her voice a little louder for his benefit. I didn't turn around as I said, "I would have thought you heard us already, they're so violent."

Whitney let her gaze flick past me, offering a playful shrug.

"Your timing is impeccable," I said to Fox as he stopped next to me and looped his arm behind my waist.

"That's how I do it," he told Whitney, making me double-over with laughter.

ASHLEY

$\mathcal{W}$e spent the day with my family. Shane and Izzy joined us at the villa for dinner and we all stayed up late, laughing and talking, even though I had to be up early to say goodbye the next morning.

That meant I had to say goodbye to my family while Mom was cooking breakfast. The rest of them were leaving swimwear out of their packing so they could enjoy the beach for a few hours before leaving for their own flight tonight.

Somewhere between the aroma of bacon, and the oatmeal scented hug that Ryan gave me, and the familiar fragrance of Whit's hairspray, I began tearing up.

"Don't be silly." Mom wiped my cheeks with her thumbs, then turned away to flip the pancakes before they scorched.

Fliss buried her face in my neck the way she used to, when she'd been Ryan's age. I held her, trying not to cry, but my heart hurt. A lot.

Fox didn't rush me. He shook hands with everyone and made promises to text the minute we landed safely. He reminded all of us that we would see each other at Christmas.

"We'll start budgeting to come to you the following year," Oliver promised.

"Really?" Fliss cautiously lifted her head from my shoulder.

"Sure. I'd love a hot, sunny Christmas. It's enough notice to work things out with Ryan's mom."

When the clock ran down, Fox set a gentle arm around me and walked me away amid their chorus of goodbyes.

"I'm sorry," I blubbered as we approached the valet stand where Shane already waited.

"You're entitled." He rubbed my back. "Feel like driving, mate?"

"So you two can snog in the back seat?" Shane asked.

"You don't have to. I'll be fine." I searched my bag for a tissue and gratefully accepted one from the valet who held out a box. I took several, anticipating I'd need them.

"Ash." Shane opened the door and pushed the seat forward so I could get in the back. "You know I would have been shite at this, right? Let Fox give you a cuddle. He won't sit still otherwise."

I had to laugh because it was true. I got in and Fox settled beside me. He pulled me into the center and clipped that belt around me so I was right against him.

Shane looked at us in the rearview mirror. "You better have booked first class tickets. I am *not* sitting in coach."

"Oh, this is gonna be awkward." Fox scratched under his chin. "I booked my own return in economy. That was before all this." He circled his finger at the way things had changed between all of us.

"You're such a cheap bastard." Shane flipped him the bird as he pulled away from the curb. "Well, I hope you enjoy sitting with the pleebs while Ash and I drink free champagne."

"Come on, mate. You're not going to do that to us," Fox chided.

"I bloody well will. Did I ever tell you about the time he rented us goddamned pedicabs instead of a car?" Shane flicked a glance at me in the mirror, still driving slow as he made his way out of the resort.

"Here's a thought. You could make your own arrangements instead of treating me like your travel agent," Fox suggested. "Then you would always get what you want."

"You *know* what I want. You're just too damned cheap to make it happen."

"I can sit in coach," I offered.

"You're not sitting in coach," Fox and Shane said together.

"He's the one who booked it. He's sitting in coach," Shane said.

"I'm going to be crying the whole way," I said to Fox as Shane pulled onto the highway and picked up speed. "I might as well be back with the fussing babies."

"We're all in first class," he murmured against my ear. "But let him have this."

"It's not like he can't afford first class," Shane continued, speaking louder to be heard over the rushing wind. "I hope you realize what you're doing, falling in with him. His wallet is sealed up tighter than a mummy's tomb. It only gets pried open every thousand years or so. Did you two eat breakfast?" Shane had to slow for the inevitable congestion. "I haven't. Let's stop, get out of this traffic."

"The traffic doesn't quit. They'll feed us on the plane," Fox said.

"They'll feed *you* on the plane. I'll get four pretzels and have to share a wet wipe with my seat mate. You cheap fucking bugger."

"Oh, my God. Just tell him," I begged under my laughter.

"Absolutely not." Fox said, offering in a louder voice, "I packed protein bars. You want one?"

"One?"

"Okay, two."

I tucked my smile against Fox's shoulder. "You're so mean."

"Are you feeling better?"

I nodded. "I missed this. I feel like I'm home."

He pressed a kiss to my forehead. "You are."

EPILOGUE

 *our years later...*

"You're here!" I had heard the honk of the van, but didn't even get out the door and down the stairs before Fliss was bursting in and throwing herself into my arms.

I hugged her tight, pulling back to see she was still not one for make-up, still wearing her hair in a scrappy knot, but was maybe a bit taller than when I'd last seen her. Taller than me now, anyway.

"How was the flight? How was New Zealand?" I asked.

"Good. Oh my gawd." She broke away to move through the doors I'd opened between the living room and huge veranda. She hung her mouth open as she stared at the surf curling toward shore. It wasn't right below us, but it was an easy walk down a well-worn path and a few flights of wooden stairs.

"Technically the bank owns more of it than we do," I

hurried to remind her. And I ran it like a hotel, so it didn't always feel like ours, but we had no regrets.

This property in Margaret River had been showing its age when we'd driven here two years ago, taking a rare day off from opening a T&B shop in Perth. Fox had been acquainted with the owners through Shane and we'd only stopped in to say hello literally because we were in the neighborhood.

The owners, former pro surfers, had been sweet, but were getting on. This had been their retirement plan, but they had mentioned wanting to downsize and move closer to their grandchildren, but they were reluctant to sell to just anyone.

The house had a full suite downstairs and there were three bungalows tucked into the trees on the hillside. The place was a bit of a fixture, being so well-situated to the beach and well-known enough by serious surfers that it rarely had vacancies for anyone else.

One thing led to another and we made an offer that afternoon. We'd actually lived in one of the bungalows ourselves while the main house was updated. Each one had a full kitchen, two bedrooms, two baths and a loft.

Everything was done and dusted now and I had booked a full week for my family and Fox's to stay with us.

"Ryan! I've missed you, mate." I hugged the eight-year-old who walked through the open door. He grinned and hugged me like he'd missed me, too.

"Where's Fox?" he asked.

"Here." Fox came out of the bedroom with our six-month-old daughter, Penny.

Okay, so, funny story. I swore I wouldn't have a baby without planning for it, but around the time we'd bought this place, my IUD started giving me issues, feeling like it was trying to migrate into my left kidney. I had it removed and started using a birth control patch. We'd been in the middle of opening the shop and buying this place, not to mention flying back and forth to Sydney every few months to keep everything afloat there. It was definitely *not* the right time to start a family.

But one day I realized I'd lost my patch in the surf. You'd think it was an oil spill, I was that upset at littering in the ocean, never imagining I'd actually lost it two days before that, in the shower. By the time we found it and realized what was going on, we'd been using condoms for a week, but it was already too late.

Because I was late.

We'd both been goofily happy, though.

Penny was blinking awake from her nap, but already kicking with excitement when she saw me. She let Fliss hold her thought, when Fliss flexed her greedy hands at her.

He gave Fliss a quick hug and said to Ryan, "Let's help your old man with the luggage. Oh hey, Whit." He came up short at the door. "Asleep?" he asked in a softer voice, nodding at two-year-old Jayden hanging lax against Whit's shoulder.

She nodded, both arms wrapped under the boy's bum.

"How's he been going?" I asked as she gently settled him on the sofa.

"I can't say I'm looking forward to the flight home," she said wryly. "But it was worth it to be here and see you." She held out her arms to hug me. "How *are* you? And where— Fliss. Tsk." She dropped her arms and frowned at her daughter. "I called dibs."

"You should have been faster up the stairs," Fliss said, unrepentant as she nuzzled her nose against Penny's cheek.

"So it wasn't me you were in such a hurry to see," I teased.

Fliss lifted a shoulder and kept cuddling my baby.

Whitney stepped outside to squabble with Fliss over Penny. I left them to it and trotted down to where Fox was pointing out the bungalows.

"Gary and Stephanie are in that one. Vicky and Mitchell have that one. We thought we'd let the kids take over the suite downstairs, unless they want to bunk with their parents. You guys get that bungalow and Joanna, you're upstairs in the guest room again. Does that work?"

"That sounds good— Oh, there you are." Mom hugged me and so did Oliver. "How are you?" Mom had flown out to be with me when Penny was born, so she was less agog at than everyone else. "You look good," she added with a critical eye.

"I am. My iron's back to where it should be. How was New Zealand?"

"Really good. Lots to see. I wish we could have stayed longer, but next time." Mom talked like that now, like flying around the globe was a thing that was normal for our family because it kind of was.

Whitney met me at the door with a squawking Penny. "She's hungry. But I get her next."

"Yeah, she's been up a whole five minutes and my boob isn't in her mouth. That means I'm clearly starving her to *death*."

Penny curled her fist into the collar of my shirt and bobbed her head, complaining rather loudly that I was, in fact, guilty of human rights violations.

"All right. You're going to wake your cousin. Shush." I sat and hurried to get her latched.

As she settled to suckle, I stroked her curly hair. Fox's hair and Fox's eyes staring up at me while her little baby nails scratched lightly against the swell of my breast. God, I loved her.

"Water?" Mom asked.

"Thanks."

Mom moved to the kitchen while Fliss came and sat on the sofa near Jayden's feet.

"Okay, be real," Fliss said. "Are we here for a surprise wedding?"

"Ha! No. And you're not the first to ask." I had chatted with Izzy a week ago, telling her about this family reunion we were hosting.

Don't you dare get married without me, she had warned.

Same, I had said of the woman she was living with. Her parents had met her girlfriend, but I hadn't. Izzy had promised to come see us as soon as they could line up their vacations.

"Fox and I actually talked about it a few times, but we just don't have the bandwidth right now. And we can't do it without Izzy and Shane." He was Fox's first choice for best man.

"Shane's still with Gillian? How's she doing?" Whit asked, scooping up Jayden as he stirred and crawled grumpily into her lap, eyeing me and these unfamiliar surroundings with suspicion.

I smiled at him, then answered Whit.

"Continuing with her world domination." T&B had sponsored Gillian when she'd first gone pro a few years ago. She was twenty-five and killing it on the Championship Tour— which was awesome for T&B from a marketing and publicity standpoint, but it put even more eyes on the company.

That meant T&B was growing like mad while Shane was personally managing her, ensuring her support team was the absolute best from coach to equipment manager to photographers to nutritionists. They were also a couple and yes, she was a little too young for him. Or he was a little too old for her, but maturity-wise, they were very evenly matched and they did seem to actually adore each other so Fox and I were very happy for both of them.

But Shane's traveling meant Fox was the man on the ground here, keeping the business running. T&B had a lot more managerial staff now, but we were still really freaking busy all the time. It was all nice problems to have, though, so we didn't complain.

"How are things with Josh?" I asked Fliss.

"We broke up a couple weeks ago."

"Oh, hon."

"No, it's okay." She grimaced, but pushed her mouth to the side, kind of resigned. "I mean, it was gross at school. Everyone kept asking me about it, but..." She shrugged, then looked to the windows. "I thought, um, Fox's brothers and sisters were coming?"

So subtle, but I didn't tease.

"Vicky and Mitchell took them to see some friends up the coast who moved here a while back. Gary and Steph took their kids to Perth for the day, but they all got here yesterday. Look at this photo I took." I reached for my phone and showed her Fox sitting with Penny on his knee, his five brothers and sisters around him. "That's the first time Fox has ever had all his brothers and sisters in one place at one time."

"Really? Aw. Look how happy he is."

"I know." He hadn't stopped grinning.

"Michael's gotten taller," Fliss noted.

"He has." I kept to myself that Michael had asked me if Fliss was going to be here.

My family had met Vicky and Mitchell and their children when they'd come to Sydney two Christmases ago. Michael was two years older than Fliss and very academic, like Fliss. He also loved gaming and was funny as hell. He wasn't hard to look at, either.

By dinner, everyone was back. Fox was on the veranda flipping burgers on the barbecue. I was setting out salads and buns. Our parents were chatting in the shade, Vicky holding Penny. Oliver and Whit were enjoying some quiet time in their bungalow while Mom and I kept an eye on Jayden who was building a puzzle I'd got for him. Ryan was downstairs with the teens. Music and laughter were coming from that direction, assuring us they were all getting along.

"We're really lucky, aren't we?" I said, nudging Fox with my elbow.

"Couldn't have done it better if we'd planned it." He flipped the last burger then switched the spatula to his other hand, drawing me into his side and giving me a kiss. "Do you wish we were getting married this week?"

"I don't... I mean, I don't *not* want to marry you. But the only reason I would want a wedding is this. Getting everyone together." I nodded at the way Mom reached forward to help Jayden turn a piece to make it fit. "It'd be nice to have another excuse to do it, I suppose. Something to consider for next time."

"Okay, so, um, let me be more specific." He closed one eye. "If I offer you a ring later, in front of everyone, what are you going to say?"

"Oh." I couldn't help the grin that was spreading across my face. My heart began to swell with all the swoony feelings this man still effortlessly provoked in me. "Are you really planning to do that?"

"Is it too corny?"

"It's exactly corny enough. I will say yes. I promise."

"*And* go through with the wedding?"

"Pinky swear." I held mine out to him.

He caught it with his, then brought it to his mouth so he could kiss my knuckle. "I love you, you know."

"I love you back." I hugged his waist and kissed his chin. "I love my life with you."

"Same."

And when he called everyone together later, and went down on one knee to offer me a very pretty solitaire on a platinum band, everyone made gasping noises of surprise except me.

Until he began to speak.

"Ash, I love your big, brown eyes and your laugh and the way you let down your hair only to twist it up again when it was fine in the first place. I love that you're brave enough to try new things, even beetroot on a burger or driving on the left. I love the way you walk on your heels after you've painted your toenails and that you can make a joke and take one, but will stand up for yourself if it goes too far. I love hearing you sing in the shower and talk to your family and I *love* being a parent with you. I love that after all this time, you still fail so spectacularly at the Aussie accent. I love that I get to spend the rest of my life learning what else I love about you. Will you marry me?"

My eyes were wet. I had to blink and blink to see him. My cheeks hurt, I was smiling so hard.

I cupped his face, thinking back to a long ago conversation we'd had about marriage.

"I feel like I have to. Not for Penny or a big wedding or a piece of paper or any reason except that I can't imagine my life without you in it. Yes," I said, voice shaking as my love for him welled in my throat and chest and against the backs of my eyes. "I would love to marry you, Felix Wiley."

He rose and we hugged and pressed our smiles together while everyone sighed, "Ahh."

Except Ryan, who said, "Will they get married in Hawaii?" And we all cried, "*No.*"

The End

I HOPE you enjoyed Fox and Ashley's journey to Happily Ever After.

If you want another slow burn romance with laughter, angst, and complex family dynamics, try *Afternoon Delight* where a nearly-forty divorcee abandons her accounting career to run her friend's adult toy shop. Meg wants to try new things, but does that include 'sampling the merchandise' with her charming new neighbor?

Read on for an excerpt!

AFTERNOON DELIGHT

It's never too late to toy with change...

Freshly divorced and nearing forty, Meg regrets making all the safe choices. When her best friend needs surgery, Meg puts her accounting career on hold to run her friend's racy adult toy shop—but her vanilla life never prepared her for this!

At thirty-two, Zak leaves the tech world for his dad's antique store, wanting time with him before dementia erases his father's memories. He's Meg's landlord, but she becomes his confidante, distracting him from his troubles with her suggestive puns and amusing misadventures.

Flirty banter leads to test-driving toys together, but Meg knows they won't last. Their age-gap puts them in different life-stages and she lives in Toronto. A few afternoons of delight can't change her life. Or can they?

Afternoon Delight is a stand-alone, slow-burn to steamy older woman/younger man romance. No cliffhangers, no cheating, just laughs, chemistry, and heart.

MEG

$\mathcal{I}$ hadn't suffered this much gut-crunching anxiety and loin-tingling thrill since I'd been Meg Crutcher, lying to Mom about staying at Georgia's house on graduation night when I was actually meeting Joel at the Island Value Inn on Gorge Road.

I slowed my rented SUV, and the steering wheel grew slippery in my sweaty palms. My skin tightened with the pressure of holding in my lewd secret. My ears filled with a rushing noise. I kind of had to pee.

Screw parallel parking—I found a spot where I could nose in.

My conscience writhed with snakes that hissed, *You're being bad*, but I was a grown-ass woman. I could do what I wanted.

Which was exactly what I'd told myself twenty-one years ago, when I'd left my virginity in room twelve of the I.V. Inn.

That act of rebellion was supposed to turn me into an adult. It had. Except, I'd thought growing up meant making choices for myself, when in reality, cells had met and combined and divided without my permission. From there, one responsibility after another had appeared in front of me like stepping stones leading into a cave where a neon sign above the opening flashed, *Where did my life go?*

Now I was a few kilometers east of my youthful misconception. I had lied to my mother again, this time texting her that I was running an errand for Georgia.

It was kind of true. I had agreed to run Georgia's *store*. Actually, I'd agreed to open the doors and figure out if there was a way to keep it running—even if she couldn't come back right away. Or at all.

I cut the engine and sat there, listening to the February rain patter on the roof. Winter never really arrived in Victoria, BC. Not the way it did in the rest of Canada. Snow rarely stuck to these streets, but spring wasn't here yet, either. It was a messy, unpredictable shoulder season, and very much a metaphor for the state of my life.

This wasn't even *Victoria*. Not the downtown waterfront that looked so pretty on the postcards. No, this was Milestone —one of the oldest suburbs of the city. It was the name of the most popular streetcar stop back when those were a thing here. Locals called it 'Mild Stone.' I'll give you three guesses why.

It had had its rough years, but it was still where the broke creatives came together. Its commercial area was a colorful hodgepodge of brick storefronts and people running businesses out of their Victorian-style homes.

Georgia had picked this location because it was busy but affordable. And because they had said 'yes' to an adult toy store. Sometimes people were picky about that sort of thing.

I studied the two-story building through the drips that gathered and ran down the windshield. There were four windows on the second floor. Georgia had told me there were two apartments up there. She'd been cagey when I asked about the tenants, making me think she knew someone up there. A man? I hadn't pressed her. She was either in pain or drowsy from painkillers these days. All I'd really needed to know was that she had asked me for help.

She'd shocked me by asking. Georgia was the poster girl for independent women—meaning she would kick the ass of anyone who dismissed her as a girl or tried to put her face on a poster without her permission.

She had called me out when I began moaning about how envious I was of my daughter. Shelby was living the university life I had never experienced because I'd had her straight out of high school.

"You just got divorced. It's the perfect time to reinvent," Georgia had said an hour ago.

"I know, but I have to get Mom moved closer to me in Toronto first. Then get Roddie through high school and off to uni. *Then* I can start making changes to my life."

"Seriously, Meg? Do you hear these excuses you're making? Just jump."

I have responsibilities, I wanted to say, but this was Georgia. She'd always been able to throw herself off cliffs and then yell, *Just jump.* She'd always known how to keep her head above water.

Three weeks after grad, she'd been the one to say, *I'll go with you if you want an abortion.* She also had a healthy respect for leaps that were truly too big, but I had been convinced I was getting everything I wanted—independence, a husband,

and a life off this damned island. I moved to Montreal with Joel, and Georgia went to California. She didn't get into the movies like she wanted, but she danced on cruise ships, sang backup in a studio, and had thousands of colorful stories that spoke of a life well lived.

I had two kids I loved beyond measure, a steady job as an accountant, and a Final Divorce Order.

"I'm scared," I had admitted to Georgia with a laugh that didn't disguise any of the painful truth in that statement. "What if I make a wrong choice? It's easier to blame Mom and Joel and work than accept that I've wound up with exactly what I settled for. Which is what will happen again unless I get it right this time."

"You never change. You know why? *Because you never change.*" Georgia had shaken her scarf-covered head.

Her spinal tumors weren't cancerous, but she was in so much pain her hair had become more work than she wanted to fuss with. She'd shaved her head, and because it was still winter—and winter in southern BC was a damp cold that settled into your bones—she had to keep her head covered. Her light brown complexion was wan, her mouth strained with tension and worry, but she still managed to make me feel like the pitiful one.

"There's no 'getting it right,'" she had scolded. "Shake things up. You know what you should do? Quit your job and run my store for me."

"Can you imagine? Mom would shit a brick."

"I'm serious."

"Right," I scoffed. That store was her baby—still spanking new and something she'd worked hard to make happen.

"Meg. I actually am." Her expression had sobered into

pensive. Desperate. "I'm really worried about it. The landlord is calling about rent and..." Her eyes welled up.

"Hey." I reached out to squeeze her hand. "You know I'll do anything. I can cover rent for a few months if you need me to."

"It's not that. I need my business to *run*. To generate income. For bills and the bank loan. I put all my savings into this. If I lose it, I'm starting from nothing at forty."

"You're not going to lose it. That's the pain pills talking." They cramped her mood, she'd told me.

"I'm high as a kite," Georgia had agreed as she ran a thumb under her leaking eye. "Otherwise, I wouldn't ask for help. But I really don't want to lose my store, Meg."

"I know, but—" I bit back the protest that rose from sheer cowardice.

I thought of Roddie, who lived with Joel and kept insisting he was fine. And Mom, who was fighting me at every turn when it came to cleaning out the house. She wanted to keep everything the same. I didn't want to be Mom—stuck in the past. We both needed to start moving forward.

"You don't want to let me down, do you?" Georgia prodded.

I dropped my jaw in exaggerated outrage. "You ruthless bitch."

Georgia showed all her teeth in a slow, wide grin, knowing she had me.

So here I was, shaking things up.

Shaking.

Afraid.

Imagining I could hear Georgia yelling, *The water's fine.*

I studied the awnings on the brick building—one blue, the

other pink—that sheltered the storefront windows and the stoop in between. Under the pink one, the building looked gloomy and dark. Below the blue one, a golden light beckoned.

No use waffling. I had said I would do it, but I couldn't help wondering if this decision would leave me as screwed as last time.

Mom was going to *hate* it. Helping a friend meant dropping off a casserole or donating bone marrow. It didn't mean becoming the face of an adult toy shop. As for what Joel would say—

Ugh. No more Joel. No more spiraling through old choices, wishing I'd made different ones. No more sitting in a cubicle promising myself things would get better.

Get out of the car, dipshit. *Make* it better.

I threw open the door. A gust of wind caught it, nearly smashing it into the side of the SUV parked next to mine. I managed to hang onto it, stepped into the puddle of water backed up from the clogged drain in the curb, swore, slammed the door, and trotted the half block until I was under the pink awning of the building.

I gasped against the frigid air filling my lungs. I *really* needed to start some cardio.

At the darkened window, I cupped my hands above the gold-stenciled *Afternoon Delight* on the glass. A translucent white curtain hid the window display, but there was nothing to see. The display was empty. A tall wooden shelf was strategically placed to limit the view of any stock it might hold. Sheets were draped over odd shapes on the table in the middle of the room. There was a cheerful area rug before the cash desk, open rafters in the ceiling, and a slatted wall at the back peppered with hooks. Bagged goods hung on either side of a door that presumably led to a stockroom and bathroom.

For me, it was Room Twelve all over again—filled with mysteries both titillating and intimidating. It was filled with *sex*.

I felt in my coat pocket for the key and moved to the door.

The two shops were mirrors of each other. I glanced through the door where Twice is Nice Emporium was painted on the glass. Their Open sign glowed extra bright on this gloomy Thursday.

Inside their window, a flowery ceramic basin and jug sat next to a small pendulum clock atop an ornate wooden dresser. A lazy Susan stood on a fancy coffee table with pretty china cups arranged on it. Old-timey tins were stacked on shelves lit beneath a lamp with a fringed shade.

The crowded display reminded me of the books my kids used to love—the ones with busy photos and rhyming lists of things to search for: five buttons, a dime, three yellow tins, and a thing that tells time.

Twice is Nice had an additional selling feature hand-written on a piece of paper taped to the inside of their door:

We specialize in wood revival.

Same, I snickered to myself as I unlocked the door to Afternoon Delight.

"It was the whitest name I could think of," Georgia had said of the store's name. The inside of her door held a hand-written sign that read:

Closed for medical reasons.

I pushed in, and a sleigh bell tied to the door jangled. At the same time, the steady chime of the alarm system sounded from across the room. I hurried to the box on the wall and punched in the code Georgia had given me. It silenced, and I felt ridiculously proud of myself for not causing a SWAT team to descend on the street.

I slid the thermostat from frigid to survivable and hit the switches to illuminate the track lighting in the rafters. No harsh fluorescent office lights here. Intimate pools of gold landed on a rotating stand of books. A hammock-like contraption was suspended from the ceiling, and a number of whips and crops were mounted on the wall. The shelf that formed the privacy wall held a selection of vibrators in a variety of shapes, colors, and sizes. Several were displayed out of their boxes.

One monster compelled me to pick it up to see how heavy it was. Honestly, even though my eight-pound children had come out of my vagina, I was intimidated by the breadth of this goliath.

I tried to close my fist around it, using my grip to brush away the dust from its silicone coating while thumbing the dial to check the different vibration speeds. I resisted the impulse to press it into the notch of my jeans, but I was intrigued enough to consider it.

The sleigh bell jangled.

I threw the elephantine penis back onto the shelf in the most obvious Nothing, Mother in history. It knocked over two other vibrators and lay there buzzing, the sound amplified by the boxy shelf.

I scrambled to pick it up but couldn't figure out how to turn it off. I called out a high-pitched, "I'm not open!" while I turned the dial, accidentally increasing the vibration. Why hadn't I locked the door? Oh, right—because of the alarm. Note to self: Grab a brain, not a dildo.

"I'm from next door," a deep voice said as I finally silenced the vibrator. "I have a question."

Shit. The landlord Georgia had warned me about?

I set the vibrator back on the shelf and brushed my hands on the seat of my jeans, then slapped a compassionate smile on my face before stepping out where I could see him.

Double-shit. Georgia had made it sound like the guy was a senior. How did a man in his mid-thirties have dementia? There were glints of gold in his beard, not silver. Same with his hair. His thick dark crew cut needed a trim, but it was kind of sexy, all disheveled like that. He was tall and fit and had a smile that skewed left in a very charming way.

"Hi, Dale," I said gently, repeating what Georgia had told me to say. "Debra doesn't work here anymore. I know this might feel confusing, but if we go back into your shop, your daughter can explain." How old was this guy's daughter anyway? Seven? And she was knee-capping Georgia for rent?

His face moved through a comical set of emotions, landing on bemusement.

"Dale is my dad. I'm Zak. Are you not Georgia?"

"What? No. Ha." I wanted to die. "I'm Georgia's friend, Meg. Hi." I moved forward and offered my hand. "I'm helping Georgia for a couple of weeks." I kept it vague, since I didn't really know what I was doing.

"Nice to meet you." Zak stepped forward. He had a firm grip. There was a hint of callus on his warm palm and, for some bizarre reason, that caused a zing of electricity to ground out between my legs.

For the first time in years, I remembered that I owned a clitoris and briefly considered looking for it. I wanted to blame the vibrator, but it was him. Or me—and my utter lack of experience with being single. Whatever it was, I was regressing into prom-night Meg, smiling dopily because he wore his flannel sleeves rolled back, showing off his muscled forearms. His jeans hugged his thick thighs, and his sturdy work boots were oddly reassuring, like he knew how to take command of a situation.

I dragged my attention back to his crooked smile and straight dark brows. The combination made him seem both approachable and stern.

Too young, I cautioned myself. He didn't look like he'd collected my level of disenchantment with life. People in their thirties tended to fall into two categories—those like me, creeping up on forty and punch-drunk with family responsibilities, or those like him, who still had the bandwidth for clumsy soccer on a soggy day.

His eyes were really blue. They brimmed with amusement, and I wanted to fall right into them.

I was staring. Damn. I'd caught a case of insta-lust, and he knew it.

"So, um." *I'm due to step into traffic.* "Georgia said her landlord had a daughter. Zara? Is that your wife?" Did I really just ask if he was married? Yes, I did. I wanted to bite my tongue off.

"My sister."

Right. Duh. He had just told me his father was Dale. Could I be more uncool?

He scratched his beard, possibly trying to hide the fact that he was struggling not to laugh.

"We own the building with Dad," he said. "Fun fact—when he signed this lease, he told us the new renter was a toy store.

It wasn't until Zara stopped by after it opened that we learned what kind of toys."

"Oh." I widened my eyes. "Is that a problem?" Was he here to break the lease? Nooo.

"The neighbors aren't thrilled. But we're only hanging onto the building for Dad, so..." He lifted one well-built shoulder.

"So don't get comfortable?" My heart was sinking on Georgia's behalf.

"I honestly couldn't tell you." He shoved his hands into his back pockets, palms out, and braced his weight between his widely set feet. "At first, we thought it was funny that Dad had missed such an important detail. Then Georgia told Zara that Dad was coming in here and getting confused. Zara got him to the doctor, but she has kids and works full-time. She can't run point on him, too. I moved back after Christmas to live with Dad and..." He shrugged again. "I don't know how long this will work."

Oh. I bit back saying how nice it was that he had come home to help. No one—least of all my husband—had praised me when I helped my mother-in-law after she broke her hip. I'd put school on hold and left our kids with my own mother so I could take care of Mrs. Boyd, because Joel hadn't wanted to cancel any of his lucrative root canals and crowns. It hadn't occurred to any of us—least of all me—that he would. Or that he would look after his own mother. His parents had since moved to the Okanagan, or Joel would still expect me to check on them.

"You're here to ask about rent?" I guessed. "Georgia said Zara let her skip January while she figured things out, but she texted the other day, asking what her plans are."

"I actually forgot Zar was doing that. Yeah, people have

been asking what's going on over here." Zak glanced over his shoulder. Brim Stokers Coffeehouse was across the street next to the new microbrewery, Tap That. "There's been some revitalization lately. By that, I mean gentrification. They don't like staring at a dark window."

"Understandable."

"One of them offered to buy the building, but we want to keep it for now. Dad's used to getting up for work every morning. His doctor says it's good for him to stick to a routine. He likes dinking around with his knick-knacks, so..." Another shrug.

Oh. I bit back a laugh, adoring how affectionate he sounded.

"Where do you usually live?" I asked.

"Vancouver. You?"

"Toronto. But I grew up here."

"Me, too. I'm a programmer. I had a good job, but I was burning out again. This is a nice break. Mostly I dink around, too. Strip wood. Post photos."

Don't say it.

"That sounds like I post dick pics." His grin flashed. God, he was gorgeous. "Actually, they're chests." He waited a beat. "Of drawers." His mouth twitched with irony.

"I was trying not to ask." I was trying not to ogle his chest, but I could feel a smile teasing my lips.

"How is Georgia?" he asked with concern. "Zara said Dad was making things awkward with her staff and customers. There's been a lot of turnover in this shop the last few years, actually. We should have clued in to what was causing it. Can you let her know I'm here, though? That shouldn't happen as much now." He glanced right as he spoke.

I realized he had done that a few times. He had stationed himself so he could see his own door through this one.

"She'll be off sick for a while longer. She's staying with her sister in Sidney." It was about thirty minutes from the shop, but close to the ferry, which was good since she was seeing a specialist in Vancouver. "She should be back on her feet soon." I was staying positive.

"That's good news." His gaze flickered down, taking in my mint green rain jacket over peg-leg jeans stuffed into ankle boots with faux-fur cuffs.

When his eyes came back to my face, I was prickly and humid inside my damp clothes.

"That you're planning to reopen, I mean." He cleared his throat. "And yeah, rent would be great. My wages over there are circa most of the furniture."

"I'll see what I can do. Today I just dropped by to get the lay of the land." My voice faltered at the double entendre. "I wanted to see what I'll be working with." I fought the urge to glance at the vibrators but couldn't look at him either, certain he'd be laughing at me again.

"Sure," he said easily. "I won't bother you, but one thing has been driving me crazy since I spotted it through the window. That's why I came roaring over here the second I heard you come in. What the hell is that?" He pointed at the cash desk. "I can't find anything like it online."

I blinked at what looked like a three-pronged candelabra made of clear plastic dildos, all of different heights and widths, arranged like a tripod, not a fork.

"Um..." I was equally mystified and walked over to gingerly pick it up.

"Are they flexible?"

I tested one branch. "No." It was solid and weighted at the base so it wouldn't tip over.

"Who uses something like that? I'm not being judgmental." His expression became boyish, one eyebrow quirking upward while his hand flailed in bafflement. "It's a real question. What goes where? How? There's not enough room for three people to use it at once. I honestly don't think it would be comfortable for one. Maybe that's the point?"

I was just as perplexed. If someone wanted to rotate through poking me with three differently sized dildos so vigorously that they needed a common handle, I would have a lot of questions first.

"I can't figure it out," he continued. "And believe me, I've put in the hours."

"I'm picturing you over there with a corkboard and red yarn."

"Mostly doodling on the back of provenance certificates, but it keeps me from worrying about Dad."

I tucked my smile into the zipper of my jacket. "Perhaps it would be kinder to keep you in the dark, then."

"Please don't. I've reached my limit for edging my curiosity."

Oh heck. I was really starting to enjoy this.

I lifted my chin, trying to project some level of competence while I admitted, "Full disclosure, I'm new to all of this. Fortunately, I can phone a friend." I snapped a photo and texted it to Georgia with a question mark.

"So you don't... do this?" He drew a circle with his finger to indicate the store.

"Sell adult toys for a living? No, I'm an accountant. Helping small businesses pay their taxes is my day job. I'm friendly and punctual, and Georgia says it's no more awkward than selling cans of soup, so I agreed to pinch-hit." I was starting to think she'd misled me on that front. I was feeling extremely awkward as I set down the X-rated version of the Cat in the Hat's moss-covered, three-handled family gradunza, trying not to imagine which one went up my bum or how much it would sting.

How hard could it be had been my naïve assumption about working here. And there I went with the dirty puns again.

"Pro tip? You can sell anything with a story. This trunk was supposed to be on the Titanic." He waved at an imaginary trunk at his feet. "It was accidentally left behind and went to the passenger's cousin, who found a pearl-handled knife inside—one that was later found to have been used in a murder."

"You make stuff up?"

"No." He frowned, insulted. "I'm saying you need to know what you're selling so you can pique curiosity. I guarantee you could sell that thing if you told your next customer that your vanilla neighbor has been obsessing about it for weeks. They won't care what it's actually for. They'll buy it for the story."

"Maybe I'll keep it as a conversation piece, then."

"No," he warned sternly. "Never get sentimental. If you can *sell it,* sell it. You can tell I haven't had anyone new to talk to in a while, can't you?" His mouth twisted with self-deprecation. "I should get back, make sure Dad's okay." He canted his head. "But if you find anything else that stumps you, run it by me. I'm genuinely interested."

"I will, thanks. And I'll let you know what I learn." I nodded at the trident of dildos.

"Great. See you tomorrow." He left with a jangle of the sleigh bell.

I opened my jacket to air out the trapped heat. Talk about trial by fire!

I had gotten through it, though. Maybe I could handle this job after all.

My phone buzzed. I tilted the screen to read Georgia's reply:

GEORGIA:

It's a condom tree. Change it up for the holidays, but don't use flavored ones.

People will lick it.

ZAK

$\mathcal{T}$he phone was ringing as I walked back into the shop.

I looked for Dad, but the place had always been a rabbit warren of tallboys, standing mirrors, and folding screens. As a kid, playing hide-and-seek in here with Zara had been a riot. Playing hide-and-seek with Dad? Not so much.

"Dad?" The phone was still ringing, which didn't necessarily mean he wasn't in the office. I'd caught him in there two days ago, watching it ring, but yesterday he'd answered it like he always used to.

From the back of the shop, I heard a cry of pain and the thump of something hitting the floor. I veered toward the workroom, where I'd been stripping a table.

Dad was standing next to it, clutching his own hand, looking at it with a mix of confusion and agony. The heat gun was on the floor.

Fuck me.

"Let's get that under cold water." I yanked the plug from

the wall on my way to bringing him into the bathroom, then guided his hand so cold water washed over the pink crescent in his palm.

How had we missed that he was getting this bad?

It wasn't actually a mystery. I hadn't been here because I was a workaholic who'd been saving for a wedding and a house. Zara had a husband, a job, and three kids. I suspected her marriage was also on the rocks, but maybe it was just this situation with Dad putting stress fractures into their relationship. I didn't have the nerve to ask.

"I thought it was your mother's hair dryer," Dad said, giving me a baffled look.

"It's the heat gun for stripping paint. I was using it on the table." He'd been using it himself last summer when I'd visited. "It's my fault. I shouldn't have left it out."

I had to start thinking of him like Ollie, Zara's youngest, but it was a mental shift I didn't want to make. Dad had taught me how to refinish furniture, for Christ's sake. As well as how to drive, how to get a car loan, and how to change the oil. Sure, this was the YouTube generation. Every life skill you needed was one skip of a five-second ad away, but *he* was my Google.

Nothing in me wanted to accept that he couldn't remember the difference between a heat gun and a hair dryer. Or that Mom was dead.

"Does that feel better?" The mark had faded and didn't look like it would blister. "Let's get some gauze on it, then you can hold a cold bottle of root beer. Sound good?" I needed to stop pushing sugar on him. We didn't need him diabetic on top of the Alzheimer's, but part of me wanted to believe his absent-mindedness was just low blood sugar.

"That does sound good," he said, and I thought, *What the hell. If it makes him happy.*

I got Dad settled in the office with his root beer, then went back to the workroom and put away the heat gun, the scrapers, the turpentine—anything I thought could be a danger to him. There was only a wooden turning latch to keep the cupboard doors closed. It felt like a dick move to put a padlock on it, but I guessed I'd have to.

I added it to my To Do list, a living document in my phone that still had "pick up ring" on it. Then I returned to the office to listen to the message from the call we'd missed. The recording from the credit bureau warned me that my credit card was blah, blah, blah.

I deleted it without listening to the rest, but now I had to wonder how easily Dad could be tricked into entering his credit card number. I would talk to Zara before removing his cards from his wallet. We were in the middle of getting power of attorney for his finances anyway, but this felt like the next-level piss-all-over-his-self-esteem move. Maybe we could just lower his available credit to an amount we were willing to lose.

I heard a muted jangle and got out to the front of the shop just in time to see the door to Afternoon Delight go dark again.

At least I had a cute neighbor now. One who knew even less about sex toys than I did.

I'd never really fucked with them. Literally. Erica had had a vibrator, but she'd never wanted me to use it on her. I'd wandered through stores now and again and seen shit online, but my hand did the job—and it was always there.

My curiosity had grown since I'd seen that trident through

the window, though. I'd spent way too much time trying to find it online. Turns out, looking at toys was almost as effective as looking at porn. It made me really horny.

Now I would be picturing Meg in her snug jeans, dark-blond hair, and flustered blushes as she fondled those things. Yes, please.

"Zak? Did that couple ever call back for this coffee table?" And just like that, he was back—shrewdly running the least profitable business in Canada.

"I think she wanted it, but he wasn't as keen."

"I think you're right." He took the 'reserved' sign off it and set a bowl filled with wooden fruit in its place. He gave the arrangement a little adjustment, always so loving with the clutter in here.

I had a lot of feelings about this place. Some were nostalgic, some were overwhelmed and annoyed. These days, I had to wonder if this smorgasbord of disarray was a peek inside Dad's mind. It was filled to the brim, but everything was jammed together and unusable. The thing you might actually want was buried behind an umbrella stand, covered in dust so you couldn't see it. That didn't mean it wasn't here.

"I was thinking of pork chops for dinner," he said.

"Sounds great. Should we knock off early and pick them up on our way home?"

"Let's do that. It's good to have you home, Zak. I like the company." He gave my shoulder a pat, smiling in a way that made me feel goofy, like a kid earning Dad's praise for catching a ball.

It's okay, I thought. He's okay. Everything was going to be okay.

But then he noticed the bandage on his hand and began to

pick at it with puzzlement, trying to figure out why it was there.

My heart sank. He was not okay.

~

More *Afternoon Delight*

BECOME A VIP

Do you want to be notified when Dani's next book comes out? You'll also get behind-the-scenes gossip and hear first about exclusive deals, sneak peeks, bonus content, and special offers. Join now:

DaniCollins.com/VIP

ABOUT THE AUTHOR

Award-winning and USA Today Bestselling author Dani Collins thrives on giving readers emotional, compelling, heart-soaring romance with laughter and heat thrown in, just like real life. While she's best known for contemporary romances written for Harlequin Presents and Tule Publishing, she also writes historical and erotic romance. When she's not writing —just kidding, she's always writing. Dani lives in an empty nest in Southern BC, Canada with her high school sweetheart husband.

ALSO BY DANI COLLINS

Afternoon Delight

Raven's Cove Trilogy

Harlequin Presents

Fancy Foibles Collection

Visit danicollins.com for a full list.